CARVED IN DARKNESS

A NOVEL

MAEGAN BEAUMONT

MIDNIGHT INK
WOODBURY, MINNESOTA

FIRST EDITION
First Printing, 2013
Published in association with MacGregor Literary, Inc. of Hillsboro, OR

Book design by Bob Gaul
Cover design by Kevin R. Brown
Editing by Nicole Nugent

Midnight Ink, an imprint of Llewellyn Worldwide Ltd.

This is a work of fiction. Names, characters, places, and incidents are either the product of the author's imagination or are used fictitiously, and any resemblance to actual persons, living or dead, business establishments, events, or locales is entirely coincidental.

Library of Congress Cataloging-in-Publication Data
Beaumont, Maegan, 1975–
  Carved in darkness: a novel/Maegan Beaumont.—First edition.
     pages cm
  ISBN 978-0-7387-3689-1
1. Policewomen—Fiction. 2. Murder—Investigation—Fiction. 3. Mystery fiction. I. Title.
  PS3602.E2635C37 2013
  813'.6—dc23

                          2012051406

Midnight Ink
Llewellyn Worldwide Ltd.
2143 Wooddale Drive
Woodbury, MN 55125-2989
www.midnightinkbooks.com

Printed in the United States of America

For my parents—thank you for loving me.

ONE

Yuma, Arizona
December 22, 1998

WAITING WAS THE WORST part. The sporadic stretches of time between his visits—when he came and hurt her—were the hardest torture to bear. She had no idea how long she'd been in the dark. No longer trusted herself to count the days. It'd been October first when he took her. What month it was now was impossible to figure out, but if every time he raped her marked the passing of a day—every time he cut her, the passing of an hour—then she'd been locked away for centuries and everyone she loved was dead and gone.

Shifting, she felt the pull of dried blood and unhealed wounds across her skin. She couldn't see them—the only kindness the darkness granted her—but she could feel them. Smell them. They were everywhere. Cuts, long and thin, ran the length of her spine. The inside of her thighs. Along the swell of her breasts. The soft flesh under her arms. The soles of her feet. The stench of old blood and infection mingled with the warm, revolting smell of the bucket she was forced to use as a toilet. She tried not to think about it. About what had been done to her body. About what she'd been forced to do to survive…

Sounds penetrated the dense folds of black that surrounded her. Footsteps. Slow and measured.

Terror gripped her, forced movement into limbs no longer totally under her control. Lurching to her feet, she swayed beneath the almost impossible heaviness of her own body weight. She took a few shuffling steps, kept one hand braced against the wall, while the other hovered out in front of her.

He wanted to play.

Her hands closed on the knob and grappled with it. Her hands were encased in duct tape—wrapped round and round until her fingers were fused together and rendered useless. Without working fingers, getting the door open was difficult but not impossible. Using both hands, she gripped the knob and turned. The door unlatched and swung inward.

Step by step, she forced her legs and feet forward until she slammed into the wall opposite the door. Pressing her battered cheek against it, she dragged cleaner air into her lungs in ragged gulps.

Light glowed a dull, muted red against her lids. Instinct seized her, her brain sent the signal, tried to open her eyes even though she knew she couldn't. Her lids wouldn't budge—they hadn't since she woke in the dark.

Experience told her that going right was wrong. There were stairs to the right, but they led to nothing more than a locked door. He wanted to chase her. It was his favorite game. She could feel him, standing at the base of the stairs.

Staring at her.

Her heart started its frantic kicking. It bounced around her chest, tried to claw its way up her throat. Turning left, she moved her legs as fast as they'd go, her shoulder hugging the wall to keep herself upright.

Footsteps echoed after her, slow at first but then faster and faster. He was coming.

———

He reached the bottom of the stairs and smiled when the door flew open. Watched her stumble across the hall and slam into the wall in front of her. He took a deep breath—pulled the sweet smell of her blood into his chest and held it.

Even at a distance, he could feel the heat of it. The way it tingled across his skin. His mouth began to water. The need to taste her was a fire in his blood. He'd fought against the burn for years. Not because he felt like what he wanted to do to her was wrong, but because he *knew*.

Eventually he'd go too far and end up killing her. Killing wasn't the problem; the problem was the more he had of her, the more he tasted her, the less he was able to control himself. Every time he drew his knife across her skin, the urge to push the blade in just a little deeper grew stronger and stronger. Sooner or later, he was gonna snap. Wouldn't be able to stop himself. The thought worried him. He could feel it, circling closer and closer. Not that he didn't like killing—no, killing was fun. He'd killed lots of times. Animals, cats and rabbits mostly. A dog here and there.

Some people said animals didn't have souls, but he knew that wasn't true. Felt them plenty as they wriggled free of the meat and bone that trapped them. Sometimes he had to force it out, and sometimes that slippery thing seemed almost grateful to be set free. He liked it better when they put up a fight. Liked to peel back the skin—layer by layer—until the screaming thing beneath him simply ... stopped.

But his Melissa was different.

There was fight in her. More than he'd bargained for—it thrilled him beyond measure. He'd had her for eighty-two days—eighty-three, if he counted today—and she hadn't given in. Hadn't wriggled free.

Not yet, anyway.

She lurched forward, her gait made slow and uneven by the drugs he kept her on. Her naked body was smeared with blood he'd drawn. Covered in wounds he'd inflicted.

Beautiful. Almost too beautiful to be real. He swept his gaze over her face before it settled on her eyes and the neat row of stitches that kept them closed. He was sorry for it, not being able to see her eyes. He wanted to rip those stitches out of her lids and force her eyes open, make her look at him. Make her see him. But he couldn't; seeing him would ruin everything.

His eyes traveled downward. The blood was freshest between her thighs. Thick and dark. Moist and warm. Seeing it killed his amusement, dried it up. The thought of nesting there—pumping himself into that slippery hole between her legs, cutting her while he did, over and over—moved him forward. He could see it. Her blood-slicked skin, marbled with his semen. His hands and cock covered in both.

Reaching into his pocket, he pulled out the KA-bar he always carried. The knife had been a gift from his father for his twelfth birthday. If he knew what he'd been using it for, his daddy wouldn't be too happy. Thinking about it made him smile. He flicked the blade open and gripped it tight.

Looking at her always made him hungry.

He started after her, took the distance slow at first, but every inch forward pushed him harder and faster until he was nearly running. He fell on her, dragged her under, and she went down swinging and screaming.

Just how he liked it.

———

She hit the floor, her skull bouncing off the unforgiving pad of concrete that had only seconds before been under her feet. Her arms swung wildly, hitting him again and again.

The sound of his laughter told her he found her efforts amusing. Anger roiled around with the terror. The scream forced its way out, nothing more than a dry croak that burned her throat as she drove the flat of her foot into something soft. He grunted in pain and let go.

Suddenly free, she rolled over. Tried to crawl but couldn't. Digging her fingers into the rough floor, she pulled—dragged herself until she had nowhere to go.

Dead end.

Pressing herself against the wall, she drew her legs to a chest that heaved and wracked with dry, wordless sobs. He'd recovered from whatever minor damage she'd managed to inflict and was standing over her. He wasn't laughing anymore.

She heard the jerk and snap of his belt as he yanked it off. Felt the bite and hiss of his zipper as he drew it down.

Battered knees forced themselves harder into her chest. Her swollen face buried itself against her thighs.

Please…please let me die this time. Let me go. Please—

His hand fell on her head, gripped her hair and flung her to the floor. He crouched beside her, his warm breath excited and hurried against her face and neck. Grabbing her arms, he looped his belt around her wrists, yanked them above her head. Bent them back until they felt like they'd snap in two. Her eyes rolled in her sockets. The red burn of light behind her lids went black.

Hands fell on her thighs and yanked them wide. A fierce burn, accompanied by the horrible pressure of him inside her as he rammed his hips against her—faster and faster—his grunts and moans a dull roar inside her head.

"Mine. Mine. Mine…" He muttered it over and over, each thrust accompanied by the only word she'd ever heard him say. She knew him, but every time she tried to focus on the voice behind the guttural tone, she got lost. Let herself drift away from what was happening to her until the pain and horror faded away into nothing more than shadow.

The tip of his knife sank in, dragged along her breast, skirted around the rapid, uneven rhythm of her heart, but she hardly felt it. His tongue came next, flat and wet against her breast, lapping at the blood his knife had drawn. The feel of it turned her stomach—she was almost glad when he pushed the blade in farther, and she prayed this time he'd force it deep enough to kill her. It bumped along her rib cage, its journey made jagged and broken by each brutal thrust of his hips. The blade skated along her belly. His muttering became frenzied, almost enraged. The pounding between her thighs came even faster, even more violent.

Over. It was almost over—

The blade at her belly sank in deep, a vertical breach that stole her breath and answered her prayers.

The lift and drag of the knife being yanked from her torso set her on fire, followed by another thrust of both hips and knife. "*Mine.*" This time he sank the blade in at a diagonal angle.

Lift. Drag. Thrust. "*Mine.*" Diagonal.

Lift. Drag. Thrust. "*Mine.*" Vertical.

It was the letter M.

Something inside her broke free and floated away. The legs she'd tried so desperately to close, even with him between them, went lax. A sudden warmth stole over her, and she smiled.

She was dying. She was finally free.

———

He felt for a pulse. Nothing.

He watched her gore-splattered chest for the rise and fall of breathing. It was still.

He bathed her and put her in the trunk before driving toward the place he'd picked out a few weeks before. It was far from where he'd kept her, even farther from where he'd taken her. A small building appeared to the left of the road, and he turned. It was a Catholic church, Saint Rose of Lima. The structure was squat and brown, hunkered in the dirt it sat in, as if afraid of the wide night sky and endless desert that surrounded it.

Saint Rose served a transient congregation. Mostly migrant workers who labored in the cotton and melon fields that dotted the landscape. He drove around the back of the structure and killed the engine. He watched the building for a few minutes to ensure it was empty.

The first time he'd ever seen her was in a church—one much different from Saint Rose. It'd been a Baptist church. Tall and proud, surrounded by trees. He'd seen her sitting in the front pew with her grandmother—her stunning face so serious, her Sunday dress clean but faded and nearly too small for her growing frame—and knew she was meant to be his. She belonged to him. Looking at her, one word pounded through his brain, over and over:

Mine.

She'd been young, too young to be alarmed when she caught him staring at her. She'd looked at him from across the aisle with the bluest eyes he'd ever seen—and smiled. Just remembering it took his breath away.

He popped the trunk and got out of the car. This time he cradled her in his arms like he was crossing the threshold with his bride. Hunkered down, he freed one of his gloved hands from his bundle and unlatched the gate to step into the tiny prayer garden behind the church.

It was nothing more than a few trees and some rosebushes planted next to a marble bench, but he imagined it was paradise as he stretched his Melissa out over the bench. Kneeling beside her, he pulled a pair of cuticle scissors from his front pocket and used them to snip the sutures from her lids. As careful as he was, each pass of the scissors tore the delicate flesh. Blood leaked from the corners of her eyes and he swept it away, smearing it across her temple with his gloved thumb. After the stitches were removed, he peeled her lids open, eager to see her beautiful blue eyes. Anticipation soured in his belly as soon as his eyes locked onto hers.

They were empty.

The blanket fell open, gave him a glimpse of naked flesh. Distracted, he moved it aside completely to give himself some more. He cupped her breast, still warm from the blanket, and fondled it—felt himself go hard at the sight and feel of her. His eyes travel downward until they found her stomach and the collection of stab wounds he'd left there. His groin began to throb and his free hand fell to it, began to stroke it through the rough fabric of his jeans.

He considered having sex with her one last time, but the thought was fleeting, chased away by a flutter—weak and sporadic—beneath his hand. The hand on his crotch went still and he flattened the other against her chest and pressed down. Searching for the heartbeat he was sure he'd just felt, but there was nothing there. A minute passed, then two. He dropped his hand. She was gone.

He was unsure of how much time had passed, but when the lone howl of a coyote cut across the desert, he took it as a warning.

It was time to leave.

TWO

IT WAS OCTOBER FIRST.

Sabrina rolled over and stared at the wall. She knew the date. Not because she'd checked her calendar or because the leaves on the trees outside her bedroom window were turning from green to gold.

No. It was because she hadn't been able to take a deep breath for weeks now. The feeling that someone was watching her. The long hours stretched between the setting and the rising of the sun spent wandering her silent house, kept awake by the certainty that if she closed her eyes, she'd never be able to open them again. That was what told her what day it was.

Fifteen years ago, today, she'd been kidnapped. Held for eighty-three days. Raped. Tortured. Left for dead in a churchyard.

It was October first.

She looked at her alarm clock. It was five a.m. Rolling out of bed, she made her way to the bathroom to splash cold water on her face in a vain attempt to wash away another sleepless night. Afterward, she pulled on a pair of yoga pants and a plain black T-shirt over a tank of the same color. Socks and her trusty running shoes came next. They fit her like a second skin from the countless miles they'd pounded out together. Under her bed was a shoe box. In it was her Ruger LCP .380. She strapped it to her ankle and stood, the full leg of her pants concealing it perfectly.

Jogging down the set of exterior stairs from the attic's third-floor landing, Sabrina took the cobblestone path she laid herself around the side of the house. The rambling Victorian, situated on an oversized lot, was a complete nightmare, defensively speaking. Too many trees and bushes offered an obstructed view from the street. Too many exterior doors and windows presented multiple points of entry. Its saving grace—the only reason she'd agreed to buy the place, was that it had a finished attic, set apart from the rest of the house, with its own entrance. As much as she loved her family, she needed her own space.

Her running partner waited on the sidewalk for her, as he did most mornings. He whined with excitement just beyond the pretty picket fence bordering her front yard. Seeing him, she pulled up short with a shake of her head.

"We can't keep meeting like this, Noodlehead. One of these days we're gonna get caught." Opening the gate, she stepped onto the sidewalk. Noodles, the neighbor's chocolate Lab, whined in response. He danced around in a tight circle at her feet before planting his rump on the cold concrete. He lifted a paw and cocked his head, tail going a mile a minute.

"Fine, you can come, but if we get caught, I'm blaming it all on you." She heaved an exaggerated sigh and grabbed his paw. He pulled his paw from her grasp and shot down the sidewalk toward the park at the end of the street.

Sabrina's feet absorbed the shift from hard pavement to soft earth as they hit the trail winding through the woods surrounding the park. Once swallowed by the trees, Noodles ran off into the brush, his occasional happy bark sounding back to her.

She opened herself up. Let her legs set a brutal pace, eating the trail with hungry strides. Forced her mind to pull free of the nightmares of just a few hours before. Her legs burned, but she didn't slow. Instead, she used the pain to sandblast the dregs of last night from her thoughts.

Footsteps pounded behind her, the sound of them almost perfectly matched to her own. It made her uneasy, and she pushed herself harder. Ran a bit faster. The footsteps behind her faded for a moment then doubled, catching up with her. No more than fifteen feet now. Shifting across the trail, she hugged the tree line to give the person behind her room to pass. They didn't pass but seemed intent on closing the gap between them.

Forcing out another burst of speed, she widened the gap momentarily, but the advantage was short-lived. The man, judging from the heavy sound of his footfalls, closed the space between them again.

Shooting through a gap in the trees, Sabrina ran for the open area of the park. Faking a cramp, she gripped her side before stumbling to a stop. Bent forward, her elbows braced on her knees, she took deep breaths. Her arms dangled loosely, waiting for the man behind her to make an appearance. He burst through the trees and continued on the trail without even a glance in her direction.

He ran past, not more than twenty feet away from her. Eyeing him, she took in his black track pants and white muscle shirt. Extensive ink decorated his shoulder and upper arm. The Celtic design was distinctive.

His hair was dark, cut shorter than she remembered, and his face was leaner, harder than it had been the last time she'd seen him. His name was Michael. They'd grown up in the same small Texas town, gone to school together, attended the same church. Her heart was pounding so hard it hurt, and her palms were suddenly slick with sweat.

They'd never known each other well, but he'd often stared at her a little too long, gotten a little too quiet when she was around. He'd always made her uncomfortable; seeing him now scared the shit out of her.

Every instinct Sabrina had was screaming, telling her she was in danger, urging her to run. He didn't appear by accident. This wasn't a coincidence.

Michael knew exactly who she was, and he'd come here for her.

THREE

Two people. Only two people knew who she really was—that she survived those eighty-three days of rape and torture. Valerie, her roommate, never knew Michael. If Val had run into someone claiming to be from her past, she'd sure as hell say so.

That left her Grandma Lucy.

Factoring in the time difference, she hesitated, but Lucy had always been an early riser. Walking home from the park, Noodles ambling along beside her, Sabrina unclipped her cell and dialed.

"Hello?" Lucy sounded like she'd been up for hours.

"You want to explain to me why Michael O'Shea nearly ran me down while I was out for my morning run?" Her question was met with silence. "Lucy, what did you do?"

"Would it kill you to call me Grandma?" Lucy said in her usual no-nonsense way.

Yes.

"Please . . . please explain to me why you told Michael O'Shea where I am—*who* I am. Of all people, why him?"

"He was headed your way, and I asked him to look in on y'all," Lucy said.

"I can take care of myself."

"I know." Lucy sighed. "But I'm your grandmother, no matter what you call me. I'm allowed to worry about you."

"Call him. Tell him to leave. Tell him I don't want him here." Her demands were met with silence. "Lucy—"

"He's only there for a few days, and then he'll be gone. He just wants to help," Lucy said.

"Why would he want to help you?"

"He's my friend."

"Your friend? Michael O'Shea doesn't know the meaning of the word. He's manipulative and self-serving—he uses people. If he's claiming to be your friend, it's because he wants something from you, Lucy. Don't be stupid."

Lucy was quiet for a few seconds. "You never did give him a chance," she finally said, sounding wounded. Sabrina instantly felt horrible for speaking so harshly, but she continued on, intent on making Lucy understand that trusting Michael O'Shea with anything was a horrible mistake.

"He didn't deserve one. After how he treated his parents, the hell he put them through … he spit in their faces every chance he got. Sophia and Sean adopted him when no one else wanted him, loved him in spite of all the pain he caused them, and he didn't even have the decency to stick around after they died. He just dumped his sister off on the first relative he could find and took off," she said. It was something she'd never been able to understand—the way he'd turned his back on his sister without a backward glance. It was that, more than anything, that told her what kind of person he really was.

15

"You aren't being fair. Michael changed after Frankie was born, though most folks didn't care to notice. He loved his sister … he only did what he thought was right. He was in no position to raise Frankie—she was practically a baby," Lucy said.

"Sounds pretty fucking selfish if you ask me."

"You'll watch your language, little girl." Lucy's tone was firm, one she remembered well. Suddenly, she was a child again, desperate for her grandmother's approval.

"Yes, ma'am. I'm sorry." Sabrina took a calming breath. She'd allowed Lucy to pull her off topic. None of this mattered. What mattered was why Michael O'Shea was here now. She started again. "I know you wouldn't have done this without a reason; tell me what's going on. Please, help me understand."

"I asked a friend to look in on you. I hardly see the crime."

"He's still there, the person who took me. Michael could *be* the person who took me—"

"Girl, you're talking nonsense. Michael was nowhere near here when you … when you left." Her voice drifted off on a ragged breath.

"What if he knows the man who hurt me? He could've told him, led him here … do you understand what you've done?" She hated the way her voice sounded: scared. Scared and desperate. Something she swore she'd never be again.

Opening the Harpers' front gate, she urged Noodles into the yard. He turned a mournful look her way. Their run had been cut short. She gave him an absentminded pat on the head over the fence before walking away.

He could be the person who took me … he could've led him here. Her legs felt rubbery and unsteady beneath her. Her heart still galloped in her chest. She took a deep breath and then another in an effort to steady her nerves. It was useless. It'd felt like someone had

16

been watching her for weeks now. What if Michael had been following her this whole time? What if he wasn't alone?

Walking up her driveway toward the back of the house, it hit her. There was no one there, but the feeling of being watched was so strong, it was a physical weight on her back and shoulders.

The key almost flipped out of her hand when she tried to jam it into the lock. Next door, Noodles let out a series of sharp barks. She shot another glance over her shoulder. Still no one there, but the feeling intensified.

"Michael isn't the one who hurt you and he'd never tell anyone. I'm sure of it," Lucy said, her tone firm. Lucy had always been too kind, too trusting.

Wrestling the door open, Sabrina ducked inside. The alarm system was flashing, counting down the seconds until it could start squawking. She punched in the code to keep it quiet. A flick of her wrist drove the deadbolt home, and she sagged against the doorframe for a moment. Relief did little to calm her nerves.

"How do you know for sure?" she said. The faint whirl of Lucy's KitchenAid filled the line between them.

"I trust him," Lucy said, and Sabrina had to bite back a harsh laugh.

"Why would you send someone here to spy on me anyway?" The idea of anyone, let alone Michael O'Shea, skulking around in the shadows, watching her, made her skin crawl. The fact he was here at Lucy's request did nothing to put her at ease.

"*Why*? Girl, you never were one for stupid questions. Don't start askin' 'em now. You know why." Lucy sounded angry, but she was right. If Lucy sent Michael here to watch over her, it was understandable why she'd do so without telling her. The last time she had felt danger breathing down her neck, she grabbed her brother and sister and took off.

Fifteen years ago she'd been Melissa Walker. She loved a boy named Tommy, a short-order cook in the diner where she worked, and he loved her back. She worked hard, labored under the long shadow cast by her mother in order to prove she was nothing like her. She took care of her brother and sister. Made sure they were fed and cared for. Protected them from their mother when she got too drunk or high to know where she even was. Tommy was the one bright spot in her life. She saw herself with Tommy forever, saw them growing old together. She allowed herself to believe it was possible. That she could be happy.

She should've known better.

Tommy was half Apache. In a backwoods, East Texas town of less that fifteen hundred, that set him apart. The fact that his mother was white made him good enough to cook their food and clean up after them, but no matter who his mother was, his father's blood ensured he would never be good enough to marry one of them. Even if the person he wanted to marry was the bastard daughter of the town whore.

At Tommy's urging, they kept their relationship a secret, being careful not to touch or even look at each other while other people were around. The night he slipped that lapis and sterling silver band on her finger and asked her to be his wife was the happiest of her life. She'd said yes... and twelve hours later he was found, stripped naked—bludgeoned and stabbed several times on Route 80. Obviously they hadn't been careful enough. They hadn't been careful enough.

She stayed with him, sleeping in the chair next to his hospital bed. She didn't care who knew about them—she never had. She left his room for only a moment, long enough to fill a pitcher with ice chips from the nurses' station. When she returned, there was a piece of paper stuffed in Tommy's slackened grip. It was a note: *Leave him or I'll finish what I started.*

She left the hospital then, collected the twins from her grandmother's, and was gone before sundown. She never looked back, never doubted that the decision she made had been the right one. Not even when the person who tried to kill Tommy came after her. Not even when that person dragged her into the dark and kept her there for eighty-three days.

Time had done little to dull the memories. It all seemed like it happened yesterday, and yet she felt like she'd aged a century since she'd been that stupid girl who said yes. And now here was her grandmother, desperate enough to confide in a man like Michael O'Shea and refusing to tell her why.

"Tell me what's going on. Why *him*?"

"Not my place to say. Next time you see Michael, you'd do best to ask him yourself."

Next time. "Lucy—"

"And you're wrong about him. I'm telling you, he changed after Frankie was born. Sean and Sophia's dying nearly killed him … he's far from perfect, but I trust him."

"What does he do for a living?" Sabrina said. The question was meant to throw Lucy, and it worked.

"He never said."

"It's a pretty basic thing to know about a friend, don't you think? Maybe he sells life insurance or roadies for a Neil Diamond cover band … or maybe he's something a hell of a lot worse. Ever think of that? Do you have any idea what kind of man you've trusted with my life?"

Sabrina tightened her grip on the cell for a second before snapping it shut. Something *had* happened. Something bad. Nothing short of disaster would have pulled the truth about Sabrina out of her grandmother.

Thoughts of Michael caused her apprehension rise. Why had Lucy told him about her, and why would he even care? If Lucy could be persuaded to tell someone like Michael O'Shea something as important as the fact of her survival, what else had she told him?

Finding her way downstairs to the kitchen table, Sabrina sat. Pulled her shaking hand into fists, felt angry with herself for being so afraid. The trembling crept up her arms and settled into her shoulders before inching downward until her whole body shook. She'd known this day would come. That the man who'd kidnapped her would eventually find her.

She stared out the kitchen window, but the view was lost on her. All she could see was the dark...

She couldn't see—couldn't open her eyes. The dark was absolute. No cracks of light, no pinpoints in the black to guide her way as she crawled around the room he kept her in. She couldn't see, but she could hear and smell. Her ears and nose told her everything she knew about the place he kept her. Dripping water pinging off a metal pipe, the distant passing of an airplane overhead. The frantic scurry of rats; she could smell the unclean stench of them. Other smells surrounded her. The smell of the bucket she used as a toilet... the metallic tang of blood. Her blood. Every breath she took brought her the smell of it, and with it, the memories of what had been done to her.

Next door, Noodles let out another series of barks. The sound of them snapped her back to reality. Blinking hard, her gaze settled on the cabinet above the coffee pot. In the back, hidden in the hand-painted mug Jason gave her for Mother's day when he was eight, was a prescription bottle with her name on it. *Ativan—3mg PO, PRN for anxiety.* Before she knew what she was doing, she was out of her seat. Reaching out, she gripped the cabinet knob with trembling fingers but stopped herself from pulling it open.

No. Falling apart wasn't an option and neither was relying on drugs to keep herself together. She *was* stronger. She wasn't that stupid girl anymore.

The clock display on the timered coffeemaker read just after six a.m.

Pouring herself a cup of coffee, Sabrina carried it up stairs, in a hurry to be dressed and out the door before Val woke up. Her roommate would know right away something was going on, and she didn't want to get into it.

It was clear she'd get no answers from her grandmother. Luckily, she had other ways to get what she needed.

If she hurried, she could get to work early and run his name through the computer, figure out what Michael had been up to for the past fifteen years and what it had to do with her.

Sometimes, being a cop had its privileges.

FOUR

SABRINA SHOWERED QUICKLY, NOT bothering to comb out her hair before throwing it up into a damp ponytail. Afterward, she pulled on a pair of black cargo pants and a plain black T-shirt. Reaching into her nightstand, she pulled out her SIG P220 and attached the holster to her waistband. Socks and boots came next, and she sat down on the edge of her bed to lace them. The floorboard outside her bedroom door creaked, and her head snapped up. She dropped the laces of her boot and stood. Years of training dropped her hand to the SIG strapped to her hip, and she waited. Knuckles rapped softly a moment before the door was pushed open.

"It's me—can I come in?" Val said.

Nodding, Sabrina dropped the hand on her hip. The movement wasn't lost on Val. Sabrina sat back down to pull her boot laces tight, ignoring the worried glare she was getting. Val leaned against the doorframe and crossed her arms over her chest, saying nothing.

———

She'd known Valerie only a handful of months before her abduction, but they'd formed a close friendship. So close that when she finally opened her eyes in the hospital, Val's was the first face she saw. She'd taken care of Jason and Riley during her absence and the long and brutal recovery.

She'd been a minor and the fact that the detectives investigating her case had no leads into who'd kidnapped her made her survival an easy secret to keep. As her guardian, Lucy had her case records sealed and helped her with getting her name changed. Then she let her go.

Even though Lucy never believed the person who raped and tortured her was from Jessup, she knew there was no forcing her to come home.

As soon as Sabrina had made a full recovery, she and the twins made the move to San Francisco with Val, who attended interior design school while Sabrina waited tables, biding her time until she was old enough to apply to the police academy.

Most days it was easy for her to remember how much she owed her friend. Today was not one of those days.

Boots laced and tied, she stood again and crossed the room to her closet. Reaching up, she pulled her tactical bag off the top shelf and turned to drop it on the bed. She pulled out her Kevlar vest and strapped it on. Val finally looked away. She never liked to watch her put it on.

"What's going on? Some nut job holding his cats hostage?" Knowing Val, she was trying for flippant but ended up sounding angry.

"We're doing an eight-thirty serve and search." Her team was serving a high-profile search warrant connected to a string of bank robberies. She and the boys would take point and clear the way for the Feds to come in and do their thing.

Her coffee was still hot, but she slammed it anyway. The search and serve was nothing she hadn't done a hundred times, but she was going to need the blast of caffeine to get through the next few hours. This was it though—her last assignment with SWAT. She'd finally given in and transferred out. Val should've been doing backflips. Instead, she looked like she was about to come unglued, which meant they were about five seconds from a full-fledged fight.

"You look like shit."

Right—shut your mouth, grab your gear, and leave. "I have to go." Hefting her bag onto her shoulder, she shot a look at the clock—it was six thirty. She had less than an hour to get downtown and behind her desk before the seven thirty briefing. By the time they got back from serving the warrant, her partner would be there. All she needed was for him to catch her running a background check on Michael. One look over her shoulder and the questions would start flying, and she'd be stuck. If she wanted answers, she'd have to get to the station before Strickland did. She turned and headed for the door.

"It's starting again, isn't it?"

The question came out of nowhere and stopped her retreat mid-stride. "Don't be ridiculous, Val. I'm fine."

"Ridiculous? *I'm* being ridiculous?" Valerie stared at her. "You know what's ridiculous? That after all this time, you still feel the need to lie to me—or think you *can* with any degree of success."

"I don't have time—"

"How long have the nightmares been back? How long before you convince yourself he's found you?" Val straightened and began to pace. The question was a good one. She'd been working herself there for the past few weeks, making slow and steady progress toward an inevitable breakdown.

"I'm *fine*. No nightmares. No crazy paranoia. There's nothing to worry about."

"You're a liar. I heard you last night—up the stairs, down the stairs. Back and forth in the hall. How many times did you check on the kids? Four times? Five?"

Seven. "Val—"

"Happy birthday." Val walked out without a goodbye.

It was October first. Not only was it the fifteenth anniversary of her kidnapping, it was also her thirty-second birthday.

FIVE

The lot was nearly empty when Sabrina arrived at the station. She scanned the cars as she pulled into an empty space. Strickland wasn't there yet. Thank God. Aside from a few early birds straggling in to catch up on paperwork, she was alone.

She sat down at her computer and clicked the icon linked to what she referred to as the Dirtbag Database. Typing in the name *Michael O'Shea*, she selected Texas from the list of states provided. Within minutes, his picture popped up on her screen.

This was the boy she remembered. Vacant gray eyes stared out at her framed by dark, unkempt hair that looked like it hadn't been washed in weeks. Sallow skin stretched tight over a thin face. This kid wasn't tough or angry. He was an emotional void.

She tore her eyes away from the picture on the screen and scrolled down, scanning the list of offenses littering Michael O'Shea's juvenile record. Loitering. Vandalism. Unlawful entry. Robbery. Assault. Each was worse than the last, culminating in a missing person report, filed by his foster mother when he was fourteen. He'd run away and stayed gone for over a year before being found and brought home.

Continuing to scroll down, she grew more and more puzzled. It was like the second half of his story had been lost. Where was the continuing string of crimes, growing steadily worse, until it ended in felony assault or rape? Where were the adult convictions, the prison terms he must've served? She scrolled up the page, searching carefully for what she was sure she missed, but there was nothing. It was as if he ceased to exist.

You're wrong about him. He changed after Frankie was born, though most folks didn't care to notice. He loved his sister.

As soon as the words popped into her head, she dismissed them. Lucy was too soft-hearted. She saw the good in everyone. Even when it wasn't there.

The absence of arrests meant nothing except that he'd gotten better at hiding his crimes. That didn't make him innocent; it made him smart.

"Who's that?"

Minimizing the window, she turned to find her new partner standing so close she could've reached out and touched him. He was holding two large to-go cups, and he offered her one. It'd become tradition for the last partner in to bring the other coffee. Strickland had been bringing her coffee every day since they'd partnered up a few months ago.

She took the cup and shook her head "No one." Taking a drink, she churned over everything she'd ever known or possibly forgotten about Michael. His foster parents died when he was seventeen. Both had been killed in a head-on collision, leaving him and his sister, Frankie, all alone. True to form, Michael dumped her off on an aunt and uncle and took off and ... he'd joined the Army. Maybe she could request his service records.

"I thought we liked the Tillman kid for the Weston case," he said, referring to the double homicide they were working.

"We do. We're still waiting on the warrant to search his apartment. It should be in by this afternoon—wait. What are you doing here?" It was way too early for her partner to be in already.

"This is it, right? Your last day on SWAT? The last day I have to ride solo so you can go play cowboy with that troop of primates you call a team?"

"They're good guys." *For the most part.*

Strickland smiled. "I'm sure they are ... anyway, one of us should be here in case the warrant comes in earlier than expected." Strickland tipped his chin toward the computer screen. "Who's the low-life?" He wasn't going to let it go. His tenacity was the best, worst thing about him. She took a long drink from the coffee cup and avoided making eye contact.

"Just some punk that's been calling Riley a lot lately. He wants to take her to homecoming." She thought of her little sister. At sixteen, she was beautiful enough to get plenty of male attention. What would she do if Riley brought someone home like Michael O'Shea? Murder came to mind.

Strickland gave her an odd look, followed by a boyish grin. "Please tell me you said no," he said in a conspiratorial tone she'd watched loosen the tongue of dozens of witnesses.

"I was trying to keep an open mind but now it's a definite *hell no,*" she said, making the lie up as she went along. Hopefully all he'd seen was the picture and none of the dates attached to the arrests. Pretending to get busy with paperwork, she continued to chew on the problem. She needed probable cause to request Michael's service records. No way could she get hold of them without raising questions. Another dead end.

She was suddenly angry. In the space of a few hours, her carefully constructed life had spun out of control, and the lies she'd built it on were on the verge of being exposed. Taking a deep breath, she weighed her options.

First things first, she had to figure out where Michael had been for the past fifteen years. Getting his service records through the department was out of the question, but there might be another way. Nickels, her old SWAT teammate, had been in the military, maybe he could help—

"What's goin' on with you? You're jumpy as hell." Strickland took a seat at his landfill of a desk and kicked his feet up on its top. Papers and wrappers he didn't seem to notice hit the floor.

"Nothing is going on. You gonna pick that up?"

"I need to start sneaking you decaf," he said, barely giving the clutter a passing glance. She laughed and rubbed a hand over her face.

"Bringing me caffeine is the only thing keeping you alive at this point." She stood, needing to get away from Strickland until she could get herself together. He was a rockstar interrogator in a rumpled suit and a twenty-dollar haircut. His Average Joe persona disguised a brain that could pick you apart without you even knowing it.

Her desk phone rang, and she practically dove for it.

"This is Vaughn," she said, but her relief was short-lived. She could practically feel the color drain from her face. It was her SWAT sergeant, Richards. He wanted to see her. *Now.*

Dropping the phone in its cradle, she turned away from her desk.

"Where you going?" Strickland got a good look at her face and sat up, his feet pulling a styrofoam take-out box off the desk on their way down.

"Richards wants to see me before the briefing."

"You think it's about what happened with Sanford?" Strickland looked worried.

She thought about Officer Steve Sanford. It was a safe bet that whatever Richards wanted to talk to her about involved him.

A little over a month ago, her SWAT unit participated in a drug raid on a house Narco had under surveillance for months. Once the door came down, bangers and crackheads scattered like roaches. Sanford charged in, chasing his quarry into a bedroom. He grabbed the kid's ankle while he was trying to shimmy his way under a mattress and pulled him out of hiding. When Sanford dragged him clear of the bed, the kid came up with a 9mm and got off a couple rounds.

Hit in the chest, Sanford was knocked on his back. The kid must've realized he was wearing Kevlar because he stepped up on him, intent on finishing him off with a round to the head.

She saw it all happen, kneeling in the doorway, handcuffing her catch. Sure she wouldn't be fast enough to stop what she knew was about to happen, she pulled her gun and fired. The kid went down, dead before he even hit the floor.

She *knew* Richards's call was about what happened with Sanford, but it was more than that; it was about what she'd failed to do as a result. Psych services were mandatory for officer-involved shootings within thirty days of the incident. The raid had happened five weeks ago, and she'd failed to attend her sessions.

"I don't know. He didn't say." She evaded his question, not wanting to admit she was more than likely going to be taken off active duty. She left her desk and headed downstairs, in the general direction of Richards's office.

Finding Nickels and asking him to help her track down Michael's records was more important than getting yelled at over her lack of follow-through. She briefly considered ignoring the call, but only for a moment.

Ignoring Richards would only make things worse. If she got fired, she'd have zero resources in tracking Michael down. Her best bet was to go see Richards and throw herself on her sword, make excuses he would know were bullshit, but he might accept them if they sounded plausible enough. Hopefully she'd be able to get out of his office without a suspension around her neck. After that she'd find Nickels and ask for his help in figuring out what Michael O'Shea wanted from her after all these years.

SIX

MICHAEL TOSSED THE BINOCULARS on the bed and started to pace the length of his rented room. He'd watched her get ready for work, strap on her guns, and rush out the door, intent—he was sure—on finding him. He wasn't worried though. Finding him would be impossible. Even for her.

Shooting a glance at the unopened bottle of Glenfiddich on the dresser, he felt a twinge, wanting nothing more than to drown himself in it. He'd been carrying the same bottle with him for over a year now. He hadn't drunk a single drop. Not since the day Lucy told him the truth about her granddaughter.

———

He'd come home the moment he gotten the call from his Aunt Gina—*Mikey, you've got to come home. Frankie's missing*—just dropped his life and hopped on a plane. After nearly three weeks of round-the-clock search parties and sleepless nights waiting for the phone to ring, they found her. She was in the woods along a stretch of Route 80, propped against a tree not more than ten yards from the road. It was a spot they'd searched a dozen times.

After that, he'd stayed drunk for days. Every morning he woke with a black hole in the center of his chest growing bigger by the second, an eight-man demolition crew inside his head seemingly intent on tearing his shit down from the inside out, and a liver that begged for mercy. He'd reach for the bottle and start drinking.

Days stretched into a week before the call came from the coroner, telling him Frankie's body would be released for burial. He muttered a thank you and snapped his cell in half. Frankie was all he'd had left, and she was gone. Her funeral was the next day, and he was seriously considering eating a bullet afterward. Until then he planned to keep drinking.

The banging grew louder and louder, until he was sure one of those hammer jockeys inside his head busted through his skull. No, wait. Someone was at the door. He didn't even bother to peel his face off the mattress. "No housekeeping," he shouted but the sound was muffled by the mouthful of sheets he was chewing on. He turned his face to the side. "*Go away.*" The external banging stopped. The internal hammering picked up the pace—his punishment for yelling so close to his own ears. Swiping the near-empty bottle off the nightstand, he finished it off. He managed to roll himself over to eyeball its replacement on the dresser.

The banging started up again, louder than before, like someone was going at the door with a sledgehammer. "What the *fuck* … " Somehow, he found his feet and lurched his way across the room and wrestled the door open. He hadn't seen the sun in days, and it greeted him with a stiletto to his eyeballs. *Shit.* Squinting, he raised a hand to block another attack. "Look, you can take your clean towels and shove 'em up—"

He opened his eyes just wide enough to see Lucy Walker standing on the thin stretch of sidewalk outside his no-tell-motel room door. She looked pissed, and she was holding a tire iron like she was Babe Ruth swinging for the fences. Confused, he looked past her for dancing bears or polka-dotted elephants, maybe a fish riding a bicycle, because this had to be some sort of psychotic break. "Are you real?" he said but didn't expect an answer. Chances were he was standing in his doorway talking to an unmanned housekeeping cart.

"I got your number from Charlie. He said he just talked to you, so I called but you didn't answer." Charlie. Good ol' Charlie, the town coroner slash funeral director. He and Charlie went way back. Charlie'd been the one to call him when it was time to bury his parents. He hated Charlie.

"Yeah, I broke my phone … look, I'm a little busy. Come back tomorrow." *After I've given myself a .40-caliber lobotomy.* Ignoring him, she used the business end of the tire iron to push him out of the doorway, back into the blessed dark. She followed, shutting the door behind her.

Clicking on the bedside lamp, she used her tire iron to root around in the pile of dirty clothes at the foot of the bed. She unearthed a pair of boxers and hooked them with her magic wand.

"Here." She held them out to him, and he stared at her for a second or two before he remembered. Oh, yeah—he was naked. No need to get dressed when you had no plans to go anywhere, and really, pants were a chore he could do without. Taking the boxers, he sat down on the bed. The effort at modesty turned the room into a Tilt-A-Whirl. He replanted his feet on the floor and his elbows on his knees, breathing through the spins until they subsided.

"Hand that to me, will ya?" he said, flinging his arm in the general direction of the dresser. Glancing in the direction he'd indicated, she saw the bottle. Her frown deepened into one of disappointment and concern.

"I certainly will not."

Fine. He struggled to stand, but she pushed him off his feet with that freakin' tire iron again. He went down and kept going. Sprawled out on the bed, the spins hitting him again. "What do you want?" *Just say it and get the fuck out.* He was a disappointment ... Sophia and Sean would be ashamed of him ... what would Frankie think. Nothing he hadn't been saying to himself for the past decade or so. Still, he wasn't sure he could handle hearing it right now, but she didn't say any of that.

When she started talking, he became *sure* he was having some sort of psychotic break. She couldn't possibly be saying what he was hearing.

She told him Melissa, her granddaughter—the one who'd been murdered years ago and a thousand miles away—was alive.

He had no idea what any of it had to do with him, and he didn't care. He just wanted Lucy to leave so he could get more blind drunk and hopefully pass out again.

"Look ... it's been a really long day. I just want—"

"Drinking yourself to death is gonna have to wait. Aren't you listening to me? Melissa's not dead. When they found her, she was damn close, but she managed to pull through. She's living in California. She's a police officer," she repeated when all he did was stare at her.

Melissa was *alive*? She was a *cop*?

"What are you saying? What does this have to do with Frankie?"

"I'm saying my granddaughter survived what that man did to her, and I'm saying he's the same man who killed your sister," she said plainly, pacing his room in tight circles while her fingers twisted together in an endless series of intricate knots. "I know it sounds crazy, but it's true. She's alive." She was babbling so fast he could barely track what she was saying. "She always knew he was from here. He followed her to Arizona when she ran away. After Tommy. I always thought maybe she was wrong. I mean, who around here would do such a thing? I never told her so because I didn't want to upset her, but what happened to your sister proves she's right."

"How?"

Lucy sighed and sat on the bed, next to him. "I saw what he did to Melissa. From what I hear around town, it sounds like he did the same things to Frankie."

It had taken less than a week for the police chief, in his infinite wisdom, to decree what had happened to Frankie was the work of a transient just passing through. Popular opinion latched onto this idea and held on tight. Frankie's case was closed before it was ever really opened.

He took a long look at the bottle of scotch beckoning him from the dresser. She was right—drinking himself to death would have to wait. "Tell me everything you know."

———

Lucy knew a lot, but the information came at a price. She wanted him to go to California to watch over her granddaughter, and she wanted him to do it sober. He agreed to watch her, protect her if needed, and he agreed to do it dry. Nearly a year later, he had every intention of keeping his promises.

He'd watch her. Get to know her, so to speak. Find her soft spots. When the time was right, he'd approach her and exploit them. He'd convince her to go back to Jessup with him, to help catch the man who raped and tortured her by making her survival public. If the man who killed his sister knew Melissa was still alive, he'd make a play for her—Michael was sure of it. He'd persuade her to help him, and if persuasion didn't work, he'd have to get creative.

It was a plan. Not the perfect plan, but it was action and purpose after almost a year of spinning his wheels. It was the only plan he had, and he'd fucked it all up by practically attacking her in the bushes like a goddamn crazy person.

Not his smartest move ever.

That morning he'd started on the higher trails as usual. From his vantage point he could see her while remaining undetected. Keeping up with her brutal pace, he heard nothing but the crunch of gravel beneath his feet and the occasional happy bark of her neighbor's dog, her image flickering behind the screen of dense foliage separating them.

He liked the way she moved—efficiency and confidence in every stride. Her ponytail bobbed a jaunty rhythm, at total odds with the rest of the picture she made. It made him smile ... and then it happened.

He forgot about Frankie. Forgot he was following her for a purpose, that he had a responsibility here. For a few seconds, Sabrina was just a pretty girl—not the reason his sister was dead. It was only for a moment, but it carried the jarring sense of a free fall. In those few seconds, he'd been totally lost.

Then it all rushed back. Before he knew what he was doing, he took the bisection connecting the upper and lower trails, running at full speed until he caught up with her.

Angry. He was angry at her for surviving, and he hadn't cared if she recognized him or not. If he looked at the situation objectively, he'd admit Sabrina was as much of a victim as Frankie had been. But knowing that didn't change the way he felt, and it didn't bring his baby sister back either. It was ugly and irrational, this anger he harbored toward her. He shouldn't hate her or blame her. But he did. He'd let his emotions get the best of him. And now she knew he was there.

A mistake. One he wouldn't make again.

His phone rang. He didn't have to look at it to know who it was. Lucy had been calling him all morning, which meant she knew what happened. He hit Ignore. He couldn't handle talking to her right now. That last thing he needed was a blow-by-blow replay of what an idiot he was.

Tossing his cell on the dresser, he started to pace, examining the situation from every angle. He'd probably screwed up any chance he had of approaching her on a rational level with his stalkerish behavior, but he'd try anyway. No matter what, she was going home.

He'd drag Melissa back to Jessup if he had to and stake her out like a sacrificial lamb in order to draw out and kill the man who had butchered his sister. But there was a problem, one he hadn't counted on: *Sabrina* was no lamb. She was a lion, and she wasn't going anywhere without a fight.

SEVEN

RUMORS WERE NECESSARY IN a town like Jessup. Gossip about who was sleeping with who and who got fired for drinking on the job wore away at the monotony of small-town life. People felt important knowing their neighbor's dirty little secrets. Jessup needed something to talk about, and Lucy Walker's granddaughter was a favorite subject.

Not a month went by he didn't hear someone go on and on about how she ran away after the mess she caused. How she'd seduced her mother's boyfriend and got poor Tom Onewolf stabbed near to death, only to get herself killed for her trouble. Speculation and embellishment were common; some folks made stuff up outright, but most of it was bullshit. She never tried to seduce anyone. As for what happened to Tom . . . it was that asshole's fault for thinking he had a right to even look at Melissa, much less touch her.

It was ridiculous, really, the lies people told. Nonetheless, when he heard people talking about her, he always listened, and last week was no different.

"I heard just the other day, in this very diner, she ain't dead. Way I heard it, she's livin' out in California with those kids she took from her momma. Shameful, if you ask me—the mess she caused around here…"

That was a new one. He'd never heard she survived before. At first he took it about as seriously as an Elvis sighting—he'd been the one to kill her, after all—but the words burrowed into his brain like a parasite. What should've sounded outlandish began to sound plausible. What he knew couldn't be possible changed shape and began to look like a miracle.

The thought that she might be out there somewhere kept him up at night, and the more he thought about it, the faster the infection spread. It began to make sense. Why, after countless attempts, he was never able to find another woman who could give him what he needed. Why, no matter what he did to them, he was never satisfied.

He decided to visit Lucy. She'd know the truth. Plastering a smile on his face, he knocked on her back door, and when she opened it, she smiled at him in return. He came here often and was always welcomed in. Sometimes he'd offer to fix a creaky porch step or adjust her hot water heater. Sometimes they'd just sit in her living room and gossip about small-town affairs. All the while, no matter what he was doing, the eighty-three days he spent raping and torturing her granddaughter played on a constant loop in his head.

Today's visit was for sitting and talking.

"You'll never guess what I heard in town yesterday. Someone started a rumor that she's alive, Lucy. Who'd be cruel enough to do that?" he said, watching for a reaction under the guise of barely contained disgust.

She visibly stiffened for a moment before scowling at him. "My guess is someone with nothing better to do than make up stories."

"It's not true, is it? She's not alive, is she?" It was a bold question but one he had to ask. She sharpened her gaze and let out a disdainful sigh.

"Don't be dense, boy. If she were alive, I'd know about it." Her tone closed the conversation, but he was unconvinced.

She got up to take a lemon pound cake out of the oven, and he seized the rare opportunity to peruse the space. He was looking for proof—anything that would tell him what he needed to know. He moved to the small writing desk tucked in the corner to yank at its drawers and rifle their contents. Nothing.

He quickly leafed through books and mail left out on the coffee table. Nothing. Just when he thought he'd truly lose it, he spotted it. A single sheet of paper folded around a photo and tucked into her sewing basket. He plucked it out with trembling fingers, rattling the paper a bit as he unfolded it.

Dear Lucy,
This picture was taken the day they got their driver's
licenses. You can't tell, but Sabrina is terrified! I hope you
are well.
—Valerie

The picture was of Melissa's siblings—fraternal twins, a boy and a girl. They were posed on a set of porch steps, a woman was wedged between them. His gaze lingered on the girl. She looked so much like her sister, with her bright blue eyes and auburn hair swept away

41

from the delicate bones of her face, but she failed to hold his attention. Inexplicably, his eyes were drawn away from her and came to rest on the woman by her side.

As with all women, her eyes attracted him first. They were dark brown. Not the right color. Melissa's eyes were the most amazing shade of blue. Her arms were draped over the twins' shoulders. She looked confident and comfortable, like she was right where she belonged.

Something about her pissed him off.

He brought the picture close to his face and looked for a reason this woman should compel him. Despite the smile on her face, she looked tough. Dangerous. The tingle of fear he experienced when he looked at her was something new. This woman looked like she'd laugh in his face even as he stabbed the life out of her.

He didn't like it.

He studied the photo intently, looking for a reason … and there it was. A starburst scar, the size of a half-dollar, on the back of her hand.

He'd been there when she burned herself at the diner where she waitressed. It was a splatter burn from the fryer. They'd been swamped and she'd been helping Onewolf in the kitchen …

He looked away from the scar and studied the face. A thin sheen of sweat broke out on his upper lip, and he wiped it away with the back of his hand. Was it possible?

He saw Melissa in countless women, nearly every day, but this woman was nothing like her. Melissa had been beautiful. Looking at her had been like looking at the sun. She'd been dazzling. This woman wasn't beautiful. She was barely pretty. But still, he couldn't look away. Where Melissa had been softly curved, this woman was lean, almost hard. Her face was harshly angled, her jaw almost masculine. Her mouth was wide and full. The nose sitting above it was slightly crooked, like it had been broken more than once. The feline tilt to her eyes gave her a predatory edge that made him feel uneasy.

She was different. Every muscle, every pore. Only the eyes remained the same. Not the color, but he looked past their wrongness and saw something he'd searched for in countless women for over a decade. He saw the truth of himself staring back at him.

Only Melissa had seen him for what he truly was, and he saw it in this woman's eyes.

She was alive.

Lucy was coming. He carefully placed the picture in its sleeve and slipped it into his back pocket.

"I made an extra cake for company. Would you like a piece?" she said.

He wanted to grab her and shake the truth out of her. He wanted to make her bleed for hiding his Melissa away from him. Instead he smiled.

"A piece of cake would be great, Miss Lucy," he said and made himself sit still.

"Coffee?"

"That'd be fine, but I'd hate for you to go to any trouble on my account." He forced the smile to stay put when she fluttered her hand his way.

"Nonsense, it's already made," she said before heading toward the kitchen. He waited for her to disappear into the kitchen before he moved.

He pulled a pair of thin latex gloves from his back pocket and put them on while he crossed the room. He locked the front door and slid the security chain home. He cocked his head to the side and listened. The soft murmur of her voice came to him from the kitchen.

"Miss Lucy?" he said loudly. Who was she talking to? He turned to follow her in to the kitchen.

She stood with her back to him, humming to herself. He took a quick glance around the kitchen and saw it almost immediately. The cord attached to the wall-mounted rotary phone swung slightly from side to side.

She'd made a phone call.

"*Mmm, mmm.* Lucy, that coffee smells almost as good as your lemon pound cake," he said, and she laughed without turning around.

"Well, you can hardly have one without the other," she said, placing cups and saucers on a tray along with a sugar bowl and creamer. It made him smile. She'd always been so formal.

"Who'd you call?" He kept his tone conversational and closed the distance between them.

"What? No one. I didn't call anyone." She looked up at him and smiled back.

"Miss Lucy … " He laid a gloved hand on the side of her throat and traced a thumb over her pulse. The drum banging away inside her vein thrilled him. "You're lying to me. You shouldn't do that—I really hate being lied to."

EIGHT

RICHARDS'S OFFICE WAS ON the basement level of the precinct, down the hall from the practice range. The muffled *pop, pop, pop* of gunfire followed her down the corridor, the loud bark of an angry dog. For a moment she wanted nothing more than to simply turn around and leave. Not just the corridor or the precinct. She wanted to leave this life. A life she never asked for. One she never wanted.

Without thinking, she reached inside her shirt and wrapped her fingers around the silver and lapis band hanging from a chain around her neck and gave it a squeeze. The metal, warmed by her skin, bit into her palm and the sudden sting grounded her.

The door was shut. She could hear the muted drone of conversation coming through the door. Someone was in Richards's office with him.

Sabrina leaned against the wall, crossing her arms over her chest. She closed her eyes, tried to look bored, like she didn't know what was waiting for her on the other side of Richards's door. He'd want to know why she'd ignored department protocol, why she'd skipped her psych sessions. A question she had no ready answer for. Not one she'd want to give, anyway.

If the raid had taken place a few months ago, she would've been able to sit through the sessions without a problem. She would've been able to nod her head and make appropriate comments and facial expressions. She would've hated every second of it, but she would've been able to do it. But the raid happened in September. The paranoia had already kicked in, and so had the nightmares. No way in hell could she have sat through a counseling session. Any therapist worth their salt would've seen her for what she was: a cop on the verge of a major crack-up. She would've been out on her ass before she'd even had a chance to sit down.

Skipping the sessions had been a risk, one that would cost her. Her chances of sliding on this were between slim and none, but she'd rather be tagged as non-compliant than crazy.

The door suddenly opened, and she jerked her head up. All thoughts of her suspension disappeared. Nickels, the one person who could help her find Michael, was standing right in front of her.

He began to open the door wider to allow her to pass through, but she shook her head and moved down the hall toward the gun range. She shot him a look; he instantly fell into step behind her.

"What's up?" he said.

"I need a favor." She forced the words out and had to beat down the guilt when he readily nodded his head. He'd want to know why she needed O'Shea's records, and the lie she'd worked up to explain herself wasn't one she wanted to tell.

"You got it."

She pressed on before she lost her nerve. "You were in the military, right?"

"Yeah, I served in the Gulf—so?"

"If I asked you to help me get a hold of some service records, no questions asked—could you?" The open expression on his face closed up tight, and she instantly regretted asking him. "You know what? Never mind. Forget I asked." She stepped to the side, but he shifted his body to block her exit.

"You just asked me to help you get confidential military files. Not exactly something I can just forget. What's going on?" he said, his usually pleasant face clouded with concern.

"It's stupid, really. Val wants to fix me up with this guy she knows. He said he's ex-military, but you know how it is. He could be lying just to try and impress me. Being a cop is hell on a girl's love life." This was the lie she didn't want to tell. She watched her words sink in, and his face changed again. His concern took a back seat to the protective possessiveness he felt where she was concerned. She felt horrible exploiting his feelings for her, but she'd do whatever it took to protect her family.

"What's his name?"

"Michael O'Shea."

"What branch?"

"Army." She thought she remembered Lucy telling her it was the Army, years ago when he left, but she wasn't sure. Nickels nodded his head and scrubbed a hand over his face.

"What do you want to know?" He was all business now.

"I don't know… service dates, where he was stationed. If he committed any crimes while he was in," she said. She had no idea what she needed, but it seemed like a good start.

"Basically, you want his entire jacket. Shit, Vaughn—you're not asking much, are you?"

"I know it's a lot, Nick. I just don't know who else to ask." If there was any other way, she'd jump on it in a heartbeat, but there wasn't.

"Okay. I'll see what I can do but I'm not promising anything." He gave her a crooked grin. "A date, huh? I don't know—you don't seem like a dinner and a movie kinda girl."

She forced herself to smile back. "I'm not. I'm a taco stand, gun range kinda girl, but Val thinks I need romance or some shit." She rolled her eyes.

He threw a glance over his shoulder before looking her in the eye. "Ya know … you could just tell Val thanks but no thanks and grab a drink with me after work," he said. She instinctively took a step back and dropped her gaze to the floor. With his light brown hair and whiskey-colored eyes, Nickels was no hardship to look at. If she thought they could keep it casual, she might consider it, but she knew Nickels didn't do casual. He was a long-haul guy. He couldn't handle her brand of relationships, which was no relationship at all. He caught her hesitation, and the disappointment she saw on his face compounded her guilt. She opened her mouth to agree to a drink, but he cut her off.

"I'll do it regardless, but the drink offer still stands," he said. Nickels was one of the good ones. He didn't deserve to be used. The last thing she wanted to do was string him along, but she didn't want to hurt him either.

"I better go see what Richards wants."

"Yeah, I'll see you inside," he said, nodding in the direction of the briefing room. He took a few steps down the hall before she called out.

"One condition: I buy the first round." She ignored the little voice in her head telling her this was a bad idea.

"As you wish." He gave her a slight bow and another grin before he turned and walked away.

NINE

"You wanted to see me, sir?" Sabrina nudged the cracked door open with the toe of her boot and wrapped her knuckles on the frame. Richards's head popped up from the small mountain of paperwork crowding his desk.

"Sit." Richards leaned back in his chair and steepled his fingers under his chin, studying her with enough intensity to make her want to squirm. Seemingly out of thin air, he produced a piece of paper and held it up for her to see. "You know what this is?"

"No, sir." She knew exactly what it was. Richards cracked a smile and nodded his head.

"It's your four-forty."

She said nothing. When an officer discharged their weapon in the line of duty, the case was taken before an incident review board. A committee of fellow officers, administrators, department shrinks, and civilians were asked to review your actions and decide whether or not they were justified. The 4-40 form documented her side of the story along with the board's findings and recommendations. Richards continued to stare at her for a few moments before speaking again.

"It was a good shoot. Witness accounts were able to corroborate your report. The bullet holes in Sanford's shirt didn't hurt either." He cracked another humorless smile, and she returned it. "Why didn't you come to me?" he said out of nowhere, throwing her off balance.

"Sir?"

"Sanford. Why didn't you tell me?"

Instantly, she understood what Nickels was doing in Richards's office so early in the morning. "Nick needs to learn how to keep his mouth shut."

"Wasn't just him. Lloyd, Tagert, McMillan, Davis ... there's been a steady stream coming in since you filed for a transfer. Nick was just the latest," he said. The names of her SWAT teammates closed her throat. Suddenly she missed them almost as much as she wanted to kill them for getting into her business and dumping it on Richards's desk. He leaned forward and put his elbows on his desk. "You want to tell me what happened after the raid?"

She thought of that day, of the ride back to the station. Kevlar stopped bullets, but that didn't mean getting shot didn't hurt like a bitch. Taking two to the chest had Sanford laid out in the back of the wagon. All she could hear was the excited buzz of the other team members. Her actions and the fact they'd saved Sanford's life were all anyone could talk about. She didn't have much to say, just endured the shoulder slapping and knuckle bumping with a vacant half-smile while Sanford glared at her through the slits cracked in his eyelids.

He'd said nothing to her after she dropped the banger, just lay flat on his back, staring at the ceiling. Someone yelled her name. More shouts sounded from unseen rooms. The heavy tread of pounding boots shook the floorboards under her knee, getting heavier and louder. The guy she had cuffed and pinned to the ground with her knee in his neck threw up all over her boot. She barely noticed. She stood and rushed forward. She knelt, first in front of the kid she'd shot—he couldn't have been more than twenty—to check his vitals. He was dead. She kept her gun trained on him while she removed the 9mm still in his grip and jammed it into her waistband. It took only seconds, and when she looked at Sanford, he was watching her.

"Are you hit?" she said. She moved to run her hand along his chest and sides, checking for possible wounds.

"Get the fuck off me." He practically snarled at her, shoving her hand away while he struggled to sit up. She looked up to find Nickels in the doorway, a look of sickened relief plastered all over his face. She stood and shoved her way past him. The rest was a blur.

On the way back to the station, Nickels watched them both, his temper showing plainly. "You're an asshole," he said to Sanford, his voice loud enough to quell the incessant chatter that filled the small space. "She saved your life, and you practically shit on her."

Sabrina felt her stomach hit her boots. The last thing she needed right now was a confrontation.

"Nick—don't," she said quietly, but they both ignored her.

"Fuck her and fuck you. Just because you got a hard-on for the unit dyke doesn't mean I have to kiss her ass." Sanford tossed her a snide glare. Before she knew it, Nickels hauled Sanford off the bench and the two of them were tossing each other around the back of the wagon.

Without thinking, she dove in and wedged her shoulder between them to pry them apart. Sanford took the opportunity to punch her in the mouth with a sharp jab that snapped her head back. It took the entire unit to drag Nickels out of the wagon when it finally pulled into the station lot. She'd had a busted lip she blamed on a takedown during the raid, and she'd expected the rest of the unit to back her story. Apparently, her expectations had been too high.

"I can handle it, Sarge." She wasn't saying a word.

"You know I'm required to investigate the matter."

"I never filed a formal complaint, and I'm not going to. So you're not required to do anything." It was a technicality, but she exploited it shamelessly.

"I can't let it go, Vaughn."

"I said I can handle it." The abruptness of her answer caused Richards eyebrows to shoot up on his forehead. Great, now she was noncompliant *and* insubordinate. She took a deep breath and let it out slowly. "He's having a rough time, sir. His wife left him."

"When?"

She sighed, picked at a loose thread on the knee of her pants. "A few days before the raid."

Richards's eyebrows slammed down over his eyes, and she knew she'd said too much. "How do you know?"

"Come on, Sarge. The guys around here gossip more than a sewing circle," she said and was rewarded with a snort that might've passed for a laugh.

"He drinking again?"

Last week she'd stopped at the corner market a few blocks from the station to pick up a gallon of milk on her way home. Sanford had been at the register when she walked in, a fifth of Beam on the counter in front of him. She strode past him, pretended not to notice him or his purchase. When she made it up to the counter with the milk, he was gone.

She shrugged her shoulders, "Not that I've seen."

Richards wasn't buying it. "I'm pulling him in here because of what happened. Whether you want to file a complaint or not, he assaulted a fellow officer. Not something I can let slide. I'll get the rest out of him and treat it accordingly."

"It's really not a big deal." She wished the floor would open up and swallow her whole.

"See this?" He rooted around under a stack of papers and pulled out a brass nameplate that read *Sgt. Daniel Richards.* He slapped it down on his desk in front of her face. "This gives me the right to decide what's important and what's not. You transferred out of my unit because of Sanford and his schoolyard bullshit. That's a big deal to me."

She shifted in her seat, uncomfortable. Her leaving the unit had everything to with that raid. Sanford had his hand in it, sure— but it had just as much to do, if not more, with Nickels.

When she'd looked up from where she knelt next to Sanford, she'd seen Nick's face in the doorway. He'd looked wrecked, on the verge of losing it. If it'd been her laid out on the floor, he would've fallen apart, compromising not only himself but the entire team.

She decided then and there she couldn't work with him anymore. Backing your teammate was one thing—letting your emotions lead the way was entirely another. He'd be exactly the kind of idiot to ignore his own personal safety in favor of hers. She didn't need that on her conscience.

"Okay." She looked at her watch. It was seven thirty. Time for the briefing. "Can I go?" She stood, ready to hit the door.

Richards frowned at her. "Yeah, you can go. *Home.*" He held up her 4-40 again and pointed to a box at the bottom of the page marked *Office use only.* "Do you know what this says?" he said, and she shook her head, not trusting her voice to stay steady. "It says *Special Services Recommendations.* Below that it says you're required to attend three, sixty-minute sessions with the department therapist within thirty days of the incident. It's been more than thirty-five days since the shooting, and you still haven't complied with department policy. That's a problem, Vaughn."

"I'm sorry, sir. I forgot—"

"You forgot?" He looked at her like she was on drugs. "Okay ... well, since you're so forgetful, you must have *forgotten* you scheduled an extended vacation before you transferred out of my unit."

"A vacation? I can't just take a vacation. This is my last day on the team, Sarge. We have an eight thirty—"

Richards just shook his head. "*We* have a warrant to serve—*you* don't. Your discharge from SWAT is effective immediately. Go home, Vaughn."

Go home. The words caused panic to swell in her belly. She shook her head. "Strickland and I are working a double homicide, we're waiting on a search warrant now," she said, the panic rising up from her stomach to choke her.

"You don't seem to understand. This isn't a suggestion, or a request. You're either going to take the vacation, or I'm going to suspend you for thirty days for noncompliance with department policy."

She grasped at the few straws she had left. "I'm in my first ninety days in Homicide. Mathews hates me enough as it is—"

"I'll take care of Mathews," he said, referring to her new boss.

"Please." She was begging. She was actually begging.

Richards stared at her for a long moment before looking down at his desk. "You can finish out the day so you and Strickland can make your arrest, but come tomorrow morning, you're gone."

She nodded, felt hopeful. "The serve and search?"

"No. Your discharge stands. I don't want to see you until you've completed your sessions. You read me?"

She moved toward the door. Drawing a deep breath then another, she struggled to rein in her boiling temper. She knew better than to turn around and look at him. She was being forced out on vacation because she saved Sanford's life. What kind of shit was that?

"Vaughn?" He was waiting for an answer.

"Yes sir, loud and clear." She opened the door and left, slamming it behind her with a resounding bang, blending perfectly with the gun shots from the range as they bounced down the hall.

TEN

CAREFUL TO CLOSE THE curtains, he dropped Lucy's limp body into the nearest kitchen chair. He found a roll of duct tape in a kitchen drawer, along with a few other items that might prove useful. He used the tape to strap her to the chair and slapped a piece over her mouth for good measure, then set the rest aside for later.

First things first.

Bypassing the rotary phone, he made his way into the living room. He remembered seeing a cordless handset tucked in her knitting basket. He hit Redial with no real hope. It was unlikely the person she called would be the same number she last dialed on the cordless phone, but—

"This is Michael. I'm unable to get to my phone. Leave me a message, and I'll try to call back."

O'Shea. The end of the outgoing message gave way to a prolonged silence. He listened for a few moments before ending the call. He knew the two of them were close. Lucy lived in his foster parents' old house, and he'd taken to staying here whenever he was in town, but why call him? Had Lucy called Frankie's brother to tell him her killer was eating lemon pound cake off the good china in her sitting room?

It was doubtful. O'Shea was protective of Lucy, took care of her. If he knew the fox was in the henhouse, the phone would be ringing off the hook right now, but it was silent.

O'Shea had no idea he was here.

He walked through the house closing curtains and drawing blinds. Lucy lived miles from the nearest town—between Jessup and Marshall—so he wasn't too concerned someone would drop in unannounced at this hour. She said the cake was for company, but he knew it was really just for Melissa's birthday. Still, people were unpredictable. Caution was always prudent.

He perused the bookshelf next to the small fireplace. It held an odd mix. Dime store trinkets mingled with pricey collectables. The historical romance novels and Westerns he knew she loved shared space with Hemingway and Steinbeck. O'Shea—had to be. Tiny signs of him were all over the place.

Finding Lucy's record collection, he flipped through the worn jackets until he found one he liked. He slipped the album out and placed it on the turntable, setting the needle down carefully so as not to scratch it. He raised the volume when Gene Kelly began singing in the rain.

He set the turntable on repeat and headed back to the kitchen. The music followed him through the house and he whistled along, the tune putting a spring in his step.

He went back into the kitchen and was pleased to see Lucy was waking. Her head lolled on her scrawny neck, her creased lids fluttered open, but she remained silent.

He smiled at her.

The look she gave him said she was only mildly surprised at the sudden turn of events. That irked him.

"Who is this woman? Is this Melissa?" He spoke calmly and showed her the picture.

She stared at him for a moment before shifting her eyes to the photo. She studied the picture as if considering his question, and his excitement mounted. He peeled back the strip of duct tape he'd stuck to her mouth. "Tell me the truth, and I'll let you go."

She shifted her eyes to his. Her face was calm—resigned, even. "No, you won't."

"It's okay, I won't hurt her," he said. This made her laugh—the sound saying, *like you could*. The rage, always simmering in his gut, started to bubble. The bouncy rhythm of Gene singing about the sun in his heart and being ready for love filled the space between them for a moment. He took a deep, cleansing breath, determined to stay calm.

"See this?" He showed her the knife he held. The folding blade was roughly the length of a child's forearm and nearly as wide. It sported a double edge—one smooth and sharpened to a razor's edge, the other serrated with teeth that looked like they were made to bite. His father had given it to him for his twelfth birthday, but despite its age and countless uses, it showed little wear. He took care of what was his.

"This is the knife I used on Melissa." He leaned in close and whispered in her ear. "Did she tell you, Lucy? Did she tell you what I did to her with it? You know, a gentleman never kisses and tells but I have to tell you, it was ... *magical*." He pressed his lips to her cheek and she reared back, twisting her face out of reach. He grabbed her by her hair and yanked, pulling her back to him with a laugh. "She fought me in the beginning, and toward the end she just begged me to kill her, but between you and me"—he smiled and lowered his tone to a whisper—"I think she kinda liked it."

Lucy started to cry. Tears coursed down her wrinkled face, dripping off her trembling chin, but they only seemed to strengthen her resolve. She looked away, terrified but still silent. A thumping scratch signaled the end of the record before the needle lifted and set itself down to repeat the song.

He decided to change tactics. He loosened his grip on her hair and smoothed his hand over her head before letting it fall to her cheek for a moment. Gently, he took her chin in his hand, lifted her face to his, and waited for her to look at him.

"Why did you call Michael O'Shea?" he said, and she looked surprised.

"I didn't."

"You're lying." It bothered him that she would be so bold. "Does he know where Melissa is?"

"You killed Melissa." The words stuck in her throat, hitched on a sob.

"Stop lying," he said loudly. His fingers dug into her face, deep enough to bruise, and she fought hard not to cry out. He let go, took a step back to steady himself. Losing control now would serve no purpose.

She *was* lying. She had to be. But doubt crept in, and the absolute certainty he'd felt only moments before began to waver. Could it be he was so desperate to have her back that he fooled himself into seeing things that weren't there, into believing things that couldn't possibly be true? He looked at the picture in his hand and instantly felt the connection. The woman in the picture *was* Melissa, he was sure of it. Somehow, some way, she'd come back to him.

"This is Melissa, I know it is." He flashed Lucy the picture he held and grinned. "She's mine. She belongs to me, and you've been hiding her from me all this time ... you're smarter than I gave you credit for."

"No. Melissa's gone. Been gone for years." She turned her face away, dismissing him. He felt himself bend, his control threatening to break. He slipped the picture in his pocket and picked up his knife. He leaned in close, putting his face within inches of hers.

"You are a stubborn one, Miss Lucy ... " He drew the blade down her cheek. Blood mingled with the tears, but she remained silent. "Where is she?" he said quietly, not at all surprised when Lucy refused to answer. "Okay ... we'll do things your way." He straightened and returned to the counter to take a quick inventory of what he'd collected there. A hammer and nails. A roll of trash bags. An extension cord. A dishtowel.

Whistling along with the music, he opened an upper cabinet and rifled its contents. He found a carton of salt, gave it a testing shake— nearly full. He added it to his collection. Not at all what he was used to, but he'd worked with less. He retrieved a mixing bowl from the sink and rinsed it out before filling it with hot water.

"You know, of all the things my daddy taught me, the value of hard work stuck with me the most," he said to her over his shoulder. "'*Nothing worth having ever comes easy, boy.*' Every time he said it to me, I wanted to cut out his tongue. But he was right." He chose the hammer and nails and showed her what he held. Cocked his head to the side and gave her a lopsided grin. "Last chance," he sang and waggled the hammer at her.

She spat at him.

His smile widened. "I was hoping you'd say that."

He carried it all to the table and set it out carefully, prolonging the pleasure he felt at the prospect of what lay ahead. Breaking them was always the best part.

He opened the carton of salt, poured it into the bowl of water. He shook out the last few grains and tossed her a wink over his shoulder. "Every bit counts," he said before he dropped the dish-towel into the briny mix.

"You're insane." She said the words quietly, but he heard her and for a split second, hated her.

"There's no cause for name calling, Miss Lucy." His tone was light, but she shrank away from the look he gave her. "I tried doing this the easy way. What happens next … well, you got no one to blame but yourself."

He picked up the trash bags and unrolled them, tearing them off one by one. He started whistling again, picking up the tune where Gene sang about September seeming as sunny as spring. The music buoyed his spirits, and he forgave her.

"It's alright Miss Lucy. I'm not mad, and I want to apologize ahead of time. This is gonna get messy," he said. He laid the trash bags on the floor, overlapping them around and beneath her chair. When he finished, he picked up the roll of duct tape and ripped off a strip.

"I'm gonna go ahead and gag you again. As far as screaming is concerned, I've found a little goes a long way." He slapped the tape over her mouth and gave her cheek an affectionate pinch.

She began to cry in earnest, though she tried hard to fight it. She breathed heavily, dragging air into her lungs through her nose, so fast and hard, each whistling intake flattened her nostrils. She sounded like a teakettle set to boil.

"You need to try and calm down, now. You keep breathing like that, you're gonna pass out and miss all the fun." He knelt down in front of her, pinning her left foot beneath his knee and reached for the right. Her eyes squeezed shut, and she jerked her leg to the side, fighting to stay out of his grasp. He captured it easily—his fingers circled her bony ankle and pulled it back in place. He forced her foot flat on the floor and held it there, a nail pinched between his fingers.

He could feel her foot straining against his hand, but it was useless. "You prayin' Miss Lucy? You beggin' God to save you—deliver you from evil? Deliver you from me?" He lifted the hammer and tightened his grip on her foot. "I'll tell you something else my daddy taught me. *God helps those who help themselves*," he said and drove the nail home.

Shrieks ripped from her throat, got caught behind the strip of tape and collected there—building to a high-pitched hum he was sure only a dog could truly appreciate it. He grabbed another nail and forced her other foot flat.

"Where is she?" He raised the hammer, held it high over his head and looked up at her. She writhed and moaned in pain but shook her head, still refusing to tell him what he wanted to know. He shrugged and brought the hammer down on the second nail.

One high-pitched hum bled into the next.

Without pause, he picked up his knife, dragged it up her calf, then down. First one and then the other. Back and forth until her legs were covered in dozens of thin, shallow cuts.

He took the towel out of the bowl and bathed her cuts in the salty water. Salt seeped into the wounds, and she began to jerk in her chair. He repeated the process. First the knife and then the towel, each time dipping into the saltwater before applying it to her legs—until dozens of cuts became hundreds. They overlapped, creating an intricate pattern resembling the scales on a fish. Using the tip of his knife, he lifted the edge of one of these scales and pulled, peeling a thin layer of skin from her leg. First one … and then another and another until blood streaked her calves and puddled at her feet. Occasionally, he bathed her wounds in the salty water while she hummed and convulsed with pain. She jerked at her feet, tried to escape the relentless peeling, but it was useless. The nails in her feet trapped them in place.

He gave the towel a final squeeze over her feet, brine pooled around the head of the nails for a moment before sinking in. Now the hums came in short bursts. She sounded like a siren, wailing in the distance.

He sat back on his haunches and swiped a forearm over his brow and waited. After a while, her muffled screams tapered off into a series of snuffling whimpers, sounding more animal than human. He reached for her face, but she jerked her head away.

"Be still now, I'm just gonna take the tape off so we can chat." His hand darted out and snagged a corner, ripping the tape off and some skin along with it. Blood peppered her bottom lip and she cried out from the sting of it.

"I'll tell you Miss Lucy, this sure makes for thirsty work. Got any lemonade?" He stood and crossed the room—hammer in hand—to open the refrigerator. Disappointed, he pulled out a pitcher of iced tea. It'd have to do. He carried it to the counter and retrieved a glass from the dish drainer. The cake dome set in the corner caught his eye. "Mind if I cut myself a piece of cake to go along with it?"

"… choke on it."

"Now, that ain't Christian-like, Miss Lucy." He splayed a hand across his chest and shook his head, but truthfully he found her rebellious attitude amusing. He used his knife to cut the cake. Her blood leached into the yellow of it, creating an orange ring around the outside edges. He liked the way it looked. Like one of those bright crayon drawings of the sun kids did in elementary school. He set it on the plate she'd laid out on the tray along with the coffee and grabbed a fork.

"I'm gonna find her, one way or another. I did it once, I can do it again." He poured tea into the glass and took a long drink. It wasn't lemonade, but it was sweet, just the way he like it. "This can all end now, Miss Lucy. I'll kill you quick, cross my heart. All you gotta do is tell me where she is." He took a bite of cake and smiled. It even *tasted* like sunshine.

"Go to hell," she said. Her voice sounded strange, garbled from the pain. He nodded his head and took another drink.

"Figured as much. Obviously, Melissa got her sass from you. She sure didn't get it from her mama." He smiled at her when she looked at him. The mention of her daughter surprised her. "Kelly was all talk. She acted tough but folded like a bad poker player the very first time I cut her." Lucy's eyes, glassy with pain, jerked to his face. He lowered his tone to an exaggerated whisper. "I did her just like I did Melissa. Just like I'm doing you now—but you knew that, didn't you? Only difference is, I know for a *fact* Kelly liked it." He took a final bite and washed it down with the last of his tea. It occurred to him he'd now had three generations of Walker women under his knife. He thought it was sweet. It felt right. The way things should be.

"Alright, Miss Lucy, time to get serious. What'd you say to O'Shea when you called him?"

"Told 'em the man ... killed his sister ... in my sittin' room ... send the law," she said between labored breaths, and he laughed.

"*Send the law* ... good one, Miss Lucy." He set his plate down and picked up the hammer. "How 'bout I use this to shatter your knee. Bet you'll tell me then."

He stepped toward her, purposely bringing the heavy sole of his boot down on the tops of her feet.

"No, no, I lied ... I didn't tell him anything. I swear—nothing, I swear." She was babbling and crying, her face twisted tight with terror, eyes squeezed shut against the sight of him.

"Liar, liar." He brought the hammer down. It hit the kitchen table, the loud crack of it echoed in the small space. Her eyes popped wide, and she yelped like a whipped dog.

"I promise, I promise, please ... please, don't," she said in a pleading rush. He dropped the hammer onto the table and smiled at her.

Finally, he was getting somewhere.

"Why'd you call him?" He knew he should be focusing on where to find Melissa, but the phone call was bothering him.

"He's ... my friend." The tears started again.

"That ain't sayin' much. Up until about an hour ago, I was your friend, too," he said with a sad shake of his head. "Do I have to worry about him busting in here tryin' to save the day?" When she didn't answer right away, he applied pressure to her feet with his boot. Already, the area surrounding the nail holes were bruised and swollen. When she cried out, she croaked so she sounded like a frog on the wrong end of a gigging fork.

"No."

He watched her face for lies, but she only shook her head. The hopelessness in her eyes told him she was telling the truth. "That's good. Real good, Miss Lucy." He leaned back against the table and pulled the picture from his pocket. "This is Melissa." It wasn't a question but he held the photo up to her face for confirmation anyway. She

66

said nothing, but when he stepped heavily on her wounds, she croaked again and nodded. "She's calling herself Sabrina these days?"

She said nothing, even when he twisted the heel of his boot, putting pressure on the head of the nail, driving it deeper into her foot. "That's alright. I know the answer. Got it right here." He fished the note from his back pocket and waved it at her. "I hear she's living in California. What've you got to say about that?"

She must've found her second wind, because she spat at him again.

"Lord, save me from stubborn women," he said under his breath. He flipped the picture over to read it out loud. "*Jason and Riley Vaughn, age 16.* Riley sure is a peach, ain't she? Don't think I've seen a beauty like her since … well, you know." He looked up from the photo and smiled at her. "Either you tell me where Melissa is, or when I *do* find her, I'll add little Riley here to my list. What I did to her big sister won't even come close to what I'll do to her," he said. She looked him in the eye and swallowed hard, running her tongue over her teeth, trying to clean away some of the blood.

"She won't let you." Her ironclad belief that even if he did manage to find the woman in the picture, he would be no match for her— that she was *better*—brought the rage screaming to the surface.

The picture crumpled in his fist and he stepped into the swing, landing a haymaker on the side of her head. The force of the blow would've knocked her over in her chair if not for the nails. She was unconscious now, but he slapped her again anyway. He picked up the knife and grabbed her by her hair and shook her. Used the grip he had on her scalp to revive her.

"Wakey, wakey, Miss Lucy." He grinned when her eyes fluttered open. She was terrified, but not of him or what he would do to her. No, she was terrified because the words she'd fought so hard to keep to herself were near the surface, threatening to break free. She was on the edge, he could see it. All she needed was a little push.

"It's there, right there on the tip of your tongue. Can you feel how close you are?" he said into her ear, and she shook her head against his grasp.

"I won't … I won't … I won't … "

"Yes, you will. Where. Is. She?" He was close enough to feel her heart slamming around in her rib cage. It beat so hard and fast he was surprised it didn't burst through her chest. She took a deep breath, held it for a moment before she exhaled.

"No," she said, but they both knew this was her last stand. The next words out of her mouth would be the ones he wanted to hear.

"Have it your way." He straddled her and yanked her head to the side to wedge the jagged edge of his knife into the crease behind her ear. "Tell me, Miss Lucy. Tell me where she is, and I'll stop," he said, but he knew the promise was a lie. There was no stopping now, not even if she talked. She said nothing, and he took her silence as another refusal.

He began to saw the knife back and forth. The serrated edge bit into the tender flesh behind her ear and chewed. Blood bloomed, a bright red flower behind her ear, and ran thick and warm down her neck.

He stopped for a moment, wiped sweat off his brow with the sleeve of his shirt. He caught sight of her arms, still bound to the chair. Her hands fluttered rapidly, like the tiny wings of a frightened bird. Music still flowed into the kitchen, and he imagined she was moving them in time with the melody.

He forced the knife deeper, separating the fleshy cartilage of her ear from the meat and bone of her skull. He pulled on the lobe and cut the last bit of if free, tightening his fist around her ear. It felt warm and wet in his hand. Her hands were suddenly still, and she stopped screaming. She'd passed out again.

Blood poured from the jagged hole and coursed down her neck. It soaked the front of her faded house dress, but she didn't make a sound. He reached for the towel again and brought it, salty and wet, to the side of her ear and squeezed. Still nothing.

He stood back to drop the towel into the bowl and tossed her ear on the table. He'd do the other one next and maybe start on her fingers. She'd tell him where Melissa was soon enough. First, he needed to wake her.

He traded knife for extension cord, fashioned it into a makeshift noose, and slipped it over her head. He gave it a sharp yank, tightening it around her throat until it disappeared into the soft skin of her neck. Seconds passed. The sudden loss of air did nothing to rouse her. He jerked it again and her head tipped forward, her chin hit her chest with no resistance and stayed there. Something close to panic settled into his chest.

No, no, no, no. He dropped the cord and lunged at her. His fingers fumbled at her throat, looking for a pulse. Nothing. The blood covering her chest was cool and tacky against his hand. She wasn't breathing. He slipped his hand under her chin and tipped it upward. Her eyes were open but empty.

She was dead.

This wasn't happening. No fucking way was this happening. He shook her, slamming her head against the back of the chair with each thrust. What the hell happened? A heart attack? A stroke? Who the fuck knew? He didn't really care. She was dead, and she hadn't given him what he wanted.

"Selfish bitch, she's *mine*. She belongs to me, and I want her back!" He gave her a final, neck-cracking shake, but it did nothing to staunch the steady flow of rage coursing through is veins.

His field of vision narrowed, all he could see was her face, all he could hear was the roar of blood pounding in his head. His knife was suddenly in his hand and he brought it down again and again, ripping into her soft flesh, tearing the papery skin that covered it. He stabbed and hacked, even though Lucy was well beyond his reach now, one motion blurring into another until his arm was tired and his vision cleared.

His rage finally spent, he stood over her, chest heaving as his breath came in deep, gasping gulps. His sweat and her blood mixed together, plastered his shirt to his chest. Looking down at the mess he made, at the lump of flesh barely recognizable as a human being, he felt no remorse. Only a need for more.

He felt a tingle, a crackle of electricity danced along his skin. His hands and face were covered in the old woman's blood … but it was Melissa's blood too, wasn't it?

He could feel it seep into his pores—currents of electricity dove deeper and deeper. No longer skin deep, they jolted his bones, moved his muscles. On impulse, he brought the broad blade of the knife to his mouth and ran it along his tongue. Heat flooded his veins and settled heavily in his groin. God, he'd missed the taste of her.

Lucy's sightless blue eyes, so like her granddaughter's, seemed to stare at him. Beckoned him.

More. He needed *more*.

He folded his knife, slipped it into his pocket and picked up the hammer. He used the claw end to remove the nails from her feet and tossed them aside. Whistling along with Gene, he gripped the back of Lucy's chair and dragged her to the doorway leading to the basement. The door swung shut behind them, and he was careful to lock it. He was with his Melissa again.

They were alone in the dark, and he didn't want any interruptions.

ELEVEN

IN THE END, THE Glenfiddich went unopened. Instead, Michael took a few aspirin and washed them down with a bottle of water. Sabrina was a machine. She and that goofy-ass dog ran eight miles every morning. No matter how little sleep she got or how bad the nightmares were, she never missed a run. Running with a hangover was never a good idea.

And her nightmares *had* gotten bad. So bad that if she wasn't pacing the length of her room in the dark, she was thrashing around on her bed, trying to pull clear of whatever nightmare held her. She usually gave up around one or two in the morning. Sometimes she'd make her way through the house, checking and re-checking windows and doors to ensure they were locked.

Other times she'd clean her collection of firearms. Make sure they were all loaded and easily accessible. Her behavior bordered on compulsive. He'd been watching her long enough to know the shield and armor she'd fashioned herself out of lies and years of denial was starting to crack.

His watch read just before noon. She wouldn't be home for at least another five or six hours. He tossed the binocs on the bed and hit the shower. What the aspirin couldn't fix, he was hoping hot water would take care of. He took his time; with Sabrina at work, he had plenty to spare. He shaved away a few days' worth of stubble before stepping into the shower stall. The spray of scalding water loosened the stress-induced knots, and he stayed in long after the water began to cool. He stepped out of the stall just in time to hear his cell issue a muted beep from the next room. He'd missed another call.

He threw a towel around his waist, left the bathroom to retrieve his phone from the dresser. The screen display showed six voice-mails. Scrolling through the missed call log, he saw every one of them were from Lucy.

On speaker phone, he guided his cell through the menu until he reached the first message.

"Michael, it's Lucy. Call me, please…" Delete.

"Michael, this is Lucy. I need to talk to you…" Delete.

"Michael, I know you're avoiding…" Delete.

"Boy, if you have the sense God gave a turnip…" Delete.

"Michael—who did you tell?"

He almost deleted the message before he fully comprehended what was said. He hit the playback option instead and listened to it again.

"Michael—who did you tell?" Lucy said, her voice hushed, like she didn't want to be overheard. In the background, he heard someone call out. What was said was indistinguishable. The voice was too low and faint to make out the words. Apprehension tightened the skin on the back of his neck.

She hadn't been alone when she left that last message.

He saved the message to his archives and played the next one, hoping it would offer a clue to what was wrong. No one spoke. On the other end, all he heard was a deep well of silence.

His gut screamed at him. Something was wrong. Lucy was in trouble.

Problem was, he'd told no one about Sabrina or even where he was going when he left Jessup. What little family he had left were long used to him tossing what few possessions he owned in his duffle and leaving as abruptly as he came. Only one person knew where he was, but he trusted Lark with his life. No way would he betray him. He glanced at his watch. The call came through an hour and forty minutes ago.

He hung up and dialed Lucy. The phone rang and rang. No answer.

Calm down. Panic is the enemy. He took a cleansing breath and dialed a different number. This time the call was answered on the fourth ring.

"Wander-Inn, this is Tom."

"Tom, it's Michael. I need a favor."

TWELVE

When he was finished, he gathered his clothes and put them back on. The blood and gore, dried stiff, abraded his skin, but he didn't mind. He dragged Lucy to a corner of the basement and laid her out. Finding an open bottle of bleach above the washer, he washed her thoroughly.

Once she was clean, he wrapped her in the freshly-laundered sheets he found in her dryer and concealed her beneath a pile of old boxes. She'd eventually be found, but by then the bleach would have done its job. Any DNA he might have left on her would be long gone.

The muffled sound of Gene, still singing in the rain, drifted down the basement steps, and he sang along while he worked. He brought the chair and Lucy's house dress back upstairs and rummaged under the sink. He found more bleach, a bottle of ammonia and a bottle of lighter fluid. He rolled up the makeshift tarp he'd laid out on the kitchen floor and placed it in a trash bag along with the dress. He poured the undiluted ammonia onto the kitchen floor and chair. While ammonia didn't destroy DNA, any evidence gathered there would be corrupted by the chemical and rendered useless. The ammonia was strong-smelling, so he opened a few windows for ventilation. The early afternoon breeze made the chore of cleaning up his mess almost pleasant.

Castoff was a problem, and he silently chided himself for losing control while he wiped down the walls. His actions would do nothing to eliminate the blood evidence but it didn't concern him. He knew Lucy's home would eventually become a crime scene but the longer things appeared normal, the better.

Finished cleaning, he took the other bottle of bleach and the trash bag into the bathroom with him. In the shower, he washed himself with the lavender soap he'd smelled on Lucy's skin and it made him smile. After his shower, he used the bleach to clean the tub and dumped the remainder down the drain. He added his clothing and the soap he'd used to the bag and pulled on a fresh pair of gloves.

Wandering down the hall in a towel, he found the room he knew O'Shea slept in when he was in town. The room was sparse. The only thing that made it Michael's was a framed photo of Frankie and his parents.

He opened a dresser drawer and found what he was looking for. The jeans were a little long, but they'd do for what he needed. In the closet he found an old sweatshirt and pulled it on before tossing the towel he used into the bag of clothing. Down the hall, the kitchen phone began to ring. Even without the benefit of caller ID, he knew who it was.

Michael O'Shea to the rescue.

The idea of O'Shea as anyone's savior made him laugh. He ignored the phone but understood what it meant. If O'Shea was worried, he'd find a way to check on her. There was no way of really knowing what Lucy had told him.

Time to finish up and leave.

He swiped the lighter fluid off the counter and emptied it into the bag. He carried the bag into the living room, and set it next to the small, brick fireplace.

He thought of the girl he'd picked out for today. She was a plump little waitress from some backwoods town in Oklahoma. He'd been priming the pump for weeks now, chatting her up, flirting with her. He had her panting after him—one smile was all it'd take to get her to follow him anywhere. Just the thought of her made him sick to his stomach.

She was nothing. Less than nothing, compared to his Melissa. She wouldn't do ... no one else would ever do again. Not now that he knew she was out there.

Finding her wasn't going to be easy.

He stood at the bookshelf and scanned its contents. He was looking for something ... *there.* It was tucked away, safe, on a high shelf. He picked it up, marveling at how light and delicate it felt in his hand. He'd been there when Lucy gave it to Melissa. A birthday gift—he remembered it like it was yesterday. It was the first day he'd ever seen her up close. The first time he'd ever looked into her eyes and realized she belonged to him. He palmed the treasure and slipped it into the pocket of his borrowed jeans for safekeeping.

Back at the fireplace, he crouched down and removed the screen. There was ash and cold cinder in the hearth. The smell of a recent fire drifted up to his nose. He used the small shovel to clean out some of the ash to make room for the bag. Reaching back, he scraped the shovel toward the front of the fireplace and pulled out what looked like a piece of charred paper. He almost dismissed it as nothing more than kindling, but when he pulled it from the ash, he felt it was a heavier stock than newspaper. It took him a few seconds to realize what he was holding. An envelope. Or at least part of one. Lucy had thrown an envelope into the fire.

He turned it over, eyes darting here and there, looking for anything that would tell him where, or who, it came from. He carried it into the kitchen and found the letter where he'd left it on the counter. He spread it out and laid the charred scrap next to it. The return address was burned away, as was most of Lucy's, but there was enough to make a comparison.

The handwriting was the same.

He could feel Melissa's blood pounding away inside him. Guiding him, showing him the way. The scrap was badly burned, but the corner that held the postage stamp was still intact. He rubbed away some of the char and soot, revealing the postmark faintly visible beneath.

San Francisco, California.

He felt a smile spread across his face. He'd found her.

THIRTEEN

THE ARREST WARRANT FOR Adam Tillman came in while Sabrina and Strickland were eating Chinese takeout at their desks. The minute the paper hit his desk, Strickland jumped up—ready to go. She tossed her carton of Kung Pao in the trash but didn't move from her seat. As wrong as it was, she'd been hoping their investigation would hit a snag. They'd have their suspect in custody by the end of the day, and she'd have no excuse to use as leverage to squeeze another day's reprieve out of Richards. This time tomorrow, she'd be on *vacation*. Just the thought depressed her.

She looked at her watch. It was noon, straight up. Almost five hours since she talked to Nickels, and she hadn't heard from him since. She debated on whether she should call but decided against it. Hounding him about O'Shea's records was the wrong thing to do. If Michael was nothing more than a potential blind date, she wouldn't be so eager to delve into his background.

She was beginning to think he couldn't help her ... or maybe he just didn't want to. Helping sniff out a potential date for the woman you had the hots for didn't usually rank high on a guy's to-do list. As much as she hated it, she had no choice but to wait it out. Calling Nickels only added a layer of complication she didn't need.

"What's the matter with you, Vaughn? A warrant comes in, you usually hit the ground running, dragging me behind you." She looked up at Strickland. He was standing next to her desk, staring at her like she'd just told him she had a contagious disease. What was the matter with her? The list went on and on. "What? Did the extra chili paste in your Kung Pao fry your brain? Warrant. Arrest. Tillman. Now." He waved the piece of paper in her face. She shot him a dirty look and stood up.

"Keep your panties on. Tillman's as dumb as they come. He's not going anywhere." She retrieved her SIG from the bottom drawer of her desk and clipped the holster to her waistband, pretending not to notice the look Strickland was giving her. She recognized that she was barely holding herself together, that Strickland could see there was a problem. She hadn't told him about her forced vacation yet, but he knew something was wrong. She opened her mouth to tell him, but it snapped shut when his face fell into a wary glare.

"What?" She glanced over her shoulder and felt her stomach sink. Behind her, Sanford was steam-training his way through the bullpen, taking the express route toward her desk.

She looked at her partner and slammed the desk drawer closed. The loud bang did nothing to distract him. "Hey. Strickland." He ignored her. Shit. "*Christopher.*" She'd never called him by his first name before. The strangeness of it must've been what made him look at her. "Not a word. No matter what he says. Got me?"

He looked away from her, continued watching Sanford stalk toward them. He shook his head. "Sorry partner, no promises."

Double shit. This was going to be a train wreck.

She pushed her chair into her desk and turned around just in time to greet the Sanford Express. He ground to a halt in front of her desk and glared at her.

"What the fuck did you say to Richards?" Several inches taller, he loomed over her, his face a collection of harsh lines and jutting bones, twisted with rage.

Behind him, Sabrina saw Nickels standing in front of a rapidly growing crowd, a grim expression on his face. Of course he'd show up *now*. He'd probably been dogging Sanford all day, waiting for him to make his move.

Catching her eye, Nickels inclined his head in silent question. Did she want him to intercede? With a barely perceptible shake of her head, she told him no. He conceded, but she could tell it cost him a hell of a lot to keep out of it.

"He asked me if I wanted to lodge a formal complaint against you, and I told him it wasn't necessary," she said.

"Bullshit. He suspended me. Three weeks without pay. *Three weeks*. What the hell am I supposed to do?"

"Maybe you should take the time to get your head straight." She looked him in the eye, aware almost every badge in the precinct was crammed into the Homicide bullpen, and her desk was the eye of a storm.

Sanford took a step forward, fists clenched. "You still haven't learned to keep your mouth shut and mind your own fucking business." He gave her the up-down, letting his eyes travel slowly from her face to her feet. His gaze popped back to her face. "Maybe it's about time someone taught you a little life lesson."

She held her ground. It'd take a hell of a lot more than anything Sanford could dish out make her squirm. She didn't know what she did to attract assholes, but it sure seemed like they found her wherever she went. "You got the last one for free. You swing on me again—I'll kick your ass." She gave him the warning in a low tone only he could hear.

"You think you're so smart, but you're nothin' but a dumb bitch with a badge and a raging case of dick-envy." He drilled his finger into her chest, and it took all she had not to snap it off. She was on thin ice with Richards. The only reason she wasn't getting the boot was because her paperwork hit his desk, and not Mathews's. If she lost it in front of the entire department, she was as good as gone. Not even Richards would be able to save her. This job and her family were all she had. She couldn't afford to lose either one.

"You need to think about what you're doing," she said. She wasn't sure whether she was talking to Sanford or herself.

"Fuck off, Vaughn," Sanford muttered. "Don't act like you give a shit, alright?"

"I cared enough to stop that punk from turning your head into a spaghetti strainer," she said, instantly regretting it. The last thing she needed to do was bring up what happened.

"Who asked you to?" The words were said low—only she heard them, and they set off an alarm. It was suddenly obvious why he'd been so angry. Why he was *still* angry. She hadn't saved his life. She'd stopped his suicide.

"Sanford—"

He ignored her. "Why'd you lie to Richards to get me suspended?"

"I never lied. I didn't have to," she said and watched his scowl deepen into a snarl.

"Someone told him I was drinking again, *which is a lie.*" He stepped even closer. Sabrina instinctively dropped her leg back, shifting her weight to the balls of her feet, and waited for him to take a swing. Before he could, the sea of blue parted and Richards waded through, followed by Mathews.

"What the hell are you doing here?" Richards said to Sanford.

Before Sanford could answer, she said, "He was just apologizing for the other day." She gave Sanford a look, warning him to shut the hell up. "It's all good. Sanford and I are square."

Richards looked like he knew he was being fed a line of bullshit, but he swallowed it anyway. "Good. Glad to see you two work it out."

"Okay, party's over!" Captain Mathews shouted over the crowd. "If you aren't assigned to this department, exit now. Everyone else, back to work!" He gave her a frustrated once-over before he stalked back to his office and slammed the door.

"Get out of here," Richards said to Sanford. He flicked a glance at her and walked away.

Sanford caught the exchange. "This isn't over," he said before he backed away from her.

"Yeah, I figured." She moved around him to follow Richards. She hurried to catch up and she reached out, touched the sergeant's arm to stop him. "Sarge, wait."

He turned around and looked as tired as she felt. "Vaughn, it's done. Leave it alone."

"Three weeks unpaid? Sir, I told you I was fine. Don't bounce him out just because he has a big mouth. He's a good officer, he just—"

He produced a business card. "You're loyal Vaughn, even to people who don't deserve it, but this is *his* shit creek, not yours." He pushed the card into her hand. "Keep your paddle. You're gonna need it." Before she could say another word, he left her standing in the middle of the precinct. She looked down at the card. It belonged to a department therapist. It was like he'd handed her a live snake.

"Hey."

She jammed the card into her pocket and turned to see Nickels a few feet away. She'd forgotten he was even there, but seeing him stirred up a whole different set of problems. He motioned her to follow him. She shot a look at Strickland, found him leaning against her desk, staring at her. He gave the warrant a shake: *Can we do some police work now?* She held up a finger and nodded. He threw his hands in the air and took a seat at her desk, kicking his feet up on its top. He gave her a shit-eating grin that raised her hackles. He knew she hated it when he put his feet on her desk.

She turned her back on her partner and followed Nickels. They walked down the hall toward Homicide's interview rooms. He pulled her into an alcove housing a few vending machines and an industrial-size coffee urn.

Nickels gave her a long, hard look. "You want to tell me what's really going on?"

She forced herself to hold his gaze. "What are you talking about? Sanford? You tell me. You're the one who got Richards all riled up this morning—"

"Fuck Sanford. Don't play dumb, Vaughn. It's insulting." He sounded angry, but it was more than that. She held onto her bluff and said nothing. He laughed—a nasty, pissed-off sound.

"Okay. Fine. I'm talking about Michael O'Shea. Ring a bell?"

"What about him? I told you it was no big deal. If you can't drum anything up, then whatever. I really didn't want to go out with him anyway," she said. She was digging herself a hole but there was no turning back now.

"Really? Okay, you want to cut me out? Go ahead, but let me tell you how it went down. I called a friend, who called a friend, who called a friend that's still in the service—I drop O'Shea's name, and it's all good. One minute we're bullshitting about baseball, waiting for his computer to catch up, and the next I'm told there's no file available. I ask the guy to run it again, just in case, and he puts me on hold. After fifteen minutes, I figure I'm getting the Army shuffle, and I hang up. Five minutes after *that,* my cell rings."

"Who was it?" she said, suddenly sure she didn't want to know.

"I don't have a clue, but I can tell you whoever it was, wasn't Army. I'm told my *inquiries are unwelcome* and *further investigation will result in immediate and unpleasant consequences.* Now, I'm going to ask you again. What the hell is going on?"

It felt like all the air had been sucked out of the alcove they were standing in. What the hell was happening? Who was Michael O'Shea? What had he become?

Whatever was going on, she needed to end Nickels's involvement. Now.

"Huh. Guess my mystery date was a dud. Oh well, thanks for trying." She moved around him and went for the coffee. She'd already downed a gallon of the stuff today, but she needed something to keep her hands busy.

"*Dud* isn't the word I'd use. *Scary son of a bitch* might be closer to the truth." Nickels reached out and grabbed her by her arm before she reached the coffee. He gave her arm a small yank. "Damn it, Sabrina. Talk to me."

She looked down at where he held her arm and deliberately raised her gaze to his to give him a warning look. "Don't," she said and slowly pulled her arm out of his grasp.

"Shit." He took a step back and squeezed his eyes shut for a second, the picture of frustration. "I'm sorry. I just—"

"Don't be. Sorry if I got you jammed up."

"I'm not jammed up—"

"Then what's the problem?"

"I wasn't jammed up. I was shut down. Forcibly. Threats were insinuated. You're not stupid, Sabrina. Quit acting like you don't know what I'm talking about." He laughed again at the blank look she gave him and took a step away from her, hands in the air. "Okay, I surrender. You want to play it that way? Fine. But whoever this Michael O'Shea is to you, be smart and stay away from him." Then he was gone.

FOURTEEN

IT HAD BEEN OVER an hour since he'd talked to Tom and still no word. Michael was beginning to worry he'd sent him into a situation he couldn't handle. He was just a regular guy. Hell, his idea of home defense was a Louisville Slugger. Not someone he'd prefer to send into a potentially dangerous situation, but there was no one else to call. When his phone rang, he answered it without hesitation, but it wasn't Tom.

"Tell me something—are you out of your fucking mind?" It was his friend Lark.

He stifled a sigh of frustration. The last thing he needed was Lark's dramatics. "It probably depends on who you ask."

"I'm being serious, asshole. This whole Charles Bronson, *Death Wish* thing you got going on is beginning to wear thin," Lark said.

He began to pace, in no mood to play. "What the hell are you talking about?"

"Does the name Devon Nickels mean anything to you?" Lark said.

Michael stopped pacing. He knew Sabrina would come after him. He just hadn't counted on her being this creative or resourceful. He figured she'd just pull his juvi record and make a few calls. Maybe track down a few of his old probation officers, maybe even call his Aunt Gina. Instead, she'd sicced her ex-soldier boyfriend on him. He was impressed. He hadn't even known she remembered he'd been in the military. He wasn't someone she used to pay much attention to.

"Should it?" He'd play it careful until he knew more.

"No? I'm sorry, how about *Staff Sergeant* Devon Nickels. He was an armory gunner in the Gulf." Michael said nothing. Lark was baiting him, but he wasn't biting. "Still don't know him? Huh ... that's weird, because he knows you. He flagged your service jacket this morning," Lark said, practically biting each word in half.

Too bad there was nothing to flag. His records were locked down. Gaining access would take a hell of a lot more juice than Staff Sergeant Devon Nickels could muster.

"Look, Lark—I don't have time to play around." He looked at his watch. *Where the hell was Tom?* "If you've got something to say, just spit it out."

"When I agreed to this crazy Lucy and Ethel scheme of yours, I distinctly remember you telling me contact would be kept to a bare minimum." Lark knew about Frankie and, for reasons Michael couldn't figure out, had offered to help find the man that killed her. He also knew about Sabrina and had been instrumental in keeping tabs on her.

"She made me this morning."

"You've been doggin' this chick for over a month now and all of a sudden *you get made?* Give me a break O'Shea—you're better than that."

"We had a ... situation. It's no big deal. Everything is under control." The lie came as easy as breathing.

"It better be, because if your girl keeps sniffing around, we're all in trouble. And when I say trouble, I mean dead."

He didn't have to elaborate. The organization he and Lark worked for was very sensitive when it came to information—any information—being made public.

His phone buzzed. He had another call. It was Tom.

"I'll take care of it, don't worry. Gotta go."

"Goddamn it, O'Sh—"

He clicked over to Tom. "What do you see?" he said.

"Nothing out of the ordinary. Her car is gone, and there's a note on the door. It says she drove to Shreveport to see her sister."

The note did little to put him at ease. Lucy'd been using the same three or four notes over and over. She kept them in a kitchen drawer by the door. If she left, she just fished out the appropriate one—*gone to town, gone to church, gone to Shreveport*—and clipped it to her screen door with a clothespin.

"What's going on, man?" Tom said.

"I called her, and she didn't answer." At least that much was true.

Tom laughed. "Come on, Mikey. You know how much she hates the phone."

"It's the first of October. She wouldn't ignore me. Not today."

Silence settled across the line while the implications sank in. October first wasn't just another day for either of them.

"Do you want me to go in?" Tom said. He wasn't surprised Tom knew where she kept her spare key—shit, half the county knew. Lucy did mending and alterations out of the house she now lived in. If you wanted to pick up or drop off things to be fixed or altered when she wasn't going to be home, the answer was always the same—"The spare key is under the potted daisy." He often wondered why she bothered to lock her door at all.

"No." If something *was* wrong, having Tom go inside would be disastrous. He'd leave all kinds of prints while potentially contaminating any real evidence that might've been left. The police chief would have Tom in a cell before sundown. *Shit*. He sat on the bed and rubbed a rough hand over his face. He couldn't believe what he was about to say…

"You're going to have to call Carson."

Silence stretched out for a few seconds. "You can't be serious." From the sound of Tom's voice, Lark wasn't the only one who thought he was insane. He dropped the phone to his shoulder for a moment. He couldn't tell Tom why he was worried. He couldn't tell him anything. He lifted the phone to his ear.

"I am. Do it," he said.

"You don't think—"

"I think we need to find Lucy. She could be in trouble, and he's the only one who might be able to help her." He understood Tom's feelings about Jed Carson—he harbored a few of his own—but he couldn't let them get in the way. Not when it might mean Lucy's life.

"What if he's the one who hurt her?" Tom said exactly what he'd been thinking. Jed Carson, Jessup's police chief, just happened to be Michael's number one suspect in his sister's murder.

FIFTEEN

THE PICTURE OF FIFTEEN-YEAR-OLD O'Shea popped up on Sabrina's screen along with the mile-long list of juvenile offenses. She hit Print.

She was out for at least a week. Probably two. This was her only chance to gather whatever information she could about him. She'd go over it at home, hopefully find something she missed.

"You're killin' me, Vaughn. Tillman's stewing in the tank. We found the murder weapon *and* the shoes he wore that night. Dumb shit never stood a chance." Strickland threw up his hands and mimicked a three-point swish.

She laughed. When they finally got there to serve the warrant, Tillman didn't answer. Big surprise. She'd gone around to cover the back of the house and caught sight of Tillman's size ten slipping over the neighbor's fence. She'd chased him down while Strickland followed by car. When he finally caught up to her, she had Tillman pinned against the block wall she'd pulled him off of. Their suspect was cuffed and Mirandized before Strickland had even thrown it in

Park. "By the way, I love the way you toss the term *we* around so loosely," she said, but she was joking. She didn't mind doing the footwork. She didn't run eight miles a day for nothing.

"Hey, I'm the brains of this outfit—you're the muscle." He grinned when she rolled her eyes. "Seriously, let me buy you a beer. I owe you one."

"I can't. Sorry, partner."

"Okay, how about *you* owe *me*." On their way back to the station, guilt got the better of her. So she'd told him about her "forgotten" vacation. He'd been less than pleased and now seemed hell-bent on taking full advantage of her guilt.

"I did the arrest report and cleaned your desk. What more do you want?" she said, gesturing toward his now empty desk.

"Doesn't count. You always do that," he said, shuffling papers into a folder in a half-hearted attempt to look organized. "Come on, you can insult me the entire time just so I don't get the wrong idea and assume you might actually like me." He stood to pull his suit jacket up his arm and across his shoulders.

His offer reminded her she was supposed to have drinks with Nickels. As angry with her as he was the last time she saw him, she seriously doubted he'd even speak to her, let alone allow her to buy him a beer.

"I can't. It's taco night, I'm on cheese-grating duty," she said. Michael's juvenile arrest record sat in the printer tray, waiting for her to retrieve it. Which she couldn't do with Strickland breathing down her neck. He knew something was going on with her, and he knew it went far beyond what happened with Sanford. He'd been shooting her looks all day, like he wanted to say something but kept deciding against it. She had the feeling asking her to go for a drink was his way of getting her into a more relaxed environment so he could pick her brain.

He looked at her and cocked his head to the side. "I'm trying to envision you in a Betty Crocker apron and a shoulder holster." He righted his head and shook it. "I can't see it."

"Which is why I'm the designated chopper, grater, and slicer," she said. "Sometimes, Val lets me stir." She popped her collar, and he laughed.

"You'll make someone a wonderful cop someday." He switched off his computer. "Last chance . . . "

She just smiled and shook her head, silently urging him to leave. They'd just closed their case and hadn't caught another. There was no legitimate reason for her to print anything. If she pulled the file while he was still there, he'd want to know what she was working on. He'd pester and insist on being let into the loop. Michael O'Shea was one loop he was safer being kept out of.

Muttering something about bullshit and pantywaists, he pushed his chair in. He stopped for a minute, glared at his newly cleaned desk, and shook his head. "You won't be here tomorrow."

"Nope."

"You know what this means, don't you?"

"You're gonna have to do your own paperwork?"

"Exactly. How friggin' depressing."

"I'll be back before you know it. Go, drown your sorrows. Have a few for me." She waved him off. Just as he turned to leave, a uniform dropped by her desk to let her know Sanford had been spotted in the parking lot. The news stopped Strickland dead in his tracks.

She gave him a vague smile. "Go on, I can get one of the guys to walk me out," she said.

"Yeah, you *could*." He plopped down in his chair and leaned back. "But you won't."

"Really, Strickland—"

"I'm not leaving this building without you," he said, his tone stubborn enough to give her pause.

She stood up. "I don't need a babysitter."

He just stared at her.

"I'm not afraid of Sanford." The petty insistence she heard in her own voice was like an ice pick in her ear.

Strickland nodded. "Yeah, I know." He laced his fingers together before propping them behind his head. The definition of *I'm not going anywhere.* "Which makes you bat shit crazy." It was no secret Sanford fought dirty; how he'd managed to hang onto his badge was a mystery.

"I can take care of myself."

"Yup, I know that, too." He looked at her and smiled. "But I'm your partner, which means I'm watching your back whether you want me to or not. Now, are you going to walk or am I pulling a caveman and dragging your ass out of here?"

In the three months they'd been partners, she'd come to know that look. He'd sit there all night rather than leave without her. "Fine. You win. But touch me, and I break something important." She scooped up O'Shea's file and jammed it into her bag before shouldering it.

He watched her swipe the papers off the printer tray. "What's that?"

"None of your business, *Lancelot.*" His coddling was almost more than she could stand.

He gave her a deadpan expression. "Perhaps you're confused about how a partnership is supposed to work—let me break it down for you. We help each other. Trust each other." He leaned forward in his chair and glared up at her. "We tell each other when we decide to commit career suicide and pursue suspects off the clock." He delivered the last line in a low tone meant for her ears only.

Her stomach did a slow roll, tickling her tonsils on the upswing. "What are you talking about?" she said, but it was useless. Strickland was a pit bull. Once he caught the investigative scent, there was no shaking him. It was what made him so good at his job.

"You're good. *Really* good, but I know you lied to me this morning about the junior dirtbag you were checking out on your computer." He smiled and pointed at her. "I don't know what you're doing." He stopped smiling. "But whatever it is, I know you shouldn't be doing it alone."

"I told you—"

"A lie. I know this because I refreshed the search history on your computer while you were off playing grab-ass with Nickels. That *kid* you were running background on is thirty-five years old," he said without an ounce of remorse.

"You did *what*?" Her tone was loud, and she cast a quick glance around the room. Several of the remaining inspectors were openly staring at them. *Just get him out of here before he really starts running his mouth.* "Get up, let's go. People are staring."

He stood and gave her a look that said *after you* and fell into step behind her, herding her toward the elevator. Once the doors slid shut, she turned on him. "Who the hell do you think you are?"

"I think I'm your partner. And I think you're in trouble."

She scoffed. "Trouble? Really? Jump to conclusions much?" She shoved her hands in her pockets and rocked back onto the heels of her boots.

"Okay then. Let me look at the file. What was his name? Michael O'Shea? If it doesn't have his name on it, I'll let it go." He nodded and rolled his eyes when she didn't move. "Right. Trouble. Capital T."

"You're wrong." She couldn't even look at him.

"I'm wrong? I might look like a mouth-breather, but I'm a fucking bloodhound when it comes to this shit. I know something is going on with you. You've been on edge for weeks now. At first I chalked it up to us working out the new-partner kinks. And then I thought maybe it was that shit with Sanford." He leaned against the wall of the elevator and crossed his arms over his chest. "But that's not it, either." He jerked his head toward her bag. "Whatever's going on, I'd bet my pension it's got everything to do with that file full of *nothing* you shoved in your bag."

"Why do you even care?" she said.

He looked at her like she'd slapped him in the face. "I don't know what pisses me off more: the fact you'd have the balls to ask me that, or that you genuinely don't know the answer."

"What I do on my own time is my business, not yours." *God, she was such a bitch.*

He opened his mouth like he was about to say something but clamped it shut and looked away from her. He worked his jaw, like he was chewing on a mouthful of words he wanted to spit out. Finally, he looked at her again. "You're right. Your personal life isn't any of my business. But if *I* were in trouble and pulling a sphinx? You'd ride me till I caved, and don't try to tell me otherwise."

"There is no trouble. The file means nothing. *He* means nothing." She looked at him, that familiar tightening in her chest making it hard to look him in the eye.

"People don't lie over *nothing*, and you know it." He made it easy on her by averting his eyes for a moment but when he glanced back at her, he looked more hurt than angry.

She suppressed the urge to reach out and shake him until his teeth rattled. "You need to let it go, Strickland." *For your own safety.* The military wasn't usually in the business of scrubbing the records of its discharged soldiers. Whatever Michael O'Shea was into, it was dangerous. Too dangerous to let her partner get mixed up it in.

"Sorry. Not gonna happen."

"I don't need—"

"Yeah, I know. You don't need me in your business. Well, tough shit because that's exactly where I am." He leaned forward and narrowed his eyes. "When things get crazy, I know I can count on you. You've got my back. You just won't let me get *yours*. That doesn't work for me." She could tell it was something he'd wanted to say to her for a while. She looked away. She'd been about to say, *I don't need to worry about you too.*

She lifted her shoulder in a half-assed shrug. "I've got some personal stuff going on right now. But it's not something I want to talk about." *It's not something I can talk about.*

Strickland studied her face for a moment and relaxed. "That's the first truthful thing you've said to me all day," he said. He uncrossed his arms and nodded. "I can take a lot of shit, Vaughn. Being lied to isn't one of them."

When she made Homicide, Sabrina told herself it didn't matter who they stuck her with. That she didn't care. Suddenly, she realized she cared a great deal. Strickland was close to her age and still had the drive needed to solve cases. He cared—not only about the people they tried to help but about the people he worked with. She couldn't have asked for a better partner, but she couldn't change who she was, and telling him the truth about Michael was out of the question. She nodded and dropped her gaze. "I'm not good at relying on people."

"I get that, but if this partnership is going to work, you're gonna have to try, " he said.

"Okay," she said, and his face lost its pissed-off look. For fifteen years, lies had been her stock and trade. She didn't remember telling the truth being this hard.

The elevator dinged and the doors slid open on a deserted lobby. As soon as they reached the parking lot, he nipped her keys out of her hand. She let him open her door and check the back seat. "Wanna call the bomb squad?" she said.

"Nah, Sanford isn't the bomb-making type," he said, moving aside so she could slide behind the wheel. "See, quick and painless." He shut her door and handed her the keys.

She started her jeep and shot him an evil grin. "I bet you say that to all the girls."

"Such a pain in my ass…" He propped his arms on her door and leaned his head through the open window. "Look, I'm not gonna push about this O'Shea guy—I think we've both had enough personal growth for one day." He leaned his forehead against the outside of her car and looked down. "Just promise me if things get tight, you'll let me in." His tone was easy, but she knew he wasn't going to let her leave until she gave her word.

She pressed in the clutch and threw it into Reverse. Letting him in would be a mistake. She had no idea who or what O'Shea had become. All she knew was just thinking about it scared the hell out of her. She'd already made the mistake of involving Nickels, and look where that got her. "If things get tight, there might not be room for you."

"Then we'll make room. Partners—remember?"

She nodded. "Partners. And for the record, Nickels and I are friends. Just friends."

"That's too bad. Nick's a great guy." He stepped back so she could leave. She pulled out of the station lot and turned right, toward home, then took a glance in her rearview mirror. She wasn't at all surprised to see a truck pull away from curb and force itself into traffic.

She was being followed.

SIXTEEN

Taco night was in full swing at Casa Vaughn when Sabrina arrived. Val liked to match music to food, so tonight's selection, old-school Vicente Fernandez, blasted through the open windows of the house. Grateful Val and the kids liked their music loud, Sabrina killed the headlights before she pulled into the drive and quietly shut her car door. She'd hoped to stay below the radar until she could get rid of her unwanted guest, but he had different ideas.

"Alone at last," Sanford yelled at her from the street. He vaulted the pretty picket fence and crossed her lawn in broad, uneven steps. He was drunk. Perfect. Just friggin' perfect.

"Why are you here, Sanford?" She watched him advance, closing the space between them to just a few feet.

"*Why am I here?* I don't have a job, I'm living on a barstool, my wife took out a *restraining order* against me, and you're at least partly to blame. So you tell me, where else would I fucking be?" He leaned into her space and jabbed her in the chest with his finger. *What was it with this ass-clown and the poking?*

She took a deep, slow breath and a step back. "Don't touch me." Drunk or sober, Sanford was an asshole, but at least he had slightly better judgment when he was sober. She shifted her body into a defensive stance, ready for a fight.

He smiled. "Whaddya gonna do," he sneered and closed the gap between them. "Shoot me?" He drilled his pointer into the center of her chest again.

Okay, asshole. Game on.

She snatched his finger off her chest and bent it back until she heard the pop. Sanford howled and swung wildly with his free arm. She blocked the blow with her forearm and gave him a hard crack in the nose with her elbow. Stunned, he tried to stumble back, but the grip she had on his finger kept him tethered. She delivered a face-crushing head-butt that drew blood, and he swung again, this time clipping her in the side of the head. Pain shot through her temple, but it was fleeting.

He caught her in the ribs with a ham-handed jab that stole her breath. She used the grip she had on his finger like a rudder and shoved him backward, jerking him to the side before she let go. The force, and the fact he smelled like he was sweating pure booze, sent him stumbling away from her. She used the time and space that created to shed her jacket.

As soon as it hit the ground, Sanford zeroed in on her SIG. He stood a few feet away, cradling his abused finger, dripping blood all over her cobblestone walkway. Instead of giving him second thoughts, the sight of her gun seemed to give him hope.

"Now we're talkin'." The relief in his voice was obvious.

Holy Hell. He really wants me to shoot him. "Don't do it, Sanford," she said. He ignored her warning and started toward her. She closed her hands into fists, raised and ready for round two.

"Is there a problem?"

She shot her gaze to the right to find Michael O'Shea standing on the sidewalk just a few yards away.

Sanford turned toward him and glared through the blood. "Mind your own business, asshole."

Michael appraised Sanford with cool amusement. "When I see a drunk guy harassing a woman in her own front yard, I tend to see that *as* my business." He spoke calmly, but she saw it—the shifting of body weight, the cool amusement turned to cold calculation in his eyes. It told her if she didn't intervene, Sanford would get exactly what he was looking for.

"Who the hell are you?" Sanford said.

"Just a guy, out for a walk, who happened across a situation he feels uncomfortable with ignoring," he said, welcoming Sanford's full attention.

She took a few steps back, widening the distance between her and Sanford, before she unholstered her SIG and aimed it downward. "Sanford, give me your car keys."

"What?" He rounded on her belligerently, saw the gun held at her side.

"I said give me your goddamn car keys."

Without a word, he fished them from his pocket and held them aloft. "What if I don't?" He gave them a little shake before closing them into his fist. "What if I just charge you, see who comes up the winner?"

"Take one step in my direction, I'll put a bullet in your knee. It won't kill you, but you'll have to hang up your tutu and kiss your dance dreams goodbye." She gave O'Shea a quick glance. "That goes double for you, Mr. Can't-Mind-My-Own-Business."

"Smart-mouthed bitch ... one of these days, you're gonna get what's comin' to you." He tossed the keys at her feet, and she stepped on them. He snarled and started toward her. She aimed her gun directly at his knee. The movement stopped him cold.

"Yeah, one of these days ... but not today." She waved him off. "There's a bus bench in front of the park. Go sit on it, I'll call you a cab. Your truck will be at the station tomorrow. You can pick it up there," she said to Sanford.

"I'm not taking a fuck—"

"Yes, you are. You're too drunk to drive. Leave. Now, before I put one in your leg for bringing this shit to my house. And don't ever come here again. If you do, I *will* kill you," she said.

He smiled. "Good to know," he said and took a few steps toward the street. He passed through the gate, eyeing Michael the entire time. Michael leaned against the fence, hands stuffed into the kangaroo pocket of his hoodie, watching him walk away.

Sanford stopped just past gate and turned toward Michael. "What are you looking at?"

Michael chuckled then shrugged. "I don't know ... you've got"—he took a hand out of his pocket and waved it at Sanford—"something on your face."

Sanford used the back of his hand to wipe away some of the blood. He smiled and took a half-step in Michael's direction. Sabrina intervened before he had a chance to respond.

"You," she jabbed her finger at Sanford, "get the hell out of here." She turned to Michael. "And *you*—shut the hell up."

"This isn't over." Sanford turned his back on her and started walking.

"Yeah, that's what you keep telling me. See you later." The tension leaked from her system with every step he took, but she didn't holster her gun.

With little more than a glance in his direction, she bent down and collected Sanford's keys before making her way toward the front porch. She took a seat on the top step and stared across her yard at the man by the fence.

Michael looked at her for a few moments before he pushed the gate open and crossed the lawn to retrieve her jacket. Bringing it to her, he held it out, but she refused to accept it. She preferred to keep both hands wrapped around the gun dangling between her knees. Waiting another beat, he tossed the jacket on the porch.

"You broke his finger." The thought seemed to amuse him.

"No, I didn't. I dislocated it."

He laughed. "You can put that away now," he said, nodding toward the SIG.

"I like it just where it is." Her eyes locked on his face. "What are you doing here, O'Shea?"

He flashed her a killer smile. She tightened her grip on her SIG and waited for him to start spitting lies.

"Melissa—"

Her spine snapped tight, encased in ice. "Don't call me that."

"Okay, *Sabrina* ... I wanted to apologize for this morning. Lucy knew I was going to be in the area, and she asked me to look in on you. I really didn't think you'd recognize me." The explanation sounded completely reasonable, and it would have been enough to placate her if it were true.

"Liar."

The smile didn't fade; it blinked out like a switch had been flipped. In its place was a carefully guarded expression that gave away nothing.

"He killed my sister," he said quietly. The words carried the force of a wrecking ball. They hit her square in the chest, nearly knocking her over.

"I don't know what you're talking about."

"Liar." He threw her word back at her with vicious smile. It held for a moment before his face gave way under the weight of his grief. He looked away from her for a moment, seemed to be wavering, choosing his words, before he turned back to look at her. "I need your help."

She stood and reholstered her gun at her side.

"No."

He made a noise that sounded like a strangled laugh and nodded his head. "You don't even know what I want."

"I've got a pretty good idea, but it really doesn't matter. The answer stands." She turned to leave. What he wanted from her was obvious. It would be what she'd want from him if she were in his place: he wanted her to go back to Jessup with him so he could bait the hook.

Not gonna happen.

"Let me ask you something… do you feel even a tiny bit guilty you're alive? I mean, don't you feel like all those dead girls are at least partially your fault?"

"What?" she said. His words rooted her in place. She turned to stare at him while the porch steps rolled beneath her feet like the deck of a ship. She turned around to face him. "What girls?"

"Really? You thought he stopped with you? Guys like that don't do what he did to you and then just *stop*." His tone was hard. Cold.

She shook her head, still unwilling to believe. "No. I would've heard—"

"He likes waitresses. Young ones with blue eyes. Spreads it around—Texas, Oklahoma, Louisiana, Arkansas. Sticks to small towns with podunk sheriffs who couldn't find their asses with both hands and a map. He's disciplined. Careful. He only takes one a year. Guess when?" he said.

His words sucked the air out of her lungs. She couldn't breathe. *October first.* Today. He was hunting today.

"He takes them and—*poof*—they're gone, never seen again. Frankie was number fourteen last year. My guess? He's looking for number fifteen—if he doesn't have her already."

Liar. He's a liar. He'd say anything to get her to do what he wanted.

"How do you know? If the police can't put it together, how did you figure it out?"

"I have unlimited resources, and I'm highly motivated."

His answer reminded her she had no idea who or what he was. Not anymore. She turned her back on him, surprised she found her way up the last of the steps without stumbling. She turned to give him another look. "Stay away from me. Stay away from my family."

"I'm not going anywhere. You're going to help me." He bared his teeth in another vicious smile. "One way or another." He backed away from her until he was standing in the glow of the streetlamp. The sullen young boy she remembered was gone. In his place was a hardened man who would not take no for an answer.

"Oh, and a word of advice? Stop digging into my background. You're going to get your boyfriend killed. I'm staying at the Brewster place. You want to know something, just ask."

"Are you threatening me?"

"No. I'm warning you."

"Don't come back here." She wanted to run. Instead, she crossed the porch slowly and pushed through the door. She closed it with a quiet click and engaged every lock in an impressive row of chains and deadbolts.

I'm staying at the Brewster place. You want to know something, just ask…

The Brewster place was a B&B, one street over—directly behind her house. She looked out the foyer window. He was gone.

SEVENTEEN

SABRINA DID HER BEST to bury it. The fear, the worry—she tossed it in a hole she'd dug in the back of her mind and did her best to cover it up. But it was still there.

Her life was unraveling.

Valerie made dinner while she helped the twins with homework. Afterward they played Scrabble. For just a few hours, she'd tried to pretend everything was fine. She'd laughed and joked, teased and played—but every time she looked at Riley, she imagined her trapped in the dark, with nothing but the sound of her own screams and the smell of blood to reassure her she was still alive. That she hadn't died and gone to hell.

"Mom? Can I?"

She looked up. Jason was staring at her, Scrabble tiles in his hand and a concerned look on his face. Game over, she and Jason were putting the game away while Val and Riley loaded the dishwasher. Somehow, over the years, she'd become *mom* instead of sister—a natural progression of time and the love they both felt for her.

"What's up, kiddo?"

"I asked if I could use the car this weekend," Jason said, tossing the handful of tiles into the box. "I asked Staci Greene to the movies."

"Ohhh, the infamous Staci with an *i*," she said, and Jason blushed. He was a good-looking kid with hair a few shades darker that his twin sister's auburn color. Where Riley's heart-shaped face was finely boned, Jason's was more masculine, his features a bit broader. But they both had the most heart-breaking blue eyes Sabrina had ever seen. Sometimes looking into them was hard, but she did it now, ignoring the twinge of fear she felt in her gut.

"Yeah, Mom, Staci with an *i* ... so, can I?"

Her hand found the lapis band around her neck and squeezed.

The look of concern on Jason's face deepened into a scowl. "Mom, are you okay?"

She smiled again, quickly averting her eyes, concentrating instead on folding the game board and placing it in the box. Jason had always been the sensitive one. He noticed things.

"Fine." She nodded. "I'm fine, kiddo. Long day, that's all. If you can wrestle the keys from your sister's iron grip, then I don't have a problem with it." She arched an eyebrow at him and narrowed her eyes. "You *do* understand that I expect you to treat Miss Staci with an *i* with respect, right?"

"*Mom*."

"Just sayin'," she said with a shrug.

"I understand. Besides, getting the keys from Ry won't be hard. She has a date," Jason said in a sly tone that had Sabrina's head jerking up.

"A date. Riley has a date? With who?"

Jason cast a quick glance at the door connecting the kitchen and dining room to assure they weren't overheard.

"Jimmy Bradshaw."

"Jimmy? Little League Jimmy? Braceface Jimmy?" She felt marginally better.

"He's nose ring, blue mohawk Jimmy these days. Anyway, he asked her out." Jason didn't seem pleased, and truthfully, neither was she.

He killed my sister . . .

Worry gnawed at her. Somehow she'd managed to delude herself into thinking that even though he was still out there, the man who kidnapped and tortured her had stopped with her. That he hadn't hurt anyone else. Michael was right—she was smarter than that. "Would I be completely terrible if I asked you to push for a group outing rather than a one-on-one thing?"

Jason looked reluctant. "Me and Jimmy don't exactly hang anymore."

"Why?"

"I don't know. He got all weird after he didn't make varsity last year." Jason put the cardboard top on the game box and put it away.

"Sounds like he needs a good friend."

Jason laughed and shook his head. "My mom—the gun-toting humanitarian."

"Jason."

He rolled his eyes at her but softened it with a smile, "Okay, okay—I get it. I'll talk to him tomorrow, see if he's down with it."

"Thanks, kiddo." She leaned over and gave him a quick peck on the cheek. When she pulled back, he was giving her that look again.

"I know something's wrong. You always do that when you're upset," Jason said, jamming his hands into the pockets of his jeans.

"Do what?"

"Hold on to your necklace."

She looked down. Her hand was wrapped into a fist on her chest, the lapis band clutched tight. She hadn't even realized she was doing it. She looked up to give Jason a half-hearted smile and a lame excuse, but she found herself alone.

EIGHTEEN

Michael let himself into his room and locked the door before taking a quick look around. Other than fresh sheets and clean towels, the room was untouched.

He stooped and pulled out the case, set it on the bed. He punched several buttons on the coded keypad and popped its top. Guns. Laptop. Prepaid cells. Cash and documents. He bypassed it all and pulled out his binocs. He took the chair from the small writing desk and set it in front of the window before retrieving the bottle of Glenfiddich from the dresser.

Sabrina didn't believe him. She didn't trust him—had no reason to. Goddamn it, he'd come at her straight on, been honest, and she'd flat out refused to help him. She was the beginning, the point from which all roads led. Way he saw it, she was the reason girls were dying.

And she didn't care.

He wasn't surprised, though. Not really. He'd dismissed everything he'd been told about her. Lucy warned him she was different.

Not just the way she looked, that *she* was different, but he hadn't believed her.

A person couldn't change who they were. They could break habits and make conscious decisions that altered their behavior, but deep down, they were still same the person. No one knew that better than him, but she *was* different.

What had been done to her changed her on a fundamental level. It'd killed the sweet, naive girl she'd been and left a stranger in her place. A stranger who didn't give a shit about anyone or anything but herself. A far cry from the girl he remembered. He'd barely known Melissa back then beyond good looks, but she'd been kind and quick to smile—compassionate, like her grandmother. Thinking about Lucy tied his stomach in knots.

Taking the bottle with him, he settled into the chair he'd placed in front of the window and broke the seal with his teeth. *To hell with it*, he thought. Promise keeping had never been his strong suit anyway. He wedged the open bottle between his knees and lifted the field glasses to his face, seeing her almost instantly.

She was on her back porch, a file folder in her lap and a borrowed dog at her feet. He imagined the file was full of whatever information she'd managed to scrape together about him. It wouldn't be much. Everything since he'd joined the Army was well beyond her reach. The set of her shoulders suddenly stiffened. She raised her head and stared across the yard, in his direction.

She knew he was there. Her eyes scanned the back of the house he hid in and settled on each of the windows for a few moments before she flipped the bird in his general direction and mouthed the words *fuck you.*

He cracked a half-smile and lifted the bottle, tipped it in her direction. "Right back at you," he said out loud, but he didn't take a drink. Melissa was long gone. There was no way the woman she'd become was going to help him. Not willingly.

He checked his watch. It was just past seven. Jessup was a few hours ahead, so he should have heard from Tom long before now. He couldn't decide if the fact that he hadn't was good news or bad.

NINETEEN

She poured a glass of wine and took it—and O'Shea's painfully thin arrest file—out onto the deck. There were eighteen pieces of paper inside. She counted them, put them in chronological order. Read them and reread them. According to his file, he'd run away when he was thirteen. Just disappeared without a trace.

He'd been found almost a year later, OD'd on heroin in the closet of some shitty rent-by-the-hour motel. She found the missing persons report and reread it. His foster mother filed the report in Jessup. The police chief, Billy Bauer, had filed it himself.

Sabrina took a deep breath. Billy Bauer was her father. Her mother, Kelly, had been fifteen and beautiful, with a reputation that kept her hip-deep in trouble. Billy had been older, newly married, with a baby on the way. Little Melissa Walker was born a year and four months after Billy's son, Wade.

Kelly had taken one look at the baby and decided motherhood wasn't for her. She dropped her in Lucy's arms and walked away. Lucy took her in, and they moved away to Marshal, far from Jessup and the ugliness of schoolroom gossip. The pair visited the Jessup community every Sunday, though, to attend Lucy's lifelong church, and she'd felt the sting of being excluded.

None of that had really bothered her. She was raised with love. Did well in school. She worked hard to be all the things her mother wasn't. She lived to make her grandmother proud, tried to do the right thing. Which is why, when she was fifteen and Kelly showed up on their doorstep, claiming to have had a change of heart, she listened.

It wasn't the words that got her—they were all lies—it was the fact that Kelly was pregnant again. And so at fifteen, she agreed to leave the life that Lucy had given her. Not because she wanted to, but because she knew the babies Kelly was carrying wouldn't survive without her. She'd moved back to Jessup for them.

———

Sabrina shoved the useless pieces of paper back into their folder and set it aside. She picked up her wine and took a drink, pushed her bare feet under the dog that lay at the foot of her chaise. He groaned, rolling his eyes to look at her.

"I didn't ask you to stage a prison break, you know. I'm aiding and abetting, here. The least you can do is keep my feet warm." Noodles licked her ankle.

She was cold but refused to go inside, even for a moment. O'Shea was watching her. She could feel it. She wouldn't give him the satisfaction of thinking she ran from him. Nearly an acre of land separated her deck from the back of the Brewster place, a three-story Victorian much like her own. Her eyes scanned the windows that dotted the second and third floor. A few were lighted, but most were dark. O'Shea was behind one of them, she was sure of it. She gave into her fear and frustration and flipped the bird in the general direction of the Brewster place and mouthed the words *fuck you*. Childish, but it felt good anyway.

The porch light snapped on.

She craned her neck around to see Val standing in the open doorway.

Ding, ding—round two. "Hey."

Val stood where she was for a second before coming toward her. She dropped a pair of socks and a sweatshirt into her lap.

"I know you'd rather freeze than come inside when you've got a class-A brood going on," Val said.

She shot a look across the yard before she understood. Val thought she was refusing to come in because they were fighting. "I'm not brooding. I'm thinking." She pulled on the socks.

"Same diff." Val sat down on the chaise across from her and looked at the dog. "Dog-napping again, I see?"

She tugged the sweatshirt down over her chest. "He 'napped himself—what am I supposed to do?"

"Fill in the tunnel he dug behind the hydrangeas?"

"Did you really come out here to fight with me about the neighbor's dog?"

Val sighed. She picked up Sabrina's wine and drank the last of it. "No. I came out here as an exercise in futility."

"Uh, oh—in that case I'm gonna need more wine." She stood, but Val's hand shot out and gripped her wrist. She gave it a tug, but her friend held firm. Val was the only person who could get away with grabbing her like that without consequence, and they both knew it. Val pulled her back down until she was once again sitting across from her, but she didn't let go.

"Something's going on. Don't bother lying—you're terrible at it."

117

She pulled a hurt look. "I happen to be an excellent liar."

"Not when it comes to me."

She yanked her arm out of Val's grip and settled back into her seat. "I got tossed off the job today for that shit that went down with Sanford." She pinned the blame on him without guilt. There was no need to tell Val she skipped out on her psych sessions.

"Is that why he was here?"

"You saw that?" *So much for flying below radar.*

"Yeah, I saw that. I also saw the guy you were talking to after he left. Who was he?" Val asked.

She shrugged. "I don't know. Some guy walking by who happened to catch the show." There was no need to get Val riled up. She could handle O'Shea on her own.

Val wasn't buying it. "Who was he, Sabrina?"

I wish I knew. "I told you, just some guy."

"You looked pretty angry for someone who was talking to just some random guy."

"I *was* angry. I had to chase Sanford off our front lawn at gun point," she said, but Val just stared at her. Frustration and fear had kept her stretched thin all day. She finally snapped. "What do you want from me?" She threw her arms in the air, practically shouting.

"The truth. For once, goddamn it, tell me the truth," Val said, her voice just as loud.

Sabrina's mouth snapped shut, and they glared at each other. Tears stung her eyes. She ignored them. "The truth ... okay. The truth is, fifteen years ago today, the girl I used to be was kidnapped. For eighty-two days she was raped and tortured. For eighty-two days, things were done to her that I will *never* talk about. And then on the eighty-third day, she was murdered." She swallowed hard, shoving memories and emotions aside. "Melissa is gone. She's dead, and I'm all that's left. I can't be her. I *won't* be her. Not for you—not for anybody, so … if you can't handle that, then you should just leave." It was the most she'd ever talked about her disappearance. For a moment, all Val could do was stare at her.

Then Val shook her head. "You know what? Fuck you." She stood and glared down at her. "We're in this together, you and me. I don't run. You taught me that. *You*—not Melissa. I know who you are and who you aren't, so you can take your lone-wolf speech and shove it up your ass." Val walked back into the house and slammed the door shut behind her.

TWENTY

Michael was certain she'd cancel her standing date with the law student. He was surprised when the flood light she had set on a motion sensor clicked on and he caught sight of him trotting his ass up the third story landing on the side of the house. The kid straightened his shirt and knocked on the exterior door leading to her bedroom. He was holding something... *Christ, are those flowers?*

"You've gotta be kidding." He glanced at his watch—eleven o'clock. Right on time. When she answered the door, they got down to business. Five minutes later the bedroom light clicked off, leaving only the bathroom light to see by. The bed, and what was going on in it, was thankfully cast in shadows.

The phone on his hip let out a chirp. It was Tom.

"Did you call Carson? What did he say?"

Tom was quiet for a second. He cleared his throat. "I can't find him. Looked high and low. He's nowhere to be found," Tom said.

"What? What do you mean you can't find him?"

"I mean, I can't find him. I tried the station, his house, every bar and roadhouse between here and Marshall. Hell, I even checked his parent's house. He's gone."

The hairs on the back of his neck stood straight up. Jed Carson was gone, and so was Lucy. This was it, the proof he needed: justification to kill Carson.

"What about Wade? Zeke?" he said, mentioning Carson's uniformed officers.

"Zeke's at the station, holding down the fort. I harassed him into driving out to Lucy's place with me."

"And?"

"Nothing. He went inside, said everything looked fine, neat as a pin. No signs of a struggle, no signs of a robbery. He's convinced she went to Shreveport—hell, it's even marked on her calendar. Said if we don't hear from her in a couple of days, he'd file a missing person's report."

"*A couple of days*? What the hell kind of good is that going to do? She's in trouble Tom, I don't give a shit what her calendar says. I know it," he said, his tone hard and even. "What about Wade? You find him?"

And where the hell are Wade and Carson?"

"Wade's gone too."

Both of them? What the fuck was going on? Before he could ask, Tom pushed on. "I talked to Shelly. She said Wade left for work this morning as soon as she got home from the hospital. From what Zeke would tell me, he sent her a text around noon saying that he and Carson were headed up to Caddo to do some fishing." Shelly, Wade's wife was a pediatric nurse at Good Shepherd in Marshall. And she was pregnant with their first child. No way Wade just disappears on her like that. Not without a good reason.

"Fishing? They just loaded up the poles on a random Monday and skipped town? Bullshit." That Wade was also gone meant nothing. He and Jed had been best friends since grade school. Wade followed Jed around like a puppy. He'd do anything Jed said—no questions asked. Even if it involved dumping Lucy's body in Caddo Lake.

"It's a hardly a random Monday. For any of us." Tom said.

He was right. From what Tom had told him, Carson had lost it when Melissa disappeared. He'd come home from college and never went back. "I still don't buy it," he said stubbornly. "Why not tell Zeke or Shelly they were leaving? Whatever they're doing, wherever they went, they didn't want anyone to know until they were already gone."

"Yeah, well, unfortunately, if you're going to accuse the police chief of murder and his number one of offering a false alibi, you're gonna need more than a gut feeling." Tom's voice was tight with anger. "When are you coming back? I'm probably gonna need help strong-arming Zeke into filing that missing person's if Lucy doesn't show up soon."

Lucy. He was torn between his need to get back to Jessup and the promise he made her.

"I'm on a job . . . I can't leave for a few days." At least. He'd promised Lucy he'd stay the entire month, but if anything happened to her, all bets were off. "Besides, I'm the last person Zeke is gonna listen to." How many times had Zeke tossed his ass in the back of his squad car and taken him to the station to sleep it off? Hauled him up the front porch steps at three a.m. to turn him over to an angry Sophia and worried Sean? Too many to count. Zeke knew him too well to take anything he had to say seriously.

"We need to find Carson," Tom said.

"Caddo Lake State Park is almost a thousand square miles of wetland, Tom. If he *is* there, we ain't finding him." The frustration he felt had him raising the bottle to his mouth, but he lowered it without taking a drink. "Our best bet is to look for Lucy. Do you know where her sister lives?" He knew he was grasping at straws. Lucy wasn't at her sister's; Lucy was dead, but he couldn't give up on her. Not yet.

"I never met her. All I know is her name is Loraine, and she lives in Shreveport," Tom said.

"I'll get you an address by morning." He wedged the bottle between his knees and swiped a hand over his face. Getting an address meant calling Lark. Calling Lark meant listening to his bullshit.

"Where are you?" Tom never asked where he was—usually knew better—but he seemed surprised that work would take precedence over Lucy's disappearance.

In a rented room, watching your high-school sweetheart play naked rodeo with her flavor of the month. "Nowhere special. Look, I'm gonna try to get some shut-eye. I'll give you a call in the morning. If you hear something—"

"Yeah, I'll call," Tom said before hanging up.

TWENTY-ONE

SABRINA ROLLED OVER AND stared at the ceiling, listening to Matt's heavy breathing from where he lay next to her on her bed. She'd made a mistake. She should've called him and cancelled. He was a sweet kid, good in bed—undemanding, willing to follow her lead, too busy to feel slighted over unreturned calls. Perfect for her, really. She used him because he was okay with it, but she could see that was changing.

He'd brought her flowers.

"So … what do you think?" Matt said. He reached for her hand, splayed her fingers to link them with his own. She wanted to bolt off the bed and tell him to get the hell out, but she stayed put, forcing herself to at least appear calm.

"What? I'm sorry, I must've zoned out. I didn't hear what you said." That was a lie. She'd heard him. She was just hoping he'd rethink his question.

"I said maybe I could stay the night. Be kinda nice to wake up next to each other for a change." The second the words left his mouth, Sabrina knew their casual, no-strings affair was over. They didn't do sleepovers. They didn't do flowers and holding hands. He came over, they had sex, and he left—that was it. All she wanted. All she had in her to want.

"Yeah, I don't think that's such a good idea. Early roll-call." Another lie. She didn't have anything to look forward to tomorrow except watching *Family Feud* in her underwear and eating Cap'n Crunch straight out of the box.

"That's okay. I've got a nine a.m. study group. I can lock up when I leave," he said, willing to take any crumb she tossed his way. It made her feel angry and guilty all at once, and she couldn't help but think of Nickels. The way he'd looked at her in the hallway outside Richards's office and again, later on, when he'd tried to get her to confide in him.

Matt, Nickels, O'Shea. Even Strickland. They all wanted things from her she just couldn't give.

"Sabrina—"

"Sounds great. Let's shoot for next time." She stood and pulled on a pair of boy shorts in addition to the tank she was already wearing. She never took her shirt off during sex, and Matt had never asked why. The majority of her scars had faded with time, and what hadn't was easily explained away by the hazards of her job. But there was no explaining what had been done to her stomach. Looking down, she saw the bouquet of daises he'd ambushed her with was on the floor, next to his pants. She kicked them under the bed.

"I'm gonna hit the shower. Lock the door on your way out," she said, heading for the bathroom. She shut the door between them before he could offer to join her. She was hurting him, but she didn't care.

Her hands shook so hard that she fumbled with the lock for a few seconds before forcing it into compliance. She cranked on the shower and sat on the side of the tub, listening for the faint sounds of him dressing and leaving. She was unable to take a deep breath until she heard the quiet click of the door, signaling his departure.

Her hands slowed from a fast rattle to a pathetic twitch. *Next time?* There wouldn't be a next time. She'd dodge his calls, delete his voicemails, make vague excuses, and avoid him like the plague. Eventually, he'd get the hint and give up. That was the type of guy he was. The only type she'd allow herself to become involved with.

She stood over the sink and removed her coffee-colored contacts. The eyes staring back at her didn't belong to her. They were dark, sapphire blue. They were Melissa's eyes.

They made her sick.

She backed away from the sink and lowered herself to the edge of the tub again. Her hands picked up the pace—they were jittering so hard she had to trap them between her knees to keep them still. She closed her eyes and took a few shaky breaths. She was fine. She was safe.

She needed to stop lying to herself.

He takes one a year—guess when?

No matter what she said to Michael, no matter what she told herself, she knew he was telling the truth.

You thought he stopped with you? Guys like that don't do what he did to you and then just stop.

Somewhere, a girl had been taken. She was in the dark, trapped and terrified. Somewhere, she was bleeding and screaming…

———

She pulled the lapels of her sweater closer against the stiff October chill. It was only three blocks. She was safe. She was going to be fine—she'd walked it alone plenty of times.

She crossed in front of a dark alley, a black mouth—wide open—just waiting for something to swallow.

Picking up the pace, she looked around. The street was deserted. Her legs moved faster, carrying her across the mouth of the alley when she felt a prickle. An uneasy slide, like steel wool against her skin. Her throat went dry. Footsteps, crunching across gravel, falling into time with hers, echoed behind her. She looked over her shoulder, felt herself tumble headlong down the rabbit hole.

He was here.

The hood of his sweatshirt was up and pulled low, concealing his face, hands jammed into the front pocket. His stride was long and full of purpose. Even though his face was hidden, she knew he was smiling.

He'd found her.

A strangled sob escaped her, and she bobbled the cake box. It dumped out of her hands, her leftover birthday cake instantly forgotten. She ran down the sidewalk, her legs clumsy, her breath ragged in her chest. Slow... she was too slow. He was close, so close, but she didn't look back.

She tried to run faster but knew it wouldn't be enough. Please, please, please...

She couldn't hear him behind her anymore. Hope dug deep and spurred her on. She was almost there. She could see the row of apartment mailboxes in front of her building, illuminated by the street light. She was fine, she was safe. She was going to make it—

A hand fell, hard and heavy, on her face. An arm hooked her from behind, lifted her off her feet, and dragged her into the dark.

———

The memory hit her hard, sending her reeling inside her own skin, scrambling for a place to hide from what waited for her in the dark. She slid off the side of the tub, landing on the cold tile with an audible smack that barely registered. The edge of the tub bit into her shoulder blades and she curled them, pulling herself inward. Her knees pressed together tighter and tighter at the memory of being pried apart again and again. Her hands clenched into fists, and the sobs that built inside her gut were shaped by the pain and rage that was always with her, barely kept at bay. It crashed into her, wave after wave, knocking her down, dragging her under. She let go, let it pull her apart, too tired and ashamed to keep fighting.

TWENTY-TWO

It was dark.

Her eyes were still tightly closed, but she didn't need to see the dark to know it was there. It pressed in close—molded itself to every curve and plane of her body. The sensation sent a jolt of panic down her spine. It pinged off her arms and legs, radiated through her fingers and toes until it settled, low and tight, in her belly. She knew the bathroom light had been on when she came in because she never shut it off. Light was important, light kept her safe. She'd spent eighty-three days in the dark. She knew what waited for her there. Now she was never in the dark if she could help it.

Sabrina forced her eyes open. The black she stared into softened, and the watery light of the moon pulled faint shapes into focus. She could make out the dim outline of the sink. The light porcelain bowl glowed in the gloom. A slice of light reached for her from beneath the door, brushed against her toes. She had no idea how long ago the light went out, minutes or hours, as she curled there on the floor. She pulled herself to the side of the tub again and leaned over to flip the switch. Off and on, off and on—*nothing*.

How long ago did she lock herself in the bathroom? It felt like days. The liquid hiss of the shower told her it was still running. The water had gone cold. She turned it off.

Someone was on the exterior stairs—third step from the landing. The sensor attached to it registered movement and the outdoor floodlight snapped on. Light fell through the window set high in the wall. The tub and sink were bathed in light. The rest of the small room was cast in even deeper shadow. *Someone was coming.*

Her breath came in sharp gasps, shredding and ripping out of her mouth with every push and pull of her lungs, while her heart stumbled around in her chest, tripping over itself in its effort to push its way into her throat. *Too loud ... she was too loud.*

He was going to find her. She slapped a hand over her mouth and pushed herself back and over, across the bathroom floor, until she was wedged between the sink and tub.

She made herself as small as possible, squeezed her eyes shut, and waited for the hand to reach out of the dark and drag her back into the nightmare.

She saw herself—pathetic, curled in a ball, pressed into the corner. White-hot rage erupted inside her chest, decimating the fear that crippled her only seconds before. She wasn't weak ... not anymore. Not ever again.

The quiet click of her door being opened pushed her onto the balls of her feet. Matt had left the door unlocked.

She crouched in the corner, listened for the sound of the door being shut. It came a few seconds later, and she didn't hesitate. Under the sink, shoved toward the back, was an empty tampon box. Inside was a 9mm. She had it in her hand within seconds.

She stood, pulling herself upright. The gun was loaded, she'd checked it hundreds of times, but she checked it again anyway. Her hands shook so badly that she couldn't get a firm grip on the slide. She yanked it back, barely registering when the slide bit into the skin of her hand and chewed into in, drawing blood.

She waited. Quiet footsteps made the short journey from the door to her bathroom. She reached out and unlocked the door. The footsteps stopped, a shadow stepped into the slice of light. She raised the gun, leveled it at the door.

The waiting had always been the worse part. More horrible, more torturous than the pain and shame of what he did to her.

She'd spent hours listening for his footsteps, waiting for him to come back for her. She'd listen to every scrape and creak, every groan and sigh until the sound of her own breathing, the knock of her own heart, was cause for panic. It stacked, higher and higher, emotional bricks pressed around and above her. They'd shake and wobble, teeter on the edge of her sanity until the sound of his footstep sent them tumbling down, burying her alive.

Now, fifteen years later, Sabrina could feel it build. Stack high and higher, until a tower of fear surrounded her. Held her prisoner inside her own skin. It began to wobble and shake. Each footstep beyond the dark was an earthquake.

TWENTY-THREE

If asked at gunpoint what the hell he thought he was doing, he'd have had to take the bullet, because he didn't have a clue.

When the bathroom light went off, Michael had to dig his toes into the floorboards to keep himself in place. *Maybe she just turned the light off* ... bullshit. She never turned the light off.

He waited a few seconds to see if it came back on. When it didn't, he was torn between not wanting to leave his post and tearing across the backyard to get to her. No one was there. The floodlight she had pointing at the door was dark. She was safe. She was fine.

Seconds turned into minutes, and the bathroom light stayed dark. He thought it out, let his brain run through the facts. Carson was missing and so was Lucy. Lucy was the only person in Jessup who knew Melissa had survived ... or so he'd thought.

Michael, who did you tell?

No one. He'd told no one, but someone knew she was alive. What if that someone told Carson? What if he'd taken Lucy some place quiet and ...

Jessup was fifteen hundred miles away, but it was less than a hundred miles from Dallas and one of the largest airports in the country. He hadn't talked to Lucy since yesterday. Plenty of time for Carson to pull information out of her and catch a flight. He could know Melissa was alive. He could know where she was. He could be here, right now.

Michael dropped the binocs into the case on his bed and picked up his .40 Smith & Wesson. Tucking it into the small of his back, he headed out the door.

The B&B was quiet. He made it to the back door and across the yard without incident. Vaulting the block wall between yards, he landed in a crouch. His eyes instantly found the spot where the window would be—still dark.

The floodlight pointing at the landing clicked on, bathing the side yard and rear deck with light. He drew his weapon and crossed the yard fast, rounding the house, gun raised.

Noodles sat at the top of the landing, looking down at him.

He almost turned around and went back. The dog whined and managed to look worried. Most nights, he'd scratch to be let in while Sabrina was doing her laps around the house. She'd let him in for a few hours, and they'd wander the house together. The fact that he was still out on the landing was all the proof he needed that something was wrong.

He started up the stairs.

Three steps from the top, the tread groaned beneath his feet. The light sensor had already tripped, so his approach went unannounced. He took the rest of the stairs in silence and stood outside the door. Pressing himself flat along the jamb rather than standing in front of it, he listened. Nothing but his own shallow, even breathing and

133

roaring silence met his ears. The door was cracked open. He looked down at the dog. "You're not going in," he said quietly.

He pushed the door farther and waited. No sound, no movement beyond the threshold. Pushing the door open, he stepped inside, leading with his gun. The lamp next to her bed emitted a soft glow, but it was enough to see that the room was empty. He nudged Noodles back and shut the door in his face, resisting the urge to call out to her. Hearing his voice wouldn't exactly ease the situation.

He rounded the corner and stepped in front of the bathroom door. It was closed but beyond it he heard the unmistakable sound of a bullet being racked into the chamber of a gun. She was armed. He shifted to the side, making himself as small a target as possible.

If he even thought of opening the door, she'd shoot him without hesitation. Obviously, she was okay. He should leave before things got messy. He imagined she'd stand in the dark until sunrise, gun aimed at the door, waiting for her nightmare to come for her. The thought of her like that made leaving impossible.

Shit. Shit. Shit.

This was not a good idea.

"Sabrina … it's Michael. Are you okay?"

———

He said it like the fact that it was him on the other side of the door was supposed to be a relief.

"Leave." Sabrina tightened her grip on the 9mm, and something dripped off her wrist, splattering the top of her bare foot. Blood. She was bleeding. Bleeding in the dark … a fresh wave of panic assaulted her. Memories came in waves, one after the other. Crouching in the dark, bleeding and crying, listening for the footsteps, waiting to be used and hurt. Seconds ago it had been manageable, but the blood brought memories that sent her into a tailspin.

She wanted to reach out and open the door, let the light inside. But she was stuck. She couldn't move. The fact that she was frozen with fear caused heat to creep up her neck, burn her cheeks.

"Sorry—can't do it. Not until I know you're okay." He sounded angry. She wanted to tell him to get the fuck out, she could take care of herself, but the words wouldn't come. All she could do was bleed. Helplessness added a new level to her rage. She could feel the white-knuckle grip she kept on her emotions begin to slip. Suddenly, shooting him through the door made perfect sense.

TWENTY-FOUR

JUST LEAVE, SHE DOESN'T *want you here, idiot…*

Michael glanced around the corner at the door he just came through. Six steps and he'd be gone.

Goddamn it. He swiped a hand over his face. "I'm opening the door." He tucked the .40 into the small of his back. "Just… don't shoot me."

She said nothing for a moment, as if she was actually weighing the pros and cons of giving him a lead enema.

"Okay," she said from the other side. He reached for the knob—twisted but didn't pull—giving her time to adjust to the situation. He eased the door open, dim light fell across her face and she squinted against it.

She looked like hell. Her knees were jumping all over the place, her bare legs shaking. Her gun hand was hanging on by sheer force of will. Blood ran over it and dripped off her wrist. Long, dark hair hung in loosely tangled sheets, licking at her hips, framing a face that was drawn and pale.

He held up his hands. "I'm strapped." He left one hand in the air while the other reached behind him, slowly. He pulled his piece with two fingers and backed away at a snail's pace until he was across the room. She watched him with glassy blue eyes that seemed to barely register movement. He set the gun on the dresser beside him.

"We need to talk," he said, and she nodded. Finally she came toward him on shuffling legs that seemed reluctant to follow directions. "I find it difficult to carry on a conversation while dodging bullets." He gave her a pointed look and lowered his gaze to the gun she held on him in a bloody, two-fisted grip.

She dropped the gun on the bed behind her as though it weighed fifty pounds instead of two. "What do you want?"

"I saw the bathroom light go out. I got worried." Telling the truth was turning into a bad habit.

"*Worried*? You're worried?"

He ignored her attempt at confrontation. "Look, Sabrina … you're scared. I get it."

"Scared?" Her eyes snapped blue fire at him. "Of you? Please." She took a step toward him, a little steadier on her feet now.

That was obviously the wrong thing to say. "No, not of me. Of him. Of what he did to you. I understand why you don't want to go back, but he's killing—"

"Shut up." Her eyes were blazing. There was more, behind the rage and hatred. She was terrified. Her eyes seemed to shift focus between the past and present right in front of him. Like she was unable to tell the difference between what was real and what was in her head.

"PTSD, right?" She didn't answer, but she didn't have to. Post-traumatic stress disorder. He knew she'd been diagnosed with the disorder shortly after her recovery. He also knew that she completely ignored it and refused to deal with the symptoms. He'd seen it plenty in the Army. Soldiers who ignored the psychological effects that being surrounded by death and killing had on them were the most affected. Haunted by their own memories, forced to relive, over and over, the thing that nearly destroyed them. Anxiety, paranoia, insomnia, and—when they could sleep—nightmares. The worst was the flashbacks. The actual reliving of the events that were at the root of the disorder. While in the throes of them, the afflicted person was at the mercy of their memories, unable to separate reality from the nightmares inside their head.

She glanced at the gun on the bed behind her. He looked at his own on the dresser, called himself an idiot for putting it down. "You don't want to do that."

"I'm not gonna shoot you. I'm gonna beat you stupid." She closed the distance between them, leading with her knee and he instinctively moved to block. She dropped back at the last second and caught him in the face with a right-cross that gave the gift of stars.

Adrenaline surged, triggered by the blow. Slammed back into the dresser, surprise was fleeting. He circled around, gauging her excellent stance and flawless technique. "I don't want to hurt you," he said, surprised that he actually meant it.

She said nothing, just circled right to cover his dominant hand, surging again, this time to the left. She caught him with a devastating combo, cracking her elbow against his temple before she tattooed her fist into his kidney. Grabbing onto his shirt, she jerked him forward to deliver a flat-palmed jab to his mouth and nose. The stitches holding the fabric of his shirt together gave way under her grip. The shoulder seam separated, and she shoved him away.

"You're not fighting back." The fact that he refused to hit her seemed to rile her temper even more.

"I don't hit girls." He reached up to massage the feeling back into his jaw. She said nothing, just growled and charged. She was a blur—arms and fists, knees and feet raining down on him. He became not only the catalyst for her rage but its conduit as well.

"Fight back!" she screamed. She was out of control, too far gone to be reasoned with.

"Enough!" He barreled through her defenses and slipped his hands around her throat. He planted a leg behind her and took her to the floor. He straddled her, knees bracketing her chest.

She continued to fight, switching to dirty tactics without batting an eye. She slipped her thumb into his mouth and hooked it around his face before pulling back. He felt the corner of his mouth begin to separate. Her other thumb sought the soft spot of his eye. She was no longer sparring. She was brawling, and she wouldn't be satisfied until he bled.

With no small amount of relief, he slipped his pointer and middle finger under her jaw, against the nerve that rode high, just under her ear lobe. Pressing ruthlessly, he managed to avoid blindness but couldn't slip the fish hook in his mouth until he bit down on her thumb with enough force to draw blood. "Stop it!" he yelled, inches from her face, and she gave once final surge, trying to buck him off.

She struggled to get his hands off her throat. "Fuck you!" For a split second he thought the pressure point wouldn't work. Then her eyes fluttered and slammed shut, the applied pressure finally knocking her out.

He stayed where he was. He had the insane notion that she was faking so he'd let his guard down, but when he eased off her it was clear there would be no round two—not anytime soon. He had no idea how long the pressure point would last. He'd seen a person come to within seconds; in a few rare cases, he'd seen it last for as long as a few minutes. Eventually she was going to wake up; if he was smart, he'd be gone before she did.

Sitting back on his haunches, he rubbed a hand over his face and listened to the roar of silence that surrounded him now that she was still. He half-expected Valerie or the kids to pound up the stairs, but their bedrooms were on the other side of the house. Chances were the hadn't heard a thing. He stood, fully intending to just walk away, leave her sprawled out on the floor.

The knuckles on her left hand were cut and swollen. They leaked blood from where they'd tried to break his face, and there was a contusion forming where he'd jammed his fingers into her jaw. Seeing the fresh bruise bloom under the soft skin of her neck, he felt like the biggest asshole that ever lived.

In the bathroom, he flipped the switch. Nothing. He unscrewed the bulb and gave it a shake. Burnt out. He found a pack of bulbs under the sink and screwed one in. Bright light flooded the small space.

All this over a light bulb? *Fucking figures...*

He wet a washcloth and opened the medicine cabinet. Rifling through it, he found Neosporin, some Q-tips, and a few Band-Aids. He flipped off the light and shut the bathroom door before settling down beside her.

He applied ointment and bandages to her knuckles, then used the cloth to clean the dried blood from her other hand. Under the blood, he could see the damage. It was a slide bite, where her 9mm cut into her palm.

He knew the instant she woke. Her hand went stiff, her shoulders rigid. He looked down at her. She was staring up at him with those burning blue eyes, a quiet rage simmering in their depths. He met her gaze and said nothing, just held her hand in his lap and waited.

"I don't want you to take care of me," she said and tried to pull her hand out of his grasp.

He held on to it. "I know."

She pulled harder. "I want you to leave."

"When I'm finished."

"No—now. Let go." She pulled again, struggled to sit up. He pushed her back down.

"I'll just knock you out again. As many times as it takes, so ... just relax, let me finish, and then I'll leave," he said, surprised when she stopped struggling.

She watched silently while he bandaged her hand. Finished, he stood and before she could protest, bent over and scooped her into his arms. He carried her to the bed and dropped her on top of the covers.

She stared up at him. "Leave." Her voice was shaking. At first he thought it was from fear, but then he understood. She wasn't afraid. She was ashamed. Knowing that made him angry for some reason.

"Just go to sleep, I'll leave in a minute," he said, throwing the fleece at the end of the bed over her. Incredibly, she gave up, just rolled away from him and buried herself beneath the blanket. She was asleep within a few minutes.

He waited a few minutes before palming her gun. He ejected the clip and racked the slide back, popping the bullet out of the chamber. He caught the bullet, shoving it and the clip into his back pocket. He laid the SIG on the nightstand and just stood next to her bed, staring at her.

He was leaving.

He was walking away.

He watched the dark flutter of lashes against pale cheeks, heard the soft, even noises of her breath. He saw himself slip out the door without a backward glance.

He didn't need this crazy bitch or her two tons of emotional baggage. He'd find Frankie's killer on his own.

He was leaving.

He clicked the lamp off and circled the bed. Retrieving the ladder-back chair she kept in the corner, he dragged it across the floor and planted it in front of the window. Sitting down, he stared into middle space, watching the darkness, ready to battle the shadows that came for her.

He wasn't going anywhere.

TWENTY-FIVE

"Morning, Sunshine." The voice on the other end of the phone was alert and awake.

Lark.

Michael scowled at the cell's display screen—four a.m. He'd been sitting bedside for three hours now, trying to make himself leave... *Just walk out before she wakes up.*

He poked at his swollen cheek. "Dumb bastard..."

"Excuse me?"

"Nothing. What do you want? " He was so not in the mood.

"Man, you called me—"

The address for Lucy's sister. "Did you get it?"

"I'm trying really hard not to be insulted right now," Lark said. There was nothing Lark couldn't accomplish with a computer. Finding an address would have taken him all of three seconds.

He got up to find a piece of paper and something to write with. "Okay, give it to me." He'd call Tom in a few hours. Hopefully he'd be able to get away from the diner long enough to make the trip to

Shreveport. They should know by noon whether Lucy was…he didn't want to think about it. Lark rattled off the address and Michael scribbled it down, eager to get off the phone.

"Thanks—I owe you." He was up, out of the chair—now was the time to walk out. *Just keep moving.* He was trying to keep his voice down. The last thing he needed was for Sabrina to come up swinging while he was on the phone with Lark. The last eight hours hadn't really been the definition of *minimal contact.*

"Yeah, whatever. Shaw wants to know when you're coming back," Lark said matter-of-factly.

His eyes found Sabrina in the dark. *Just leave—walk out, before things get messy…* but who was he kidding? The situation had passed *messy* a few miles back. He felt the unmistakable weight of another brick being tossed on his back.

"A month off between jobs is company standard."

"Your last job was North Korea. Six weeks ago. I don't know how much longer I can hold him off."

Livingston Shaw, his boss at First Security Solutions, was a jealous man. Long-term distractions were frowned upon, and outside interests were discouraged. For him, neither were allowed. Ever. Lark managed to keep his weekend pop-ins on Lucy under wraps, but this was the longest he'd kept off-grid since he signed his life away to FSS.

"Where does he think I am?" He sat back down.

"I got you high-rollin' in Vegas, baby, but if you don't come in soon, the boss man's gonna send the Pip squad after you," Lark said. Pips—the nickname Lark gave Livingston Shaw's private security team—were the last thing he needed right now.

"I need a few more weeks," he said, even though he knew that asking for a few more *days* was pushing it.

"So you can play stalker," Lark said. He hadn't been happy that Michael had agreed to look after Sabrina, and his tone said he thought the whole thing had gone on long enough.

The word *stalker* made him frown. "It's not like that." His words were edgy, defensive. He squeezed his eyes shut for a minute. His brain began to throb—talking to Lark was almost always headache inducing.

"Whatever you say." Lark cleared his throat. "Look, if you don't surface soon, they're gonna figure out I'm pulling a *Where's Waldo* with that chip of yours, and if that happens—"

He didn't have time for this toeing-the-company-line crap. "If you have a problem—"

"Man, shut up. All I'm saying is that I can't hide you from him forever."

Lark was right, and he knew it. His free hand pressed into the small of his back. There, nestled dangerously close to his spine was the choke collar and leash used to keep him in check.

When he'd agreed to come in and play nice, FSS decided it would be wise to keep track of their newly acquired asset. They'd chipped him like a dog and tracked his whereabouts nonstop. They claimed it was for his own safety, but Michael had never bought that. As his handler, it was Lark's job to monitor him and report his activities to the boss. At the time it had seemed like a small price to pay for the protection and resources FSS would provide. Now, given the unforeseen turns the situation had taken, FSS was proving to be more hindrance than help. Without Lark, he'd probably be dead by now. Without the possibility of finding Frankie's killer, he wouldn't care.

He looked at Sabrina. She turned on her side, facing him. Her face was relaxed, eyes closed, hands curled under her chin. It happened again—that sudden sense of free fall he'd experienced yesterday on the trail. *This can't be happening…*

Where had he been while Frankie was dying? Raped and tortured, waiting for him to rescue her for days and days? He hadn't been sitting at *her* bedside, ready to protect her.

The free fall ended in a bone-splitting splatter against the rock-hard surface of his anger.

"Find me a job. Something close and quick."

"That's my boy. I'll call you back." The relieved tone in Lark's voice told him just how critical the situation with Shaw was becoming.

"Thanks, Lark." He flipped his phone shut and stared out the window. That douche-bag Sanford's truck was still parked in front of her house. The guy shows up at her house, drunk and looking to put a beating on her, and she calls him a cab and promises to bring his truck to him. He couldn't even begin to understand her.

Standing, he retrieved the clip from his back pocket and shoved it into the gun's grip. He racked a bullet into the chamber and put the gun back on the nightstand.

He scribbled a quick note and tossed it on top of the gun before he fished the asshole's keys out of her pants pocket. The bouquet of daisies she'd kicked under the bed peeked out at him. He frowned and gave them another boot. Before he left, he opened the bathroom door and turned on the light.

TWENTY-SIX

AFTER LEAVING LUCY'S, HE drove all night, stopping only for gas. Each mile added to his sense of urgency, built his excitement until he could think of nothing except seeing his Melissa again. He relived every second of every moment he'd ever spent with her. Every smile and look she'd given him before he'd made her his, every sob and scream he'd ripped out of her afterward. It was almost too much to believe, too impossible to be true. All he had to do to convince himself that it was real, that she'd come back to him, was think about the picture. The look he'd seen in her eyes was all the proof he needed.

A sudden storm brought rain in El Paso. The surrounding desert offered little shelter from the torrent of water. The girl sat on a bus bench, huddled beneath her coat, arms wrapped around her middle to ward off the biting wind. The moment he spotted her, he knew she was meant to be his. He brought the car to a stop in front of the bench and rolled down the passenger side window.

"Hey, are you alright?" He fixed a pleasant smile on his face—the perfect mix of regret and concern with just a dash of exasperation. She looked at him, wary.

"Yeah, I'm just waiting for my dad." She glanced in the direction he'd come. He caught it and gave her an apologetic expression.

"If he's coming off loop 375, he's going to be a while. The storm caused a six-car pile-up," he said. The lie was convincing enough to make her shoulders sag beneath her coat. "Tell you what—hop in, I'll take you home." His look now was one of reluctance, like he really didn't want to give her a ride but decency forced his hand. But now she didn't look defeated—she looked skeptical and a little scared.

"No, that's okay. I'll wait, but thanks anyway," she said, the rain practically drowning out her refusal. He shrugged his shoulders and nodded his head, careful to look a little relieved that she said no. This was the delicate part—he couldn't force it. She had to come to him.

"All right, suit yourself. You try to stay dry, now," he said and in a move made casual by years of practice, he flipped his visor down for just a moment and flashed the badge he clipped there. Her eyes caught the reassuring gleam of it, and she stood.

"Hey," she said just as he put the car into drive and prepared to pull back into traffic. He suppressed the urge to smile and looked at her but said nothing. "It's just a few miles from here." She was still wary but she wanted to trust him.

"No problem," he said and reached over to open the door for her. She slid in, shooting him a shy smile, folding her hands in her lap.

"Thanks a lot. I'm Katy, by the way." The color of her eyes—a cornflower blue—deepened and darkened until they weren't her own anymore.

They were Melissa's.

He fixed that pleasant smile on his face again and put the car in drive. "Nice to meet you, Katy. I'm Detective Conway. And don't worry, it's my pleasure."

TWENTY-SEVEN

SABRINA IGNORED THE KNOCKING. When it didn't stop, she sandwiched her head between a couple of pillows to muffle the sound. A cold nose nudged her cheek, and she lifted the blankets without looking. The dog dove under the covers and snuggled his furry body into hers. She flipped the covers over him and continued to ignore the pounding until it abruptly stopped. She started to drift off again, relaxed by the sunlight that surrounded her.

Knocking again. This time closer—on the door that led from her room to the rest of the house. Again, she ignored it. Noodles buried his head under the pillow next to her. The door opened. She ignored that too.

"I know you're awake, dumbass." It was Valerie.

"No, I'm not." Her voice echoed inside the pillow cave she'd built for herself and her fugitive.

"The Harpers want their dog back." She sounded amused.

"What dog?" She looked at Noodles and rolled her eyes. He licked her face.

"Sabrina." Now she sounded annoyed.

"*Fine.*" She tossed the pillow away and pulled the covers back. Noodles tried to burrow himself deeper. She stroked his muzzle a few times before pointing toward the door. "Sorry, Noodlehead. Warden's here." He slunk off the bed and out the door. She closed her eyes and listened to him shamble down the stairs like a dead man walking. A moment later, Jessica Harper shouted, "Thanks," and shut the front door behind her.

"You know ... "

"I don't want a dog." Sabrina opened her eyes and looked at her friend.

"Okay," Valerie said. She leaned against the door frame and looked down at her. "How'd you sleep?"

Okay. So they were going with the old stand-by—*let's just ignore the fact that we've been fighting for days and call an unofficial truce.* "Like a baby." It was true. She hadn't slept that hard in months. Her eyes wandered to the window and the chair Michael had placed below it. She rolled over and stared at the ceiling. She'd woken up at some point during the night to see him sitting there, staring out the window. He hadn't left like she'd told him to—like he said he would—and instead of throwing back the covers and kicking his ass out the door, she'd stayed quiet.

He sat, slouched in the chair, knees parted, hand wrapped around a gun while the other drummed its fingers against his knee. His short, dark hair stuck up in random tufts and spikes like he'd been pulling at it in frustration. His handsome face, tired and grim, as he watched the front yard.

She'd closed her eyes, but she was pretty sure he knew she was awake. He'd been talking on the phone with someone but she'd been

151

unable to make out much of what he said. Instead of threatened, his presence made her feel something she hadn't felt in years.

Safe. She'd felt safe...

"Whoa. What the hell happened to your neck?" Valerie pushed herself away from the doorframe and sat on the bed. She prodded at the spot on her neck her friend was staring at. She sucked in a hissing breath and sat up.

She remembered Michael sitting on her chest while she tried to blind him. She'd screamed at him, tried desperately to make him hit her. It would have drawn a line, thick and dark, between them—a barrier to keep him out. Instead he took what she threw at him and watched over while she slept.

"It's nothing. Matt wanted to know how to do a rear naked choke. He caught on quicker than I thought he would." She gave Val a sheepish grin.

"Charming."

"Whatever. I think I'm done with him, anyway."

"Why? I thought things were going good between you two." Val was forever trying to force her into what she called *normal relationships*.

She flexed her grip, felt the pull of bandages across her knuckles. Thought of Michael's dark head bent over her hand while it lay in his lap. His calm gray eyes looking at her while hers spat fire at him. "Look under the bed." She pulled her knees up to her chest and looked at the chair under the window again. Valerie leaned over and ducked her head under the bed.

"Ohhh..." Val came up with a sad-looking bunch of daisies. "That bastard." She pulled a flower free and took a whiff.

"It's not funny." Sabrina snatched the bouquet and tossed it in the general direction of the trash can. Valerie arched an eyebrow at her and stood up.

"I agree. It's not."

"Don't start—"

"Start what? I'm not starting anything … but if I was, I'd say that letting someone love you isn't such a terrible thing," Valerie said.

"I let the kids love me."

"They don't count."

"I let *you* love me."

"That's cute." She cocked her head to the side and smiled. "You say it like you have a choice in the matter." Valerie reached over and tucked the bloom she'd pulled from the bunch behind her ear. "You know what I'm talking about. I'm talking about a norm—"

She slapped Val's hand away, grabbed the flower, and crushed it in her fist. "Yeah, yeah—*normal relationship* … I'm thirty-two and afraid of the dark. Not exactly conducive to normalcy."

"You have good reason to be," Valerie said as she straightened.

She did have a good reason. She knew what waited for her in the dark, but it didn't make her any less pathetic. Her eyes wandered over the windows again. Sunlight streamed through the bare expanse of glass. You'd think that she'd hide behind curtains, keep her windows covered to block prying eyes. Nope. She'd tried curtains and blinds, but waking in the dark sent her into a panic spiral. *Pathetic* didn't even begin to cover it.

"I just—I just want you to be happy," Val said.

No, you want me to be normal. "I am." For some reason, saying the words brought on the sudden sting of tears.

"No, you're not."

153

"What about you? You've saddled yourself with a paranoid whack job and a couple of kids that don't even belong to you. Tell me *you're* happy." She was lashing out, regretted every word.

Valerie recoiled as if she'd spit on her. "Don't do that."

"Don't do what?"

"Pretend you don't matter."

"I matter more than I should." She reached for the hand she'd avoided only seconds before. This time it was Val who pulled away. She sighed. "You can't keep doing this."

Val shook her head. "I don't know what you're talking about."

"Yes, you do," she said. "I'm not the one who needs normal—a husband, kids of your own—*you* could actually have those things."

"I have what I want," Val said forcefully.

She shook her head. "It's not enough. You can't spend the rest of your life sitting vigil over me—"

"Stop—just stop." Valerie pressed the tips of her fingers into her eyes and took a deep breath. She let it out slowly. "I'm not doing this again." She shook her head before dropping her hands. "I'm not fighting with you."

Sabrina looked down at her hands in her lap and somehow managed to feel even worse. "I'm sorry." God, she'd been saying that a lot lately.

"Don't be. *I'm* the one who started it." Val cleared her throat. "I'm meeting Greg after work, so you and the kids are on your own for dinner." Greg, a textile designer, was Val's latest attempt at normal for herself. He was good for her, but Sabrina knew it wouldn't last—they never did.

TWENTY-EIGHT

SOMETHING CLOSE AND QUICK turned out to be Chicago. Michael deboarded a commuter flight wearing the harried expression and the rumpled, moderately priced three-piece suit of a middle management office drone. His sleeves were rolled up to his elbow and his tie was askew. His suit jacket was stuffed through the handle of his wheeled carry-on. He blended in perfectly.

"Paging Kyle Day... Kyle Day, please pick up a white courtesy phone." Kyle Day was the name stamped on his ticket. It matched the name on the driver's license and credit cards in his wallet. He took the escalator to the first floor and bypassed baggage claim. Kyle Day was paged a second and third time before he reached the predetermined alcove. He lifted the white courtesy phone. "This is Kyle Day."

"Please hold, sir." A series of clicks, then a voice. Not Lark's.

"Two-nineteen." The line went dead.

He dropped the receiver in its cradle before picking up the entire phone. A small white envelope was taped to its underside. He took the envelope and left the alcove.

Each operative had one handler. One person specifically in charge of feeding them real-time information, logistics and reporting their mission stats to the Top Floor. Lark was his handler. Calling him was Lark's job; it should have been him on that phone.

He stopped at a newsstand on his way out of the airport and bought a newspaper. He gave it a trifold and tucked it under his right arm before he rolled his carry-on out to the curb and waited. A half-dozen cabs trolled by before he saw the one he wanted. A yellow cab with the numbers 2-1-9 stenciled on the side in black letters. He pulled the newspaper from under his arm with his left hand and used it to flag the cab down. This was the signal that brought the cab he wanted curbside. He rescued his suit jacket and climbed into the back seat while the cabbie stowed his carry-on in the trunk. He didn't need to tell the cabbie where he wanted to go.

All this cloak-and-dagger bullshit was just that—bullshit. He much preferred the Colombians and their straightforward approach. *See this man? He makes trouble for me. Kill him.* That was it. No trifolded newspapers or white courtesy phones. Just him and the specific level of violence needed to convey the client's message.

A year ago his life had been much simpler but essentially the same. He was a living, breathing weapon. People used him to kill other people. The only real difference was that he no longer had a choice in who or when. He could no longer pass on or take a job as he saw fit. He took the jobs they told him to; in return, he was allowed to live in relative peace. It was what he'd agreed to. No use in bitching about it now.

He leaned his head back against the seat and closed his eyes. The cabbie was watching him. Checking out the tap-dance routine Sabrina'd done all over his face. He smirked slightly. The facial movement caused him some discomfort. The swelling in his cheek had gone down enough to remain unnoticeable and the tear in the corner of his mouth was healing fast. Most of the lasting damage was covered by the monkey suit. The cabbie was still looking at him. Probably trying to find something juicy to tell the boss. He was low-level FSS—water boy to his NFL hall-of-famer. Probably staring at him in the rearview wondering, *what does this asshole have that I don't?* Guy didn't understand that it wasn't what he *had* that made him different. It was what he lacked.

Abruptly, he thought of Frankie. Missed her so much he wanted to do something. Hurt something. An image of Sabrina shoved Frankie out of the way. He squeezed his eyes tighter, tried to push her out of his mind. She wouldn't budge.

He gave up and opened his eyes. His phone buzzed inside his pocket. It was a picture text of a middle-aged man. He looked like a lawyer or a doctor but was probably neither. He studied the man's face. Memorized it. He had no idea who or what he was beyond the obvious: he was a dead man. He just didn't know it yet.

Michael finished with the photo and deleted it before tucking his phone away. He rolled down his sleeves and straightened his tie. He shrugged his jacket on and rolled his neck on his shoulders, trying to loosen some of the business-class knots that lodged themselves there during the four-hour flight.

"We're here."

He flicked a glance at the rearview. Yup, Water Boy had that look. That *you ain't such hot shit* look. He gave him a small smile. It really wasn't a point worth arguing.

The cab's tires hit the curb in front of an upscale downtown hotel, the name of which didn't matter. Water Boy flipped on the hazards and popped the trunk. He met him on the curb with his carry-on and a briefcase that didn't belong to him. "Here's your briefcase, sir."

He took the case, exchanged it for a twenty-dollar bill. Water Boy took the money and drove away.

He checked into a business suite reserved in the same name he flew under. He tipped readily but not extravagantly; he was cordial but not friendly. He declined turn-down service, made no special requests. He was forgotten by the hotel staff minutes after he closed the door to his suite.

Tossing the case on the bed, he loosened his tie again. This meant he'd have to fix it a second time, but he didn't care. It was like a noose, choking him. He opened the case and looked inside. A Kimber .45 and suppressor were nestled atop four kilos of uncut heroin. He ignored the H and the dull itch the sight of it created in the palms of his hands—like the tingling of new skin underneath a scab that was long past falling off. The itch was faint and fleeting, born more from memory than actual want or need. It faded as soon as it appeared.

He lifted the Kimber. No sloppy seconds for FSS. This baby was straight from the box and completely untraceable. His phone pinged with an incoming text that contained the only instructions he needed. *11:45.* He knew what he was supposed to do. He was supposed to make a switch. Why he was switching a briefcase full of heroin and what he was switching it for was none of his business. He didn't care—in fact, he was paid *not* to care.

He looked at his watch. He had thirty minutes.

He took off his jacket and stretched out on top of the bed, closing his eyes. He hadn't slept, *really slept*, in days. Last night was spent in a hard chair watching Sabrina sleep. For a while, he'd been afraid he'd broken her. She usually came alive twenty minutes after her head hit the pillow, but not this time. With the exception of her brief surfacing, she'd slept the entire night through. He was envious.

The minutes ticked by in his head. *Five, ten, fifteen…* When he opened his eyes, he felt relatively rested. It was eleven-thirty.

Standing, he straightened his tie. Smoothed out the rumpled bedspread. He screwed the suppressor into the barrel of the Kimber and tucked it into the waistband of his tailored pants, then put on his jacket and picked up the briefcase. He left his room and took the stairs to the tenth floor.

Inside the envelope he'd pulled off the phone at the airport was a hotel keycard. He used it to gain access to the secure floor and walked down the plush carpeted hallway like he belonged there. The number on the keycard read 1075. He found the corresponding room number and gave the door a soft courtesy knock before using the keycard. He let himself in—making sure that the briefcase he carried was visible—and closed the door behind him.

This was a business deal about to go horribly wrong.

He recognized the man in the picture instantly. He was seated at a small dinette, a briefcase of his own on the table in front of him. Two thugs that looked a lot like Pips flanked the man in the picture. They eyed him with the smug glare of the supremely stupid and didn't even bother to unbutton their suit jackets. His jacket was already unbuttoned.

The movement was fast and fluid. *Ssk, ssk, ssk.* Three trigger pulls. Three bullets drilled dead center into three foreheads. The exit wounds were gruesome, but Michael barely noticed. Pulling his cell from the inside breast pocket of his suit, he snapped a few pictures. He chose the one that best showcased the business man's spanking-new bullet hole. He retrieved a number from his short list of contacts and sent the photo. He swapped briefcases and left.

He left the way he came, exiting the stairwell and crossing the lobby, briefcase in hand. He let the doorman open the door for him but shook his head when he offered to hail him a cab. The cab that brought him would be taking him back to the airport.

A sleek black limousine pulled up to the curb in front of him. A Pip exited the driver's side in a dark suit and even darker glasses. This guy was no low-level runner. The man walked around the front of the limo and opened the rear door for him, as self-assured as the right hand of God.

Michael hesitated for a moment. Two men, cast in shadow, waited in the dark cave of the car. One of them was Lark. He was worried but hid it well. They'd been in more than one scrape together, so he knew the look. He took a step forward. The Pip smiled.

He was getting in the car—that was a given. Walking away would be like burning down his own house. A happy thought at times, but when faced with the reality of the situation, it was hardly an option worth considering.

He climbed into the back of the limo next to Lark, and the Pip shut the door behind him. He looked at the man seated on the soft leather bench seat across from him.

As far as Michael was concerned, it was Satan himself.

TWENTY-NINE

IT TOOK TWO DAYS for her to crack. Two days of wandering, restless and alone, through the house before Sabrina was ready to pull her hair out in frustration. She called the number on the card Richards had given her and scheduled her first session with the department therapist for eleven o'clock that morning. Maybe if he saw that she was compliant, Richards would let her come back to work. It was a long shot, but it was better than doing nothing.

That wasn't the only thing getting to her. Two days and not a glimpse of or word from Michael. It wasn't like before, where she knew he was there but couldn't see him. He was gone.

His little babysitting routine didn't mean a thing. He blamed her for his sister's death. He was angry with her for what happened to Frankie, and she couldn't blame him. Either way, what he wanted was obvious: for her to come back to Jessup with him. That was never going to happen.

He made his demands and got his answer. No matter what he promised Lucy, he wouldn't be back. It'd been Lucy's fear that brought

161

him here, not some unseen danger. She was sorry about Frankie, she really was, but getting herself killed wouldn't bring anyone back.

Random thoughts rapid-fired in her head while she ran down the sidewalk. Her faithful sidekick sprinted ahead of her to circle back, nose to ground, tail wagging. She began to lose herself in the pound and rhythm, the hard crunch of her shoes against the dirt, the easy pull of air through lungs that were just beginning to ache.

In a few short hours she'd be bullshitting her way through a fifty-minute with someone trained to find cracks in her psyche. Not her idea of a good time, but she was beginning to pull clear of the nightmares. She felt better than she had in weeks. She figured she had an above-average shot of making it off the therapist couch sans straightjacket. That alone was cause for celebration.

After her session, maybe she'd swing by and grab Strickland for lunch. She hadn't talked to him in days—

A sharp bark sounded behind her, followed by another and another until she was forced to slow and then stop. She turned to see the dog standing on the trail behind her—tail tucked low, head turned toward the woods bordering the trail to the north. He barked again and turned to look at her.

"What is it, Noodlehead? A rabbit?" she said, but instead of shooting off into the trees, he sat down and whined. He turned his gaze toward her again and lifted his paw. "If you want the rabbit, *you* go get it." She walked back down the trail toward the dog. This wasn't the first time her jogging partner tried to talk her into a rabbit hunt.

She hunkered down to ruffle his ears and peered into the trees. The woods were still.

Too still.

"Come on Noodlehead, I don't have time—" She grabbed his collar and gave it a gentle pull. The dog growled, low in his throat. She dropped her hand immediately, but Noodles wasn't growling at her. He was growling at something hidden in the trees.

Her eyes swept across the thick carpet of dead leaves on the ground, still hoping to see a rabbit bolt for cover. She saw them almost immediately. Drag marks. Two grooves, deep and black, cut a swath through the carpet of leaves. They led from the top of the slope, a gentle S that wound along the ground as if the person who made them had been out for a leisurely stroll. The marks continued on for about twenty yards, ending at what looked like a small mound of dead leaves.

She rose slowly and so did Noodles, his feet dancing with apprehension. "Come on."

They started down the slope together, the rustle of dead leaves sounding like a swarm of locust beneath their feet. Ten yards from the bottom of the slope, Sabrina stopped and studied the ground, looking for whatever it was that made her companion so nervous—and then she spotted it. The police officer in her told her to stop there, call it in. Keep her distance, not disturb the crime scene.

But no matter what the cop in her knew was right, there was no stopping herself from moving toward the pile of leaves and what waited for her beneath.

"Oh … please no," she said, barely above a whisper. She took a few stumbling steps before her knees gave out, landing in front of a mound of fallen leaves.

Something was buried underneath.

She brushed the dirt and leaves aside with trembling hands, but her fingers were stiff and clumsy—they didn't want to do what her brain told them to. She skimmed them along, knocking leaves and clumps of dirt loose to reveal the heel of a foot. Moist soil clung to it, reaching for the abraded ankle above it. Mottled skin covered in blackish bruises. She continued upward. Next was a calf, cold and pale.

More leaves and dirt crumbled away, the calf gave way to thigh. She'd be young and pretty. She'd have blue eyes just like...

She'd forgotten about the dog beside her, but the growl he let loose brought her back to the here and now. The noise deepened from growl to snarl.

Someone was behind them.

THIRTY

Sabrina's heart took off at a gallop. It was all she could hear. Instinct took over and she moved slowly, her hand falling away from the mound in front of her to rest on her knee. Noodles continued to snarl, quivering lips peeled back from teeth that suddenly looked razor sharp. The sound was unlike anything she'd ever heard from him. Her hand crept down her calf, skimming the cuff of her yoga pants to wrap around the .380 LCP she never left home without.

As quickly as he'd morphed into a hell hound, Noodles went still and quiet. He whimpered. His tail began to swish side to side through the leaves. She pulled the gun from her ankle holster and stood, spinning around.

"Don't move." With her free hand she unclipped her cell and pushed a button without taking her eyes off the person in front of her. "Call 911," she said into the phone—the call was answered a few seconds later.

"911. What is your emergency?"

"This is Homicide Inspector Sabrina Vaughn with Central Station—badge number six-two-six-nine-three. Requesting backup at Mount Davidson Park. I've got a one eighty-seven and possible suspect in custody."

———

Michael didn't like the way she was looking at him. Like he was filthy. Like she'd known all along that he was out to do her harm. She finished the call and clipped the phone to her waistband without taking her eyes off him.

"You're making a mistake. I didn't do this. You *know* I didn't do this," he said, his eyes locked on her face. He lowered his arms a fraction of an inch, testing her resolve.

She tightened her grip on the butt of her gun and gave her head a small shake. "The only thing I know for sure is that if you move one more muscle, I'm going to shoot you." Sirens wailed in the distance, getting louder and louder by the second. He didn't have much time.

"Listen to me—"

"No. I'm done listening to you."

"Lucy is—"

"Just … stop talking." A pair of squad cars, followed by another, rocketed down the trail, kicking up clouds of dust in their wake. They skidded to a stop a few yards away. Doors flew open, uniforms piled out.

She looked at someone over his shoulder. "Cuff him. We'll sort it out later." A heavy hand fell on Michael's shoulder and spun him into a nearby tree trunk. Instinct urged him to fight back, but he remained compliant. The officer kicked his legs apart and forced his hands onto his head.

"Lace your fingers and leave them on top of your head, sir," the cop said, managing to make the word *sir* sound like a four-letter word.

The cop kept a hand on his head, pushing him forward just a tad to keep him off balance while the other hand got down to business. "What's your name?" He ran his free hand along Michael's rib cage and down his sides.

"Michael."

"Got a last name."

"Koptik." At least that's what the driver's license in his wallet said. He looked at Sabrina. She was standing off to the side, watching the exchange. She tensed up at his lie and he regretted it, but telling the truth wasn't an option.

"You got anything in your pockets that's gonna stab or poke me?" he said. Michael shook his head. What was in his pockets wasn't the issue. It was what was strapped to his calf that would present a problem. *Deep breath. Relax.* There was no stopping it now, not without totally destroying whatever shred of trust Sabrina might still harbor for him.

The cop pulled his wallet out of his front pocket and tossed it to a nearby uniform. "Run him," he said.

"I'll do it while you guys secure the scene." Sabrina reached out and took his wallet from the other officer. Her eyes flitted over his face, and he saw a mixture of uncertainty and anger there. "I'll call the ME and CSU while I'm at it." She turned and made her way to the closest squad car.

The cop ran his hand over the outside of his leg and paused. "What's this?" He lifted the leg of his jogging pants, exposing the tactical knife strapped to his calf. The cop gave a low whistle and shoved him harder into the tree.

Deep breath. Relax.

"Don't move." The cop reached down and pulled the knife. "Nothing that's gonna stab or poke me, huh?"

Keep your mouth shut.

The cop snapped the cuffs on him in record time and spun him around with a fistful of shirt. He dumped him on his ass, knocking his head against the tree trunk in the process. "Have a seat, Rambo," he said, kicking his legs out straight in front of him. He turned to the cop he'd tossed the wallet to and showed him the knife. "Watch him while I bag this."

Michael watched the cop walk toward the cluster of squad cars where Sabrina was. That clown would show her the knife, and that would be it. She'd never trust him.

———

The Colorado driver's license she'd pulled from the wallet the uniform took off Michael was real. Sabrina sat in the privacy of the borrowed squad car and ran the name and driver's license number for the third time; for the third time, the name Michael Lee Koptik popped up alongside a recent photo of O'Shea and an address for a condo in Boulder. Registration information for a 2008 Acura Legend completed the bogus picture. According to the business cards in his wallet, Michael Lee Koptik was a computer programmer. He'd received a parking ticket last year for parking in front of a timed-out meter. He paid the ticket three days after he got it. That was it. Nothing else.

Which was complete bullshit.

She glanced out the passenger window in time to see the older patrolman kick Michael's legs out from under him. He went down like a ton of bricks and stayed there, but she had the feeling that he was simply tolerating the officer's rough treatment. She had no doubt that he could be gone if he wanted to. Instead he splayed his legs out in front of him and stayed put. The patrolman said something to his partner and started across the clearing. He was heading toward her while Michael stared after him.

The approaching uniform had something in his hand that stopped her heart mid-thump. *Please, God. Don't let that be what I think it is.* She pulled her cell off her hip and dialed Lucy's number. It rang and rang. No answer. She hung up and dropped her phone into her lap.

"Look what our guy had," the uniform said, coming up to the window. He showed her a knife with a smooth black double-edged blade that was about four inches long. "Pop the trunk for me, will ya? I'm gonna bag this bad boy for the techs and run a perimeter around the scene."

"Sure." She reached down and pulled the trunk lever. Noodles waited patiently outside, his tail swishing double-time across the dirt when she opened the car door and stood. It was a little after eight in the morning. She glanced at the squad car in front of her. These uniforms were from Ingleside. Not her station. She figured she had about an hour before a pair of inspectors showed up to take over, and about an hour and thirty seconds before they kicked her off the scene. But until then, she was senior officer in charge.

She climbed out of the car and stood in the open doorway. "I'm also going to have you cordon off a section of the road up ahead. These trails are restricted to vehicles and too tight to turn around on, so any tracks we find up ahead will more than likely belong to whoever dumped her here."

"Her?"

"The victim is a female, late teens, early twenties." She hunkered down and gave Noodles a few long strokes along his neck and shoulders. "What a good dog you are—yes, such a good dog," she whispered. She wanted to bury her face in his fur and cry.

The officer pulled a few rolls of barricade tape and the bagged knife out of the trunk and slammed the lid. He looked at the pile of leaves and dirt that lay twenty yards away. The exposed leg was clearly visible, standing out in stark relief against its nest of rotting vegetation. "You got all that from a leg?"

He likes them young.

"*Her* toenails are painted lime green with blue rhinestone flowers. She's young." She stood again and faced the officer. He was older for a patrolman, late forties, early fifties with a stout build and a neck thick enough to put a plow horse to shame.

"You think this guy did her, dumped her, and then what? Came back on foot to get his rocks off?" He nodded in Michael's direction but she didn't look.

"Maybe," she said, finding herself not wanting to believe it.

The officer tossed her the clear, plastic evidence bag. "Nasty lookin' pig sticker. Guy don't carry a knife like that unless he's got a reason."

She looked at the plastic-encased knife in her hands and had to agree. This wasn't some cheesy pocket knife with retractable cuticle scissors and a toothpick. This knife was made for killing. Her brain took a spin inside her skull, and she had to remind herself to breathe. Eighty-three days of bleeding and crawling around in the dark had taught her a lot, but the most useful was how to compartmentalize. She reached out, grabbed the myriad emotions that assaulted her in a merciless chokehold, and started stuffing them away. She would not fall apart. She had work to do.

Turning toward the clearing, she gave a shrill whistle. Heads snapped up and turned toward the sound. She motioned for the uniforms to round it up and bring it in. She pointed at Michael—*bring him too.*

She feigned disinterest while the uniform on babysitting duty pulled Michael up the slope and propped him against the rear fender. Noodles let out a single bark and started to wag his tail, happy to see his friend.

"This your dog?" the uniform said, looking from Michael to the dog.

"No," he said, looking straight at her.

"He's mine." She snapped her fingers, bringing Noodles to heel. The officer stuffed Michael into the back of the car they were gathered around and slammed the door shut.

She delegated tasks. One to head over to the visitor's parking area to look for the car that was registered to Michael under his fake license. "If you find it, radio in and get some techs down there to process it." She turned to the two uniforms closest to her. "Walk the trail—mark any tire tracks for casting and run a perimeter around those drag marks." She turned to the officer who'd taken the knife off O'Shea. "What's your name?"

"Bertowsky." He nodded to his left. "The snot-nose boot they saw fit to stick me with is Duncan." Gruff words, but they were spoken with a certain amount of affection.

She gave them both a grim smile. "Okay, Bertowsky. You and Duncan run the perimeter and wait for the ME while I have a chat with our suspect."

THIRTY-ONE

SHE WAITED FOR THEM to start moving down the slope before she opened the rear door of the squad car. Noodles tried to nose his way in, but she pushed him back and grabbed Michael by the arm. It was like grabbing a braided steel cable.

She pulled anyway and he came willingly, letting her lean him against the back of the car. He said nothing, just stared her down with those desolate gray eyes.

"I'd like to ask you a few questions, *Mr. Koptik.*"

The corner of his mouth quirked. "Call me Michael."

She read him his rights. "Are you willing to answer my questions without the presence of legal counsel?"

He gave her a look that said, *really? This is how we're playing it?* before he shrugged. "I'll answer them, but I can't promise you'll like what you hear." He rolled his shoulders and settled in against the side of the car. Again, she had a hunch that the only reason he was in police custody was because he'd allowed it. The feeling was unsettling.

"Where did you get your false identification?"

He gave her a sardonic smile before he glanced down at the dog. He shifted his body and moved his cuffed hands to one side so he could ruffle the dog's ears. "Hey buddy, sorry I scared you." Noodles forgave him and gave his hands a thorough tongue bath.

He wasn't going to answer her. She took a step back and held up the knife. "This is yours?"

The smile held. "Yes."

She nodded. "When the ME gets here we're going to uncover... the body. We'll find stab wounds, and I'm going to have probable cause to give your knife to the CS techs. They'll run a field test for blood. Will they find any?"

"Possibly." His eyes shifted away from her face. "But it won't belong to that girl down there."

She couldn't explain why, but she believed him. "Why are you carrying a knife?"

"Because guns make noise."

His answer solidified everything she'd feared about him. She looked around. They were alone. "Why did you come back?" she said.

"You know why." Again, he looked at her like she was stupid.

"I told you not to. I told you to leave," she said, practically mouthing the words.

"I made a promise to Lucy." Translation: what she wanted meant nothing.

"It's been fifteen years—"

"For you. For me, it's been a year and two days. He killed my sister, and Lucy knew it. She got scared, asked me to look after you."

"And you agreed," she said. She knew the story she'd been fed, but she didn't believe a word of it.

"Yes."

"But not so you could look out for me. You came here to bait a trap." She forced herself to look at things objectively and couldn't blame him. What would she be willing to do? Who would she be willing to sacrifice to exact revenge on the person who hurt her family? The answer was anything and anyone.

He nodded. "I hoped I could do both, but ... " he looked away again.

She took a step closer. "But what?"

"I waited too long." He looked at her again, and she watched the truth darkened his eyes to the color of coal. "I let myself—feel sorry enough for you both to get involved past my own agenda." He gave the cuffs a rattle. "I regret it now."

"Where's Lucy?"

He shook his head. "I don't know. The day you spotted me she left me a bunch of voicemails. Mostly it was just her yelling at me for being such an idiot, but on the second to last one she said ... " He swallowed hard and cleared his throat. "She said, *Michael, who did you tell?* I could hear someone, a man, call out to her in the background, but I didn't recognize the voice."

Sabrina's lungs felt dry, shriveled. "What did the last one say?"

"Nothing. There was someone there, but whoever it was didn't say anything." He narrowed his eyes. "I think we both know what happened, Sabrina."

Yes. She knew better than anyone what happened to Lucy.

"She could be hurt, maybe—"

"I sent Tom to look in on her." He said the name like she was supposed to know who he was talking about. "By the time he got there, she was gone. The note on the door said she'd gone to Shreveport."

Hope re-inflated her lungs. "She has a sister there," she said, but he just shook his head.

"No. Tom checked … Loraine hasn't heard from her in days."

"And you trust this Tom guy to tell you the truth? How dumb are you? If he lives in Jessup, he could be—"

"Tom Onewolf."

It was like he'd spoken to her in a strange language she barely knew. Her brain strained to process the words into something she could understand. "Tommy?" Her hand reached up and latched onto the ring that hung around her neck.

"Yeah." His eyes traveled down and settled on the hand she kept clutched to her chest. "He goes by Tom these days." He glanced over her shoulder, totally unconcerned with the pain he'd just inflicted. "Your lackeys are almost done." He looked back at her.

Guilt over what'd happened to him and how she'd left things began to pile up. She'd run like a coward, left him with no explanation. She pretended it was for the best and maybe it had been, but he deserved better.

She pushed Tommy out of her mind. She couldn't think of him. Not now.

"It doesn't mean she's dead. He'd keep her alive, use her as bait—" she stopped herself. She was grasping at straws and she knew it. The bait lay in the woods behind her. He'd want to punish Lucy for keeping her from him all these years. And he'd want to punish her for hiding. Lucy was dead.

Two birds, one stone.

THIRTY-TWO

SABRINA WATCHED THE ME van pull up to the scene. The sun and shadows thrown by the dense canopy of trees made it impossible to tell who'd caught the case, which coroner had been sent to the scene to collect the body and secure any evidence that might have been left on it. But she had her hopes. When Mandy Black hopped down from the passenger seat, Sabrina's hopes were realized. *Finally*, something had gone right. She could count on Mandy to do her job. She was the best the coroner's office had to offer.

She put Michael in the back seat of the patrol car. So far he was behaving himself, but she wasn't sure how long that was going to last. Studying the knife in her hand, she wondered for the umpteenth time in the last thirty seconds how in the hell she was going to fix this mess. She looked at her watch. Her replacements were undoubtedly on their way, so she didn't have much time.

The urge to hand the knife and Michael over to Bertowsky and just *leave* was a strong one. So was the one that tried to convince her that going home, packing a bag, and hitting the road was her sanest course of action. Lucy was dead. The man who abducted her not only knew she survived, he knew where she lived. He'd dumped a body in her neighborhood.

Run. It's what you do best. Run before you get them all killed…

Fourteen years ago, it's exactly what she would've done, but not this time. She wasn't running.

She was going back to Jessup, and Michael was going with her.

"Hey, I heard it was you, but I thought it was some sort of mistake," Mandy said, walking toward her. "You transfer over from Central Station?"

"No. I live over here. Found her on my morning run," she said, surprised at how calm she sounded, given what she was about to do. "Hey, you got a pen I can borrow?" She patted the front of her yoga pants and smiled, "I forgot to bring one."

Mandy smiled and unclipped a solid-looking retractable ballpoint from the pocket of her jacket. Perfect. "Keep it. I've got boxes of 'em. Ready?" She nodded toward the crime scene.

"Yeah, I'll be there in a minute, I'm just finishing up with a suspect," she said, taking a few steps back.

"Okay I'm gonna grab my gear and get started, meet you there," Mandy said before heading for the van. Sabrina watched her for a few seconds, making sure Mandy was preoccupied before returning to the squad car.

———

He was giving her another thirty minutes. If he was still in cuffs or, even better, arrested for some trumped-up weapons charge designed to hold him until they could run his prints, he was going to pull a Houdini and disappear. Getting his cuffs in front of him would take minimal time and effort. Getting them sprung would take a little longer, but it wasn't impossible. Patience and opportunity were all he needed. Michael was never really good at waiting, but it was something he had taught himself over time, something he'd needed to survive. And he'd found that if you waited long enough, opportunity always presented itself for the taking.

He shifted his gaze to the windshield just in time to see Sabrina finishing up with a cute blonde he guessed was the coroner. She turned and made her way back to the car, opening the front driver's-side door. She said nothing, just leaned in across the bench seat to tap a few keys on the onboard computer bolted to the squad car's dash. Her other hand came to rest on the back of the front seat, flush against the wire mesh that separated them. Her fingers were curled around something long and thin. She seemed to pay him no attention at all, like he wasn't even there. But he knew better.

At first he took her refusal to look at him as a childish attempt to snub him. He was about to say something snide when a faint clinking sound drew his attention away from her face. He looked down to see a ballpoint pen fall to the floorboard on his side of the mesh. She looked at him for one long second before she straightened herself and shut the door behind her. The implication was clear: she was giving him a way out.

THIRTY-THREE

Sabrina ducked under the yellow tape and made her way to where the coroner crouched over the body. From where she was, she could see that Mandy had uncovered the remainder of the body. She had to force herself to cross the distance between them.

"What's it look like?" she said, crouching next to her. She made herself look. *Just another case. Just another body.*

Mandy shook her head. "She's in full rigor and liver temp puts TOD sometime between two and three a.m. Nails were recently clipped and scrubbed but I found something fairly interesting." She gestured toward the victim's hands, encased in plastic evidence bags. Around her left wrist was a red satin ribbon, tied in a bow. Strung through one of the loops was a fancy gift tag shaped like a birthday cake.

She felt her chest constrict around her lungs. *Just another case. Just another body.*

"Glove me?" She held her hand out and smiled when Mandy slapped a pair of purple latex gloves into her palm. She snapped them on before pulling out her cell and activating the voice recorder app. "Victim has been found naked, face down in a clearing just south of trail seven in Mount Davidson Park. There are ligature marks on both wrists and ankles, indicating that she'd been bound for an extended period of time. There is a red satin ribbon tied around her left wrist. Attached is a gift tag with a hand-written message that reads *Happy birthday—sorry I missed it*. Abrasions on her heels, coupled with the drag marks found at the scene, indicate she was dragged and dumped." She looked up at the uniformed officer standing a few feet away.

"Tire tracks?" she said.

Nodding, he pointed up the hill. "Yeah, the car entered from the east and continued on like you said."

"I want casts," she said, shoving her cell into her pocket. "and a tech to process the area surrounding those drag marks. Our guy might've dropped something."

The uniform nodded and made his way up the hill while she moved around to the front of the body, kneeling directly behind the victim's head. She looked at Mandy. "Let's get her rolled over."

Mandy spread out a length of large plastic sheeting to roll the body onto in order to preserve any evidence they may have missed. Mandy knelt at the victim's feet, placing her hands on either calf, well above the ankles, giving her a look. "Ready," she said.

"*Turn.*" Sabrina concentrated on her own breathing, working to keep it steady. The body rolled, coming to rest face up on the plastic sheet.

All of a sudden there was a swirl of activity around her: gasps, someone muttering "Sweet Jesus," the click and whoosh of a camera.

Then it was gone. The sounds, the people—sucked into a vacuum they couldn't escape. She remained crouched, staring down at what had once been a face. It wasn't a face anymore. It was a nightmare.

One she couldn't look away from.

Lifting her hand to her face, she realized she held her cell. She reactivated the recorder app. "Victim is female, approximate age between sixteen and nineteen. Multiple stab wounds, concentrated in the genital and breast area, consistent with sexual mutilation. The victim's eyes have been removed and her mouth has been sewn shut with what appears to be medical suture. The word *run* is carved into her abdomen."

Just another case. Just another body.

"He's an enucleator."

She looked up. "Huh?"

"An enucleator. He removes his victim's eyes," Mandy said, indicating the dead girl's face. Mandy's eyes narrowed on her face. "You alright?"

Enucleator. Yes, she knew what that meant. She looked down— the empty sockets glared at her, accusing her for what had been done.

"Fine." She looked away, concentrated on the stab wounds. "What do you think, Mandy? These look like they might be a match to the knife Bertowsky took off the suspect?"

Mandy leaned in close and examined the wounds. "Let me see it." A nearby uniform handed the ME the knife; she turned it this way and that, visually measuring its length and width. She looked at the body again, running a light fingertip over one of the many stab wounds. "No. This knife has a double-edge, like the knife that was used, but no serration. Do you see where this skin here looks chewed? This knife wouldn't have done that kind of damage. It's like

182

comparing a steak knife to a scalpel." She handed the knife back to Sabrina. "This isn't your murder weapon. My guess is you're looking for a large hunting or tactical knife. Possibly a KA-Bar." Mandy looked up at her. "Hey, you sure you're okay?"

She looked up from the body and secured the knife in her waistband. "Yeah, let's get her bagged." Together they gripped the thick plastic sheet and hefted the body into the waiting bag. Mandy reached for the zipper to pull the bag closed. She continued to stare into it, at what'd been carved into the girl's stomach. It was a message for her.

RUN

THIRTY-FOUR

From the back of the squad car, Michael watched them roll the body over onto the plastic sheet the blonde had spread on the ground. He didn't need to see the damage to know what'd been found. Her eyes were gone. Her genitals were mutilated. Every spare inch of her body covered in lacerations and bruises. A message, some sort of taunt or slur, stabbed into her stomach. He knew because he'd seen it before. It's what had been done to Frankie.

Sabrina lifted her cell and started to take notes, the picture of detached professionalism. She searched for evidence, answered questions, and fielded comments from those around her. She appeared totally removed from the nightmare at her feet, and he welcomed the flare of anger her lack of emotion ignited. Suddenly she looked up, and their eyes locked across the distance. The anger he felt brought her into sharp focus, seemed to pull her closer. He didn't like what he saw. She was barely hanging on. Not so removed after all.

He followed Sabrina with his eyes. She was helping the blonde load the body into the black bag before strapping it onto the backboard.

She'd risked her career to help him escape. He told himself that it was only fair since it was her crazy paranoia that landed him in this shit pile in the first place, but it didn't do any good. Still, he'd be no use to her dead, and that was exactly what he'd be if he allowed himself to be arrested. Losing her badge was nothing compared to what was coming for her if he didn't get the hell out of here.

He held the pen in his hands now, behind his back. Getting it off the floor had been awkward but certainly not impossible. Quick fingers dismantled it while he stared straight ahead. He tucked the hollow tubes that housed the ink cartridge and spring into the waistband of his track pants and concentrated his attention on the metal clasp used to clip it to your shirt pocket. He stuck it into the cuff lock and bent up, shaping it before giving it a downward turn. The cuff sprung open. He pulled the makeshift key out of the lock and started on the other side. The sharp rap of knuckles on glass, inches from his face drew his attention. He looked up expecting to see Sabrina on the other side of the window, but it wasn't her. It was a man he'd never seen before, and he looked pissed.

———

"Hey, isn't that your partner?"

Sabrina's head snapped up and turned toward Mandy. She was pointing toward the road. Strickland was standing in front of the car she'd stuck Michael in. Obviously whatever was going on in the back of that car was worth his time and attention.

Holy shit.

"I'm gonna ... I'll be right back," she said over her shoulder as she stood and hustled in her partner's direction.

"Hey, stranger," she said and succeeded in drawing his attention, but when he looked at her, she could see that razor-sharp mind of his was working overtime. He looked at her then hunkered down to peer through the rear window at Michael for a moment before straightening and turning toward her.

"Please tell me that's not who I think it is." Strickland jammed his hands into the pockets of his slacks and glowered at her. She closed the distance between them and smiled.

"What are you doing here?" She ignored his question. Of course Strickland recognized Michael from his juvenile mugshot. As a cop, he was trained to focus on the parts of the face that didn't change— eyes, nose, and mouth shape. All he'd have to do was look at Michael, and he'd know exactly who he was.

"Mathews heard you were here working the case. He called Ingleside and made nice. They agreed to hand the case over since we were first responders." He glanced over his shoulder. "It's him, right? That guy you were running? What's his name, Michael—"

"Koptik. His name is Michael Koptik. I caught him lurking around when I uncovered the body and took him into custody until I could sort everything out." She reached around him and opened the rear door. "Thank you for waiting, Mr. Koptik. I apologize for the confusion." She helped Michael stand and turned him around, exposing his cuffs. They were still locked in place.

She turned to Strickland. "Can I borrow your cuff key?"

Without a word, he produced a small metal key from his inside jacket pocket. She used it to release the cuffs and handed it back. Michael turned and smiled.

"That's okay, Inspector, I understand. Better safe than sorry." He rubbed his wrists while he waited for her to retrieve his wallet from the front seat of the cruiser. The pen she'd given him was now lying on the seat next to it.

She handed him the wallet. "This is Inspector Strickland—he'll be conducting the investigation. He may have some questions for you regarding the case." She looked at Strickland, who stared blankly at her for a moment.

"Oh, is it my turn to talk? Yeah?" He looked at her and nodded before turning to look at Michael. "Good—I *do* have a question. *Who the fuck are you*?" Strickland said, stepping into Michael's space. The corner of Michael mouth lifted in a half-smile. He shot her a quick glance that said it all—*Get your boy out of my face.*

"She told you. My name is Michael Koptik. I was out for a run when I saw the inspector head off into the trees. I got curious so I followed her. Big mistake." His smile was easy, his tone neutral as he delivered the story. He was totally believable, but it was obvious Strickland's bullshit meter was going off.

"That's not your name."

"Strickland—" She stepped between the two men, and her partner looked down at her. She hadn't been sure what was going to come out of her mouth, but the look he gave her ended any thoughts she'd entertained about lying.

"Don't. Don't lie to me, Vaughn." The hurt in his voice was too much.

She turned to Michael. "You're free to go."

Strickland stepped in front of Michael, barring him from leaving. "No, you're not."

"Do you have my back?" she said to him. It was a horrible thing to do, preying on his loyalty, but she did it anyway.

He looked at her, defeated. "You know I do."

"Then believe me when I tell you that right now, the best thing you can do is let him go." She reached under her shirt and pulled out the knife and handed it to Michael. He opened the bag and bent down to slip the knife into its sheath. He stood and looked Strickland in the eye. "I am not the bad guy," he said before slipping around him, Noodles on his heels.

Sabrina watched him jog down the trail for a second or two before turning toward her partner. "I'm sorry—"

"Save it." He looked down at his watch and then back at her, but he wouldn't look her in the eye. "Don't you have someplace to be?" He flashed her his wrist. It was ten o'clock.

Her appointment. Shit. She had an hour before she was supposed to meet with the department therapist.

She backed away from him, heading in the direction Michael had taken. "I'll find you afterward to explain."

Strickland turned, pinned her with a hard glare. "You can save that too. I want you off my crime scene, Vaughn. If I have any questions, I know where to find you."

THIRTY-FIVE

THE PRECINCT'S SPECIAL SERVICES office was on the first floor, and Sabrina made it to her appointment with only minutes to spare. She walked into the small, windowless room. The first thing she noticed was the single row of weapons lockers bolted to the wall next to a sad-looking coffee cart. A hand-lettered sign rode the wall above it.

Please deposit all weapons inside a locker and retain your key— thank you.

Seriously?

Sabrina walked over and opened the nearest locker. She lifted her service weapon off her hip and deposited it into the locker. She hesitated for a moment before stripping off her jacket and doing the same with the pair of SIGs that rode against her ribs. She left the .380 strapped to her ankle where it was.

She took a seat and continued to look around the room. The chair was an orange plastic throwback to the Seventies and the carpet was a dingy low-nap that held evidence that not everyone respected the precinct's no-smoking policy. A trio of magazines sat on a small table next to her chair. She picked the one with guns on the cover and thumbed through it with steady fingers.

She was strangely calm. She looked at her watch—it was 11:01. "Sabrina Vaughn?"

Her eyes snapped up. The woman gave her an encouraging smile from the doorway "Are you ready?"

She had only one objective—to convince Richards that she was not only compliant but fit for duty. Getting reinstated meant returning to Jessup with the full backing of the SFPD. To do that, she'd do whatever this woman wanted.

———

Michael sat in his chair in front of the window long after Sabrina left. He'd taken Noodles home and came straight back to his room, calling Tom on the fly. He got voicemail and hung up without leaving a message.

He dropped the binocs in his lap and ground the heel of his hand into one of his gritty eyes. He needed Lark's help, but that wasn't going to happen. Standing, he began to pace. It had been made perfectly clear to him that Lark was no longer at his disposal.

———

When he had settled into the plush leather seat of the limousine next to Lark, seeing Livingston Shaw sitting across from him was a shock. It was pretty much like watching Lucifer climb out of the pit to mingle among the people.

"Hello, Michael. It's been too long." Shaw held out his hand. That he was sitting across from him was a sure sign that he and Lark were in some serious shit. He thought of the Kimber, pressed against the small of his back. Eight rounds, less the three he put in the businessman and his muscle. That left five in the clip. He took Shaw's hand in a firm grip—*fuck him*. If he was going down, he was going down swinging.

"It's good to see you, sir." He sat back and forced the smile on his face to stay put.

"I trust things went well?" Shaw made a vague gesture toward the building they were pulling away from.

He nodded and slid the case across the floorboard. "No problem."

Shaw lifted it onto the seat next to him and laid his palm flat on its side. "Did you look inside?"

"No."

"Not even a bit curious?" Shaw was playing with him.

"I'm not paid to look. I'm paid to pull the trigger." He had no idea what was in the case he'd taken from the dead man, nor did he care.

Shaw gave him a small smile. "When Mr. Lark suggested that we bring you into our little family, I have to confess I was skeptical," Shaw leaned back and lifted a squat crystal tumbler of icy amber liquid to his lips. He took a sip and cocked his head to the side. "Forgive me. Would you like a drink?"

Michael wanted a drink more than he'd ever wanted anything in his life. "No. Thank you."

"Ahh, well—as I was saying … I had my doubts, but I admit you've proved more than worth the considerable amount of trouble it took to make your procurement possible," Shaw said.

His *procurement*. Like he was a painting or an antique. Not a human, but something to be owned and used. "I aim to please," he said in a relaxed tone that was a complete lie.

A small smile touch the corners of Shaw's mouth. "Of that I'm sure. There's a small matter in Quebec that requires your immediate attention," he said, watching him carefully. "I trust that this won't be a problem, given the extended amount of time you just had between assignments."

Michael felt the muscle in his jaw twitch. He needed to get back to Sabrina, which meant no time for Shaw's bullshit. He'd agree for now to buy some time so he and Lark could figure out a way around the problem. "Of course, sir."

"I am pleased. Very pleased, with your performance so far, Michael." Shaw leaned forward just a touch. "So pleased, that I've decided to let you finish what you started."

He cut Lark a quick glance, but his friend wouldn't look at him. "I don't know what you're talking about."

"I'm talking about your sister and the man who murdered her." Shaw said, waving the denial away before Michael could even voice it. "You mustn't blame Mr. Lark, he really had no choice but to tell me everything." He smiled again. "You have one week to settle the matter." His magnanimous tone served as a warning. Quebec or not—the clock was now ticking. "And you'll have to do so without the aid of Mr. Lark. His involvement puts my investments at risk, and I'm afraid I can't allow that."

The limousine glided to a stop and the rear door opened. The Pip opened the door and stepped back, allowing Shaw to exit. Before he did, Shaw turned toward him. The angle at which he sat brought him much closer than Michael was comfortable with. "The locator chip. In your back. It's a marvel of modern science, designed by our weapons department, but it's not infallible." His gaze flicked over to Lark, who continued to look straight ahead. "That's why there's a failsafe built into it. A simple phone call—seven digits and one word from me—is all it will take to detonate the equivalent of a dirty bomb nestled against your spine. I can kill you from across continents, Michael. Please remember that."

Shaw exited the car, taking the case and Lark with him.

———

Quebec had proved a challenge but in the end, Shaw's confidence in his abilities was well-founded. He'd been given seven days to find his man; Quebec had cost him two. Michael had five days left to find Frankie's killer, while attempting to safeguard not only Sabrina but her family as well. He glanced out the window again, this time without the aid of his field glasses. He could see a tiny white square in the distance—a note Sabrina had stuck to her bedroom window.

WATCH VAL.

He changed into jeans and a navy blue Hanes. The knife stayed where it was. He shrugged into a shoulder holster that held his .40 S&W before putting on a light-weight hooded jacket.

Miss Ettie was in the kitchen, the smell of something sweet drifting through the open door. It reminded him of Lucy.

Five days.

It wasn't enough. He'd wasted too much time—weeks and weeks of sitting on his hands, waiting. Now that it was finally happening, now that the wheels were finally turning—time had suddenly run out.

THIRTY-SIX

FORTY-FIVE MINUTES LATER, SABRINA left the precinct the same way she'd come in. It'd gone well. She'd managed to survive without cracking up.

She walked into the windowless waiting room with a reminder card for next session clutched in her fist. She'd find Richards, show him the card. Ask him to let her quit her vacation and come back. Afterward she'd make good on her promise to find Strickland and explain as much as she could. Hopefully, that would be enough.

She was so focused on her goal that she'd closed the door to the shrink's office and was halfway across the waiting room before she noticed him.

Sanford was sitting in the ugly orange chair.

As soon as she recognized him, she looked away. No way could she afford his brand of bullshit, not with the shrink less than twenty feet away and her path back to active duty so clear. He glared at her, obviously as surprised to see her as she was to see him. It made sense though. He was on administrative leave for assaulting a fellow officer after taking two to the chest. Kevlar or not, getting shot messed with your head. Of course Richards would order him to attend sessions.

She continued to ignore him and headed to the row of weapons lockers. After a second or two of debate, she decided to leave her shoulder holster in the locker, retrieving only her service weapon. She'd come back for the holster later, once Sanford was gone.

She clipped her SIG to her hip and slammed the locker shut. She dropped the key into her coat pocket and headed for the door. Sanford said nothing, just glowered at her around a still swollen nose with the kind of malignant rage that made turning her back on him a bad idea.

She made it as far as the precinct's main lobby when she felt a light tap on her shoulder. She turned, expecting an exasperated civilian, unsure of where or how to retrieve an errant child or spouse.

What she got was a whole lot worse.

When she pivoted, her long hair swung out and Sanford took full advantage. He wrapped a heavy hand around it—again and again—until the knuckles of his fist dug into her scalp while the other lashed out and connected with her face. This was no glancing blow—this was a full contact punch that instantly split the skin above her eye. He cocked back and swung again. This time she was able to block the punch but remained unable to extricate his hand from the tangle of her hair. "Where you goin', bitch? Where you think you're goin'?" he hissed in her face as he swung a third time and a fourth. Both blows connected with varying degrees of success. She landed a few blows of her own but was unsure of where; blood dripped from the cut above her eye, making it difficult to see.

Rough hands pulled them apart. Sanford kept his grip on her hair, unwilling to let go. Hair tore from her scalp in a painful clump. Someone screamed, and she thought maybe it was her. She lunged forward—she hadn't started it, but she sure as hell was going to finish it.

"Stop. *Stop,*" someone shouted at her. Arms and shoulders barred her from charging Sanford while he shouted things she couldn't make out. Spittle flew from his mouth, and his eyes had that blind look that belongs exclusively to someone caught in the middle of a rage-induced blackout. It took six men, civilians and officers alike, to drag Sanford away. They hauled him somewhere, back down the way they'd both come. She had no idea where, and she didn't care.

She was half-led, half-dragged in the opposite direction, into an empty conference room. Someone pushed her into a chair. An impenetrable wall of blue instantly erected itself around her. A wet wad of paper towels was shoved into her hand, and someone crouched down, into her line of sight. It was Richards.

"You think maybe you want to file that complaint now?"

———

Michael went around the side of the house and knocked on the back door rather than the front. Valerie's home office was toward the back, in what was probably once the solarium, and she liked her music loud. Banging on the front door would likely draw the attention of nosy neighbors. Considering how he spent his morning, that was the last thing he needed.

Etta James wailed through the windows, and his knock went unanswered. He waited for a pause between songs and knocked again. This time she opened the door but said nothing, just stared at him.

He cleared his throat. "Ms. Hernandez, I'm—"

"Took you long enough." She took a step back and to the side, inviting him in.

He paused. "You talked to Lucy? She told you who I am?" It was the only explanation for why she'd be so willing to invite a stranger into her home.

She shook her cap of short black hair. "No. I recognize you from the other night on the porch. Are you coming in or not?" She jerked her chin at him. He hesitated for an instant before he stepped into the kitchen. She closed the door behind him and gave the deadbolt a twist. They stood and stared awkwardly at each other while she finished sizing him up. She looked at her watch. "Coffee or beer?"

Scotch. "Coffee. Please."

She nodded again and turned toward the counter. "Sit," she said to him over her shoulder, and he dropped himself into the nearest chair. "Cake?"

"What?"

"Cake. Would you like a piece?" She gestured toward the cake dome on the counter. His throat closed up. He nodded again. She took a plate from the cabinet and cut him a slice. The tangy-sweet smell of lemons and sugar drifted across the room. She brought both coffee and cake to the table and set them down in from of him.

"You make it a habit of inviting strangers into your house for coffee and dessert?" He picked up his fork and took a bite. It tasted just like Lucy's, and he knew without asking who'd made it. He tried to swallow it but it stuck in his throat like a lump of wet cement.

"You're not a stranger," she said. She returned to the table with her own coffee and sat across from him.

"You saw me for what? Five seconds, almost a week ago. I could be dangerous." He picked up his coffee and took a drink, trying to dislodge the clump in his throat.

"I'm sure you are—but not to me." She looked him in the eye.

"How do you know that?"

She shrugged. "If you were a danger to me or the kids, Sabrina would have killed you five seconds and almost a week ago." She took a sip from her mug and set it down. "Enough chit-chat. You can start with your name and how you know Sabrina, followed by telling me what the hell is going on." She pushed her cup away and leaned her elbows on the table, staring directly at him.

He followed suit, leaning into her until they were separated by inches.

"My name is Michael O'Shea, and it's not Sabrina Vaughn I know; it's Melissa Walker. As for what's going on ... well, I think you already know."

———

The cut above Sabrina's eye continued to ooze blood. She took another swipe at it with the back of her hand.

"Keep pressure on it," Richards said, forcing the handful of wet paper towels against her brow.

She hissed and jerked her head back. "Okay—*okay*, let me do it." She pulled her hand from under his but kept pressure applied. Richards let his hand drop to his side but stayed crouched in front of her.

"What the fuck just happened, Vaughn?" he said.

She looked at Richards and shrugged. "Guess he meant it when he said it wasn't over, huh?" She cracked a smile and looked up at the cluster of people in front of her. Lloyd, Tagert, and Davis stood in a tight semicircle around her. Her team. Tears prickled the back of her eyes and she had to blink them away. She looked to her left. McMillan had Nickels backed into a corner, talking quietly. He might have been listening to McMillan, but he was looking straight at her. She glanced away but everywhere she looked, she saw hard faces full of livid concern staring back at her. Her eyes bounced around, looking for a safe place to land. They settled on the trash can. Richards stood and said nothing.

"This is funny to you? That asshole jumped you—*one of our own*—and you're making jokes?" Tagert said. He was six-foot-two, black, and built like a linebacker. She gazed up into his face and gave him a long look before she stood.

"*He's* one of yours—not me. Not anymore. I transferred out, remember?" She tossed the bloody towels into the trash can while they all stared at her in stunned silence. "Look, I appreciate the assist, but I'm fine." She looked at Richards. "What are you guys doing here, anyway?"

"Shrink said she thought Sanford needed an intervention. We were on our way in when shit hit the fan," Richards said.

"The only intervention that asshole is getting is one that involves my foot up his ass," Tagert said through clenched teeth. She looked away from Tag and found Nickels still glaring at her from the corner McMillan had him backed into. It seemed like every person she knew either wanted to beat the shit out of her or saw it as their mission in life to save her. It was so tragic, it bordered on the ridiculous.

She shook her head, stifling a laugh she knew would probably earn her double sessions with the shrink she was already seeing. "No, Tag … just leave it alone."

"Like hell—"

"I can take care of myself." She moved toward the door, but the semicircle refused to break rank. They stared down at her, unwilling to let her go.

"You heard her, Tag. She doesn't need our help. Let her go," Nick cut in. She looked at him. The face she'd always thought of as open and friendly was gone. In its place was the impenetrable face of a stranger.

For a split second, she wished she was different. That she was softer. That the walls she'd built around herself weren't so thick and high.

The feeling passed.

She gave each of the men in front of her a look, and they finally shifted to let her through. She headed for the door. Nickels followed her with his heated glare but remained where he was. She stopped in front of Richards.

"Don't let them do anything stupid, Sarge. He's not worth it," she said in a low voice.

"You're right, he's not—but you are. I want you to file assault charges."

She shook her head. "No."

"So, what? He gets away with this. Again?" Richards leaned into her. "For whatever reason, Sanford has it bad for you—and not in a good way. He'll come at you again, you know that."

Whaddya gonna do, shoot me? Yeah, he was going to keep coming at her until he got what he wanted.

"Save the DV speech for someone else's punch bag. I can take care of myself." She left without saying another word.

THIRTY-SEVEN

THE LOBBY WAS BUSY. People milling around, talking on cell phones, waiting for help. She still had the reminder card for her next counseling session clenched in her fist. No way was Richards going to help her now. She dropped it in the nearest trash can. She suddenly didn't feel like looking for Strickland. One look at her face and he'd be just another guy she'd need to talk off a ledge, all hopped up on testosterone and protective instincts.

She walked with her head down, wanting to avoid letting people see the mess her face was in. She ran right into the uniformed officer without even seeing him.

"Sorry 'bout that," he said. She looked up, and his face changed. "Oh, hey—Inspector Vaughn. You okay?" he said.

"Yeah, thanks." She just wanted to go home.

"I saw what happened—I work the information desk. You sure you're okay?" He must've been one of the officers that took Sanford away. He gave her a sympathetic smile. "Looks like it hurts— shitty way to spend your birthday, huh?"

Her head snapped up. "What? What did you just say to me?"

The uniform's smile wavered. "Your birthday…it's your birthday, right?"

The gift tag tied to the dead girl's wrist flashed in front of her. *Happy birthday—sorry I missed it.*

She took a step back, her hand falling to her SIG. "Why would you ask me that?"

She must've looked as crazy as she felt, because he held up his hands and started shaking his head. "Look, all I know is some bike-messenger guy delivered a package with your name on it a little while ago. It was wrapped in paper with balloons and stuff on it, so I just assumed it was your birthday," he said in a rush.

She dropped her hand. "Who left it? Is he still here?" she said, thinking that the frantic tone of her voice sounded odd coming from her mouth. The uniform must've thought so too, because he faltered a bit before scanning the crowd.

"He was here when…everything happened. He'd just dropped off the box and was standing right over there." He pointed back the way she'd come. She turned and scanned the lobby. Nothing but civilians—all minding their own business. None looking back at her.

She turned toward the uniform. "What'd he look like?"

"Medium height and weight. Sunglasses, baseball cap. Riding gloves, backpack. No distinguishing features—honestly, once the punches started flying, I forgot all about it until I ran into you," he said sheepishly, scanning the lobby again. "He's not here. I'm sorry." He looked at her with something close to panic.

Great. She'd succeeded in freaking the poor kid out. She shook her head. "Where's the box now?"

"I gave it to Anderson to run up to you, so it's probably at your desk. I'm sorry," he said again. She had no idea who Anderson was, but she nodded her head anyway.

"No, no—it's fine." She turned and started to retrace her steps.

"Inspector?"

She turned back and waited for him to speak.

"It's not your birthday?"

According to her personnel file, Sabrina Vaughn's birthday was in July. "No, it's not."

"Then what's in the box?"

The question formed a hard knot of panic in her belly, but she forced herself to remain calm. She shrugged and gave him a smile. "I'm sure it's nothing. Probably just someone's idea of a joke."

THIRTY-EIGHT

His OUTING HAD BEEN a success. More than a success, actually. He'd just delivered Melissa's gift when a commotion broke out across the lobby. He turned to see what was going on and could hardly believe his good fortune. She was here.

He watched a man twice her size grab her by the hair and punch her—once, twice—hard in the face. Any lingering doubt he might've had as to her identity vanished.

Her level of skill had improved. He had no doubt that she'd be a very dangerous opponent in a fair fight. The shiver of fear spilled down his spine again. During their time together, she'd been a spitting cat, all claws and teeth, but the way she fought back—her will to survive—remained the same.

She swung, connecting again and again. It lasted only seconds, thirty at best, before people dove in to break it up. The man had her by the hair and refused to let go. He ripped it out when they were pulled apart. She screamed—the rage-filled sound was one he remembered well.

There was a trio of officers behind the information counter where he stood. One of them came out and charged across the lobby while the other two stayed put. The man was hauled backward, screaming and cursing with every step. Melissa was dragged into a room by what looked like a professional football team in cargo pants, and the door was slammed shut. The lobby had come to a standstill—stunned civilians gaped at the empty space where there'd been violence only moments before. Someone coughed and it was enough to break the spell. Around him life resumed, but he continued to stare, let his gaze drift down the hall where the man had been taken.

The two officers behind the counter started talking. The man who attacked Melissa was named Sanford. Had been suspended for drinking on the job, practically lived at a bar—a place called the Station—owned by a couple of retired cops.

He left with a smile on his face.

———

Valerie got up and left him sitting at the table without a word. Michael sat there for a few minutes before she came back carrying a wooden box.

"Here." She plunked it down in front of him. "Open it."

There wasn't much inside. A nametag—the kind waitresses wear. *Melissa* was engraved across the yellowed plastic in loopy cursive. He recognized the old Wander-Inn logo. A picture of Melissa and Tommy—the kind one of them took themselves. They were both grinning, faces pressed close together. It looked well-worn, like it'd been handled a lot over the years. There was a scrap of paper that looked like it had been torn from a pocket-sized notebook. On it were three words: *Make me ugly.*

Puzzled, he dropped it back into the box. There was another scrap of paper at the bottom of the box. He picked it up and read it.

Leave him or I'll finish what I started.

It was written in different handwriting than the other. He looked up at Valerie. "What's all this?"

She rounded the table and sat across from him. "It's Melissa. All that's left of her." She picked up her coffee mug just to set it back down. "I can sit here and tell you I don't know what you're talking about, that I don't know who Melissa is, but frankly, I'm tired of the lies."

He nodded. "You met her in Yuma? She got a job waitressing at the restaurant where you worked?"

She lifted a shoulder and let it drop, didn't bother to ask him how he knew. "Yeah. I was working my way through community college with plans for interior design school in LA. She just wanted to support her brother and sister. We just clicked together, you know? You ever have a friend like that?" She looked at him. "I suppose not."

He ignored that and lifted the scrap of paper. "She tell you *why* she left Jessup?"

"Sure. She got a little too flirty with her mother's boyfriend, and he decided to take her up on her offer. Melissa got cold feet, but the guy wasn't hearing it. She fought back and he tuned her up. She decided to involve the law—*her daddy*—and rather than see her man strung up, her mother kicked her to the curb and tossed the twins out after her. Then she and the guy took off for parts unknown, never to be seen again." She cracked a humorless smile. "Did I tell it right?"

He nodded. He'd heard the story plenty of times over the past year. When he asked Lucy about it, it was the one thing she refused to talk about. "But that's not what happened." He tossed the scrap of paper on the table between them.

"No. That *is* what happened. Sort of." She tipped her chin at the scrap. "The boyfriend came at her because he was a raping pig, not because she asked for it."

"Pete Conners tried to rape her?" He said it quietly but the calm delivery must've sounded as forced as it felt because for just a second, she looked afraid—like she suddenly realized that he wasn't someone she should've invited into her home.

"If Pete Conners was her mom's boyfriend, yes."

Lucy'd never mentioned it. Surely something like that would've been worth mentioning—that her daughter's boyfriend had tried to rape her granddaughter a few days before she disappeared.

"But that's not why she left." Val changed the subject, reached into the box, and pulled out the picture of Melissa and Tommy.

"She loved him. Pined for him. Called her grandmother every day to ask about him. Was he okay? Did he hate her for leaving? The answer was yes to both."

"Can you blame him, Valerie? He got stabbed and beat near to death over her only to find out she was a whore just like her mother. And then she took off rather than face the mess she'd caused." He didn't really believe what he was saying, was only trying to bait her, but she just smiled.

She dropped the picture and picked up the scrap of paper on the table between them. "He'd asked her to marry him, and she said yes. They had plans to leave Jessup together. No amount of gossip or speculation would've made her leave him." She flashed him the scrap.

Leave him, or I'll finish what I started.

"She left him to save his life." Val dropped the piece of paper in to the box along with the picture and shut the lid.

THIRTY-NINE

SABRINA STARED AT THE box. It was smaller than she thought it would be: a four-inch cube wrapped in red paper with colorful balloons dancing along its surface. It was tied with the same red satin ribbon he'd tied around the girl's wrist. Attached to the ribbon was the same kind of gift tag. She swallowed hard. She didn't want to touch it. She could still see the girl's battered face, empty sockets aimed straight at her.

The box was big enough to hold a pair of eyes.

She looked up. Strickland was sitting at his desk, ignoring her. His desk was a mess again.

He was obviously still angry. She looked back down at the box. She'd put it in an evidence bag—

"Thought you already had a birthday."

She looked up to find him glaring at her. The glare faltered when he got a load of her face, like his resolve against her was momentarily weakened, but he didn't ask her what happened. She was sure he already knew. Gossip spread quickly among cops.

"I did. In July." She chewed on her bottom lip.

"You okay?" The glare eased up a bit more.

She hesitated. She needed his help, and to get it she was going to have to play it straight. She shook her head. "No, I'm not."

He rolled his chair over and dropped down in it, close enough to whisper. "Then let me *help* you. Tell me what's going on."

She shook her head again. "I can't. Not here."

He muttered a curse, started to pull away from her.

"But you're right. Something's going on with that guy, Michael... and the dead girl I found in the park." She said it all in a rush, before she came to her senses.

He nearly shot out of his seat, she had to reach over and grab his arm to keep him in his chair. "Did he kill her?"

"No." She let her gaze fall to the box on her desk. He looked at it, vibrating like a divining rod when comprehension finally struck. Same red ribbon. Same gift tag.

"Is this evidence?"

"Probably."

"We should bag it."

She nodded, used an evidence bag to scoop it off her desk. She turned to drop it in her bag, but Strickland stopped her.

"You expect me to let you leave this building with uncataloged evidence in an open murder investigation without so much as an explanation?"

She looked him in the eye. "I expect my partner to trust me and back my play."

He gave a low whistle. "Wow... you fight dirty, Vaughn."

"I'll explain everything—I swear. I just need a little time to figure some stuff out."

"How much?"

210

She had no idea. It all depended on how much she could find out and how long it took her to put it all together. "Did you run her prints?"

Strickland worked his jaw for a second or two, probably trying to decide whether to answer her or tell her to fuck off. "Yeah. She popped as a potential runaway from El Paso. Kaitlyn Sawyer. Been missing four days."

El Paso. Made sense if he was driving, and four days gone fit the time frame of how long Lucy'd been missing. "Has the coroner's office called about the autopsy yet?" she said.

"Black called about a half hour ago. Said she's knee-deep in autopsies but that ours made it to the front of the line because of the *brutal nature of the injuries inflicted on the victim.* Autopsy is set for nine tomorrow morning." He swiped a hand over his face and looked like he wished he never met her. It stung. "I want specifics, Vaughn. A specific time and place where you're going to tell me what's going on because, I gotta tell you, this is it. I'm at the end of my rope with you."

"I'll explain everything tomorrow after the autopsy. I'm gonna be your plus one."

———

The puzzle pieces were falling into place, but they seemed to be in endless supply. The more pieces he fit together, the more confusing the picture grew. Michael stood, needing to move around before he got mired in the past. He snagged the coffee pot and topped off his mug. He did the same for Valerie without asking. He put it back and sat down.

"Did she tell you what happened the night Tommy was attacked?"

"If Sabrina wants you to know about that, she can be the one to tell it." She pushed the box aside.

"Okay. Then tell me about the night *she* disappeared."

Val was quiet. He began to think she wouldn't answer him, but she did.

"It was her birthday. Some of us brought in a cake and sang to her. After work, I was supposed to give her a ride home, but I had a date, and I—I couldn't." She faltered, cleared her throat. Took a deep breath and started again. "I let her walk. It would've taken me less than ten minutes to drive her home, but I let her walk. She never made it home. She was just *gone* and nobody knew where or how. All that was left was that damn birthday cake she'd dropped in the street when he grabbed her." Her voice broke, the guilt and sorrow she still carried after all these years were like a length of stones draped around her neck, her head bowed beneath their invisible weight.

"You blame yourself?" It was a ridiculous notion, one she clearly clung to.

She shrugged. "She was gone—stayed gone for eighty-three days and every single one of them was my fault." There was no arguing with her. He knew that kind of conviction, that absolute certainty that you were to blame. It stared back at him every time he looked in the mirror.

"A priest found her." It wasn't a question, he'd read the police reports, seen the crime scene photos of the blood-soaked bench she'd been draped over.

She nodded. "He called 911. When they arrived, the paramedics thought she was dead but when they checked her eyes, her pupils were still reactive. They rushed her to the hospital. It took seventeen hours of surgery to repair the damage." Her voice cracked and she cleared her throat. "They removed three feet of intestine. She had a lacerated liver, a punctured lung. Every bone in her face was broken—both her arms, one of her legs. He stabbed her fourteen times, obliterated her uterus. She had to have a full hysterectomy." She paused, took a shuttering breath. "She *should've* died—it would've been more merciful if she had. When she finally woke up, she opened her eyes, and I could see it: Melissa was gone."

He didn't have to ask, he knew what she meant, had thought the same thing himself. "They fixed her face."

"Yeah. They flew in a plastic surgeon from Boston who specialized in facial reconstruction. I gave him pictures of what she looked like…before. He told her that he couldn't make her look exactly like that, but he'd come close. He promised to make her beautiful again." She laughed. "Do you know what she told him? She said *make me ugly.*" She rolled her eyes. "She couldn't actually *say* anything, her jaw was wired shut. She wrote it." She jerked her chin at the box. The scrap of paper he'd seen suddenly made sense. "The poor guy looked like she asked him to perform her surgery drunk and blindfolded." She gave him a shrug. "That was when I knew that she was gone for good and there'd be no getting her back."

"But you stuck around? Why?" he said.

"Everything is different: her voice, her face, the way she takes her coffee. But sometimes I still see Melissa in the little things. The way she ties her shoes, the way she eats her French toast. Sometimes I think that having her so close but still gone makes it impossible for me to ever really let her go." Valerie smiled. "She makes a lemon pound cake every year…it used to be Melissa's favorite. She never eats it; I end up throwing half of it away, but she still makes it. Can't cook for shit, but she can bake." Her eyes filled with tears and she let them drift to the counter. "Sometimes, when I really miss Melissa, I'll go upstairs and watch her get ready for work, just so I can see her tie her shoes. Or I'll make French toast just so she'll put peanut butter on it." She looked at him and smiled. "Crazy, right?"

"Not crazy—lucky." He paused, wondered if he should continue. As soon as he told her why he was here, she'd throw him out, but he figured it didn't matter anymore. "The man who killed Melissa killed my sister a year ago. He's still out there, and I came here to ask Sabrina to help me find him," he said quietly. Valerie stared at him while he waited for her to find her voice.

"What did she say?"

Before he could tell her that she'd told him to go to hell, a voice spoke from the doorway.

"I said yes."

He turned to see Sabrina standing there, looking at them. He had no idea how long she'd been there, or how much she'd heard. Her face was a mess, the skin above her eyebrow split open. The right side of her jaw was puffy and swollen. He didn't have to ask. He knew who did it. He put Sanford on his to-do list.

She looked at him and nodded her head. "I'll do it. I'll go back with you."

Through the determination, fear shone plainly on her face. Suddenly, taking her back to Jessup was the last thing he wanted to do.

FORTY

THE PLACE WAS CROWDED for a weekday afternoon—noisy with the constant clack of pool balls and Hank Williams's country twang. He pushed his way in and headed for the bar. It was the kind of place where beer came in a bottle and ordering an Appletini would get your ass kicked. He snagged an empty stool and gave the bartender a nod. "Beer. Jack chaser."

A bottle of Bud was all but tossed at him along with the Jack. "Eight bucks," the bartender said. He threw a ten on the bar and downed the Jack. He nursed the beer and waited. He didn't have to wait long.

Sanford showed up, coming through the back door like he owned the place. He took the stool closest to the door he'd just come through. Without being asked, the bartender slapped a glass in front of him and gave him a long pour of something brown. Sanford downed it like he was dying of thirst, and the bartender hit him again before walking away. This one he took his time with. He stared into his glass between sips, like a gypsy reading tea leaves. Every now and again he'd drain it, and the bartender would come back. After the fourth or fifth trip, the bartender gave up and just left the bottle. Before long, Sanford was totally wasted, his shoulder slumped against the wall his stool was butted up against.

He couldn't help but think of the last guy who thought it was okay to touch what belonged to him. Not that dumb cocksucker Tommy—no, he'd gotten lucky and lived. He was thinking about the one in Yuma ... what was his name? Andy. That's right—his name had been Andy.

———

Ol' Andy made a lot of mistakes that night, the first being he decided he needed pancakes after a long night of hard drinking. He and his pals rolled into the greasy spoon his Melissa was working at and ordered up breakfast. Then Andy made mistake number two.

He grabbed her ass.

After finishing breakfast, he and his friends left. He'd followed them for hours. From Yuma to some little bend in the road that was nothing more than a gas station and a roadside stand that sold Mexican insurance to border-crossers. They pulled into the gas station, and Andy disappeared around the back of the building. His third and final mistake was forgetting to lock the bathroom door.

He'd cornered him in the stall and asked him his name, the tip of his knife pressed into the vulnerable flesh beneath his eye. The kid's eye rolled in its socket, skittered away like it was trying to make a run for it. Andy stammered his name out right before he stabbed him—one thrust at an upward angle. He drove the blade deep under the rib cage, puncturing his lung, making it impossible to call for help. He let him fall to the floor, blood pouring from the single

216

wound. His face was mashed against the dirty tile, lips puckered, moving like a fish out of water. He looked surprised, like he didn't understand the why of what'd happened.

"Someone needed to teach you some manners, Andy. You can't just go around touchin' what don't belong to you," he said, but the kid still looked confused. His mouth was still moving, making a hissing sound. It took him a second to understand what he was trying to say. He reached out and gave the kid a hearty clap on the shoulder. "It's alright—I accept your apology," he said.

Stepping on Andy's forearm, he pinned it to the floor. He wrapped his gloved hand around the kid's wrist, jerked up, hard—snapping it in two. He used the saw-toothed edge of his knife to hack through the meat of his arm. He took it with him when he left.

———

He looked at Sanford's whisky-bloated face, then down to the hand he kept wrapped around his glass of brown liquor. The knuckles were swollen, scraped from where they're rammed into Melissa's face over and over. Sanford was sporting a few bruises and his nose was nothing but a wad of angry red meat slapped on his face, but it wasn't enough. He drained his beer and stood, walked over to where Sanford was slumped over.

It was time to teach him some manners.

FORTY-ONE

"No. You're not leaving. I won't let you." Val sat on the sofa—arms crossed over her chest, a mutinous glare pointed her way. Once the plan was formed—once she'd agreed out loud to leave with Michael—she knew Valerie would give her trouble, but this was ridiculous.

Sabrina sat in the chair opposite the sofa, elbows braced on her knees, head buried in her hands. She threw a look at Michael. He was leaning against the far wall, hands dug in his pockets, staring at the floor. He glanced up at her then bounced a look between her and Val. Finally his gaze settled on her. His eyes said nothing she didn't already know. Putting distance between her and her family was crucial to their safety.

"I'm going," she said for the hundredth time. "I have to go, you know that."

"Then I'm going with you," Val said stubbornly. "We'll send the kids to my parents—"

She scoffed. "Are you *kidding* me? If he can't get to me, the first thing he'll do is come after Riley." She didn't know how she knew it, but she did. "Your parents can't protect her. He didn't just kill that girl in the park. You didn't see what he did to her. He *destroyed* her."

Val aimed a look of hurt disbelief straight at her. "I did see. I saw what he did to *you*—I was there when they..." Her voice hitched in her chest and she looked away.

Her shoulders sagged. "He'll kill you. He killed Lucy to punish me—"

"You don't know that for sure." Val flicked a glare at Michael. "She's missing, no one knows for sure. She might be okay." It made sense that Val would refuse to accept the inevitable. She was the one who'd insisted that they keep contact with her. If Lucy were dead, she'd blame herself.

"Val. Please."

"I can't," Val whispered. Her dark eyes flooded with tears. "I let you leave once. When you left, you disappeared and never came back."

She met Val's gaze, saw the sorrow she was usually so deft at hiding. "Is that what you think happened? That you did this?" she said. Val looked away.

She leaned forward to grab her hand. "You had no way of knowing what was going to happen. He would've come for me no matter where I was or who I was with. I'm *glad* I was alone because you wouldn't have stopped him. He would've killed you and if you were gone, I'd be totally lost. And what about Riley and Jason? Where would they be now if you had been with me that night?"

They were quiet for a moment. Michael stared at the floor. Val stared at her hands. Sabrina stared at Val. Finally Val looked up to meet her eyes.

"You have to let me go."

Val took a deep breath, let it out slowly. "Okay. But if you get yourself killed, I'm going to be pissed."

FORTY-TWO

SABRINA LAY IN THE dark and stared at the ceiling. The red, ribbon-wrapped box sat on her nightstand unopened. A grenade, just waiting for her to pull the pin.

"You need to open it," Michael said. She turned her head to look at him.

He'd stayed. Hadn't asked, hadn't insisted—just stayed. Like it was a given. He was sitting in the chair in the corner. The wash of moonlight that fell through the window illuminated his legs. Everything else was cast in shadow. She wanted to tell him to shut up and mind his own business.

She looked back toward the ceiling. "I know."

"Scared?"

The word jerked her upright. She looked at him again. "Careful. The last time you tossed that word at me I kicked your ass."

He laughed and leaned into the pale slice of light that streamed through the window. "Don't remind me, I'm still pissing blood."

She was quiet for a moment. "I'm sorry."

Leaning back, he disappeared into the dark again. "Not the worst beating I ever took."

"That's not what I'm talking about." She was sorry for Frankie. Sorry for the trail of dead girls that led back to her. Sorry for a lot of things.

He didn't answer her. Didn't say it was okay, didn't say he forgave her, that it wasn't her fault. Silence swallowed silence, growing bigger and heavier second by second, until the weight of it pushed her flat on the mattress. Finally, he spoke.

"I fought them. Sophia and Sean, I mean. They took me in, loved me, and all I did was throw shit at them. I couldn't stop it. Every time I broke their hearts, I told myself that it was the last time, that I was going to change, be the kind of kid they deserved. Let them love me or whatever, but I couldn't. I was too scared.

"Then Frankie was born. She looked just like Sophia, but with Sean's eyes. She was everything I could never be. She was theirs, belonged to them. I hated her." He said nothing for a moment, just slow, heavy breathing. "But then Sophia made me hold her. Practically dropped her in my arms. I wouldn't even look at her. I told Sophia to take her back. I didn't want her there—I was going to hurt her if she didn't take her back. But she just said, *no, you won't.* Then she said, *she needs you Michael. She's your sister—she belongs to you too.* I finally looked down and she was staring up at me with these ... beautiful blue eyes." More slow, heavy breathing. "She saved me."

She didn't know what to say. *I'm sorry* wasn't enough. There was nothing she could say that would make it better. But there was something she could do to make it right.

"I'm going to kill him," she said quietly.

He laughed—a small, watery sound—and then leaned into the light. He looked at her, and she could see something in his face had changed. "I appreciate the sentiment, but why don't we start with opening the box."

She sat up, turned on the light. "Okay ... okay." She pulled on the pair of latex gloves that were just waiting for her to find her courage, then she grabbed the evidence bag before she changed her mind. "Strickland and I dusted it for prints. He took a sample of the ribbon to run a comparison against what he used on the vic." She was all cop now; she knew it was because she wanted to distance herself from the thing waiting for her inside the box, but she couldn't help herself.

He seemed to understand. "And?"

"No prints. No particulates—nothing. The color and cut marks on the ribbon are a match to what was found in the park. The gift tags are identical." She turned it over. This one had *Sabrina Vaughn* carefully printed across the back. She took a deep breath and tugged on the tail of ribbon, pulling the bow loose. Took the paper off, careful to preserve as much of it as possible. She put it back in the evidence bag, along with the ribbon and tag.

The box was white, unremarkable. Inside was a nest of blood-red tissue paper. She pulled the top layer aside, looked into the box. Her heart snapped in two. "Oh ... " she breathed out and slowly reached into the box.

The blown glass angel was fragile—beautiful. She recognized it instantly.

No matter what she said to Val about Lucy being dead, she'd had hope. It'd clung to her like a burr, its stubborn thorns dug deep. She'd hoped they were wrong. That somehow, Lucy was still alive. She now knew for sure that her grandmother was dead. She looked up at Michael and showed him the figurine.

"Lucy gave it to me for my eleventh birthday," she said.

He sat down on the edge of the bed and cupped his hands around hers, pulling them closer. He looked down and his face fell. "I've seen it before. She kept it up high on a bookshelf in her living room. Whoever took it had to have known what they were looking for." He looked at her. "It means something to him." He dropped his hands away and stood. Began to pace. "You were eleven?"

She watched him walk the length of the bed, back and forth—hands wrapped around the back of his neck. She nodded. "Yes. I remember because I started helping her with alterations that year." She smiled. "I saw it in some gift shop and saved every dime I made to buy it. I wanted it so bad. It's a hand-blown original—some artist out of New Orleans—expensive. I didn't care about that. I just thought it was pretty, hoping I'd be able to save enough before someone bought it. One day I went in to see if was still there, and it was gone. I was crushed. A few weeks later it was my birthday and she handed me this little box wrapped in ... red paper." Her eyes snapped up to his face. "Lucy wrapped it in red paper. With a red ribbon—it used to be my favorite color."

He'd stopped pacing and looked at her. "How would he know that?"

She remembered it like it was yesterday. "My birthday fell on a Sunday that year. She gave it to me after church. There was a picnic ... half of Jessup must've been there. Anyone could've seen her give it to me."

"Does anyone stand out? Did anyone say anything to you?"

She shook her head. "A lot of people said a lot of things. It was my birthday."

He started to pace again—back and forth along the length of the bed. He stopped after a few turns and looked at her. "What about Jed Carson. Was he there?"

The sudden memory stalled her heart for just a moment before it doubled its pace. She stared up and him and nodded. "Yes."

"Did he talk to you?"

"That was the year he started following me around. He was older and I didn't really understand at first but—he told me a bunch of kids were playing hide-and-seek in the woods behind the church... I was just happy that the other kids wanted to play with me. None of them ever did before." She laughed at the memory. "I was so stupid."

He shook his head and rubbed the back of his neck. "You weren't stupid. You were a little girl. What happened next?"

"He took me into the woods, but when we got there, it was just him and me. He tried to kiss me, but I wouldn't let him. He got mad. Really mad. He pushed me down." That'd been the beginning. After that, there was nowhere she could go in Jessup without looking over her shoulder and seeing Jed Carson, especially after she moved back there with Kelly. Still... she couldn't believe it. "He was just a kid. No more than twelve or thirteen."

He dropped his hands and looked at her. "Yeah, well, he's grown now." He scrubbed his hands over his face before shoving them into his front pockets. She noticed it was something he did when he was trying to keep himself under control. There was something he wasn't telling her.

"What? Tell me what's going on?"

More pacing. She let him go, let him figure out how to say whatever it was he wanted to tell her. She counted nine turns before he stopped and looked at her.

"Billy Bauer was killed in the line of duty about five years ago," he said plainly. He watched her face closely, so she figured that he knew; he knew Billy Bauer was her father.

She was careful to keep her expression neutral, but the truth was the news hurt more than she thought it would. She looked down at her hands for a moment. "Oh." She nodded and met his gaze. She could see he wasn't finished.

"He was killed during a routine traffic stop—stabbed to death on Route 80," he said. He took his hands out of his pockets and sat down in the chair. He leaned forward, bracing his elbows on his knees, letting his head hang between his shoulders. He looked up as her. "He was killed on October first."

"You think the man who killed Frankie and took those girls—took me—is responsible. You think he killed my—Bauer. You think he killed Bauer." It wasn't a question but he nodded anyway.

"I don't think Bauer knew *who* he was pulling over that night. I do think that when he saw who was behind the wheel, he got suspicious. Something happened to force his hand," he said before standing. More pacing, hands jammed into his pockets. He still wasn't finished.

Michael was quiet for a moment, choosing his words carefully. "I don't think it was his plan to kill Bauer that night, but I think he took the opportunity to gain control of the town."

"What? You're not making sense—"

"Five years ago, Jed Carson was just one of the two deputies. When Bauer was killed, the town council held a special session. Carson's been police chief in Jessup ever since."

As police chief, Carson would be able to steer an investigation in any direction he wanted. He'd be able to kill with impunity.

She thought of the young boy who'd tried to kiss her, the way he'd shoved her to the ground when she refused. She remembered him glaring down at her, eyes narrowed, fists clenched. Suddenly, she remembered what he said to her while he stood over where she lay, sprawled in the dirt.

"You're gonna be my girl, Melissa. Mine."

Her hand pressed against her stomach, felt the thin, raised scars scattered across it. Time and more surgeries than she wanted to remember erased the majority of them, but the original scars were still there. She could still feel them.

She traced them with her fingertip. Followed the smattering of bumps and ridges across her skin, read by touch what'd been stabbed into her. Fourteen straight-line wounds, grouped together to form a single word.

MINE

FORTY-THREE

SHE WOKE TO THE sound of her shower running. Sabrina cracked a lid and peeked at the clock. It was six a.m. She'd actually slept through the night—again. She'd take an armed guard over Ambien any day. She rolled over and stared at the ceiling. After opening the box and deciding that Jed Carson was their number one suspect, she and Michael had made plans.

They were leaving for Jessup first thing tomorrow. That gave her one day to gather any information she could and ask Strickland for help. She was meeting him at the coroner's office in a few hours for the autopsy. She'd keep her promise, explain everything to him. He'd want to go with her, be pissed when he found out she wasn't going to let him. Sabrina hoped he understood that staying behind and looking out for her family was the most important thing he could do for her.

The shower shut off, and Michael walked out a few minutes later, wearing the same jeans he had on the day before, hair sticking up from being rubbed dry. He crossed the room to sit in the chair he'd spent the night in. He picked up one of his boots but didn't put it on. He looked tired.

"Rough night?" she said.

He shook his head, gave her a half-smile. "This past year has made me soft. A couple nights in a chair, I'm ready to call my massage therapist." He laughed. "The fact that I *have* a massage therapist to call is even worse."

She wanted to ask what he meant, wanted to know more about him, but she kept her questions to herself. She understood the need for secrets. Instead, she propped her herself up on her elbow and smiled back. "You could've slept here." She gestured to the bed. He looked down and began pulling on his boots.

"I don't think that's a good idea."

It took her a second to get his meaning. When she did, she flopped onto her back and laughed out loud. "Don't worry, O'Shea—your virtue is safe with me," she said, even though she wasn't entirely sure that was true. Before he could answer, she rolled over and looked at him again. His boots were on and laced up, but he still hadn't put on his shirt. "Where're you going?"

He looked at her. "With you."

She shook her head. "You can't. Strickland is wound so tight his head's about to pop off. If he sees you there, he'll probably shoot us both. Just wait here—"

"I'll stay in the car."

"What about Val and the kids?"

"He won't go after them unless he can't get to you. They'll be fine as long as we keep dangling the carrot."

He was right. She nodded and looked away. She understood that in order to catch him, they'd have to take risks. She hated to admit it, but the thought of him being only a few seconds away was comforting. "Okay."

She rolled out of bed and looked at the clock again. No time for a run. She ducked into the closet and pulled a dark blue T-shirt off its hanger. It had SFPD stenciled in bright yellow across the front. She tossed it to him. "It'll help you blend." She headed for the bathroom. "There better be hot water left."

———

Sabrina's cell rang. It was Mathews. Again. She let it go to voicemail. He'd called her four times in the past hour and a half. Probably to give her a direct order to stay away from the Sawyer girl's autopsy.

Michael rode shotgun, not saying much. He just scrolled through what she thought might be text messages with a slight frown on his face. She wanted to ask what was wrong but didn't. She pulled into the parking lot, backed into a spot that gave him a clear view of the door.

She dropped the keys into his hand and climbed out of the jeep. Crossing the lot quickly, she hurried into the building, down a hall that smelled faintly of floor wax under the heavier, cloying aroma of formaldehyde.

Her cell rang: Mathews again. She ignored it and hurried down the hall. She rounded the corner and stopped short. Strickland sat in a folding chair outside the autopsy room with his head in his hands. Two uniforms stood on either side.

One of them turned, saw her standing at the end of the hall. He motioned for his partner to look sharp. Strickland's head came up. He saw her and stood before saying something to the two officers.

The two men didn't look happy, but when he came forward, they stayed put.

The closer Strickland got, the clearer she could see the expression on his face. Something was wrong. Horribly wrong.

"What's going on?" She looked over his shoulder at his armed escort. He didn't answer right away, just looked at her like he was seeing her for the first time. Like she was a total stranger. "Answer me, Strickland. What's happening?"

"Mathews wants you back at the station." He cleared his throat. "Sanford was found dead in his truck, early this morning. These officers are here to take you in for questioning."

FORTY-FOUR

A WEEK AGO, MICHAEL's plan had been simple. Take Sabrina back to Jessup—by force if necessary—expose her for who she really was, and wait.

She'd changed everything with two little words.

I'm sorry.

He'd have to be quick; he only had four days left. Not nearly enough time, but he'd worked in tight spaces before. If he couldn't get the job done within those time constraints, he'd have to get her out of there—hide her. She'd fight him, but he didn't care. For once, he was going to think of someone beside himself, and he was going to do it before it was too late to save them. He'd failed Frankie—he wouldn't fail Sabrina.

He called Tom, let it ring.

"Wander-Inn, this is Tom."

"Anything new?" he said.

"Not much. Still no sign of Carson. Zeke finally agreed to file the missing person's after I got Lucy's sister involved and he put a … what did he call it—a bow-low? Out on her car."

"BOLO. It means *be on the lookout,*" he said, reminded again that Tom was just a normal guy. He felt guilty for dragging him into this mess, but he'd do it all over again if given the choice. "I'm catching a flight in the morning, bringing someone that might be able to help. Is it okay if we stop by the diner?"

"Yeah, I'll be here. Who is it?"

"She's a cop—Homicide. She's got a case that might match up to Frankie's. I'll explain everything when we get there." He meant to say goodbye but when he opened his mouth, he said, "Tom … did you ask Melissa to marry you?" He had no idea where the question came from or why he felt it was important enough to ask.

"Who told you that?" Tom said.

"Did you?"

The pause was long. "Yeah. I gave her my mother's wedding ring, and she said yes. We stayed up half the night talking, making plans, and then I left her house. Next thing I know, I'm waking up in the hospital a few weeks later with a half-dozen holes punched in me and she's long gone. So much for true love." He laughed, but it was an angry sound. "Call me when you land." He hung up.

Michael dropped his phone in his lap, stared out the windshield and thought. More puzzle pieces, more loose ends.

Suddenly, she was there. Sabrina, walking, head held high, being escorted from the building by two uniforms. They put her in the back of a squad car and drove away. He jumped in the driver's seat and followed.

FORTY-FIVE

LIFTING HER EYES FROM the worn conference table bolted to the floor, Sabrina found Captain Mathews's hard stare. Central Station chatter said he'd been a detective with IA before making the jump to Homicide captain. The way he was looking at her, Sabrina had no trouble believing he'd earned his promotion by crucifying other cops.

"I don't know what happened to Sanford. Last I saw him, he was being dragged away after physically assaulting me." Her tone was calm, her posture relaxed, but her eyes were spitting fire at the man in front of her.

"Way he told it, *you* provoked *him*," he said.

"I provoked him by breathing. He has—*had*—a long history of hating me."

"Sanford made speculative comments about your sexuality. Challenged you in front of your peers. Did that make you angry?" She could see Mathews was totally loving this.

"You mean was I pissed off that he kept calling me a dyke, loudly, to anyone who would listen? No. I could care less what he or anyone else in this precinct thinks about me." Her message was clear—*that includes you, asshole.*

"He confronted you here and at your home. Threatened you repeatedly. Assaulted you. Why didn't you lodge a formal complaint? File assault charges?"

"He needed help, not me throwing more bullshit at him." Her eyes shifted to Richards leaning against the wall, arms crossed over his chest as he looked at her.

"Where were you last night?"

"I. Was. At. Home."

"Alone?"

She took a deep breath. Let it out slowly. "No. Valerie was there."

Mathews cracked a smile. "You mean your girlfriend?"

She didn't even bother to answer.

"Can anyone else corroborate your story, Vaughn?" Richards said. She thought of Michael, but instinct told her to keep him out of it.

She shook her head. "No."

Mathews shot her a nasty smirk and opened a manila file folder. "You got quite the temper." He flipped a couple pages. "Says you broke a suspect's arm in your first year—"

"He pulled a gun on my partner."

"You have three career kills—"

She shot a look at Richards. "I was SWAT. I was in the sniper rotation. Everyone knows we have more—"

"So obviously, you're not morally opposed to taking a human life."

235

"I'm a *cop*. I do my job," she said, surging to her feet, meeting Mathews's glare.

"Vaughn," Richards said quietly, but it was enough to plant her ass back in her seat.

Without a word, Mathews opened another, thinner, manila folder and pulled out a stack of 8x10 glossies. He fanned them across the table between them. Looking down, she saw what had been done to Sanford.

He was sitting upright in his truck, slumped to one side. He'd been horribly beaten, his crumpled face aimed up at her—it was dented, the bones caved in, skin splattered with blood. *A bat*, she thought. *Only a bat, heavy and swung with rage, could've delivered this level of blunt-force trauma.*

"Whoever did this is either ten kinds of stupid or the cockiest asshole I'll ever have the pleasure of arresting." Mathews picked up the photo and replaced it with another. "See this?" His finger hit the picture, nudged it her way. Beneath it she could see a wooden bat propped against the bench seat between Sanford's knees.

She closed her eyes, didn't want to look at it. She could still feel the twinge in her elbows as they extended, the jolt of connection sing up her arms.

She forced herself to open her eyes and look again. The bat was hers. The one she kept propped up behind the front door of the trailer she used to live in with her mother. The one she used to threaten her mom's johns when they got belligerent.

Rusty red smears coated its surface, covered almost every inch, overlapping the black that stained it. Blood—old under new. The rust-colored smears belonged to Sanford. The black stains were older, seeped in to the wood, trapped within the grain. They belonged to Pete Conners.

His finger hit the picture again, and it snapped her back to the present. She looked up to see Mathews smiling down at her. "Your boyfriend left the bat behind."

FORTY-SIX

Sabrina leaned back in her seat, refused to look away from him, but said nothing. The day she'd killed Pete was spotty, like her memory had been punched full of holes. She remembered running down the hall, the sound of his heavy footsteps as he chased after her. She'd almost made it, had actually closed her hand over the knob, when he'd shoved her into the front door. Sprawled against it, her arms went wide, and there it was . . . her hand closed over the bat as she rounded on him in a two-fisted grip that dropped him like a stone. She hadn't checked to see how badly he was hurt. She'd assumed he was dead, and she hadn't cared.

She just ran.

"CSU has it right now. They're pulling prints and taking samples. Only a matter of time before I can prove it was you." Mathews waited a beat, then two, before he straightened.

He was right. It was only a matter of time—her prints were on that bat. Beneath the rust-colored stains belonging to Sanford.

CSU would find them. Under normal circumstances, it would take weeks, but Sanford was a cop—she had days at best.

Before she had time to form an excuse or voice a denial, Mathews pulled the picture and replaced it with another. This one was a knee to chest close-up.

Sabrina forced herself to look past the blood. Sanford's shirt was completely covered in blood, dried crusty and dark. Stab marks marred the fabric in a random scatter—dozens of them.

Stuck to his forehead was a red cellophane bow. Studying the picture, she could see something had been placed in his hand. She wanted to ask what it was, but she kept quiet. Mathews would tell her eventually. She didn't have to wait long. He slid a photo in front of her. It was a close-up of a gift tag shaped like a birthday cake. Same red ribbon. Same gift tag. Any lingering doubt she might've had about who and why evaporated. She knew the answer to both. On the tag was another hand-written message.

Who's next?

Its meaning was clear. Sanford had been a warm-up. He was flexing his muscles, giving her a brutal reminder of what he was capable of. He was going to kill everyone she knew. Everyone she cared about.

Before she could process what she was seeing and what it meant, Mathews rifled through the stack of photos and pulled one to the top. "This is my personal favorite," he said, tossing it across the table at her. It was a close up of Sanford's mouth, yanked open to show that his tongue had been crudely cut out. "Coroner found it shoved up his ass," he said, reading the silent question on her face.

"You think I did this? You *really* think I did this?" Her eyes searched out Richards, looking for an ally. He looked away from her, like he no longer trusted his judgment when it came to her.

"What I *think* is that you got tired of taking Sanford's shit," Mathews said. He stood and took a trip around the table. It was an old interrogation tactic, meant to disorient and intimidate her. She fought the insane urge to laugh.

"What are you talking about?" She wanted to scoop up the pictures and turn them over. If she did, it would be taken as a sure sign of her guilt.

"Michael Koptik." Mathews dropped the name like a bomb.

Oh, shit. "Who? Wait—you mean that guy from the park yesterday? What does he have to do with this?"

He paused in front of her. "Yup—*that guy from the park*. Know him?"

She looked him in the eye. "No."

He nodded. "Got a call from the patrol sergeant over at Ingleside yesterday afternoon. Said one of his uniforms—Bertowsky—had some things to say about you. Said a couple things happened that didn't sit well with him." Mathews took another trip around the table. She didn't even bother to try and follow his progress. "First thing was that the dog you claimed was yours responded to the suspect you collared. Wagged his tail, licked him. Like he knew him."

"Noodles is a friendly dog… kinda dumb too. He'd probably even like you."

Mathews smiled down at her and kept circling. "Funny. The dog is dumb… but smart enough to alert on a DB in the woods."

"Maybe he just has bad taste in men."

Richards cleared his throat and she looked up. The look he gave her told her to cool it. She'd have better luck winning the Nobel Peace Prize.

"I'm glad you find this so amusing, Inspector. He also said that you seemed certain that it was a woman under all those leaves, even though all you admitted to seeing was a foot."

"I don't know many men who paint their toenails lime green."

He shrugged. "This *is* San Francisco. Then he told me you and Koptik seemed awful cozy—standing real close together, talking."

"I was reading him his rights and questioning him as a person of interest in a murder investigation."

"Right … which I'm confused about because, then you just let him go. Even gave him back the knife that was identified as a possible murder weapon."

"I had the coroner do a field comparison. She determined that the knife in question didn't even come close. I had no reason to hold the suspect, so I returned his property and released him." It was true, but she still felt like a liar. She tried not to think of the stainless-steel pen she'd slipped him through the wire mesh.

"And then he left." He stopped circling. "With your dog." He sat across from her, folded his hands and placed them on the table. "I think you know Michael Koptik. I think you're in some sort of relationship with him."

"I'm confused; I thought I was a lesbian."

Her challenge brought an angry flush to his face. "I think he's as sick as they come, and I think the two of you killed that girl in the park. Together."

"I'm still confused. Did I kill Sanford, or did I kill Kaitlyn Sawyer?"

"I think you had a hand in killing both of them."

Her eyes shot across the room, landed on Richards. She shook her head. "You can't be serious. Why would I do that?"

"Trial run. I think you had plans to kill Sanford all along—that's why you refused to press charges. If he was in lock-up, you couldn't get to him." Mathews placed his hands flat on the table and stood, towering over her.

She looked up at him. "If I had anything to do with killing that girl, why would I call it in at all?"

He smiled at her. "To see if you could get Koptik out of custody if he got caught."

She'd had enough. "Am I under arrest?"

Her question was met with silence.

"Right," she said. "All you have is a complaint about my abuse of personal space during the questioning of a potential suspect and a stranger-licking dog. No actual proof that I've done anything." She stood slowly, facing Mathews down with a slight lift to her mouth. "So … I'm gonna leave now."

She was almost to the door before he hit her with what she knew was coming. "You're vacation's just became a suspension without pay pending the outcome of our investigation. Strickland will be re-assigned. Any further involvement with the Sawyer case, or you, will result in his immediate termination. You're gone, Vaughn—the suspension is just a formality, but if the two of you so much as breathe on each other, I'll charge him with accessory after the fact." He sounded happy, like it was his birthday, Christmas, and the Fourth of July, all rolled into one. "And don't even think about running. If you so much as walk past a bus stop, I'll have you picked up for absconding."

Suddenly, her plans to go back to Jessup looked a hell of a lot harder to pull off, but Mathews wasn't finished.

"I want your badge. Now."

She took a deep, steady breath. She looked at Richards, still leaning against the wall next to the door. She unclipped her badge from her waistband and placed it in his hand.

"I didn't kill him," she said quietly, looking him straight in the eye. Richards shifted his jaw like he wanted to say something but, in the end, remained silent.

FORTY-SEVEN

SHE FELT NAKED. STRIPPED without her gun and badge. Her SIG P220s were still sitting in a weapons locker in the therapist's office. She needed to get them.

She crossed the Homicide bullpen as fast as she could, aware that everyone in the room was watching her leave. They all knew what she was being accused of, and she could tell by the look on their faces that more than a few of them believed she was guilty.

"Vaughn." She looked up to see Strickland sitting at his desk, waiting for her. She ignored him, kept walking toward the elevator. He got up to follow her. "*Vaughn*." He was getting louder.

"Damn it, Vaughn—*stop*." He was shouting at her now, obviously unconcerned with the audience. She pushed the Down button for the elevator and waited. He stood three feet away, staring at her. She wanted to cry. She wanted to scream. She did neither.

The elevator slid open, and she walked in, pushed the button for the lower level. The doors began to slide shut. Strickland dove in after her.

"Leave me alone." She shook her head, refused to look at him.

He ducked down into her line of sight. "Well, we both know *that's* not gonna happen."

She sighed, looked him in the eye. "Talk fast. Once those doors open, I'm not saying another word to you." Jamming her hands into the pocket of her coat, she found the locker key she'd tossed in there yesterday. Gripped it like a lifeline.

"Okay." He reached past her and hit the Emergency Stop button. The elevator slowed, then stopped with a slight jerk. "What's going on?"

He already knew. She could see it on his face. "They think I killed Sanford." She looked away. "And Kaitlyn Sawyer—Mathews is trying to pin that one on me too."

He was quiet for a few seconds. "Maybe you should tell him about the box—that the real killer was here, that he left it for you." He was trying to help, find a way to clear her.

She shook her head. "No. He knows O'Shea is involved, he'd just spin it into me trying to cover my tracks."

"Okay." He frowned, chewed on his bottom lip for a few seconds while he tried to figure a way out. Finally he just shrugged. "I guess we're just gonna have to find this asshole and bring him in on our own."

"We?" She shook her head, hitting the button to restart the elevator. "No. No way. Mathews made it clear—you and I are done. If he finds out we've had any contact whatsoever, he'll bring accessory charges against you."

"I don't care." He hit the Stop button again.

She looked at him. "I do. I care. I can't let you do that for me."

He shook his head. "It's not up to you."

She let out a slow breath, felt tears prickle behind her eyes. He was wrong. It *was* up to her. "I'm ... sorry for all the shit that came with being my partner." She started the elevator again, stood in front of the button panel so he couldn't reach it.

"You're *still* my partner," he said. She could tell by the stubborn set of his jaw that he wouldn't let it go. He was that dog with a bone again. He'd snarl and snap at anyone who tried to deter him. Including Mathews. He'd lose everything because of her—toss it all away without thinking twice. She wasn't the only one with an over-active sense of loyalty.

The elevator doors slid open. On impulse, she leaned over and kissed his cheek. "You're the best partner I've ever had," she said. It felt like goodbye.

"Bet you say that to all the guys."

"Such a pain in my ass ... "

She stepped out of the elevator, and the door slid closed between them.

FORTY-EIGHT

She was quick about getting her guns. On her way out, she dialed Michael's number.

"Hey, look, I'm—"

"I know. I saw them take you in. Meet me in the parking lot, you can explain then," he said.

She hurried across the lobby, almost made it out before someone shouted her name.

"Inspector Vaughn, wait up."

She turned to see the uniform from the day before, watched him weave his way through the lobby.

"Hey, glad I caught you. You got a message about a half an hour ago. Not sure why it landed down here, but ... " He held out a yellow square of paper, and she took it. Read it. He looked at her. "Is everything okay? It sounded pretty urgent—"

She turned and ran for the door, the yellow square of paper gripped tight in her fist.

———

Michael watched her cross the parking lot at a run. Something was wrong.

Very wrong.

She threw open the driver's side door. "I'm driving," she said before she all but shoved him out of the driver's seat. She floored it, flying out of the station lot like the place was rigged to blow. He'd been about to ask her what the hell was going on. Instead, he read the slip of paper she'd handed him.

She took a hard right, weaved left to avoid an illegally parked delivery truck. "He killed Sanford. Cut him up and left him in his truck in an alley. They think we're involved and that I somehow got you to kill him. They think the girl in the park was a dry run to see if I could get you out of police custody if things went south." She hung a left on a yellow, gunning it through the turn. "I'm officially suspended and if I have any contact with Strickland, Mathews will hang an accessory charge around his neck. It won't stick but it'll be enough to ruin his career," she said.

Michael read the message again.

Insp. S. Vaughn @ 32nd. Girl found in SF Gen prk lot. Name is Riley—critical condition.

He'd felt pressed for time. Like they needed to make a move, force something to happen. He made a mistake, told her that her family would be fine—that leaving them unprotected was a risk they had to take. Sabrina was going to lose her sister like he'd lost his. Six weeks ago he would have called that justice.

He looked at her. "I'm sorry." The words felt small. He felt small saying them.

She wouldn't look at him. "I guess this makes us even."

The nurse escorted them down a hall, across a linoleum floor worn thin from the countless feet that had hurried across its surface over the years. "Paramedics found her dumped in the ambulance bay. No purse, no ID. She was in pretty bad shape. Broken arm, jaw, and ribs—inside was a mess. Punctured lung, ruptured spleen," The nurse said.

Riley... how could she have let this happen? Her head was spinning. "But she's going to make it, right? She's going to be okay?" She remembered the fight for her life, all those years ago. It was brutal. Bright lights and frantic voices shouting out words she didn't understand. Hands... so many hands as they rushed to save her, keep her here, when all she wanted to do was float away.

The nurse stopped, gave her a pained look. "I'm sorry, I thought someone had told you... she coded forty-five minutes ago, right after we made the call."

Dead. Her baby sister was dead.

She hadn't even known she was going down until she felt Michael's arm slip around her waist. He held her up, and she let him. He kept walking, keeping her close to his side, pulling her down the hall.

"How did you know to call her at the station?" This came from Michael. She looked up at him, wanted to hate him, wanted to ask him if he was happy now that she was suffering. What she saw was enough to quell the words that bubbled on her lips. His face looked the same, that hard emotionless mask he always wore—but she could see the ripples beneath the surface. He was completely wrecked.

The nurse looked at her. "Your name and precinct were written on one arm, her name on the other," she said.

"My name … my name was written on her arm? I don't under-stand, I thought she was asking for me. Someone said—"

The nurse shook her head. "She didn't ask for anything. Like I said, she was in bad shape. Your name on one arm, her name on the other," she said, stopping in front of a curtained alcove, gave them both a look. Her eyes settled on the SFPD splashed across Michael's chest in bright yellow. "Something else you'll want to take a look at on her back." She pulled it open. "I'll give you a minute."

Looking at the body laid out on a stretcher, she resisted the urge to turn her face into Michael's shoulder. She pulled away from him, moved forward on her own.

She was an open wound from head to foot, bruised and ripped, torn and gouged—every inch of skin bore an injury, one bleeding into the next. Her head, hair dirty and matted with blood, rested on a pillow. Her once pretty face battered and swollen. She shot a look at Michael.

This wasn't Riley.

Relief made her lightheaded. Her knees gave out and she sank into the hard metal chair, took a few uneven breaths that made her dizzy. "It's not her."

Without a word he moved forward, rolled her carefully to ex-pose her back so they could see what had been carved into it. The slashes were messy with blood, but she could just make out the fa-miliar words.

OLLY OLLY OXEN FREE

She stood, stared hard at the words that glared up at her. He was calling her home, like a child calling out after a game of hide-and-seek. *Come on out.* He'd always liked to play games.

The thought propelled her forward. She wasn't even aware she'd left or that she was walking until she heard Michael's footfalls step in time with hers. She looked over. He was right beside her. She reached for his hand and gripped it tight but kept walking.

FORTY-NINE

SABRINA DROPPED HIM OFF in front of the Brewster place and drove home. There was an unmarked unit parked across the street from her house. She pulled into the drive and killed the engine before letting herself in through the back door. Through the kitchen window she could see Michael vaulting the fence that separated her property from Miss Ettie's.

She'd explained the situation to him on the way home, told him that he was wanted for questioning and that her house would be under surveillance. Mathews would have badges sit on her place until he showed up, so it was best if he didn't. He agreed to stay out of sight but flat-out refused to leave her alone.

They were leaving for Jessup in the morning. Until then, they had to stay out of sight. It was just a matter of time before Mathews found out about the girl in the hospital and that Sabrina was connected to yet another death—another dead body tossed at her feet.

She made sure all the downstairs curtains were closed before letting him in. He dropped what looked like a large briefcase with a numbered keypad into a chair and turned to look at her.

"Flight leaves for DFW at four tomorrow morning. You're gonna have to get someone to overnight our weapons to Tom. We'll pick them up there." He looked uncomfortable with the prospect of being unarmed, even for a few hours. She knew the feeling.

She had to call Nickels. He'd been furious with her the last time she saw him, but she didn't have a choice. Besides Strickland, he was the only one she trusted.

She dialed the number and he picked up on the fifth ring, like he was going to let it go to voicemail but decided at the last minute to answer instead.

"Hello." He still sounded pissed. She could hear the faint pop of the gun range. He was at the station.

She swallowed hard. The words refused to come.

"What do you want, Vaughn."

She cleared her throat. "I didn't kill Sanford, and I didn't get anyone to do it either." It was important to her that he believed that.

Nickels breathed out a quiet sigh. "I know. But I also know there's more to that guy you had me look into than you said."

Michael... he was talking about Michael. She looked up to find him watching her. She turned her back on him, shamed by what she was about to say, not wanting him to hear her say it. "I need help." The words burned her throat.

Nickels sighed again, this one sounded relieved. "I'll round up the team. We can be there in—"

"No. No team. Just you."

Another long pause. "I'll be there in an hour."

———

The doorbell rang forty-five minutes later. Sabrina opened the front door to find Nickels standing on her front porch.

"You've got a fan club," he said, tossing a look over his shoulder. She stepped out on to the porch and looked. The unmarked sitting across the street from her house hadn't moved. She gave a brisk wave and smiled in its direction. She looked at Nickels.

"I know—Pierce and Lawrence. I already took them some coffee and gave them my itinerary for the evening." He laughed as intended but it bled into an awkward silence. She moved aside, letting him in before shutting the door.

"Strickland caught me before I left. He asked me to bring this to you." He reached into his pocket and pulled out a flashdrive. She took it, knew what it was without having to ask. It was a copy of the Kaitlyn Sawyer file. He must've downloaded it before being taken off the case. This alone could get him fired. She looked up at Nickels, and he shrugged. "Yeah, I looked at it—pretty gruesome shit. You want to tell me what it has to do with you?"

———

Telling Nickels the truth was the last thing she wanted to do, but she was out of options. She'd need his help to see this thing through, and she'd have to trust him to get it. She took him outside, onto the back deck, away from Michael. Somehow, keeping the two of them separate seemed like a good idea.

"This is you?" Nickels looked at the picture she'd showed him. His eyes bounced back to her face, searching for similarities, some kind of continuity that connected her to the girl in the picture. He was looking for an identifiable marker—something that would make her insane story believable. He could look for the rest of his life; he wasn't going to find what he was looking for in her face.

While the plastic surgeon hadn't done exactly what she'd asked, he'd made sure there was no trace of Melissa Walker left on her face.

She took the photo out of his hand and slipped it into her back pocket before lifting his hand to her cheek, guiding his fingertips over her face, letting him feel the screws and plates beneath the muscles and skin. After that he seemed ready to believe anything.

She started at the beginning and took him through it all. He stared at her while she talked. He obviously wanted to ask her things but didn't know where to begin. He glanced over his shoulder, through the open door at Michael.

"Where does he fit into all this?" Nickels said, looking back at her.

"The man who took me killed his sister last year. He came here to ask for my help in catching him." It was the condensed version, but Nickels was a cop—he knew what it meant.

"Bait." He sounded angry.

"It's my choice, Nick," she said quietly. She looked over her shoulder. Michael was staring at his laptop, poring over the flashdrive she'd given him.

Nickels stood and faced the yard, leaning against the porch railing. The set of his shoulders told her more than enough about his state of mind.

She sighed, reached out to place a hand on his shoulder. "Look, Nick—you don't have to worry, I can take care—"

He turned on her. "If you finish that sentence, I'm gonna pick up that fucking chair and throw it through a window." His voice was raised. She looked at Michael again. He was still sitting in the living room, only now he was blatantly staring at them through

255

the open door of the deck, making no attempt to hide the fact that he was listening to their conversation.

Nickels followed her line of vision, settling his gaze on Michael. By the set of his shoulders, the tight clench of his jaw, and the way the two of them were staring holes into each other, she could see things were seconds away from getting ugly.

"Hey, want a beer?" she said to Nickels, trying to distract him.

He looked at her. "Sure."

"Stay out here—away from him, okay?" she said , backing away from him toward the door that led to the kitchen.

Nickels nodded, but she wasn't convinced.

FIFTY

THE COP WOULDN'T STOP staring. Michael kept working, comparing the file Strickland had copied for Sabrina on the Sawyer girl against the file he already had on the rest of the victims.

The cop was still staring. He tried to ignore it but failed miserably. "Can I help you with something?" he said without looking up. He could feel the cop's eyes drilling into the top of his head.

"No." Nickels moved through the doorway and into the living room.

"Where'd she go?" Again he didn't look up. Leaving the two of them alone was a bad idea.

"To get me a beer." Nickels leaned against the chair across from him. He'd have to be deaf to miss the possessive tone the cop threw at him.

He just laughed... *Yeah, this is really bad idea.*

"Sabrina told me you served in the Army," Nickels said.

He gave up, closed his laptop, and sat back in his chair. "That's right."

Nickels looked down at him, arms crossed over his chest. "Where?"

He smiled. "What? Your buddy at Fort Meade couldn't hook you up with the 411?" It had taken Lark all of ten seconds to find the name, rank, and serial number of the enlisted that Nickels used to run a trace on him; it had taken less than thirty more to make it clear that doing so was unwise. His smile widened at the wary look Nickels gave him. "Friends are wonderful things, aren't they?"

Nickels recovered quickly, cocked his head to the side, and smirked. "I'd never consider dragging a *friend* into a situation that could get her killed."

Michael stood, jammed his hands into his front pockets and shook his head. "She's not my friend. And, let's be honest—she's not your friend either. You want to fuck her. There's a difference."

Nickels dropped his arms and took a step forward. He pulled his hands out of his pockets, welcoming the advance. Sabrina came out of nowhere, beer in one hand, glass of wine in the other. She stepped between them, facing Nickels.

"Come on," she said to Nickels, nudging him backward. She threw an exasperated look at him over her shoulder. Michael shrugged, curbed the urge to say *he started it*. She herded Nickels all the way to the doorway before he said anything.

"First SFOD-D."

Nickels shot him a look over Sabrina's shoulder as she pushed him out onto the deck. He didn't ask him to repeat what he'd said. Nickels had heard and understood him just fine.

———

"I told you to wait out here," Sabrina said, shoving a beer bottle into his hand. Nickels just glared at her for a second before he tipped it back, taking a long drink.

"Do you have any idea who—*what*—that guy is?" Nickels looked over his shoulder, into the living room where Michael still stood, watching him.

She shut the door on Michael and shrugged. "No. And I'm not interested in finding out."

"First SFOD-D. First Special Forces Operational Detachment Delta." He set the beer down, braced his hands on the porch railing. "These guys are scary, Sabrina. Mission-driven all the way." He leaned forward. "If your safety, your *survival,* isn't the mission, he'll sacrifice you in an instant to obtain his objective." He looked at her. "I don't want you going anywhere with him."

She stood next to him, elbows resting on the railing, staring into the glass of wine in her hand. "My eyes are wide open, Nick. I have no disillusions—he's made no promises." She looked up at him "I'm going. I have to."

He looked at her. "Then I'm going with you."

"No. I need you to stay here. Look after Val and the kids."

He shook his head. "No way. Get Strickland to—"

"*No.*" She looked him in the eye. "He's not going to lose his career over me, and you're not risking your life." She shook her head. "He killed Sanford. He must've been there when we got into in the lobby. If he can do *that* to someone who hates me, imagine what he could do to someone who—" She looked away.

He ducked his head and caught her eye. "What? Someone who what? Loves you?"

"Don't say that."

He smiled, looked around. "I can say it out loud. There's no one here."

She straightened, kept looking away. "You don't love me, Nick."

He reached for her hand, pulled her closer. "I don't know, maybe I do."

She shook her head. "No, you don't. You can't." *I can't.* She tried to make herself pull her hand from his but couldn't. "I'm not ... normal."

"*It's not you, it's me,* is that it?" he said.

"Yes. That's it exactly."

"What about him?" He tipped his chin toward the house. "Seems like *abnormal* is right up his alley."

She sighed, this time succeeding in pulling her hand away. "It's not like that."

He laughed out loud, caught her hand again. "Bullshit."

She thought of her offer to share her bed. Michael's quick decline. "He has no interest in me, and the feeling is mutual." She was lying. The look Nick gave her said he knew it.

He let it go. "I have something for you." He reached under his shirt, pulling something off his waistband. He handed it to her. It was her badge.

She stared at it for a second before looking up at him. "Where did you—"

He grinned. "You know Richards never locks his office or his desk."

She looked down at her badge. It had only been a few hours, but she realized she'd missed the weight and feel of it. She wanted to keep it. Knew she couldn't.

"You could get fired for this." *Hell, girl, let's get serious—he could go to prison for it.* She tried to shove it into his hand, but he refused to take it. "You have to take it back. If Richards finds out or, God forbid, Mathews…you have to take it back."

"You need it. How else are you going to get in with the local PD?" he said. She stopped pushing and looked at her badge. He was right. If she wanted access to case files and the investigation into Lucy's disappearance, she'd need to flash her badge to get it.

"They'll call to verify I'm on a case." She was thinking it through, trying to gauge exactly how much shit would bury her if she got caught in that big a lie.

"Not if the police chief is your guy. He'll know who you are—want you there. He won't check."

She saw the message, carved into that girl's back.

Olly Olly Oxen Free.

She nodded. "You're right."

"Of course I'm right." He moved closer, looked down at her. "Which scares the shit out of me. Please, Sabrina, let me come with you."

She shook her head. "I need you here. I *need* to know my family is safe. But I'll take the badge, and I'll call every day." She looked up at him.

He grimaced, shook his head. "Okay, I'll stay. Just…stop looking at me like that."

"Like what?"

"Like I'm never gonna see you again."

It was a distinct possibility, one they needed to talk about. "If I don't come back, I need to know that you'll look after them. Protect them. He'll come after Riley next. They'll have to run—"

He shook his head. "No. We're not doing that." His mouth was a thin, hard line, his whiskey-colored eyes narrowed on her face.

"Doing what?"

"Making auxiliary plans. You're coming home." He leaned in, lowered his mouth to hers, and she was curious enough, selfish enough, to let him.

The kiss was soft—his lips parted slightly, his eyes closed. She closed her own, tried to let herself go, to give in … but she couldn't. In the end, she did what she always did.

She held herself back.

FIFTY-ONE

A FEW HOURS LATER, the back door banged open, letting in the sounds of raucous teenager. Backpacks were dropped and shoes were kicked off amid a shouting match carried on in playful tones. Neither Jason nor Riley seemed aware that there were a quartet of adults gathered around the kitchen table, talking quietly.

Sabrina watched them for a moment. Couldn't help but think of where she'd been just a few hours earlier. The crippling loss she'd felt when she'd believed that it was Riley behind that curtain. That it had been Riley who'd been tortured and raped. That she was dead.

Riley looked so much like she had at that age—rich auburn hair and wide blue eyes. She'd been beautiful. Too beautiful.

Panic wrapped around her chest, ratcheting tighter and tighter with every breath she tried to take. Her baby sister was too bright. She shined. She beckoned. The man who took her knew about Riley. He'd seen her. It was only a matter time before he took her too.

She looked at Michael. He was watching the twins in their adolescent scramble, a slight smile on his face. His gaze settled on Riley and a shadow flitted across his features—allowed himself a second of sadness before tucking it away. He was thinking about Frankie.

She looked away, unable to stand the grief she saw in his eyes. Not when she'd caused it. Not when she was so close to losing Riley and knowing what it was like to feel that kind of grief settle into her bones and refuse to leave.

A hand reached out and laced its fingers between hers and squeezed. Nickels. She looked up and gave him a quick smile, tried to return the reassuring pressure his hand lent her. She gave up after a few seconds, pulled her hand from his, covered it up by sitting back in her chair and looking away.

"Hey, Mom—what's up?" Jason said, his questioned muffled by the fact that his head was stuffed in the refrigerator. He emerged with various containers of leftovers and dumped them on the counter.

"Yeah, why are there cops parked across the street?" Riley said. She stood by the back door and took her time hanging the car keys on the hook, studying the cluster of adults in front of her. Where her brother had always been sensitive, careful with others' feelings, Riley was blunt. She attacked whatever was in front of her, head on. "What's going on?"

Michael stood, jerked his head toward the open doorway. "That's our cue, Cop." He left and Nickels followed.

Sabrina gestured to the pair of vacated chairs. "Sit down."

Jason carried a plastic container of spaghetti to the table and sat across from her, while Riley took her time. "What's wrong? What are the cops doing outside?" She leaned back, tipped her chin at the open doorway. "Who are they?"

Sabrina shot a looked at Val. They'd decided to stick as close to the truth as possible. To tell them only what they needed to in order to make them understand that they were in danger. Val gave her a soft shrug. She had the floor.

She told them about Lucy, as gently as she could. About Michael's sister and that he had proof that linked her death to their grandmother's. She told them that the only way to make sure they were safe was for her to leave with Michael so that they could find him.

"What does this have to do with us? Why does that guy think you can do anything to help him?" Jason said, the container of spaghetti forgotten on the table in front of him.

"Because I'm a police officer. It's what I do—catch murderers," she said, falling back on the pat answer she'd been giving them for the past fourteen years.

This time, Riley wasn't buying it. "It's him, isn't it? The guy who took you. He killed Lucy, didn't he?"

"Riley—"

The look on her face must've told her sister the truth. She shook her head. "He's going to kill you this time." Riley looked down at Jason and swallowed hard. "He's going to kill you, and we're going to be left alone."

The words hit her hard. She fought the urge to look away from her little sister's seething face. "Ri, that's not going to happen—"

"You can't say that for sure." She shook her head.

"Please try to understand—I *have* to go." She looked at both of them, trying to make them understand. The man who hurt her had made it perfectly clear today that Riley was next. She'd do anything to keep that from happening.

"Why?" Jason said, finally looking up from the tabletop he'd been staring at. Riley had always been the fighter, not Jason—but he was fighting now. "Why don't we just leave? We'll take off—"

"He'll find us. It might take another fifteen years for him to do it, but he will," she said quietly. "In the meantime, he'll keep killing. I couldn't live with myself knowing that."

Jason looked away, defeated. He didn't like the answer but seemed to understand. She reached across the table and took his hand. "I love you—"

Riley pinned her with a hard look. "You're a liar. If you loved us, you'd stay." She stood and went upstairs, leaving the three of them in heavy silence.

———

A few hours later, they were ready to go. Michael shouldered her duffle without asking and stood by the back door while she said quiet goodbyes to Jason and Val. Riley had refused to come down, and leaving her without saying goodbye was breaking Sabrina's heart. Nickels leaned against the kitchen counter, waiting his turn and when she turned to him, he pulled her into his arms, giving her a hard embrace.

"Remember what I said. You're coming back." He smoothed a hand over her hair and pulled away just enough to look down at her. He dropped a quick kiss on her mouth before stepping back, letting her go.

She moved through the door, avoiding the look Michael gave her, and pulled the door closed behind them both. They stood on the dark stoop, but neither moved to leave.

"Go back in. Talk to her," Michael said. He dropped her duffle at his feet and sat on the top step.

No way was she going back in there. "No, let's just leave. I'll call her—"

"No you won't. Go." He pushed his shoulder into her knee, urging her toward the door. "Tell her that you love her, make promises you don't have the power to keep. Do whatever you have to do to make it right with her because if you don't, you'll regret it. Trust me on that." He looked up at her. "Go on—I'll wait here."

Michael reached up and turned the knob, opened the door, shoved her back into the house, and shut the door behind her. She stood in the deserted kitchen for a few seconds before she mounted the back stairs quietly and let her legs carry her down the hall. She stopped in front of Riley's bedroom door and hesitated again. *Afraid of a sixteen-year-old-girl…*

She knocked softly but got no answer. She told herself to turn around and leave. Why she opened the door and let herself in was a mystery.

The room was dark. Riley curled up in her bed, back toward the door, but she could tell by the set of her shoulders that the girl was tense—listening and awake.

She crossed the room and sat on the bed. "I know you're awake, and I know you're angry with me. I'm sorry about that, but I have to go. I have to try and make this right. For Lucy, for you and Jason, for Michael's sister—" Her heart pounded, so hard and fast her chest hurt. "For me."

Riley's shoulders began to shake with the effort to keep her emotions in check. She knew because hers did the same thing when she fought back tears. She thought about Michael's advice to lie, to say whatever she had to in order to make it right with her sister, and rejected it. She was done lying to the people she loved.

"I can't promise nothing will happen to me … but I can tell you that everything I have ever done has been because I love you and Jason. The two of you and Val—you're all that matter to me. And I promise I'll do anything I have to do to make my way back. I won't leave you alone. Not if I can help it," she said quietly, hands clasped in her lap, hands that wanted to grip Riley's trembling shoulders.

Her words were met with silence. After a few seconds she nodded, shifted herself around to leave. Just as she moved to stand, Riley turned toward her, unshed tears washed in moonlight, turning her blue eyes silver. Riley reached out to grab her hand.

"Will you stay? Just until I fall asleep?"

Sabrina nodded, didn't trust her voice to stay steady. She stretched out on the bed next to Riley and stroked her hair, watched her eyes grow heavy and close, waited until her breathing grew deep and even before she leaned over and dropped a soft kiss on her daughter's cheek.

"I love you, Mom," Riley said on a sigh, moments before she drifted off to sleep.

"I love you too, baby," she said before she finally stood and left.

FIFTY-TWO

THEY TREKKED ACROSS THE backyard in the dark, tossing her duffle and his case over the fence before hauling themselves over. They entered the B&B through the back door, moving silently through the dark house, up the stairs to his room.

Michael shut his door and locked it while she clicked on the bedside lamp and looked around the room. There was a pair of overstuffed armchairs facing a gas fireplace to the right of the full-size bed.

"I'll take the chair this time." Sabrina sat down and curled up, resting her face on the back of it to look at him. He sat on the edge of the bed and pulled off his boots. They had to leave for the airport in less than four hours. Just enough time to take a shower, get his gear packed up, and maybe grab a few hours of shut-eye.

"Take the bed. I'm not going to be doing much sleeping, anyway." He pulled off his shirt and tossed it in the corner. She was looking at him, cataloging every bump and scar, curiosity showed plainly on her face. He was used to it—most people got that look when he stripped down. He pointed to the long, raised scar that ran along his rib cage.

"Knife fight in Grenada." He pointed to another. "Gun fight in Sincelejo." He turned and showed her the scattering of scars across his back. "Shrapnel from an IED in Iraq."

She smiled, held up her hand and showed him a starburst scar on the back of her hand roughly the size of a half-dollar. "Splatter burn from the fryer at the diner." She turned and lifted her sleeve to expose her bicep. "Took a graze my rookie year, stopping a robbery in progress." She grinned for a second then went quiet, like she was trying to figure something out. She seemed to make up her mind and stood, crossing the room to stop just in front of him.

She reached for his hand and pulled it to her stomach, under her shirt. She ran the tip of his fingers along her skin and watched his face. He couldn't look away from her, couldn't pull away from the smattering of thin, hard scars across her belly.

"He stabbed me fourteen times. They spell out the word *MINE*." She dropped her hand away from his and eased herself back. She sat on the edge of the bed and pulled a Bersa .380 from the small of her back. She laid it on the nightstand and looked up at him. "I changed my mind; I'll take the bed."

———

Sabrina stretched out on top of the covers and closed her eyes. Her fingers played across her stomach, tracing and retracing her scars.

The bathroom door opened. She didn't have to look to know he was watching her, deciding if lying down beside her would be a mistake.

She smiled in the dark. "Quit being such a girl and just lie down."

He laughed before stretching out next to her. They were quiet for a while, both of them staring up at the ceiling, watching shadows play across the pale wash of moonlight.

"We're done lying to each other, right?" he said without looking at her.

She stared straight ahead but didn't like the serious tone of his voice. "Yes." He was here, risking his life to help her after losing so much. She'd tell him the truth. She owed him that.

"What happened the night Tom was attacked?"

She paused for a few seconds before lifting the ring from her chest. She showed it to him. "He used to walk me home from work. By the time we closed the diner it was late, so no one was around to see us together. That last night he gave this to me—asked me to marry him. I said yes. He dropped me off at the front door then circled back around. I snuck him into my room through the window." She squeezed the ring tight. "He left later than usual—kissed me and ducked out the window like always and just . . . disappeared." Michael reached over and took her free hand and held it. The pressure of his hand in hers trapped the words inside her throat, but she forced them out—she needed to say it. Maybe if she did, she could finally let it go.

"I must've dozed off because the next thing I remember, someone was knocking on my window. I got up to look and he was just standing there." She looked at him. "I thought it was Tommy at first. He was wearing Tommy's jacket but . . . he had the hood up. I went to the window to let him back in . . . I'd almost opened it when I noticed the blood. It was all over the place—hard to see in the dark but when I saw it, I knew something was wrong. It wasn't Tommy outside my window . . . it was him."

"You saw the man who took you? In Jessup?" Michael said.

She shook her head. "I—I didn't see anything. It was dark, his jacket hood was up. He kept his face tilted down—"

He sat up, stared down at her. "Try. Try to remember."

Michael's demanding tone opened her eyes. She narrowed them on his face. "I've tried—believe me, I've tried but there's nothing there. Nothing *to* remember." She looked away. "When I realized it wasn't Tommy, I ran for the door, tried to get out. I was sure he was going to come through the window, but when I looked, he was gone. I thought maybe I'd dreamt it. For just a second I thought everything was fine … then he knocked on the front door and my mother let him in."

FIFTY-THREE

HE STARED AT HER for a second. Blinked like he wasn't sure he heard her right. "Kelly let him in the house?"

Sabrina nodded. "She took him to her room."

He lay back down. "How do you know it was him?"

"Usually, when she was with a john, she kept the radio turned up. This time, someone turned the radio *off*, like he wanted me to listen." She looked away. "I think he wanted me to hear what he was doing to her. It was just sex at first ... but then she started screaming."

She stopped for a minute, listened to his breathing beside her, waited for him to ask her why she hadn't tried to stop Kelly from letting him in, why she hadn't been braver. Why she hadn't saved her mother. He stayed quiet, waiting for her to find the courage to finish her story.

"She screamed once or twice ... then it just stopped." She could still hear it, her mother's piercing scream, the way it was abruptly cut off, replaced by the more pedestrian sounds of sex. "After about twenty minutes or so, the radio came back on. He came out and shut the door, came down the hall and stopped in front of my room." She could still remember pressing herself against the door, holding onto to the knob, praying the flimsy privacy lock would hold.

They'd been separated by inches, nothing but pressed wood and veneer between her and the monster that murdered her mother. "He stood there for a few seconds then went into the bathroom across the hall. I could hear the water running, him whistling while he washed his hands. Then he left," she said.

"Why would he just leave? He had you right where he wanted you, and he just *left*?" His voice sounded rough, almost strangled with anger.

The waiting had always been the worst part... "It was just another form of torture. I was trapped, and he knew it—wanted me to know it too. I couldn't run, not without the twins. He wanted me to know he was coming for me. Wanted me scared and to know there was nothing I could do to stop him." She could feel Michael's palm pressed against hers, his fingers laced between her own. Her fingers flexed around his hand, held on to him tighter. "I fell asleep in the corner behind the door. When I woke up, it was morning. I told myself I was safe, that I'd make it through. I thought maybe it wasn't as bad as it sounded, maybe Kelly was okay. When I looked in her room, she was gone, but there was blood everywhere. Castoff—I know that now." She looked at him. "It looked like a lot of blood to me and I got scared all over again. We didn't have a phone, so I decided to get dressed and go get my father, to ask him for help. Kelly was gone but she left a lot of blood behind, and Tommy... I didn't know what happened to him yet." She held his hand in a death grip and refused to look away, no matter how much she wanted to.

"When I went back to my room to get dressed, Pete was sitting on my bed."

"And?"

"And he … came at me." She shrugged. "It'd been building for a while. A lot of touching, a lot of grabbing when he thought my mom wasn't looking."

His face closed up, folded around itself to hold in whatever it was he was thinking or feeling. "Did he know about Tom? That the two of you were involved?"

She nodded. "Yes. He told me that he knew I'd been sneaking him into my room. That I was a whore just like my mother."

"Could he have been the one that attacked Tom—killed Kelly?"

"No." She shook her head against the pillow.

"Why? Maybe it *was* him. He was Kelly's boyfriend. She would've let him in, no questions asked," he said, but she just shook her head again. "It makes sense—"

"The man who attacked Tommy and killed Kelly is the same man who took me," she said.

"Right. As much as I hate to say it, maybe Jed Carson isn't our guy—"

"Trust me—it's not Pete," she said in a tone that left no room for argument.

"How can you be so sure?"

Because I killed him. "I just am." She pulled her hand out of his and rolled over to face the wall. She'd already said too much.

FIFTY-FOUR

MICHAEL PURCHASED THEIR TICKETS and secured a rental car with a fresh set of ID. Michael Koptik was wanted for questioning in at least two murders—possibly three if you counted the dead girl at the hospital—and he'd be willing to bet they'd found a way to connect that one to him too. Today he was Mathew Stern, a plant manager from Plano, Texas.

When asked for her ID at the ticket counter, she'd produced a valid Nevada driver's license under the name Serena Vincent. He had no idea where she'd gotten it, but he was sure it was not the only set of false ID she had. Sometimes being paranoid paid off.

When they landed she ducked into the first bathroom they came across while he stood outside, surrounded by duffle bags, waiting for her. He started to worry that maybe he'd have to go in and get her. Before he could think too much about it, his phone rang. It was Tom.

"Hey."

"Carson's back," he said. "He and Wade came in about seven. They usually meet up for breakfast before heading to the station. They're here now."

Sabrina walked out of the bathroom and picked up her duffle, then stood there and looked at him like he was the one holding them up.

"Alright. We should be in town in a few hours." He hung up, looked her over. "You okay?"

She picked up her duffle and slung it over her shoulder. "Peachy. Let's go." She started walking, and he fell into step beside her.

He glanced at her. "That was Tom. Carson's back in town."

She shook her head but kept walking. "It's like he wants me to know it's him."

"Maybe he does—maybe he wants to force a confrontation early."

"Well then it's a good thing I'm in the mood to give him one." She looked sick to her stomach. Each stride that took her through the airport and out into the world seemed to weigh on her, drag her down. She was pale, the ashen color of her face making her look almost frail. She may have been in the mood for a fight, but she was in no condition for one.

On impulse he grabbed her arm and pulled her into an alcove under the escalator. She didn't pull away, just stared up at him. Like she trusted him. Believed in him. She wasn't the first person to make that mistake. Everyone who'd ever looked at him like that had ended up dead. It was enough to make him want to ram his head through the wall.

He squeezed her arm and shook his head. "Nickels is right. This isn't a good idea—"

"What?"

"Yeah, I can't believe I just said it myself." He leaned forward, looked her in the eye. "Think about it, he knows we're coming—wants you here. Why didn't he just make a play for you in San Francisco?" He spoke in a rush, squeezing her arm tighter and tighter.

"Because he has plans for me. Didn't we just establish that?" She looked down at her arm and then back to his face. The brown plastic lenses did nothing to hide the glint in her eyes. "You're hurting me."

He ignored her complaint. "Right. Plans." He nodded, pulled on her arm. "Come on, you're going back—"

"What? You want me to *run*? I'm sorry, have we met?" She yanked her arm out of his grip and glared at him, continued on before he could speak. "If you want to tuck tail, go ahead but that son of a bitch killed my *grandmother*. He's not getting away with that."

"Who said he would? I'll go alone. He'll be dead by lunch time." He could see himself doing it—walking into the JPD, putting a bullet in Carson's head. He'd probably have to kill Wade and Zeke too, but he didn't really care. He'd burn the entire town to the ground before he let anything happen to Sabrina again.

"You don't know for sure that it's him. Think about this for a minute, will you?" She sighed, rubbed a hand over her face. "All we have is circumstantial evidence. Nothing solid that says Carson is our guy."

"Right now, I'm okay with that."

"I'm not. We have to be sure. I have to go so we *can* be sure." She shook her head. "Besides, he wins either way. He dropped a pile of dead bodies on my doorstep. If I go home, I'll be arrested. If I run, he succeeds in separating me from everyone I know—just like last time. He'll find me eventually, and if he doesn't, there's always Riley. If he can't get to me, he'll get to her, and I won't be there to protect her."

"I'll protect her." The promise was an empty one. He only had a few days' reprieve before he'd have to leave her. He thought about the chip in his back, about what seven digits and a whim could do to him. Before all this, knowing he could die any second wouldn't have bothered him. Now his actions could get her killed. He was the last person she needed in her life.

She just shook her head. "No. I'm going. Sorry, but my grandmother and your sister deserve more than that."

He looked at her, saw the determined gleam in her eye that he both admired and despised. She was going to Jessup and there was nothing he could do to stop her. He slumped against the wall, dropped his duffle at his feet. He felt beaten, like he'd already lost her. Anger and confusion crawled around his head, churned together with the realization that losing her would do to him what Frankie's death hadn't quite managed, what nothing else had been able to do:

It would kill him.

FIFTY-FIVE

THERE WAS A PRETTY woman with caramel-colored hair sitting behind the counter. She was filling sugar dispensers, and Sabrina had a sudden flash of herself doing the exact same task, standing in the exact same spot. Next to her was a little girl, no older than four or five, sitting on a stool. She had soft brown hair and Tommy's eyes.

Tommy's head popped into the service window, gaze directed at Michael. He disappeared for just a moment before pushing his way through the door. He came toward them, pulling off his apron as he did. His face hadn't changed. The dusky pale gold of his skin was still smooth; the sharp, angular lines of his jaw and nose still spoke proudly of his Apache heritage; his blue-black hair held no gray. And for just a moment, she had the feeling that she was as she'd been, that she was the person she was supposed to be and that it had all been a terrible nightmare.

Tommy indicated a booth toward the back of the diner, away from the crowd. Michael slid in first, and she sat across from him. Tommy dragged a chair to the table, turned it around to straddle it.

"They found Lucy," Tommy said without preamble. "Sue Ellen Rouser went by this morning to pick up some stuff Lucy donated for the church rummage sale. She used the key to let herself in—she was in the basement." He turned to Michael. "I'm sorry. I'm so—"

Michael reached out, clapped a hard hand on Tom's shoulder. "Stop. Just stop. You did everything right, everything I asked."

She thought of Lucy, left in the dark. About what she knew had been done to her. It was almost too much—almost more than she could bear. She wanted to cry. She wanted to run. Instead, she did what she always did. She pulled away from the pain and grief nested deep inside her chest. Took a deep, insulating breath and buried the emotions that dogged her.

"Where's Carson now?" she said.

Tommy looked at her. His expression was mild, but his eyes on her held the stinging wrath of a whip. He didn't know who she was, she was sure of it. Not even Lucy had been able to recognize her after the doctor had gotten through with her face.

"At Lucy's, probably covering his tracks." They all thought Carson was guilty, would bet their lives on it, but she had to force herself to look at this objectively. They needed proof. Hard proof, and they weren't going to find it without digging.

She decided to open a new vein of questioning. "What about Melissa Walker? Carson had a thing for her?" she said, feeling ridiculous for asking about things she already knew and horrible for drudging up painful memories for them both.

"A *thing*?" Tom let out a disgusted laugh. "I guess you could call it that. He followed her everywhere, hounded her every step. Never gave her a moment's peace," he said.

"He knew about the two of you?" she said.

His gaze sharpened for a moment. "Yeah, he knew. After she'd been gone for a few weeks, he started spouting off about how she was calling him, telling him she realized she loved him, wanted him to come be with her. He took off a few months after she did." Tommy said this like he believed it, like he knew it was true. Before she could say anything, he continued. "He came back to Jessup three months after she disappeared."

She'd left Jessup in April—a few months would've meant that Carson had left sometime that summer. "And you believe she left you for Carson." She could hardly get the words out. This wasn't something she'd heard before, something Michael had failed to mention.

"Well, she wasn't exactly around to prove otherwise." He leaned forward. "I asked her to marry me, and she said yes. Not more than a few hours later, I was stabbed, bludgeoned, and left naked on the side of the road. I was laid up for weeks, and she just took off on me." He leaned back and scoffed. "The least she could've done was leave my mother's ring behind."

The ring—*her ring*—hidden by her shirt, burned a hole in her chest.

It was too much—the memories of the way things had been, the way Tommy was looking at her now. She stood—amazed she could without passing out.

"Will you excuse me?" she said. She headed for the parking lot, making herself measure her steps, slow and even, weaving her way through the dining room—picking up and carrying with her the stares of everyone she passed.

FIFTY-SIX

SABRINA KNEW PEOPLE WERE staring at her, but she kept moving—pressed on, stopping only when she reached their rental car.

She leaned against the front fender, pressed her palms together, wedging them between her knees to hide their shaking. Drawing in a wobbly breath, she closed her eyes for a moment, trying for just a few seconds to shut out the world around her.

Her phone rang. Strickland. She hit Ignore. It rang again three seconds later.

She snapped. "FYI—when someone ignores your phone calls, that means they don't want to talk to you," she all but barked into the phone, her tirade met with a second or two of silence.

"Oh, is that what that means? I always just thought it meant you were a stubborn bitch," Strickland said, biting back.

She squeezed her eyes shut. "I don't have time—"

"Yeah, I hear ya. Nothing says *sense of urgency* like a dead girl with your name written on her arm."

Shit. "Who caught the case?"

"Robbins and Carr. Hospital surveillance picked up the car that dumped her. A dark, late-model sedan. Didn't catch the plates or a look at the driver, so your name on her arm is pretty much all they have to go on. Oh, and the fact that the charge nurse positively identified you and a man matching O'Shea's description as being what she thought were relatives. Said he was wearing a SFPD shirt. They're looking to bring you both back in for questioning." He went quiet for a second. "They're some talk of the murder weapon used to kill Sanford. That there's a chance it has your prints on it."

The bat. Somehow, in the middle of this waking nightmare, she'd somehow managed to forget that there was actual forensic evidence that could land her in prison.

She had to call Nickels, warn him. Once the lab came through with DNA and prints, a warrant would be issued for her arrest. She'd left the state pending a murder investigation. If Richards or Mathews found out that Nickels had helped her—

"Vaughn."

"I have to go." She moved to hang up the phone.

"Goddamn it, don't hang up on me." His angry tone stopped her cold.

"I'm trying to do what's right by you."

"I'm a grown-ass man, and I don't need you to protect me—I need you to trust me. For once…just trust me," he said.

She sighed. "I do."

"Prove it. Body count is at three. Start explaining."

She hesitated, but only for a second. "Call Val—she'll explain everything." She hung up and sent a quick text to Val.

When Strickland calls, tell him everything.

The bell on the diner door dinged again. She looked up to see Michael walking toward her. He carried a pair of boxes, one beneath each arm. "You okay?" he said, leaning against the car next to her.

"Yes." She looked to the box under his arm. "What's in it?"

He dropped one of them on the hood, slid it across until it bumped into her hip. "The package from Val probably won't get here until tomorrow. Until then, this is your new best friend."

FIFTY-SEVEN

THE GUN WAS BEAUTIFUL—MADE her pair of SIG P220s look like a couple of Saturday Night Specials. A Colt Super .38—matte chrome with an extended grip. Government issue. No serial number. In the box next to the gun were extra clips and a suppressor. She stared hard at it for a few seconds, waited for fear to grip her like it usually did when she found herself confronted with the person Michael had become.

Instead of fear she felt something else. Something fierce. Vengeful.

It felt good.

She didn't ask where they were going. She already knew. Their plan had been to stop by the diner on their way to the house Lucy had lived in. She figured Michael knew the way.

She filled him in on what Strickland had told her. The description of the car that dumped the girl at the hospital had him quiet. Too quiet.

"What is it?" She looked down at her hands, needed something to do. She started loading clips from the box of ammo on the seat between them.

He bounced a look between her and the road. "I've gone through every police report filed in Jessup for the last twenty years."

"So?" She kept feeding the bullets into the clip, each kiss of metal against metal making a *click, click, click.*

"The file on what happened to Bauer is thin. Not much more than a few crime scene photos and the autopsy report," he said.

This was about her father. "And?"

"In evidence is a notebook—one of those flip-top jobs cops keep in their pockets." She knew what he meant. She used to use one before she switched to the voice-recorder app on her cell. An old-school cop like Billy Bauer would still carry one.

"Anyway, the last entry was just a quick notation—*dark blue, Chevy four-door,*" he said, turning off the main road onto a single-lane dirt strip that led off into the trees. It was hardly more than a dirt path, choked and cluttered with untrimmed trees and bramble.

"What kind of car does Carson drive?" she said, her voice tight, each word punctuated with a *click, click, click.*

"I've never seen him drive anything but the JPD Blazer, and nothing else is registered in his name." They'd reached the end of the drive, so he killed the engine. "That doesn't mean he doesn't have another car stashed somewhere. It's an easy thing to do."

She nodded. "You're right. Let's go ask him."

———

Michael could see the house as it once was. The front door Sophia had insisted on painting a bright, splashy red. The slate blue shutters—the tire swing in the front yard Sean made for him.

"This was my parent's house," he said. "When we started all this last year, I asked Lucy to move in, take care of things for me when I was away."

"And she was closer to her friends this way. You took care of her."

"We took care of each other," he said even though the words felt like a lie.

They left the car, barely cleared the gate before Carson stepped out onto the porch. He puffed out his chest and used his grip on his gun belt to hitch up his khakis. "One more step, O'Shea, and I'll have Zeke haul you in for trespassing. It'd be just like old times."

The threat didn't even break his stride. "It's my house."

"It's my crime scene," he said with a smirk flicked at Sabrina. "Looks like you and your lady-love are gonna have to find another place to shack up."

Michael instinctively reached for the small of his back, his hand closing on nothing but empty air. The Colt was still in its box, sitting on the front seat of the rental car behind him. Good thing; if it'd been within reach, he would've unloaded the clip into Jed Carson's face without a moment's hesitation. Carson's hand dropped to the butt of the 9mm on his hip. He laughed a little when Michael came up empty, but it was a nervous sound and he kept his hand where it was.

Shifting his gaze to Sabrina, Carson leaned against the porch post. "You might want to think about the kind of company you keep," he said to her. "This one here's not looked on too kindly round these parts. Being seen with him, you won't have an easy time of it."

His eyes dropped to Carson's gun. It'd take him all of three seconds to strip it from him and another four to pistol-whip him into a coma.

Seven seconds total. The thought made him smile.

Before he could make his move, Sabrina reached out and gripped his arm. She squeezed, the pressure telling him to stay put. He watched her pull her badge off her waist and flash it.

"I'm Inspector Vaughn with the SFPD, I'd like to talk to you for a minute if I could, Chief Carson," she said.

Carson flicked his gaze at her badge before letting it settle on her. He smiled. "Well, I'd be obliged to do any number of things with *you,* Miss Vaughn. But if it's talk you want, you're gonna have to put your dog in the car." Carson cut him a vicious grin.

Michael snapped his head in her direction, glared at her. "No fucking way."

"Ten minutes," she said and gave him a look that said *be reasonable.* He said nothing, just pulled his arm from her grip and walked away. He passed through the gate, could see the Colt sitting on the front seat. Getting into the car with it was a really bad idea.

FIFTY-EIGHT

SABRINA WIPED HER HANDS on her jeans and forced herself to take a few steps forward. "Chief Carson—"

"SFPD? Long way from home, ain't ya?" Carson said, taking a few seconds to look a little closer at the badge she'd flashed him.

You would know. "I'm here investigating a homicide I believe has ties to a murder your department investigated about a year ago—Frankie O'Shea."

He looked past her, his eyes narrowed suspiciously. She knew Michael was back there somewhere—that he hadn't gotten in the car. She could feel him staring at them, knew she had only a few minutes before he got tired of waiting.

"He the one that brought you here?" He cut his eyes back to her face before she could answer. "No matter. You're wasting your time, Inspector. My murder and my town ain't got nothing to do with you and yours, so if it's all the same..."

"It is the same—right down to MO and signature." She looked away for a second, trying to rein in her emotions before they ran away with her. "Do you know what an enucleator is?"

"A nuclear what?" He looked at her like she was crazy, but she knew he wasn't as dumb as he was pretending to be.

"An *enucleator*. The term is used to describe serial killers who remove their victims' eyes. They're rare. Combine that with his penchant for marking his victims by stabbing words into their stomachs and you've got a unique signature." She took a half-step in his direction, forced herself to look at his face. "Frankie O'Shea had her eyes removed and so did my victim in San Francisco. Both of them had words stabbed into their stomachs. They were killed by the same man, I'd bet my life on it." She forced herself even closer, had to be able to see his eyes when she said what came next. "And that same man killed Melissa Walker."

"What happened to Frankie O'Shea was a tragedy—an *isolated* tragedy. And what happened to her doesn't have anything to do with Melissa." He took a step back. "Now, if you'll excuse me—"

"Isolated? Really?" She pointed at the door behind him. "Did Lucy Walker still have her eyes when you found her? What word did he stab into *her* stomach?"

His face closed tighter and tighter with every word she spoke. "I'm not at liberty to divulge particulars on this or any other ongoing investigation."

"I think we both know that you're at liberty to do whatever the hell you want around here," she said.

"Now, you wait just a—"

"Did you kill them?"

He took a step back, stared at her in stunned silence. "Kill them? You can't be serious."

"Oh, I am. Dead serious."

"Melissa died a thousand miles from here. What would I have to do with that?"

"You followed her to Yuma," she said. "How'd you find her?"

"I didn't follow her. I applied to UC San Diego my senior year. She took off around the same time I left for college," he said, but that wasn't the end of the story and they both knew it.

"You told Tom she called you—said she wanted you to come be with her," she said.

"I lied. A way to hurt Onewolf. A way to make her mine, I guess."

"That doesn't explain how you found her."

Carson sighed, gave up. "Fate. Destiny. Dumb luck. Whatever you want to call it. I walked into that restaurant in Yuma and saw her waiting tables. At first I thought I'd gone shithouse crazy. No way did I walk into some truck stop a thousand miles away from home and run smack-dab into her, but I did." Carson look at her, shook his head. "Some buddies and I were on our way home from a football game in Tucson. We took a booth in the back and when it was time to leave I told them I was staying, that I'd jump a bus back in the morning. I spent the rest of her shift watching her, thanking my lucky stars that I'd been given another chance … but I was too chickenshit to take it. Her shift ended, she put her coat on, told some Mexican girl she was walking home, and left."

"And then you followed her, dragged her off someplace dark and quiet." She was reaching again, had no way of proving that it'd been him who took her, but as the words spilled out of her mouth, she became convinced that what she was saying was real.

"No—*no*. That's not what … you think … I would never, *could never*, hurt Melissa. I love her, she was everything to me." He took a step toward her, energized by his own desperation. "Most nights I lay awake, wishing I could find a way back there … maybe if I hadn't been so gutless—maybe if I'd talked to her, she'd still be here."

A touching declaration, but she wasn't swayed. She held up her fingers, ticked off her points one by one. "You had time, motive, opportunity—"

"Motive? What the hell are you talking about? What possible reason would I have to kill Melissa? I love her," he practically yelled at her.

I love her. Not *loved*. Sabrina felt her heartbeat do a double-tap against her chest. "But she didn't love you. She despised you. Tell me that didn't piss you off."

Carson opened his mouth to say something but the screen door banged shut behind him, signally an abrupt end to their conversation. She looked up to see Wade Bauer standing on the front porch. He stood still and quiet, like he knew he'd interrupted something important and had done it on purpose. His eyes and nose were red like he'd been crying.

Carson turned an unsympathetic look on his friend. "What?"

Wade stalled for a moment, seemingly stung by Carson's tone. "Charlie called, said he's on his way. I finished processing the kitchen, and Zeke's about done in the basement," he said, shooting her little looks over Carson's shoulder.

"Alright. Tell Zeke to walk the perimeter out here." He turned toward the yard and shook his head. "He ain't gonna find shit, but tell him to do it anyway. There're a few disposables in the glove box of the Blazer. Go ahead and grab 'em—give one to Zeke. He can photo the outside while you do the in." He turned to her, aimed an icy glare her way as Wade took the steps two at a time. "I think it's time you headed on out, Inspector," he said.

"Okay." Reaching into her coat, she pulled out a card and held it out to him. "My cell number is on the back." She tipped a nod to the house behind him. "If you're innocent, then let me help you find out what happened to her," she said. He took the card but made no promises as he slipped it into the breast pocket.

She left then, passing Wade on her way out the gate. On impulse she stopped him, held out her hand. "I'm Inspector Vaughn with the SFPD."

He bobbled the cameras a bit, shifting them from one hand to the other, so he could take her hand. "Wade Bauer." He gave her a hesitant smile and nod, looking over her shoulder to where Carson watched and waited on the porch.

"You were Melissa Walker's brother, weren't you?"

"Half-brother—same father. We weren't all that close," he said, shooting a confused look at Carson over her shoulder. "She was a good girl, didn't deserve what happened to her." He cleared his throat. "If you'll excuse me?" He tried to step around her, but she blocked his retreat, not ready to let him go.

"How'd they bite up at Caddo?" She threw the question at him on the fly and he stared at her blankly for a second before giving her a sheepish grin.

"Truth be told, we didn't fish much. It was just an excuse for me and Jed to get out of town. This time of year can be hard on him." He cast another worried glance behind her then looked over his shoulder at Michael. He turned back to her. "Look, I'm sure you can take care of yourself, you being a city cop and all, but that one's trouble. He may look harmless, but trust me, he ain't."

She looked over his shoulder. Michael was where she'd left him, leaning against the hood, glaring at them both. She wasn't sure who Wade was looking at—there was nothing harmless-looking about Michael O'Shea.

"Thanks, I'll keep that in mind," she said and let him walk away.

FIFTY-NINE

MICHAEL HAULED HIS BAG in and dumped it on the floor. Put his laptop on the bed and looked around. Smoke-yellowed walls and a dark brown mess stretched out on the floor that looked more like matted fur than carpet.

Same motel—same room, even—that Lucy'd found him in, blind drunk and ready to eat his gun. She'd saved him. In return, he'd gotten her killed.

He looked at Sabrina and felt that irrational flare of anger again. Added to the anger was lust. He wanted her, but his want had a possessive bend to it that was messing with his head. If it was just about sex, he'd be fine with it, but it wasn't. He *liked* her.

And didn't that just fuck everything up?

He hadn't spoken to her in nearly an hour. Wasn't really sure what would come out of his mouth if he did. He shoved his hands into his pockets and looked at her. "You hungry?"

"Starved, but—"

"Not the diner. There's a pizza place across the street these days," he said, pretty sure that the last thing she wanted was to face Tom twice in one day.

She looked relieved. "Sounds good."

He nodded and headed for the door.

———

Sabrina looked around at the people scattered throughout the restaurant. Fathers with their families crowded around tables, eating pizza. Brothers and sons bellied up to the bar. Friends and co-workers drinking beer and watching the game.

The man who hurt her was here, in Jessup—not a few thousand miles away and under the assumption that she was dead. He had her within reach and knew who she was. She kept looking, hoping that one of them would trigger something—a memory, a twinge—but there was nothing. There was only the certainty that it could be anyone, that he could be standing right in front of her and she'd never even know it.

Michael was doing the same thing: looking around, letting his eyes rest on every single face aimed their way. He was in a mood, pissed that she'd taken control of the Carson situation. What she had to say would probably make things worse, but it had to be said.

She waited for their waitress to take their order before she spoke. "Someone around here knows who I am."

He sat back and nodded. "I know. If we can find out who it is, maybe we can find a way to pin Carson down."

"You have any friends around here, besides Tommy?"

"No." It was a short answer, obviously something he didn't want to talk about.

She leaned forward, cocked her head. "Nobody? Old buddies? Old hookups? People you used to run with?"

"What are you getting at?"

She leaned back and shrugged. "Someone sold me out."

He lunged forward in his seat. "And you think it was me? You think I told someone?"

She held her ground. "I'm sure you didn't do it on purpose—"

"Oh, are you? How do you know? Maybe I did. Maybe I did it just to get you here." His tone was ice-cold but she could see it. He'd come to the same conclusion. Something he'd done or said had opened the door, and knowing that he'd somehow been responsible for Lucy's death was killing him.

"You might do some pretty awful shit for whoever it is you work for, but you wouldn't do that to Lucy. Not on purpose." She was sure of it.

He sat back. "You give me way too much credit. I *would* do that to her. That's who I am," he said.

Suddenly she was anything but hungry. She stood and looked around at the sea of faces pointed their way. "You know what your problem is?" she said, looking down at him. "You're one of them. You believe everything they've ever said about you."

"Because it's true."

"You wouldn't know the truth if it ran up and kicked you in the balls. I know the truth. You loved your parents and your sister." She leaned down, into his face until they were practically nose to nose. "You loved Lucy, and you would've died protecting her." She straightened. "*That's* the truth, whether you want them to see it or not," she said and headed for the door.

SIXTY

She walked. Just put one foot in front of the other and kept going. Didn't even stop to think about what she was doing until she heard the footsteps behind her. Her heart took a flying leap at her throat, choked her with its bulk and took off at a gallop. She nearly gave into the urge to follow it. Instead, Sabrina reached into the small of her back and pulled the .38, spun around, and leveled it in front of her.

"Whoa!" Wade dropped the pizza box in his hands and flung his arms in the air, his eyes yanked wide with surprise and a good dose of fear.

She tipped the muzzle of the gun downward, aiming it at the ground. "What are you doing here? Following me?"

In answer, he aimed the key fob in his hand over her shoulder and pushed a button. An alarm chirped and the running lights on a late-model 4-runner parked on the street behind her flashed. "Just picking up a pizza."

She sighed. "Sorry." She tucked the gun into her waistband and stooped to pick up the box, took a peek under the lid. "Pineapple and jalapeño? Yikes." She handed the box back, and he grinned.

"Yeah, my wife's pregnant with our first. Believe it or not, this is one of her more normal requests. Ever tried peanut butter and beef jerky?" They started walking, side by side.

I'm going to be an aunt.

"That doesn't even sound good." She laughed and shook her head, remembered the way small talk between them had always been easy. He was right. They'd never been close, but they'd always been friendly. She missed it.

"I know, right?" They reached his car and he turned, gave her an awkward look. "I saw you and O'Shea fighting in there," he said.

Yeah, you and everyone else. "He's upset about Lucy Walker."

Wade gave her a look, nodded. "We all are. She was important to a lot of us." He opened the passenger door. "Need a lift?" He tilted the box. "I'm on my way to have dinner with my wife, but I can drop you somewhere—"

"No thanks, I'm right across the street." She took a few steps back, watched him drop the pizza box on the front seat. "Did you know Jed Carson found your sister in Yuma, just a few days before she disappeared?"

He gave her a hard look, closed his fist around his keys. "You're lying."

"No, I'm not. He told me so himself, just this afternoon. Why would he keep something like that from you?" she said, watching his face closely for a reaction.

He didn't give her one. "If you're looking for someone to turn against Jed, you're looking in the wrong place." He shook his head.

"He's my best friend, and he loved Melissa. Too much. Even now, after all this time—it's killing him the way he can't let her go."

She knew that, had seen it when they'd talked. "An obsession like that could drive a person to do some pretty horrible things."

"Not him. Not Jed." He was still shaking his head, but she could hear it in his voice. Doubt. He was beginning to doubt his friend.

"Then who?"

"I don't know." He shrugged. "All I know is that Jed loved Melissa too much to ever hurt her, and he took care of Miss Lucy. He always found time to help her if she needed it."

She decided to shake things up. "I know you weren't at Caddo." Again, she was stretching, only this time he seemed to know it.

"We *were* at Caddo. Me and Jed. Together." He shut the passenger door. "You get home safe, now," he said before rounding the front of his car and climbing in. She stood on the sidewalk and watched him drive away.

SIXTY-ONE

SHE WAS GONE.

Michael had the pizza boxed and left, intent on catching up to her, but when he hit the sidewalk, she was nowhere to be found.

He dropped the pizza and crossed the street at a dead run. He shouldn't have let her leave—*what the fuck was wrong with him?* Panic clawed his chest, ripped him open, left him exposed.

He almost missed her, didn't see her until he was nearly on top of her.

"Hey," she said and his head snapped around at the sound of her voice. "You dropped our pizza." She leaned against the wall next to the motel office, watching the street.

Relief was almost as painful as the panic. He closed the distance between them in two steps, grabbed her by the arm and pulled her close. She went stiff, but he didn't care. He had to hold her, feel her against him in order to convince himself she was okay. She felt good—solid and strong. He held her even tighter.

"Can't breathe," she said, trying to gain a few inches between them.

"Don't care," he said. He crushed her against him, buried his face in her neck, breathed in her smell and held it in his lungs. She was okay. He didn't want to think about what those few seconds he'd thought he'd lost her had done to him. It was too much, too soon. His feelings for her were messy and unmanageable. It was unsettling, not being able to keep them in check. It was also something he didn't want to think about. Not now. Not ever.

He took a step back to look down at her, felt the frown settle on his face. "What are you doing out here?"

She looked over her shoulder. "I went in and asked the troll behind the desk for my own room." She held up a plastic key card.

He started to protest, but she talked over him. "Shut up and listen. I was on my way back to the room to get my stuff..." She looked over her shoulder again before turning back to him. "I turned the desk lamp on before we left. I hate the dark..." She swallowed hard and looked in the direction of their room again.

No light in the window. The room was completely black.

SIXTY-TWO

When he reached for his .38, Sabrina followed suit without question. He started forward and she followed, but he turned, shook his head.

"I need you to go across the street and wait for me there. If I'm not back in thirty minutes, jump a bus to Dallas and catch a flight home. No matter what you do, don't come back here," he said quickly and quietly.

"Fuck that," she said, shoving his hand away when he laid it on her shoulder to urge her back. "I don't know what's going on, but I sure as hell know that I don't abandon my partner. Not ever. Now, are you taking point or am I?"

For a second he looked like he couldn't decide whether to kiss her or knock her out.

"Wasting time," she said quietly.

"*Shit.* Fine, but stay behind me," he said.

"Yes, sir," she said and let him lead the way.

They approached the room with caution, eyes sweeping into every shadow and dark corner of the lot. The door was closed, but she could see it wasn't latched.

He crossed in front of it quickly, pressing his back against the block wall while she did the same on the other side. Signaling for her to take the secondary position, he pushed the door open with the toe of his boot, leading with his gun. She followed, training the barrel of her .38 just over his left shoulder.

Dirty yellow light followed them in, illuminating the room from black to gray. She could see a human-shaped shadow in the corner. She eased herself into the room, kept her back pressed against the wall. She wished she had her Kevlar vest on, but it was in her duffle.

Suddenly, the tension dropped from Michael's shoulders. He lowered his weapon, pointed it at the ground. "You fucking idiot. I could've shot you," he said. He reholstered his weapon and moved to the desk to switch on the lamp. Soft light flooded the room, revealing the man sitting in the room's only chair.

Except *man* was a grossly inaccurate description. He was massive, a moving mountain with coffee-colored skin and enough muscle to make Mr. Universe look like a ninety-pound weakling. His clean-shaven head, roughly the size of a basketball, swiveled in her direction. He smiled, the facial movement revealing a set of deep dimples. "You mind shutting that door, sweetheart?"

"No problem, honey," she said, kicking the door shut with the flat of her foot. His smile widened until she was sure his face would split in two, revealing teeth so large and white they looked like fence slats.

"Hostile, paranoid, a little crazy—I can see the attraction," he said to Michael without taking his eyes off her. Turning to her, Michael gave her a look. Shrugging off her coat, she let it drop to the floor. She tucked the gun into the small of her back before leaning against the wall, arms crossed over her chest. The moving mountain stared at her. She stared back.

———

Michael could see that Sabrina wasn't going to give the two men any privacy. "What are you doing here, Lark?"

Lark shook his head and gave him a shrug. "Playtime's over, bro."

Michael shook his head. "No. No way. You heard him, I have three days left."

"The Lord giveth … and then he decides he's gonna be a prick. He wants you back. *Now*," Lark said.

"I'm not leaving." He looked at her. She was clearly confused, but the look she gave him said she trusted him completely. He looked back at Lark. "No."

Lark looked at Sabrina. "Why don't you go get some ice or somethin', let us have a little chat?" Lark said to her. Sabrina turned to him, looking for guidance. Her expression was clear. She'd go if he asked, but nothing short of his say-so would move her. She was fearless, loyal—ready to kill and die for him. The sense of free fall hit him again only this time he didn't land.

He just kept falling.

"She's not going anywhere."

Lark gave him with a look of utter disbelief. "So that's how it is?"

"Yup. That's how it is."

Lark shook his head, rubbed him forehead like he felt a headache coming on. "You dumb son of a bitch … "

The three of them stood in heavy silence, each waiting for the other to break until finally Lark turned and spoke directly to her. "He has to leave with me—tonight. He can't stay here—"

"Don't talk to her." He took a step, blocking Lark's view of her.

"You wanted her to stay, so she stayed. Obviously, what I have to say doesn't mean shit anymore, so maybe you'll listen to *her*." Lark stepped to the side, looked around him to talk to her. "If he stays with you, he'll die." Lark shifted his gaze, looked at him.

The room fell into silence again. Sabrina looked at Lark then at him, the question plain on her face—*What the hell is going on?*

Just then, the bathroom door opened. Michael looked at the man who walked through it and felt the situation spin out of control.

"You brought *him* here?" He aimed a look of betrayed disbelief at his friend.

"You're kidding, right? Like I had some sort of alternative." Lark dropped himself back into the chair, giving up.

Michael looked at the man who'd just walked into the room and felt the walls close in. Looked like he was leaving her, after all. He didn't have a choice.

SIXTY-THREE

SABRINA'S FIRST IMPRESSION WAS that this wasn't a man. This was a kid. He was tall, only an inch or two shorter than Michael, with the sleek, muscular build of a swimmer. Reddish-brown hair that flopped over his forehead and clear blue eyes gave him an instantly boyish charm that was absurd, given how he was dressed. He was wearing black cargo pants, a gray thermal, and a double shoulder holster that housed a pair of .40 Desert Eagles. His thigh was strapped with the biggest tactical knife she'd ever seen.

"Hello, I'm Benjamin Shaw." He came at her with an extended hand and an easy grin. She found herself accepting it without hesitation. "Lark's told me a lot about you—it's nice to finally meet you," he said, giving her hand a few pumps before letting go.

"I'm not leaving."

Everyone in the room turned to look at Michael. He stood in the middle of the room, arms at his sides, fists clenched.

"Yes, you are," Ben said to Michael, before turning to look back at Sabrina. "Because if he doesn't, he'll be dead by morning, and there's nothing I can do about it."

She stared at him for a second. Surely she hadn't heard him correctly. "I don't understand—"

"My father doesn't believe in trust or loyalty ... or free will. Every one of his operatives is implanted with GPS at the base of their spine—think Lo-jack, only in people. It's his way of protecting his investments. O'Shea here apparently has a special model. I'm not sure what it does, but my father has assured me that if he's not on that plane with me, he'll live *just* long enough to regret it." He cocked his head at Michael, and shrugged. "So ... yeah—you're coming with me, even if I have to take out your kneecaps and throw you in the trunk of my car," Ben said calmly, giving the words time to sink in. "Good. Glad we understand each other." He looked at his watch and cocked his head at the door. "Lark and I are gonna leave, give you some time." He headed out, Lark on his heels. "See you in an hour."

Sabrina followed them to the door and locked it before turning on him. "Who the hell was that?"

He sighed. "The big, angry one is my handler—Lark. The one who looks like he should be sucking tequila out of a sorority girl's navel is named Benjamin Shaw. His father is my boss."

"Okay, next question—who are *you*?"

"It's not who, it's what. The term these days is *paramilitary professional*."

"So ... you're a mercenary," she said, not surprised at all.

"Yes."

"And you're leaving." Of course he was. Somewhere along the way, she'd allowed herself to forget just who Michael O'Shea really was.

"No. I'm not. That guy's full of shit—" He was backpedaling, but she wasn't letting him off that easy.

"Really, O'Shea? Because he sounded pretty fucking sure," she said. "And what's this about an implant? That will *kill* you?" Saying it out loud, it sounded even crazier the second time around. Things like that didn't exist. Did they?

"More bullshit. Just a scare tactic—"

"Prove it. He said it was at the base of your spine—let me feel for it."

"No."

She lunged at him, driven by anger and more than a little fear, but he caught her before she could get her arms around him. "Don't," he said, holding her wrists in a grip so tight her fingers began to tingle.

She thought of his hands on her stomach, his fingers tracing the hard knot of scars embedded in her skin. "I showed you mine, O'Shea; time to show me yours."

He stared down at her for a few seconds, that hard expression of his beginning to crack. He finally let go of her, dropping his hands to his sides. She slipped her arms around his waist, trailing her fingers around either side until they met at the base of his spine. She ran her hands against his skin. And felt nothing.

"You'll have to press harder," he said. "It's under the muscle."

She looked up at his face, but he was staring straight ahead. She pressed harder, and there it was—the size and shape of a dime. She jerked her hands away, took a step back, and he finally looked down at her with that sardonic smile of his. "Don't worry—it can take a beating. It won't go off until they're done with me," he said.

"Why?" Why would someone do that? Make a slave of another human being…but she knew. Maybe not *why*, but she knew what it was like to be held prisoner. Made to do things. Kept as a pet until the person that held you grew tired of playing with you.

"Because I'm one of the bad guys, Sabrina." He shook his head. "I've killed a lot of men and murdered more than a few in cold blood—I did it for my country, and after that I did it for money. I've used people as pawns, and now I'm a pawn. Whatever Shaw did to me—I deserve it."

———

She stared at him quietly for a few minutes, as if digesting what he'd just told her. He waited for her to get angry or maybe even scared. She'd locked herself in a room with a man who just confessed to multiple murders. She was a cop—surely she'd have some sort of reaction. All she did was look at him, her silence as loud as a shout.

He passed a rough hand over his face. "It doesn't matter. I'm not leaving. Lark'll find a way to buy me a couple days." Even as he said it, he knew his chances of that were slim. Something had happened between Livingston Shaw and Lark. There was a little voice, getting louder and louder, telling him that he could no longer trust his friend. Looking at her, none of that mattered. Trusting Lark to pull through was a risk he was willing to take.

She just shook her head, like she knew he was lying. "I don't know who you were looking at, but the Lark I met isn't in the position to help anyone." She took a step toward him. "Is there any way we can get it out? Disable it somehow?" she said.

God, he wanted to kiss her. "No. Shaw has them put as close to the spine as possible to make sure that tampering with it would result in paralysis."

She nodded, went quiet for a few seconds. "Then you'll go."

He felt like he was already dead, like what'd been put inside him had already been detonated. "I can't. I can't leave you."

She sighed, crossed her arms over her chest. "Of course you can."

"Can't. Won't. Take your pick." He hated the sound of his voice. He sounded desperate. Weak.

"I want you to go," she said. "Morning rolls around, you're gone either way. I'd rather you be gone and *breathing*."

He looked down at her. The panic was back, settled in deep. "You won't leave, will you. You won't go home? Even if I ask you to?"

"No, I won't." She shook her head. "I have to see this through."

SIXTY-FOUR

SABRINA WATCHED HIM MOVE around the room, securing windows, installing motion detectors. She wanted to tell him to stop, that it was a waste of what little time they had left, but she didn't. What he was doing was necessary because he was leaving. The thought closed her throat, and she pushed it away. She looked at the cheap digital clock on the nightstand—four minutes left.

Michael came out of the bathroom, his eyes traveling around the room until they found her. She was sitting in the corner, in the chair his handler had been sitting in. His *handler* ... she pushed that thought away, too. It was too bizarre, too real to contemplate. She looked at Michael and smiled, tried to reassure him that she'd be okay, but he had that look again—that dead calm expression that told her he was barely hanging on.

"We're all good in there. Windows and doors are locked down. If there's a breach, an alarm will sound, loud enough to wake the dead." He stood over her, something in his hands. It was her cell. He held it out to her. "If there's a breach while you're not here, it'll

313

trigger the remote alarm and send you a text," he said. "And here's this." It was the flashdrive Strickland made for her of the Sawyer case. "I downloaded copies of all the victim files onto it. Maybe you'll find something I missed." He made is sound like an apology.

She took it from him and smiled, tried to put him at ease. "I'll be fine. I can take care of myself."

He laughed, one short bark that sounded like a curse. "I know."

There was a sharp rap on the door. *Time's up*, she thought.

He backed away from her, picked up his duffle, and slung it over his shoulder, headed for the door. He stalled then, turned to her with his hand on the doorknob. "I'll call you when I'm done—as soon as I can," he said before turning away.

She wasn't even aware that she was moving until she was half-way across the room.

"I don't want you to go."

He let go of the knob and dropped his bag, turning and reaching for her before she could think to pull back. He held her close, kissed the top of her head, her cheeks. "I'll come back. I'll find a way." He looked into her eyes, cupped her chin so she couldn't look away. "I'll come back for you," he said before lowering his lips to hers.

Her eyes slipped closed and she reached up to clasp her hand around his wrist, anchoring him in place. When he broke away, she opened her eyes to look into the quiet gray of his, and felt what she always felt, wished what she always wished: that she was softer, easier to reach.

She swallowed the pithy comeback that bubbled in her throat, took a deep, shuddering breath ... and let go.

"I'll be waiting."

SIXTY-FIVE

HE LET HIMSELF IN quietly. Closed the back door and waited, listened for a sign that she'd heard him. Nothing but silence. He looked around the tidy kitchen, found the cake dome in the corner. Pleased to see it, he lifted the lid and cut himself a slice. He ate it standing up, poured himself a glass of lemonade to go with it.

He thought about Melissa. He'd known she'd follow him home—do as she was told. In their time together, she'd come to understand that he was master. He called the shots, held the power of life and death. She'd learned her lesson... the way he taught, it was not something she'd easily forget.

He rinsed his plate and put it away, carried his glass with him through the silent house, from room to tidy room.

The woman who lived here was his plan B. A placeholder of sorts—always had been. To be honest, there was nothing special or remarkable about her beyond the purpose she served. It was easy, in the soft glow of her bedroom lamp, to look at her and let go. To convince himself that she was his Melissa. That was why he kept her.

He made his way to the bedroom. Found her asleep on her stomach, her face obscured by the long fall of rich auburn hair he loved so much. He felt himself grow hard at the sight of her supple form beneath the thin white sheet. Pulling it down, he revealed her long, lean back, her firm, round ass. They were nice, but not what aroused him.

It was the scars he'd left on her over the years that made him hard. Countless thin, white scars looped and swirled across the skin of her back, intersecting and receding in a pattern that proved her absolute devotion. Lifting his hand, running it over the first cuts he'd ever made on her, she transformed before his eyes. She was young and vibrant. Bright and innocent.

She was his Melissa.

He set the glass on the nightstand and undressed in the dark. Pulled his knife from his pocket, flicked it open. The quiet *snick* it made was enough to wake her.

"You're home." She smiled, but it faltered a little when her gaze settled on the blade. "I missed you."

"Of course you did." He began to stroke himself with his free hand, liked the way she watched him. Liked the fear he saw on her face. It was the only thing making it possible for him to hold on to the illusion that she was who he really wanted. Her blue eyes drifted down, first to the hand that worked between his legs, then to the knife in the other. Her breathing became heavy, coming in short, excited pants. She sounded like a dog, eager for a game of catch. "Are you going to hurt me?"

He smiled at her in the dark. "Yes."

SIXTY-SIX

SABRINA WAS WOKEN UP by the sound of her ringing cell. She looked at the display. Local number—not one she recognized.

"Hello," she said. She'd been up all night, pouring over victim files. An early morning call was the last thing she expected.

"Inspector Vaughn, this is Chief Carson. Did I wake you?"

She looked at the clock. It was after eight in the morning. Shit. She sat up, pushed her hair out of her face. "No. I'm awake."

"Good. Our coroner just called. Lucy Walker's autopsy is today if you're interested in coming along." He said it like he was hoping she'd say no.

"Today? It's Sunday."

"That don't matter much around here. Meet me at the station in an hour," he said before hanging up.

317

She made it with fifteen minutes to spare, pulling into the station lot just as Wade pushed his way through the door.

"Mornin', Inspector." He tipped his hat.

"Good morning." She looked around. "Early call?"

"Yeah. Someone reported a possible trespassing about thirty miles out. Supposed to be my day off, but I got called in on account of where you and the chief are headed." He stopped, shifted from one foot to the other, looking anxious.

She decided to make it easy for him. "You have something to say?"

He nodded. "What you asked me last night got me to thinking about who else could've hurt Melissa." He dug a folded piece of paper from his breast pocket and shook it out at her. She took it, smoothed it open and read it. Read it again.

Her eyes shot to his face. "What is this?"

"A speeding ticket I wrote Pete Conners not more than six months ago. He was Kelly Walker's boyfriend for a time, took an unhealthy interest in Melissa. You wanted to know who else could've killed her. There's your answer."

It was a lie. Something Wade concocted to keep his friend out of trouble. Maybe even something Jed had put him up to.

"Okay. I'll call my partner, have him look into it," she said, expecting him to backpedal, to ask for the ticket back. He did neither. Instead he nodded and looked relieved.

"You do that, and you'll see it's true. Pete Conners tried to rape her. My father told me that himself, not more than a few days before she took off."

She watched him leave, climb into a JPD Blazer, and drive away before she pulled her cell from her pocket and dialed the number.

It rang twice before he answered. "Strickland."

"Hey."

"Hey, how's it going?"

"Did you talk to Val?"

He was quiet for a second. "Yeah."

"Still want to help me?"

"More than ever."

She looked down at the ticket in her hand. "Great. I need you to find me a car."

———

The JPD lobby was small, separated from the officers' area by a high counter top. Zeke was on the other side of it, waiting for her.

"I'm here to see Chief Carson," she said.

"Chief, that lady cop from California's here to see you," he said loudly over his shoulder. Turning back, he nodded toward the row of chairs behind her. "If you'd like to find a seat, he'll be right out." Zeke had been her father's number one for years and always seemed to find time for a friendly smile or kind word. She seen him come in and out of Kelly's bedroom once or twice, but he'd always been respectful to her—something most of her mother's customers never felt was necessary.

Before she could sit, Carson made his appearance. "Wade leave on that trespassing call?" he said as he set his hat on his head, tugging the brim down low.

Zeke nodded from his desk. "Yup, cruiser's got a flat so he took your Blazer," he said without looking up. "Hank said he'd be by to fix it after lunch. If there's a call, I'll take my truck."

Carson grinned for a moment and gave her a shrug. "Guess that means I'm hitching a ride with you, darlin'," he said as he fastened his gun belt in place and head for the door.

SIXTY-SEVEN

Trapped in a car with the man she suspected of raping and torturing her was not a place Sabrina wanted to be. She looked at him—let her eyes travel to his gun. The safety strap that held it snug inside its holster was snapped shut. No easy draw from him. She figured she could handle the rest.

He'd been quiet nearly the entire time, poring over the printout of the Sawyer file she'd brought along.

She thought about Pete Conners, about the ticket Wade claimed to have given him, and she wished Strickland would hurry the hell up.

Carson closed the file folder and turned to look at her. "This happened Wednesday last?" he said, and she nodded.

"You see the similarities between your case and mine? Same type of knife was used. Both victims had words stabbed into their abdomens. Both had their eyes taken. It's the same guy."

Now it was his turn to nod. "I see a lot of same—but I see a lot of different, too." He held up the file folder. "Red ribbon? Gift tag around the vic's wrist? That's pretty specific, and none of that was found at the O'Shea or Walker crime scenes." He dropped the file into his lap. "But let's say you're right. Let's say that this girl and Frankie were killed by the same guy. What does that have to do with Melissa?"

"Kaitlyn Sawyer was abducted in El Paso on October first. She was found on the third with a gift tag tied around her wrist that said, *Happy birthday—sorry I missed it.*" Frustration weighed heavy in her voice. He was either fucking with her or too stubborn to see what was right in front of him. She shot him a look. "She was number fifteen. I have a stack of files, each one on a young, blue-eyed waitress who disappeared on October first." She glared at him for a second before turning back toward the windshield. "We both know what October first is, so let's cut the bullshit."

"Melissa's birthday." He looked out his window, waited a few beats before doing a slow nod. "*Sorry I missed it . . .* why would he write something like that on a gift tag and tie it to a dead girl's wrist?" he asked, but before she could answer, he turned toward her and answered his own question. "The only way it makes any sense is if the guy who killed Melissa thinks she's still alive."

———

He looked at his watch again. He'd been gone nearly eleven hours. Michael turned in his seat and stared out the window of the private Lear. No commercial flights for Ben Shaw. There were some advantages to traveling with the boss's son.

It'd been another bullshit mission. Down to Mexico. Pull the trigger. Back on the plane. He had no idea where they were going now, but they were headed north. Texas and Sabrina were due east.

He looked at his watch again—eleven hours now. He'd been gone eleven hours.

"Mind if I sit?"

"Yes," he said, but Ben took a seat anyway.

"Sorry, I should've mentioned that was a rhetorical question." He settled back into one of the plush leather seats that dotted the interior of the plane. "That was an impressive shot you took today," Ben said, not wasting time.

He was talking about the job, and he was right. It had been an impressive shot: 2,293 yards. Only a handful of people in the world who could've made it. He was one of them. "What can I say? I'm an impressive guy," he said, still staring out the window.

"I suppose the whole 'You've stopped a very bad man from doing very bad things' speech wouldn't matter much to you, huh?" Ben said.

He just shrugged.

"Lark explained the situation. Is she in immediate danger?"

Yeah, Lark had been doing a lot of that lately—explaining where he shouldn't. He looked away from the window. "*She* is none of your fucking business," he said.

Ben leaned forward with a smile, his eyes, as clear and calm as lake water. "Curiouser and curiouser." He sat back in his chair. "You'd kill me in an instant if you thought I posed a threat to her."

He just gave Ben another shrug. "I'd kill you for a handful of magic beans and a talking donkey. I'm a killer—that's what I do."

Ben laughed. "We have more in common than you think, O'Shea," Ben said before looking out the window. "You believe I'm gonna tell my father about her, and he'll use her to keep you in line," Ben said, reading him perfectly. "Do you love her?"

He looked at Ben. "Capsule or not, if anything happens to her, you'll be the first person I kill."

"I guess that answers my question." Ben pulled out his cell phone and dialed a number.

Michael waited for the capsule in his back to detonate. For some kind of neurotoxin to drop him to the floor and take him out.

Ben spoke a few words and clipped his phone closed. Within seconds, the Lear banked gently to the right.

Michael looked out the window. They were now heading east.

"I can buy you a couple of hours. That's the best I can do," Ben said.

"What's it gonna cost me?"

Ben smiled. "Does it really matter?"

He looked away, out the window at the world below. Sabrina was down there, and he'd do whatever it took to get back to her—nothing else mattered. He stared out the window and shook his head. "No, it doesn't."

SIXTY-EIGHT

THE REVELATION HUNG BETWEEN them. Sabrina looked at Carson and waited for him to put the rest of it together. That not only was Melissa Walker alive, that she was sitting next to him. If he did put it together, he didn't tell her. If he already knew, he hid well.

"Charlie's is up here on the right." He pointed to a white stucco building with *Dubois & Son Funeral Home* stenciled on the side.

They entered though the back of the building, stepping into an office that make Richards's look like corner digs on Wall Street. Charlie Dubois looked up from the open file on his desk, looked at his watch. "Chief Carson, I was just about to call you." He stood up from his desk, extending his hand across its surface in Sabrina's direction. "Nice to meet you, ma'am, I'm Charlie Dubois." He pulled his hand back before continuing. "Are we ready to get started?"

She started to nod but the phone on her hip let out a chirp. "Excuse me," she said, taking a glance at the display. It was Strickland. "I have to take this, I'll be right back." She left through the door they'd just come through and stepped into the parking lot.

"Tell me you found it."

"I found it."

Relief, followed by a strong shot of adrenaline, hit her system. "Where?"

"You aren't gonna believe it—I sure in the hell didn't. I checked long-term parking at the airport, like you suggested. Guy I talked to said he called *us* about a car matching the description I gave him yesterday. Said he remembered because the car had both its plate and VIN pulled. Said we sent a uniform out and had it towed to the city impound lot."

"If the plate and VIN are gone, how do you know it's a match?"

"I don't. Not for sure, anyway. Both are dark blue, 1999 Chevy Cavaliers, but … "

"But what?"

"But I checked the plate and VIN you gave me. Both are registered to a Pete Conners."

Pete was alive.

Strickland was still talking and she tried to focus on what he was saying, but all she could think was that somehow, the man she thought she'd killed had survived.

" … the address on the registration matches to a storage yard for long-haul truckers in Idabel, Oklahoma, so there's no way to prove it's a match to the car I found."

In other words, they had nothing.

But Strickland wasn't finished. "What I *do* know for sure is that the tire treads on the car I found in the impound lot match the cast we took of the tire tracks left at the Mount Davidson crime scene. The car I found was the one used to dump Kaitlyn Sawyer's body."

She dug the ticket out of her pocket and read it carefully. The address printed at the top of the ticket didn't match the one on the one in the registration records that Strickland pulled: it was for a *residence* in Idabel. Which was less than a hundred miles away.

She headed for the car. "Okay. Thanks."

"I have to turn my findings over to Robbins and Carr." He made it sound like an apology.

"I know. Give me two hours, okay? I might be able to make a positive ID on the suspect," she said, digging her keys from her pocket.

"How stupid are you about to get?" he said, a panicked edge to his voice.

"I'll call you in a couple hours." She hung up the phone. The door to the funeral home banged open. She looked over her shoulder to see Carson coming at her. He had something in his hand, and he looked angry. She opened the car door and started the engine, pulled out of the lot without looking back. How stupid was she about to get?

Very.

SIXTY-NINE

SABRINA PARKED ACROSS THE street and watched the house for a few minutes. She'd made the trip on impulse, hadn't really thought about what she'd do once she got here. She needed proof that the car Strickland found belonged to Pete, and she needed to find a way to link it all together. Beyond that, she had no idea how she was doing.

With her badge clipped to her waist and her hand resting firmly on the butt of the .38 that rode her hip, she walked with false confidence up the length of the driveway. Bypassing the front door, she headed for the back, toward the detached garage. If the car was there, she was back to square one. If not, she'd check the truck yard listed on the ticket. It was a long shot but she was running out of options and time. Strickland would have to hand what they'd found over to the officers in charge of the case and when he did, it would only be a matter of time before Mathews found out she was here. She walked around the side of the garage, into the yard next to it. There was a side door next to a couple of windows. She used her sleeve to wipe off some of the dirt that obscured her view and looked inside.

There was a car inside, covered from front to back with a canvas tarp. She looked at the floor, saw that it was dirt. Its oil-soaked surface was crisscrossed with dozens of tire tracks. She'd bet anything that one of those tire tracks was a match to the ones they found in Mount Davidson. She needed to get in. Get a look under the tarp to make sure the car underneath it wasn't the one she was looking for. Snap a few pictures of the tracks pressed into the dirt and send them to Strickland for a comparison, just to be sure. She looked at the door. It was secured shut with a tough-looking padlock.

No way in.

"Excuse me, can I help you?" someone said behind her, and she stiffened. The tone and cadence was one she remembered well. She turned toward the voice, a remote, professional smile plastered on her face.

Standing not more than five yards away was her mother.

———

After Ben worked his magic, he left him alone. Michael imagined he was off polishing his knife or hatching plans for world domination—he didn't know and didn't care. All he knew was that the kid was going to help him. It would cost, but he didn't care about that either. The only thing that mattered was getting back to Sabrina.

He looked across the plane at Lark, tapping away on his computer, and tried to get a grip on what he'd come to believe. He'd turned it inside out, pulled it apart, and put it back together—all to the same conclusion: Lark had betrayed him.

He moved across the aisle and sat across from his friend, watched him for a few seconds, trying to keep himself together.

"Why?" It was all he could say, the only question he could think of. Lark looked up for a second, shooting him a puzzled look.

"Why what?" He looked at him again, shook his head. "Look, I told you—the kid's in charge. Daddy handed him the keys to this op, I'm just along for the ride—"

"No. I understand why you sold me out to Shaw, but you're the one who started the rumor about Sabrina's survival and that she was living in California. I want to know why." Even as he said the words, he couldn't believe them. Didn't want to. Not Lark. Not his friend.

Lark stopped tapping and gave him a long, hard look. He could see them, the calculations Lark was running in his head. How far could he get on a lie, how much trouble would the truth buy him. He closed his laptop and leaned back in his seat.

"I did what had to be done to get the mission back on track." That was it. No remorse. No regret. "What started as a simple re-con turned into some fucked-up babysitting job. That bitch was messin' with your head. You weren't thinking straight anymore, hadn't been for *weeks*. I knew that if we were going to get what we were after, I was going to have to *make* it happen." He shrugged. "So I did."

"I had everything under control." It was a lie, but he said it with such conviction that he almost believed himself.

Lark laughed. "Control? Please—you've been scrambling since day one, but I stuck by you. Did what I promised I'd do. But I never promised to die over this shit, and that's exactly where the both of us were headed."

"Lucy—"

"Was collateral damage. I just spun the top and set it down—I had no idea it was gonna knock her over," Lark said with a shrug.

"How? Who did you tell?" Lark was an outsider in Jessup, one that would be remembered. No way he acted alone.

Lark looked out the window. "Your Aunt Gina."

It hit him hard. Harder than he thought it would. He wasn't surprised though, not really. He'd never been close to her—she'd never understood Sean and Sophia's devotion to him. It'd been Frankie she loved and raised as her own after her sister's death. She would've done anything to find even a small measure of justice for the child she lost.

"Lucy wasn't collateral damage. She was my friend. She trusted me." It was all he had, the only reason he could think of, but for a man like Lark, he knew it wasn't enough.

"Are you listening to yourself? *She trusted you*? Really? Come on, man—how many people have you fucked over in the past? How many people have you betrayed to your own end? *Your friend*? What about me? You left me high and fucking dry—ass in the wind—while you played hide-and-seek with that whacked-out headcase—"

The draw was fast, so fast he didn't even realize what he was doing until the gun was in his hand and shoved in Lark's face. He pressed the barrel of it into his cheekbone, finger hovering above the trigger. "Yes. Lucy was my friend." He touched the trigger for a half-second, felt the urge to pull it. "She trusted me, and I trusted you." He forced himself to lower the gun and stood, shoved it back in to its holster. "She was a good woman—so good that she'd want me to forgive you. That's the only reason you're still alive."

Lark looked up at him and smirked. "Over a woman." He shook his head. "Who would've thought *El Cartero* would go soft over a woman?"

He reached for his gun again, but before he could draw down, Ben was in his face, pushing him back. "Wow. You are one intense motherfucker, aren't you?" He shoved him into a chair, pointed a finger at him and shook his head. "Wheels down in five—save it for later." He turned to Lark. "You say one more word to him, I'm gonna let him kill you."

Five minutes. Michael looked out the window and counted them down in his head. Tried to convince himself that the hard knot in his belly was just nerves, that it had nothing to do with fear. *She's fine. She's safe* ... he repeated it over and over, but the more he tried to convince himself, the more sure he became that she was anything but.

SEVENTY

It took Sabrina a few seconds to find her voice. Her mother was alive. "Are you Kelly Walker?" she said to the woman in front of her.

There was nothing, not even a glimmer of recognition to suggest that her mother knew who she really was, and she wasn't surprised. For the whole of her young life, her mother had been either drunk or high. Her children had been nothing but bothersome strangers to her.

"Yes, is something wrong?" Kelly said, her bright blue eyes settled first on the badge secured at her waist and then the gun strapped to her hip.

"I'd like to ask you a few questions about a 1999 Chevy Cavalier registered to a Pete Conners. This address is listed as his residence," she said in a tone that made it clear that Kelly really didn't have a choice.

"Alright." Kelly widened her stance to push the door open, inviting her inside. "Would you like to come in? I've just started a pot of coffee."

That was exactly what she wanted. "I'd hate to impose."

"Don't be silly—my Pete's not here, and I don't have to be to work for a few hours. Come on in," she said, beckoning her up the steps and into a tidy kitchen. The house smelled clean, like fresh laundry. Nothing like the dank smell of cheap booze and even cheaper sex she grew up with. This was a Kelly she'd never met. Sober and healthy, clear gaze and steady hands. She felt a sudden, irrational stab of anger that she and the twins had been denied this life, had never known this mother.

"Coffee?" Kelly said, pot in hand. She nodded and watched her pour it into sturdy ceramic mugs. "Cream, sugar?"

"No, thank you," she said, intent on listening to the house and its sounds. The creak of old floorboards, the faint whine of a squeaky hinge. Anything that would betray another person in the house, but it was silent. They were alone.

Kelly handed her a mug with an apprehensive smile. "Is this about the parking ticket I got last month? I fed the meter—"

"No, nothing like that," she said as Kelly gestured for her to take a seat at the kitchen table. "Are you the only person who drives the car?" she said, her eyes trailing Kelly as she moved about the kitchen.

"No, my Pete drives it when he's in town, but he's on the road a lot. He's a truck driver," she said. She pulled a few dessert plates from a cabinet. "Cake?"

She could only nod as she watched Kelly lift the lid off a cake dome, set in the corner of the counter, cutting thick slices of buttery yellow cake. Kelly sat the cake in front of her with a prideful smile.

"It's lemon pound cake. My mama's recipe, she makes the best in Texas," Kelly said proudly, and she caught the present tense of her words. Kelly had no idea her mother was dead. Which wasn't that shocking, seeing as Sabrina had had no idea her mother was alive.

After that night, no one had heard from or seen Kelly Walker again. At least, no one in Jessup.

She stared at the cake in front of her. The tangy scent of lemon coupled with the rich, buttery aroma of the cake brought a momentary flutter to her heart.

"You don't like lemon?" Kelly said with a slight frown as she sat down across from her, setting her own mug and plate on the table.

"No, it's great, thanks. How often is Pete home?" She forced his name past her lips, surprised it wasn't delivered on a gagging sound. She lifted her mug to her mouth to hide her disgust.

"As often as he can be. It really depends on the time of year," she said.

I bet. Sabrina made a neutral sound in the back of her throat. Politeness forced her to reach for her fork to sample the cake, but there wasn't one on her plate.

Kelly sighed and rose from her seat. "Look at me, forgetting the most important part. I'm so sorry." She rushed across the kitchen to retrieve a pair of forks from the drawer. "Did Pete do something in my car?" Kelly returned, forks in hand.

She shook her head. "I'm not sure. There was a hit and run a few nights ago, and the car registered to this address matches the description."

Kelly looked relieved. "Oh, then it couldn't have been Pete. He's been gone for the past few weeks now, and I usually walk to work—it's right up the street."

"I'd like to see the car if I could, just so I can cross it off my list," she said, turning in her chair to look at Kelly.

"Of course. Here's your fork," Kelly said. She took it, nodding and smiling her thanks. Turning again, it took her less than a second to realize something was wrong.

Kelly was still standing behind her.

Before she could move, Kelly jabbed something into her neck. A pinch followed by a fierce liquid burn that swept swiftly and unchecked along her muscles, seeping into her blood. She jolted to her feet, knocking Kelly backward, into the counter.

Her hand fell to the gun at her hip, but her arm was boneless, her fingers incapable of gripping and lifting it from her holster.

She turned and caught sight of her mother. Kelly's face was calm, eyes clear and free of the malice that used to plague them. The syringe in her hand looked tiny, easily concealed and as if to prove it, Kelly recapped it and slipped it into the snug pocket of her pants.

She felt her knees give way and she sank to the floor. She remembered this feeling, was no stranger to it.

"Why?" She landed gracelessly on the kitchen floor, staring up with rapidly failing eyes at the woman who'd drugged her. Her mother looked down at her, her brow slightly furrowed for a second. It smoothed in an instant as she straightened her stance.

"Because he told me to."

SEVENTY-ONE

MICHAEL STARTED CALLING HER the second the Lear touched down. No answer. He checked their motel room. The sensors and motion detectors were still in place and hadn't been activated, but the room was empty. Sabrina was gone.

He looked at Lark. Felt angry that he had to ask him for help. "Track the GPS in her phone."

Lark smirked, cut a *get a load of this asshole* look at Ben.

"Do it," Ben said.

"Oh, it's like that?" Lark said.

"Yeah, it is. Do it," Ben said again.

Lark shook his head, muttered on his way to the Humvee to boot up his computer. He was back a few minutes later—the look on his face said it all.

"GPS is disabled, but I got the name and number for the last incoming call—Christopher Strickland."

Michael dialed, paced the parking lot while Ben watched with avid interest and Lark leaned against the car, arms crossed over his massive chest, staring into middle space.

"Strickland."

"Strickland, this is Michael O'Shea—"

"Thank God." He blew out a long breath. "Sabrina's with you, right? She's okay. Can I talk to her?" Strickland said.

"No. She's not with me. We were … working different angles on the case and got separated." He turned his back on Ben. "Did you talk to her?"

"Yeah, she called me this morning, asked me to help her find a car that she thought might be involved in the Sawyer case."

"What car?"

"A 1999 dark blue Chevy Cavalier."

The car that matched the description of Billy Bauer's last notebook entry. Why would she be looking for that car?

"Did you find it?"

"Yeah, in our own friggin' impound lot. Long story—anyway, tire tracks match the ones found at the Sawyer crime scene but the plate and VIN were pulled—no way to match it to the name she gave me."

"Name? What name?" He looked up. Both Shaw and Lark were staring at him now.

"Pete Conners."

SEVENTY-TWO

HE SAW MELISSA'S RENTAL car parked across the street from Kelly's and couldn't help but smile. Knowing she was inside—that he'd played her so perfectly she practically fell right into his lap was enough to put a spring his step as he crossed the yard and let himself in.

Kelly greeted him at the door, all wringing hands and eager smile. "I did it. I did just what you told me to. She was there, just like you said she would be. I invited her in and gave her the shot." She smiled proudly. "She never knew what hit her, not until it was too late."

He ignored Kelly's rambling, pushed past her. He had to see her—had to see his Melissa. She was there, sprawled on the floor at his feet. Right where she belonged.

He knelt down, pulled the gun off her hip. Ejected the clip and tossed it under the fridge. He racked back the slide and popped out the chambered bullet.

He set the empty gun on the counter, could feel Kelly behind—could practically *hear* her thinking. She knew she was being replaced.

He made himself look at her, allowed himself to see just how old and used up she really was. She disgusted him.

He forced a reassuring smile onto his face. "You did good. Real good."

Now she looked relieved. "I just want to make you happy, baby. I'll do anything for you. Anything."

"Get me a roll of duct tape." There was no doubt she'd comply, and she did quickly, eager to please. He looked away, back down at Melissa.

He ran his hands over her face, felt the screws and plates that held it together. Changed it. The years spent running, the hiding. It had all been for nothing.

He'd found her.

Lifting the hem of her shirt, he exposed her stomach and the gift he'd given her. He traced the smattering of puckered scars with his fingertips, pleased to see the goosebumps his touch raised against her skin. Watched his fingers spell the word that made more sense to him than any other.

MINE

"You're mine. I told you that. What made you think you could get away?" Reaching up, he pried her lids apart to reveal the colored lenses that hid her eyes. Sweeping them out, he was disappointed by what he found. Her pupils, totally blown by the drugs in her system, ate up the blue he'd hoped to see. Only the slightest ring of sapphire was left along the rim.

Pushing his face to within inches of hers, he stared into her eyes. "Do you see me now, Melissa? Do you know who I am?" he said, the movement of his mouth brushing his lips against hers. Letting her lids slip shut, he continued to stare and was delighted to see tears seep between them. They swept across her lashes, down her cheeks and into her hair. Riveted by the sight of them, by the memories they stirred, his tongue snaked out, lapped the side of her face. He collected her tears, swallowed them.

They tasted better than he remembered.

There was a sound behind him, and he looked over his shoulder. Kelly was there, duct tape in hand. She must've seen her fate on his face because she fumbled the roll. It fell, rolled across the floor, bumped into his boot.

He smiled, held out his hand to her. "Come here."

For just a second, he thought she'd refuse—finally do something interesting. There was a slight shake to her head and hands. He felt his excitement rise at the thought of a rebellion, but in the end, Kelly did what she always did.

She did as she was told.

Kelly took a few stumbling steps forward, enough for him to catch her hand and pull her down beside him. He swept the hair he loved so much away from her face, exposing her jaw and neck. "Do you recognize her? Do you know who she is?" He whispered in her ear—saw the flash of deep blue as her eyes widened in confusion.

"You said she was a cop ... that she wanted to take you away." Kelly shook her head, looked at his face. "She's just a cop."

He laughed, cupped the back of her neck, traced his thumb along her pulse. It pounded beneath his hand, faster and faster with each second. "You're so pathetic. And dumb ... how I stomached you all these years, I'll never understand." He turned her head, forced it down. "Look at her."

He felt a momentary stiffening in her neck, like she was going to fight him, but like before, it lasted only a fraction of a second. She relaxed and went willingly, let him push her face close to Melissa's exposed stomach. "Do you see it?" He used his other hand to grip hers, made Kelly trace her fingers along the scars that glare up at her. "It says *mine*. I did that…" His voice trailed off, mesmerized by the reminder of all the damage he'd done. "She belongs to me."

Kelly shot a look at his face, began to shake her head. "No—no, *I* belong to you. I'm yours. That's what you said. You said I belong to you."

"You do." He gave her a shrug, tightened the grip he had on the back of her neck. "But I don't want you anymore. I finally have what I really want. The only thing I've ever wanted. I have my Melissa back."

The name was like a bracing slap across her face. Kelly jerked away, struggled to stand. Chuckling, he pushed her even closer and made her look at the face of her long-dead daughter.

"You know, I didn't see it at first either. I had to really look at her, look past the face to see the truth." He proved his point by peeling back one of Melissa's lid again, exposing a lone blue eye.

It must've been like looking in a mirror because Kelly started to shake her head, "No. No. No…" she said it over and over, like a broken record.

"Yes." He said it once, turning her face back to his.

She stared at him with wide blue eyes. "You killed her—you killed Melissa," she screeched at him. She hit him. Actually swung and clipped the side of his jaw with her fist, more out of sheer luck than actual skill. He would've laughed it he hadn't been so surprised. Finally—here was the fight he'd been waiting fifteen years for. Too bad his didn't have time to play.

"Well, I *thought* I'd killed her, but here she is—right where she belongs. Thanks to you." He winked at her just to rile her some more and it worked.

"You son of a bitch," she screamed, swinging again, over and over. This time he was ready and batted her clumsy fists away with a few playful swats of his hand.

"Watch where you're swingin' those things," he said, laughing harder, and she doubled her efforts.

"You raped my child."

"She's not yours—never was. She's mine."

She stopped swinging and jolted upward, like she'd been shot from a cannon. She was making a run for it. He reached out and snagged her ankle so she went down hard, her face slamming into the worn linoleum floor.

Stunned by the blow, blood gushed from her nose, and he was able to drag her toward him without a fight. He lifted her into a sitting position so he could latch both hands around her neck and squeeze.

The sudden lack of oxygen brought her around. She fought, swatted and scratched at his hands and arms, gagged and choked against the hold he had on her throat. Kelly's face went red, then purple—then almost black from lack of oxygen. She finally went limp, but he kept squeezing. He glanced at the kitchen clock. A minute passed, and then another. He kept squeezing, just to be sure. He watched the sweep of the minute hand, counted five of them.

That should do it.

He let go of Kelly, and she dropped to the floor. He looked down at his Melissa, let his eyes roam—go where his hands and knife would follow. Her arms were flung out from her body as if she'd hoped for wings to carry her away from the nightmare she'd been plunged into. But this nightmare had only just begun.

This time his Melissa would not fly away.

SEVENTY-THREE

STRICKLAND RATTLED OFF AN address for a truck yard in Oklahoma, but he didn't bother to write it down. A place like that would be constantly busy—truckers coming in from off the road, while others spent hours gearing up for cross-country trips.

Not exactly private.

He had questions, and there was only one person he could think of that might have the answers. A quick call to Tom told him that the person he was looking for had decided to make himself easy to find.

The diner was busy, the Sunday after-church crowd filling the space to near capacity. Michael and his companions pushed their way in, and he stood in the doorway for a second, surveying the crowd. He zeroed in on the back of Carson's head and started for him.

Carson never moved, never looked up from the counter he sat at. He seemed totally unaware of what was going on around him, but Michael knew better.

He looked away from Carson for a second. Tommy's wife and daughter were on the other side of the counter, not more than three feet away. He smiled at the girl before looking at her mother. "Take her home," he said in a low voice.

She nodded once, picked up her daughter without a word. She gave Tom a look through the service window as she went, one he imagined that was meant to urge her husband to come with her. Tom shook his head—never once taking his eyes off Carson. He seemed to understand that this was it: the time for retribution had finally come. Tom wasn't going anywhere.

Ben turned to the crowded restaurant. "Alright, folks—today's your lucky day. Lunch is on me," he said with a smile, but the message was clear. People stood, looked at the pair of Desert Eagle pistols riding Ben's rib cage, and looked away. It was time to leave.

The restaurant cleared in record time. Ben ushered them all out and locked the door behind them while Lark pulled the blinds. He stood over Carson, joined by Tom on the other side of the counter. He looked at him. "Package come for me?"

"Yup," Tom said. "In my office."

He looked at Ben. "Gun's in the back. Some assembly required."

Ben looked at Lark. "Take care of it."

Lark shook his head. "When did I turn into the unit bitch?"

"When you opened your mouth and started squawking like one," Ben said.

He waited for Lark to leave before he pulled the .38 off his hip and laid it on the counter between him and Carson. "Where is she?"

Carson finally looked up at him, seemed absolutely unconcerned with the fact that he was hemmed in by a couple of gun-toting thugs. He looked at Tom. "You're just lovin' this aren't you, Tomahawk?"

Tom shrugged. "It doesn't suck."

Michael snapped his finger in front of Carson's face. "Sabrina's missing. I left her last night and now she's gone." He placed his hand on the gun. "Where is she? That's the last time I'm gonna ask nice." He watched Carson's gaze drift down, settle on the hand that rested on the gun between them. Carson looked up. Smiled. *Go ahead and try.*

The invitation was clear, but apparently Carson recognized that going for the gun would be a mistake. Instead, he leaned away from it, looked over his shoulder at Ben standing behind him. "Where is she? I don't have a fucking clue, but I can do you one better, O'Shea." He shifted to the side, pulled something out of his back pocket. Carson slapped it on the counter, nudged the gun out of the way to do it.

He looked down, felt his throat go tight. It was a picture of Sabrina and the twins on the front porch of their house.

Carson tapped the photo with a calloused finger. "*Who* is she?"

SEVENTY-FOUR

SABRINA WOKE IN THE dark, riding wave after wave of nausea as the last of whatever Kelly had stuck her with worked its way through her system. Feeling the gorge rise in her throat, she breathed, drawing air into her lungs in deep, slow pulls meant to calm her rising panic.

She was in the dark.

Closing her eyes, she focused on her breathing. Used her hands to feel around and recognized almost instantly that she was in the trunk of a car. Her hands were bound together at the wrist. She twisted and tugged. It felt like duct tape. She moved her hands to her side to confirm what she already knew. Her gun was gone and she didn't have a backup.

Panic climbed another notch. More deep breathing. She tried to listen to the sounds outside, but all she could hear was the frantic knock of her own heart. She focused on it, reined it in from a fast gallop to a steady trot. More deep breathing took it from a steady trot to a slow walk. The sounds outside came into focus, and she listened carefully.

Nothing.

She could feel the panic push its way up, but she shoved it down, refused to give in. She listened closer, held her breath. There was nothing. No cars in the far off distance. No airplanes overhead. No sound of water. Nothing...no, wait. The faint rustling of wind through treetops. The soft chatter of birds. Wherever she was, it was secluded.

She was in the middle of nowhere, trapped inside the trunk of a car. Michael was gone. No one knew where she was. Strickland would put it together, but that would get him only so far. He had no way of finding her, no way of sending help.

She was on her own.

SEVENTY-FIVE

MICHAEL PICKED UP THE wrinkled photo and flipped it over. On the back was Sabrina's name along with the twins' names and age. It was recent. A picture he'd never seen before. "Where'd you get this?"

"Charlie found it crammed inside Lucy's mouth." He shot a look at Tom. "Take a look, Tomahawk. See anything familiar?" Carson aimed the picture at him—that callused finger pointing the way. He watched Tom's face go blank for a moment before recognition dawned. He looked at Carson before shooting him a disbelieving look.

"That scar … " Tom looked at the picture again, couldn't seem to look away.

"It's her, isn't it?" Carson tapped the crumpled picture again. "That's Melissa."

Michael ignored him, looked at Ben. "How far are you willing to go?"

Ben cracked a smile made for charming coeds. "Miles and miles." He clapped Carson on the shoulder. "My boy asked you a question, Mayberry. Where's the woman?"

Carson moved to shove Ben's hand off his shoulder. "Fuck—"

Ben grabbed his wrist and twisted, used the stool to swivel him around and his forearm to bounce his head off the counter. "Wrong answer, Mayberry." He took the cuffs off Carson's belt and slapped them on his wrists before he could blink. Ben lifted the gun off Carson's hip and glanced at Tom. "Ever shoot someone before?"

Tom shook his head.

Ben flipped the safety off and racked back the slide. "Easy-peasy— just point and pull."

He looked like he was giving Tom a tutorial on how to knit a sweater. "Now you're one of the cool kids. If he moves, shoot him. Aim for his balls—you'll probably hit his face." Ben handed the gun over the counter to Tom.

Tom took the gun. "I can do that."

"He's all yours," Ben said on his way toward the back of the restaurant. "I'm going to see what's keeping Lark—you kids play nice."

As soon as Ben was gone, Michael picked up the picture. The sight of her face, that rare smile, hit him low in the gut.

He looked over the top of the photo and found Carson's baleful glare. "I'm going to kill you—that's a given. But if you don't tell me where Sabrina is, I'm going to do things to you that'll make what you put her through look like a trip to Disneyland."

———

Waiting had always been the worst part. The part where panic found the time to build and grow into something uncontrollable and ugly. Something that could break her down. Destroy her. Yes, waiting had always been the worst part ... but not this time.

This time she used her time in the dark to remind herself that she was strong. Capable. She was no one's victim. Not anymore.

First order of business was to find a weapon. She wormed her way onto her side and searched the dark interior of the car. Used her hands to take stock of what was in the trunk. Not much. A plastic bag. What felt like a bottle of water. Her throat was on fire and he mouth felt like it was full of sand, but she didn't trust it. He used to drug her food and water. She left it unopened and moved on but found nothing but empty space. Nothing that would serve as a weapon. All she had was herself. It would have to be enough.

She began working her wrists back and forth, twisting them inside the tape. It would take some time, but if she could work them loose she'd have a chance. She was awake. He wouldn't expect that. She'd have to strike hard—strike first.

Another gust of wind rustled the treetops. Birds chattered softly. A rumbling ... faint and far off in the distance. The sound of the engine grew louder, joined by the crunch of gravel and brush beneath tires until the vehicle drew to a stop no more than a few yards away. The rumbling engine was cut short, magnifying the silence that followed until it almost hummed in her ears.

Boots, hard and heavy, landed on dirt as whoever was out there left their vehicle. There was the sound of a car door slamming. No. Too heavy for a car. A truck. It was a truck. The person out there wasn't trying for stealth. They were announcing their presence.

They began walking, footsteps growing faint, then louder and louder as they slowly circled the car, coming to rest in front of the trunk.

"Is someone here?" a voice called out. It was one she recognized. One she trusted.

She swallowed the sob locked in her throat. "Yes! I'm in the trunk—get me the hell out of here!"

SEVENTY-SIX

MICHAEL GLANCED AT THE clock above the service window. It was just after one. Strickland said he talked to her around ten thirty. Two and a half hours. Long enough for Carson to grab her, put her somewhere, and keep her there while he played the part of concerned police chief.

Two and a half hours was a long time.

He looked down at the .38 in his hand, then at the 9mm in Tom's. He tucked the .38 into his waistband and gestured for the gun in Tom's hand. Tom turned it over without protest.

He pressed the 9mm against Carson's shoulder and pulled the trigger.

The gun roared, bucked in his hand. The bullet tore through the meat of his shoulder on its way out. It traveled fast, burrowed into the red vinyl booth across the room. Carson flipped off the back of the stool, landed on his face and cried out. Fight or flight kicked in, and he tried to use his other shoulder to pull himself across the carpet.

Michael stepped on him, flipped him over with his boot and pinned him to the floor. He pointed the gun at his other shoulder. "Nothing worse than getting shot with your own gun."

"Fuck you, O'Shea," Carson said through clenched teeth. "You think you're gonna get away with this? Zeke and Wade are on their way here right now. *You just shot a cop.*" He was sweating and bleeding everywhere, snot and tears running down his face.

He looked around the empty diner and shrugged. "No Wade. No Zeke." He reached across the counter and grabbed the towel off Tom's shoulder. "No one is coming for you. No one cares," he said and shook his head. He tossed the towel onto Carson's shoulder and stepped on it to control the bleeding. Carson screamed, looked like he was about to pass out. He stepped harder. "No, you don't—you wake the fuck up. Where is she?"

"I don't know!"

"Right, just like you don't know what happened to my sister," he said dispassionately.

"I didn't kill your fucking sister!"

He turned to Tom, who was watching the whole thing with a look that said he wasn't sure he wanted to run with the cool kids anymore. "Hey." He waited for Tom to look at him. "You with me?" he said.

Tom hesitated, looked down at Carson then back at him. He nodded.

"Good." He looked back down at the man under his boot. "Got a corkscrew in that kitchen?"

"Yeah. Got a few."

He smiled. "Fabulous. Go get 'em." He stepped harder on Carson's shoulder. "I'm also gonna need an ice pick, a paring knife, and something that'll separate joints."

"Got a cleaver," Tom said.

Michael smiled down at the man beneath his boot. "That'll work."

Carson started to jerk around like he was in the middle of a full-blown seizure. "No, no—don't. I'm telling you the truth. I didn't kill Frankie, I swear to God," he said, frantically bouncing a look of sheer terror between him and Tom. "I loved Melissa. I couldn't have hurt her. I'd have died for her."

Michael looked down and didn't like what he saw. A man telling the truth.

"Where's Sabrina?"

"Okay ... okay." Carson swallowed hard. "Last I saw, she was hauling ass out of the parking lot at Charlie's. I called her this morning to ask her if she wanted to sit in on Lucy's autopsy. We hadn't been there five minutes before she got a call and left," he said, shaking his head. "Haven't seen or heard from her since, I swear."

"That was a call from her partner, telling her the car that dumped her murder victim in San Francisco was a match to one owned by Pete Conners," he said.

"Pete Conners?"

"Yeah. Wade told her this morning he wrote Pete a ticket, driving a car that—surprise, surprise—matches the car involved in Billy Bauer's murder." He shook his head. "Only trouble is, no one's seen or heard from Pete Conners in nearly twenty years."

"That can't be right." Carson said, dividing a confused look between him and Tom. "Are you sure?"

Something cold rattled down his spine. He used his boot to put pressure on Carson's wound. "What do you mean?"

Carson yelped. "Conners is dead. Melissa killed him. He tried to rape her—she nearly took his head off with a bat. Afterward she showed up at the station, looking for Billy, freaking out. He took care of everything, covered it all up."

"Who told you that?"

"Billy—Billy did. Right before Wade and I helped him bury the body."

SEVENTY-SEVEN

"Hold tight miss, I'm coming," he said, circling his way around the front of the car. The sound of his work boots made a scuffling sound as he hurried through the dirt. Sabrina could hear him testing doors, could feel the jerk of him pulling on the handles. "Doors are locked. I have to break the window," he said.

Seconds later she heard the shattering of glass. A moment later the trunk popped open, the blinding light of day reaching through the crack to stab her eyes. A wave of nausea, brought on by the light, hit her but passed quickly.

The trunk opened, revealing the shape of her savior, his features thrown into deep shadows by the sun that sat high in the sky behind him. "Inspector Vaughn?" he said incredulously, staring down at her for a moment as if he couldn't quite grasp what he was seeing.

"Last time I checked," she said, her hands shielding her narrowed eyes. She pulled herself into a sitting position, the sudden movement causing the dregs of the narcotics she'd been hit with to take a drunken spin through her system. She swung her legs over the edge of the trunk despite the roll of her gut and closed her eyes for a moment. Something slipped through the tape around her wrists, cutting her free. "Thanks. Where are we?" she said, pulling the rest of the tape off and dropped it into the trunk.

Looking around, she noted the dense line of trees that hemmed them in on three sides. A rundown cabin stood at her back. He'd left her in the trunk, not expecting her system to fight off the effects of the drugs so quickly.

But he'd be back.

"Not sure really. Private land, looks like someone's hunting cabin. Did you see who put you in the trunk?" he said, his face taking a wary cast as he scanned the trees and cabin for potential threats.

"Pete Conners … I think. What're you doing here?" she said, scoping the area for clues as to where she was and who'd brought her here.

"Got a call from a trooper on the BOLO we put out on Lucy's car. Said he saw it taking a rural turn-off on I-80. I was in the area, so I told him I'd come check it out." He looked down. "This is it. This is Lucy's car."

She wasn't surprised. It was probably under the tarp in Kelly's garage. She looked at him. "Wait, we're in Texas?" she said. His eyes narrowed on her face, a wary kind of concern crawled along his features.

"What the hell is going on here, Inspector?" he said, his eyes darting around the clearing.

"We need to get out of here, *now*." She pushed herself away from the car. The sudden movement was like a blow to the back of her knees, and they buckled slightly. She threw out a hand to steady herself and he caught it, holding her up.

"You don't look so good. Do you need some water? Here—" He reached past her and into the trunk to pull out the water. "Drink this. You look like you could use it." He tried to press the bottle in to her hand.

She pushed it away. "No, I'm not drinking that. He drugged it."

"What?" He looked down at the container in his hand. "How do you know?"

"I just do . . . look, I don't need water. I need a cell phone, a gun, and a ride into town." She stood with care, bracing her hand on the rear fender of the car to steady herself.

"The battery on my cell is dead, and this is the only piece I carry," he said, dropping his hand to the butt of a 9mm. "But I can give you a lift back to town. You want to check the cabin for a phone before we head out?" He moved toward the squat log structure even before she answered, leaving her little choice but to follow him.

He walked a few steps ahead of her, his gait sure and confident, his hand resting on the butt of his gun, the holster snap thumbed open to ensure an easy draw in case they ran into trouble. Another gust of wind swept through the clearing, kicked up dust, blew it into her eyes.

She stopped in her tracks. "Shit." She reached up to shield her face from the assault. After years of wearing them, it took her only a second to realize, as she was rubbing her eyes, that there was no synthetic slide of plastic against her eyes. Her colored contacts were gone.

He had seen her. Stood no more than a few feet from her. Looked into her eyes while he talked to her. He was a cop. A trained observer. He had to have noticed the sudden color change—but he'd said nothing, displayed no reaction whatsoever. Her heart stalled in her chest, her hands dropped away from her face, her discomfort forgotten.

"Wade."

She said his name quietly, but it was enough to stall his stride. He turned to look at her and she felt the rolling nausea that'd been plaguing her swell inside her gut, but this feeling had nothing to do with the drugs. This had everything to do with the way he looked at her. Head cocked in a predatory tilt, a slight half-smile lifting the corner of his mouth.

She could see just how easily he'd fooled them all.

He closed his eyes for a moment, dragged a deep breath into his lungs, and let it out on a sigh.

"Finally."

SEVENTY-EIGHT

MICHAEL LOOKED UP AT Tom. "Go get Ben—the kid. Go get the kid." Tom took off for the back.

Carson had lost a lot of blood. A Band-Aid and a lollipop wasn't gonna cut it. "Did you and Wade go to Caddo?" he said.

Carson hesitated, looked like he was going to hold on to the lie. Michael shook his head, applied pressure with his foot. "Lying? Not a good idea right now. Did you and Wade go to Caddo?"

Carson groaned and shook his head. "I went but not Wade. He's got a side-piece in Shreveport. He sees her every few weeks or so."

"What's up?"

He looked up to see Ben coming at him. "I need a field dressing."

"So much for playing nice," he said and hurried back into the kitchen.

Michael lifted his foot to check the wound. The towel was completely saturated. He reapplied pressure. "Where's Wade now?"

"Out on an early call—trespassing. He was still gone when I got back to the station. He radioed in, told Zeke he caught a call from a trooper that said he spotted Lucy's car on I-80, so he was going to check it out."

He stopped, thought about what was logical. If Wade had Sabrina, he'd need somewhere to keep her. Somewhere secluded. "Wade has a place—somewhere he goes to be alone. Where is it?"

"What? No—no. You think Wade killed … no. No way." Carson shook his head, tried to sit up.

"Think about it." He felt the pieces fall into place, could actually hear them click together. "You told Sabrina that you found Melissa in Yuma. Who did you tell?" he said, and Carson started to shake his head again. "Look, no way you kept that to yourself. That's something you'd tell a best friend. Something you'd tell her brother."

Carson went still—his face pale as much from blood loss as it was from the blow the truth dealt him. "Oh God … "

"Who told you Melissa was missing? How'd you find out?"

"I … Wade. I was back at college in California. He called, told me she was missing … Lucy'd come to his dad and told him she hadn't called in weeks." Carson blinked slowly, his words began to slur and drift.

Where the fuck was Ben?

Carson opened his eyes. "I came home for Christmas break—that was when they found her … I never went back. I stayed here … for her."

Just then, Ben brushed past him with a stack of clean towels and roll of plastic wrap. He uncuffed Carson and used his tactical knife to cut his shirt off at the shoulder. Ben examined the wound, looked up at him. "He needs a hospital. This'll slow it down, but he's in pretty bad shape."

"I know—just do what you can."

Ben padded his shoulder with the towels and used the plastic wrap to bind them tightly to the wound. Finished, he clapped Carson on his wounded shoulder. "How's that feel, Mayberry?"

"Fuck you." Carson looked up at him. "Is it her? Is she Melissa? Please, just tell me … "

"Yes." He had to force the word out and had a hard time looking Carson in the eye when he did it. He could feel Tom behind him, knew he'd heard. "Yes, it's her."

Carson closed his eyes. He'd thought he finally passed out, but then he opened them, looked up at him. "A hunting cabin—used to be his dad's. Billy used to take us there when we were kids … fifty miles north of here. If he has her, that's where he took her."

SEVENTY-NINE

SABRINA'S EYES DARTED AROUND, looking for an exit. There was none. She looked at the cabin behind him, knew without a doubt that if he managed to get her into it, she would never get out. The 9mm on Wade's hip promised that her chances of running for it were slim.

"Look at me, Melissa," he said, and suddenly it was a voice she recognized, one that haunted her nightmares. "Look. At. Me," he said again. He lifted his gun from its holster, pointing the muzzle downward, but the implication was clear. She looked up, found his face, unable to comprehend what she was seeing—stubbornly refused to believe it. It wasn't possible. It couldn't be him—not him.

Anyone but him.

"You're my—" She gagged on the last word. It snagged on her tongue and refused to leave her mouth.

"Brother," he said with a shrug. "That's what makes us perfect for each other."

She needed time to think—would need to stall him for it. "My mother?"

He laughed. "I'd been a regular of hers since I was fifteen. Pretty sure she enjoyed the irony of it all."

"You killed her."

He cocked his head to the side and winced. "She no longer served a purpose—so, yeah."

"And our—Billy ... "

"Well, now—ol' daddy-o didn't leave me much choice. He caught me with a Waffle House waitress from Texarkana in my trunk." His smile broadened. "But you ... you killed Pete all by yourself."

That night was a blur, one she tried not to think of. "He's really dead? Kelly said—"

"Kelly said and did whatever I told her to. A bit of misdirection to keep you guessing. Couldn't have you figuring it out before I was ready. Pete's been dead since you pulled a Barry Bonds and cracked his egg with that bat of yours. Jed, Dad, and me, we buried him in these woods—was supposed to bury the bat too, but I kept it. I'm sentimental that way."

"You used it to kill Sanford." She thought of Sanford—his crushed face, covered in blood. *Time.* She needed more time.

He shook his head. "No. I'm pretty sure it was all the stabbing that killed him." He took another step closer, but not close enough for her to go on the attack without catching a bullet for her trouble. Her gaze drifted to the gun in his hand.

"You think I'm gonna kill you?" he said and laughed. "Where's the fun in that?" He matched her movements as she slid along the body of the car, just a fraction of an inch, toward the trunk. "To tell the truth, I hate guns. Too impersonal." He winked at her. "You remember what I like, don't you, Melissa?"

"I remember you're a sick, twisted son of a bitch who can't get it up unless he's in the middle of killing something," she said. He took a few steps back before he stopped and smiled at her.

"You say that like it's a bad thing," he said, feigning hurt moments before he lifted the gun and pulled the trigger.

EIGHTY

THE BULLET TORE THROUGH the flesh of her thigh, ripping muscle as it punched through the other side. The force of it knocked her off her feet and into the dirt, flat on her back. Teeth gritted, she refused to cry out as white-hot pain seared her leg from hip to toe. She stared up at an impossibly blue patch of sky surrounded by green treetops and tried to remember how to breathe.

Wade holstered his gun and leaned over to examine her thigh but kept his distance. "Yup. That ought to do it."

She refused to look at him. "Fuck you."

"It's a through and through, what's the big deal? You're a badass, remember? I'm just a dumb hick cop—had to level the playing field." He grinned down at her.

"Gutless piece of shit," she hissed through gritted teeth.

He came toward her, two steps closer than was prudent, and had no time to stop the attack. Her good leg whipped out, the heel of her boot hammering into his kneecap, and he dropped like a stone.

She fisted a hand in his hair and drove her knee into his face, but it struck the hard bone of his forehead instead, doing little damage. Her other hand grappled for the gun in his holster, her fingers closed around the butt of it. Before she could pull it clear he stopped her cold, landing a heavily-fisted blow to her thigh, dead center on the hole he'd put in it.

A scream tore through her throat, taking her fight with it as it rushed up and out into the sky. She went limp, her vision going gray around the edges while she fought to stay conscious.

"I gotta hand it to you, you're a helluva lot feistier than I remember," he said. Standing, he leaned against Lucy's car. "That's good. I like it. Most girls I bring here just cry and beg me not to kill 'em ... sooo boring." Wade looked down at her, the corner of his mouth lifted in a crooked smile. "Don't worry, Melissa, I thought about you the whole time. You know what they say—you never forget your first."

She rolled onto her side in the dirt, clutched her thigh, and said nothing. The nausea from the drugs was nothing compared to the pain that crowded her, pushed in and crushed her from all sides.

He stood up straight, taking a glance at his watch. "Alright— enough lollygaggin'," he said, giving the bottom of her foot a playful kick. "We're gonna play, you and me. I want you to run."

He wanted to chase her, run her down like an animal. "Eat shit, you crazy hillbilly."

"*Crazy* ... okay." He point the gun at her other thigh and pulled the trigger. The bullet slammed into the ground, bare inches from her leg, kicking up a plume of dust that stung her eyes. "Consider that a warning." He sighed. "You're either gonna run, or I'm gonna make that hole in your leg a matched set. Then I'll drag you by your hair into our little love nest, and you'll never see the light of day again. Maybe I'll hop a plane and go get us a new playmate. You think little Riley is ready for some fun and games?"

She thought about her baby sister. About how bright and innocent she was. About the things he would do to her if ever given the chance. Rage and hate flashed, white-hot, in her gut, blinded her for just a moment. Gripping the bumper, she pulled herself up, leaning on the car, favoring her injured leg.

A steady river of blood flowed from her thigh, into her boot. The tacky warmth of it between her thighs ignited a hellish nightmare of memories that flashed in front of her, random and out of sequence.

"Nearest neighbor is ten miles from here—just a short stretch of the legs for you, which is why I had to slow you down a bit. I'll give you five minutes and then it's game on. I'll even leave the gun behind, maybe you can circle back around and get to it in time," he said.

"Why? Why not just take me inside and get started?" *More time…* she needed to steel herself against the pain that would careen through her body the moment she applied pressure to her leg. The smile perched on his face tightened around his mouth, drawing it into a sneer.

"Because you need to remember what you are," he said. "You're mine. No matter what you do, no matter who you try to become, you can't change that." He looked at his watch and then back at her. "Four minutes."

Without warning, she spun on her good leg, dug the heavy sole of her boot into the soft earth of the clearing and pushed herself away from the car. She did the only thing she could do. She ran.

EIGHTY-ONE

SHE WON'T LET YOU.

Wade watched her run into the trees. Truthfully it was more of a hobbling lurch, but Lucy's words stuck with him. They'd been pushing him since she'd said them, worrying him that maybe she'd been right.

She'd changed. No helpless cowering. No begging for mercy. He realized that he'd had a hand in her metamorphosis. That it'd been the pressure and pain he'd applied during their time spent in the dark that had changed her.

She was different. She wasn't his Melissa anymore.

That fucking trooper had ruined it all—spotted him in Lucy's car on I-80 and called it in. With the trooper about to investigate, he had to leave her in the trunk and double back to the main road in the JPD Blazer. He cut the trooper off at the pass, assured him that he'd patrol the area and keep him informed. It had taken longer than expected. By the time he'd gotten back to the cabin, he wasn't sure she was still entirely under the influence of the Ativan

Kelly injected her with. He left a bottle of water laced with GHB in the trunk, but he had little hope that she'd actually drink it.

He'd thought of popping the trunk and hauling her out at gunpoint but knew doing so would be a mistake. He'd seen her in action, knew how dangerous she could be in a close contact situation. He decided to err on the side of caution and called out to her under the guise of potential rescuer. If she responded, he'd let her out of the trunk and lure her into the cabin. If not, he'd know she was still out cold and just drag her inside. She'd been awake and it had gotten messy. Things hadn't gone as he'd planned, but they were still salvageable.

He frowned down at the gun in his hand, momentarily regretting his decision to challenge her. His daddy's words came back to him: *Nothing good ever comes easy, boy.*

His daddy was right. The truth was that he could never look at her, touch her, hurt her, unless he knew for sure that *he* was the thing to be feared. Not a piece of metal. And she had to know it too.

He ejected the clip from the gun and thumbed the bullets into the dirt before slapping it back home. He popped the last bullet out of the chamber and laid the gun on the lid of the trunk as promised. He found his knife folded up in the pocket of his khakis and flicked it open. He looked at his watch.

Time was up.

"Ready or not, here I come." He tilted his head back and yelled it to the sky. Suddenly, he felt strong. He felt ready. His Melissa was in there somewhere, hiding.

He just needed to peel back the layers until he found her.

EIGHTY-TWO

SABRINA RAN. EVERY STEP she took made her feel like a coward and a weakling, but she ran anyway. Survival was the only thing that mattered. She thought of Riley, of what would happen to her sister if she was dead, or worse—captured. The only way to save Riley was to kill Wade. Survival was key.

The moment she hit the trees she changed direction, traveling for a few steps before changing directions again, this time traveling for a few hundred. Weaving this way and that, blindly through the brush—low-slung branches slapping at her face and arms as she rushed forward in a blind panic. Her only thought was to get as much distance between her and Wade as possible before her leg gave out.

Wade…

The thought of him, gun in hand, grinning down at her pushed renewed power into her legs but she knew it'd be short-lived. She was bleeding badly, her thigh coated in it, the loss making her dizzy, but she pushed on. Her initial burst of speed lagged to a shuffling lurch and she fought to keep her feet beneath her. What should've been easy now took every ounce of strength she possessed. She changed directions even though she knew she couldn't outrun him, not with a bullet hole in her leg. She needed to find a place to hide, assess the damage done to her leg. But she was too close to the clearing to stop and dress the wound.

She'd never make it, even if he were telling the truth about the neighbors. Ten miles might as well be a hundred in her condition. Every step was agony. A pain so intense that every footfall brought her to the brink of unconsciousness, but she'd learned long ago how to pull away from it, to float above the pain. She did so now, thinking of nothing else but putting one foot in front of the other.

Four minutes. She had four minutes to get as far away as possible, and that was only if Wade played fair. His face, handsome and earnest, shoved its way to the forefront of her mind.

It was Wade. Her brother.

She heard him call out, tease her that he was coming, that her time was up. Her heart sank.

He sounded so close.

She wasn't far enough to keep running and expect to survive. Without the hole in her leg, she would've been nearly a mile away by now, but she hadn't even managed to cover a quarter of that distance. If she kept going, he would simply run her down. Scanning the area, she spotted a fallen tree a few yards ahead and gunned for it. Diving behind it, she hunkered down in an effort to conceal herself.

With shaky hands, she stripped her shirt off in favor of the black tank she wore underneath. Her shirt was red and would be easily spotted, even through the dense screen of trees she hid in. Next she unbuttoned her cargo pants, sliding them down to mid-thigh in an effort to survey the damage to her thigh.

It was a bloody mess. The hole punched through it a deep, weeping well of blood. Twisting her shirt around itself, she wound it around her leg, high above the wound, tying the sleeves together in a tight knot in an effort to, if not stop the bleeding, slow it down. Yanking her pants back in place, she tried to think about what came next.

A weapon. She needed a weapon. She raised herself on her haunches, felt the binding around her thigh squeeze tight. She leaned to the side, taking pressure off her injured leg and began scrounging in the dirt for a stick, a rock ... anything that would serve as a mean to hurt him.

Her fingers closed on something small and hard, but smooth. Too smooth to be a rock. She picked it up, examined it—and knew almost immediately what it was.

It was a bone.

A vertebra—from the size and shape she knew that it was human. That it belonged to a young girl who used to have blue eyes. She looked into the surrounding trees and felt ill. They were here. This is where all those girls disappeared to. Left in the open, exposed to the elements and the wild animals she was sure inhabited these woods. Grief and panic came for her, but she was ready. She broke away—detached herself from what she held in her hand. There would be time for grieving, but not now.

Placing it gently on the ground, she scrounged, found more bones, and placed them in a growing pile until she found what she was looking for.

EIGHTY-THREE

WADE WOUND HIS WAY through the dense cover of trees and brush—zigzagging through the woods. There was no pattern—some distances were covered for a few feet, others for several yards, but they always changed direction. He had no idea where she had gone.

Truth was, his neighbors were more like fifty miles away. But if he'd told her that—that there was no possible way she'd ever find help—it would've ruined everything. He'd learned over the years that it was when he gave them hope that he had the most fun.

Finding a fallen tree, Wade hopped over the bulk of it, ignoring the twinge in his injured knee. He crouched, took a few seconds to look the spot over. Bent foliage, tacky smudges of blood congealed on them. She'd taken brief refuge here. The small pile of bones was interesting—she'd found one of his toys. The terror she must have felt when she realized what she held in her hand was almost palpable.

He imagined her binding her wound, resting the frantic gallop of her heart as she lamented over the futility of it all; and he smiled, taking a deep breath, drawing in her scent. He ran his fingers along the leaves that bore her blood and brought them to his lips. His tongue slipped from his mouth of its own volition, needing a taste.

The power that zinged through his veins lit him up like a bucket of fireworks. Stars exploded in front of his eyes. Every fiber, every synapse, every molecule of his being was electrified, set on fire. He stood slowly, feet shifting themselves, pointing in the right direction.

Pointing toward her.

He moved with purpose, weaving through the trees, as sure of where he was going as he was of the blood that pulled him along—and that the woman he was being pulled toward belonged to him and him alone.

EIGHTY-FOUR

MICHAEL CRANKED THE WHEEL, took the turn fast. The road was little more than a footpath, narrow and caged in by trees. The Hummer ate the terrain, slinging rocks and debris out of its way. A few miles in was a fork in the road, forcing him to slow to a crawl.

They'd split up. He'd sent Tom home to his family, and Shaw and Lark had taken Carson to the hospital while he went after Sabrina. The coordinates Carson had given him, fed into the Hummer's GPS, said to take a left. The road was supposed take him around the back and bring him in behind the cabin that sat on the property. He began to wonder and worry that Carson was playing him. He hesitated, but only for a second. She was here. She had to be. He cranked the wheel to the left and punched the gas.

After a few miles he checked his progress. Carson had told him that the cabin sat pretty snug against the surrounding foothills. He could see the craggy outcropping of rock dotted with scrub brush. He braked and killed the engine.

He geared up quietly and thought for the hundredth time that this whole thing could be a setup—that maybe Carson and Wade were in this together. He dropped the Kimber into his holster, tucked a few *just in case* items in various pockets. It didn't matter. Wade was going to die bloody, and if he was involved, so was Carson. He'd make sure of it.

It was an easy walk and he made it silently, his head on a constant swivel. The cabin came into view. It was little more than a run-down shack with boarded-up windows, a dilapidated back porch, and a sagging roof.

Weapon in hand, he approached the porch. Taking the steps quickly, he studied the back door. On rusty hinges, it looked surprisingly sturdy. So did the industrial-size padlock that bolted it closed.

Shooting off padlocks looked cool in the movies, but it didn't always work. And it would alert whoever might be nearby that he was there. He pulled out his lock-pick set and had the padlock free within a minute.

Hand on the knob, he gave it a testing turn. It rolled in his hand without protest. Waiting a few seconds, he rushed in, gun raised. It took a moment to see that the cabin was deserted. Then he lowered his gun and took in the horrors around him.

From the outside, the cabin was old, rotted wood, but it was a clever deception. The interior walls had been covered in cinder block, including the boarded-up windows, and the floor was a thick pad of concrete. He stared at it. Stains bloomed across almost every square inch, overlapping in variegated shades of rust, some years old. Some newer.

He recognized them instantly for what they were: bloodstains. He surveyed the room. There were surveillance cameras mounted in every corner, all of them pointed directly at the large stainless-steel table bolted to the floor in the middle of the room. There were lengths of chain also bolted to the floor. At the end of each was an iron manacle, some big enough to fit a person's neck, others the size of the average ankle.

On the opposite wall stood a sink and hot plate, and on the short length of worn countertop were tools. Pliers and knives. Lengths of wire and straight edge razors. A blow torch. On the shelf above the sink were jelly jars full of cloudy liquid. In each were floating masses he recognized as human eyes. Inside one of those jars were eyes belonging to his baby sister.

This is where Frankie had been taken. Where she'd been kept and killed. Her blood was here, seeped into the rough concrete floor.

Just another stain in the countless layers beneath his feet.

He felt grief and anger well up inside him, as it always did when he thought of his sister, but he pushed it down. He couldn't do what needed to be done if he allowed himself to be pulled under by the riptide of emotion that tugged at him. Frankie was gone; he couldn't help her. Sabrina was alive; she needed him. In order to save Sabrina, he'd have to let Frankie go.

He turned away from the jars and tools and noted that none of the blood on the floor was new. Any blood that was Sabrina's would've been fresh. That and the fine layer of dust settled on the table said that wherever she was, she hadn't been brought into the cabin.

She wasn't here, had never been here, and he felt a homicidal rage coming on. He'd been played, lied to. Sabrina was fighting for her life somewhere, and he'd let her down. Why he allowed himself to hope that this time, this woman, would be any different, he'd never understand.

He found his phone, about to call Ben and have him kill Carson for lying when it came to him: the woods.

She was in the woods.

EIGHTY-FIVE

THE FIRST THING MICHAEL saw was Lucy's car, parked haphazardly in a clearing just on the other side of the cabin. He ran for it, hating the hope that pushed him forward. He reached through the shattered window and popped the trunk before heading toward it. He saw the gun resting on the lid and picked it up. It wasn't the Super Colt he'd given Sabrina. It was a 9mm, exactly like Carson's. Wade's service weapon.

It felt light. He ejected the clip and saw that it was empty. He racked the slide back and checked the chamber. Empty.

He tucked the empty 9mm into his waistband and lifted the lid of the trunk. Saw the balled-up wad of duct tape. Thought about Sabrina, bound and trapped in the dark.

Hunkering down, he surveyed the ground in front of him. This time the blood he found was freshly spilled, soaked into the soft dirt of the clearing. Two shell casings and several unspent bullets littered the ground. He scooped a few out of the dirt and jiggled them in his hand while he studied the casing. Wade had shot her.

If it'd been the other way around, he'd be crouched over Wade's corpse rather than a patch of fresh blood. Why he shot her was something he couldn't figure out. But *why* didn't matter.

What mattered was that Sabrina was wounded and on the run. Wade's absence told him that he wasn't far behind her. It was the only logical explanation. He studied the blood, tried to make sense of what he was seeing and what he held in his hand. Why the bullets were on the ground and not in the gun was something else he couldn't figure out. He surveyed the clearing, saw the JPD blazer parked a few yards away. He stood to check it out and wasn't at all surprised to see that the radio inside it had been gutted.

Michael gazed into the trees for a moment—tried to listen for her. He wanted to yell her name, let her know he'd come for her, but he held his tongue. He had no idea where she was or how long she'd been running. Wade's whereabouts were unknown. Calling out to her could put her in danger. If she was injured, she'd know that making a run for it wouldn't be possible. She'd do her best to double back to the clearing, try for either the radio in Wade's truck or the gun he'd left behind. Only, if she did manage to make it back, all she'd find was a broken radio and an empty gun. She'd need at least one of them is she was going to survive.

He couldn't do anything about the radio. The gun was a different story.

He pulled Carson's 9mm from the small of his back. After depositing it onto the trunk lid of Lucy's car, he headed into the woods.

———

It'd been nearly an hour and Wade hadn't seen hide nor hair of his quarry and quite frankly, he was getting pissed. Rage rose up, drowned out everything else. This was wrong. All wrong. The rage grew, burned in his blood.

Blood ...

He came to an abrupt standstill and closed his eyes. He was forgetting he was connected to her. He could feel her, find her, if he let her blood lead him. Taking a few deep, cleansing breaths, he felt the connection grab hold, clutch him tight in a desperate fist that kicked his pulse up to a rapid hammering against his temple. He could *feel* her.

She was close.

He snapped his eyes open. Piloted by the whiplash turn of his neck, he caught a flash of movement to the left. A bare arm pumping frantically as his prey ran through the trees some distance away, going much faster than she should've been able to with a hole in her leg. Another deep breath brought him her scent, that sweet smell he missed so much. She was making a run for it, hoping to make the clearing and the gun he left there in time to kill him.

He smiled. Clipped his knife closed and dropped it into his pocket

She was never going to make it.

EIGHTY-SIX

Fueled by an adrenaline she knew couldn't last, Sabrina ran full speed. Nothing more than an easy jog for her, pre-GSW, but it was fast enough to put distance between her and Wade. At least for the time being.

She'd circled around, followed him at a safe distance, watched him amble through the woods, knife in hand, following the trail she left for him.

The element of surprise was an important advantage, one she would have to seize when the opportunity presented itself. He was frustrated. Angry. Things were not happening the way he envisioned. Disbelief rolled off of him in waves and she knew that if she was going to attack, it would have to be soon. Staring at the huge blade gripped in his fist, she ignored the throbbing in her leg and the tingling sensation that snaked its way from boot to hip.

She was about ten minutes from passing out and maybe another fifteen from dying. Too much blood had been lost for her to wait much longer.

He stopped midstride, closed his eyes, and took a deep breath. Driven by pure instinct, she ran, the pain in her thigh fading beneath the pounding surge of adrenaline.

Stomping the urge to look behind her, she ran past him, not more than twenty yards away. The sound of snapping twigs and crunching leaves fell heavily upon the silent wood, amplified by her instincts but also muffled by the rush of blood in her ears. She knew the instant he spotted her, and she pushed even harder for the break in the trees.

If she'd planned correctly, she'd emerge from the east, behind the car and the gun. She could hear him behind her. His footfalls fast and heavy beneath the sounds of her own terrified scramble.

He was close. *Too close.*

Her plan was falling apart. It was too soon. She tried to force another burst of speed from her battered leg, but there was nothing left. She faltered. Her leg buckled, turned to pudding, and she knew it was over. The hairs on the back of her neck started to prickle mere moments before she felt the painful yank of his hand as it fisted in her hair, pulling her off her feet and tossing her face down in the dirt.

"I told you, Melissa, you're never gonna get away from me." He gripped her shoulder, rolled her toward him, a sadistic glimmer in his eye. "I own you—you're *mine*," he said.

He didn't see the strike—didn't see her bring the broken length of bone up. She drove it forward, aimed for his gut but struck too low. Its jagged tip punctured his khakis and skin, made a quarter-sized hole in his groin. His eyes widened in surprise, his mouth went slack as all the clever words he had for her tumbled away on a low moan that was both pained and stunned.

His hand shot out, gripping her wrist like an iron clamp. Holding her and the bone in place, Wade closed his other hand into a fist and swung heavily into her face. Stars exploded in her eyes, fusing together into a solid field of white that seared away her vision.

She held onto consciousness, ripping herself from his grip with a snarl that sounded more animal than human. Crabbing back on her hands, she was unable to take her eyes off of him. Blood poured from her ruined mouth and nose, soaked her chest and hair. Even though she needed to run, she watched, horrified, as he lifted his bloodied fist to his mouth, running his tongue along his knuckles, lapping at the blood that coated them.

"That all you've got?" he said.

Revulsion tried to root her in place, but she kept moving backward. At a safe distance she flipped over and crawled, trying to find her feet.

The clearing, some fifty yards away, shone like a beacon she might never reach.

EIGHTY-SEVEN

THE MOMENT HE ENTERED the woods, years of training and instinct took over. Michael honed in on Sabrina's trail, following it swiftly.

He stopped, planted a hand, and vaulted a fallen tree, coming to rest in a crouch on the other side. She'd hunkered down here for a few minutes. Regrouped, probably dressed her wound. He touched the leaves of a nearby bush, holding them up to see. Blood.

He saw what looked like a pile of debris—nothing more that rocks and sticks. They puzzled him for a moment, and then he realized what they were.

Bones.

He stood, fought back the rising tide of rage that threatened to sweep him away. He looked away from the pile.

He reminded himself that she was a fighter. Tried to convince himself that she would survive. He wanted to believe it—*needed to*—but couldn't.

Find her... that was his focus, was all he cared about. He picked up her trail without a moment's hesitation, started to detect a subtle arc. She was doubling back on Wade, trying to get behind him. He lifted his field glasses, surveyed the woods slowly. He did a full sweep, caught movement almost directly behind him.

Sabrina was running—making a break for the clearing.

Wade was only a few steps behind.

EIGHTY-EIGHT

SABRINA MANAGED TO GET her legs beneath her again, took a few lurching steps before she was able to find a staggering rhythm that moved her forward. She bounced off of trees, stumbled over feet that were slow to respond to the frantic commands her brain was sending them.

It seemed to take years, but she finally burst into the clearing, nearly blinded by the explosion of light brought by the high afternoon sun. Wade was behind her; she'd wounded him, but it hadn't been enough.

He was coming at her fast. The knowledge spurred her to move faster, but her leg was slow to respond. It was over. She wasn't running another step.

She fell, those last few feet covered in a frantic stumble that had her throwing herself at the trunk of Lucy's car. She saw it. Couldn't believe it.

The gun was there.

She palmed it, kept a bracing hand planted on the lid of the trunk as she rounded on him. He stood at the hood, the knife in his fist held casually at his side.

"I gotta say, Wade, you don't look so hot." She pushed herself up, stood as tall as she could, and tried to raise the gun, which weighed heavy in her hand. Too heavy. It took every bit of strength she had just to hold on to it.

"You should talk. Awful pale, Melissa...whadd'ya think? Another minute or two before you pass out and this is all over?" He looked at the gun in her hand and seemed unconcerned that she held it. He smirked at her. "I think I'll wait."

The unsteady sway of the ground beneath her said he wasn't far from wrong. She could feel the darkness—see it from the corner of her eye. It was waiting...but it wouldn't wait forever. She had seconds, a minute at best, before it came for her.

She was dying. It was now or never.

The smirk on Wade's face deepened into a lopsided grin. "Guess you're not such a badass after all," he said and took a few steps toward her.

Her arm jerked upward in response, her finger tightening around the trigger. The bullet slammed into the ground that separated them. The loud bark of it knocked the smile right off Wade's face. He stopped midstride, his head cocked toward the woods.

"Well, ain't that interesting," he said and started forward again, closing the distance between them in long, confident strides.

She tried to move back, tried to keep distance between them, but her legs were a tangled mess beneath her and she went down hard, slamming into the rear fender of Lucy's car as she did. Desperate, she pulled the trigger again as she fell. This time the shot went wide, shattering the rear window of the car.

Even though she knew it was only midafternoon, Sabrina watched, flat on her back, as light faded from her field of vision. The darkness was tired of waiting.

She widened her eyes, tried to steal as much light as possible, but all she could see was Wade, standing over her. Laughing at her. "I'm gonna need that gun back, now—"

A final surge of strength cycloned its way through her body. It wrapped around her bones, fortified her muscles. She screamed, jerked the gun up, and carried by that final surge, drowned out his words with one last pull of the trigger.

The bullet slammed into Wade's face, ripped through his cheek—splintering bone as it burst through his opposite temple in an explosion of torn flesh and blood.

He fell to his knees. She pulled the trigger again. And again.

His ruined face was the last thing she saw before the darkness took her.

EIGHTY-NINE

MULTIPLE SHOTS FIRED, JUST beyond his line of vision. Michael broke through the trees, at a dead run. "Sabrina!" he shouted, stopping short at what he saw.

Legs, those black lace-up boots of hers, stuck out from behind the car. He rounded the hood and found Sabrina sprawled in the dirt, motionless. He fell on her, gathered her into his arms. She was breathing, but barely. Her skin, gray and cool, the gun he'd left for her held in a grip so tight her knuckles were white.

She was alive.

He looked at the body that lay a few feet away. Wade's face was gone, torn away by bullets. The only distinguishable feature—the only thing that that made him recognizable—was the badge pinned to his chest. Michael resisted the urge to stomp on it, tear him apart with his bare hands.

He held her, buried his face in her hair. She was alive, but he could feel her slipping away, like water between his fingers.

This darkness was different.

This time it was a healing void into which she retreated. The cool black pressed around her. Held her. Kept her safe.

Sounds penetrated its dense folds. The far-off approach of a helicopter. The mindless drone of voices sounding hurried and authoritative all at once. Someone spoke in angry, frantic tones while another someone spoke in a calm, quiet voice.

Through it all the warm, protective pressure of her hand being held in the grasp of another.

It was Michael. He was here with her, had come for her. It was a good thought and she clung to it. Needed it to see herself through.

NINETY

The pilot put out a restraining hand, barring him from boarding the air-evac helicopter. "I'm sorry, sir, there isn't room for extra passengers. We'll fly her to Good Shepherd in Marshall, if you want to follow along on the ground," the pilot said.

Michael looked down at the hand on his chest then bounced his glare back up. The pilot took one look at his face, dropped his hand, and took a step back, but still refused to move out of his way.

He looked at her, stretched out on a gurney, tubes and needles sticking out of her arms, her hair matted with dirt and blood, her pants hastily cut away to reveal the gruesome hole punched into the grayish skin of her thigh. Her eyes were closed, and he found himself wishing she would open them, just for a moment so that she could see that he was here, that he'd come for her. That he'd kept his promise.

Realizing he was being stared at, he tore his gaze from Sabrina's face to find the pilot still standing there, wedged between him and the chopper, waiting for him to either press the issue or relent. He was wasting time. He gave one terse nod before stepping back, letting her go.

The helicopter lifted off the ground, carried her away.

She's going to be fine... the words were worthless, and they rang false even as he thought them.

The blood loss had been tremendous; the fact that she was even still breathing was a miracle.

Miracle.

She was a fighter. A survivor. That she was even alive was a testament to that. She *was* a miracle. She was going to be okay. He had to believe that.

She'd survive—but he wouldn't be there to see her through. He stared up at the sky, watched until it was silent and clear. The helicopter was gone, and so was she.

NINETY-ONE

THE FAINT, RHYTHMIC, BEEP that punctuated the silence and the gnawing pain in her thigh told her everything she needed to know.

She was alive.

"I'll hate you—do you hear me? If you die, I'll never forgive you, I'll hate you for the rest of my life." It was said low, but the terrified tone pulled Sabrina out of the dark.

She felt her face crumple into a frown, but she didn't open her eyes. "Shhh ... sleeping," she said, in a weak, thready voice she barely recognized.

A sharp intake of breath delivered a strange half-laugh, half sob. "You aren't sleeping, jackass. You've been out of it for almost a week." It was Val.

She forced her lids open a crack, but through the slits, she could see her. It was just like last time ... Val staring at her, hoping against hope that she'd be whole when she finally opened her eyes. Denial and grief when it became clear she'd never be the same.

It was too much.

She wanted Michael...loved him. She loved him. Needed him here with her, but she knew he was gone. That he wasn't coming back.

She didn't want to be here. She could just close her eyes and float away. She'd done it once before. Escaped from the horror that was her life. Let go. Shut down.

She could do it again. The thought was tempting.

She looked her friend over. "You look like shit," she said, taking in the total lack of makeup, the deep smudges under Val's eyes that said she hadn't slept in days. "...smell too."

Val smiled, looked relieved. "Oh, yeah? When was the last time you brushed your teeth?"

"Been busy..." She tried to smile, but it felt weak and faded quickly. "Wade?"

Val face went blank. "Dead. When he took longer than expected to radio in after checking out the BOLO on Lucy's car, Chief Carson went after him. Found him trying to drag you into his little shop of horrors. Carson ordered him to stop at gunpoint, there was a struggle for his weapon. Carson killed Wade but not before taking one in the shoulder at close range. Some hunters in the area heard the shots and found the two of you. Two of them took Carson to the hospital by car while the other stayed with you and saw you onto the chopper."

Sabrina was quiet for a moment. Remembered pulling the trigger. Watching Wade's face explode under the impact of several bullets before she let the darkness take her. Carson hadn't been there. It was Michael. He'd been the one to follow her into the black.

He'd saved her.

It was a bogus story. One that Val had an entire week to rehearse. One with holes big enough to drive a truck through. Holes that must've been plugged with Carson's badge and slicked over with a thick topcoat of lies. How Michael got Carson to comply and how he got shot were a mystery. One she didn't want to think about just yet. "Carson. Is he okay?"

"Yeah. He's been by a few times. They were keeping him down the hall, but he was released yesterday," Val said before going quiet. She looked uncomfortable. "Tom stopped by too. He had a little girl with him."

Tommy had come to see her, probably looking for answers. Her hand settled on her chest. Her ring was gone.

"It's in an envelope," Val said, nodding her head toward the stand by her hospital bed. "They had to take it off when they took you in for surgery." Val reached for the drawer. "Do you want it?"

"No." She shook her head against the pillow. "If he comes back, give it to him. Tell him I'm sorry for ... everything."

"Tell him yourself," Val said, her voice taking on a slightly panicked edge.

Her mouth quirked for a moment. Seeing Tommy was something else she didn't want to think about. She changed to subject. "Kids?"

Val smiled. "At home with Devon. Worried."

Her eyebrows raised a bit at Val's use of Nickels' first name but she didn't say anything. He'd kept his word. Protected her family. "Tell them I'm fine." She tried for another smile but couldn't quite make it stick.

"Are you?"

No. She wasn't fine. Michael was gone. Her career was in shambles. She was more than likely facing twenty-year-old murder charges. The foundation of lies she'd been living on for the better part of two decades had crumbled away to nothing. She was floundering. She was heartbroken. She was alone.

But she was free.

"No, I'm not," she said, answering honestly. "But I will be …" She was exhausted. Her eyes slipped closed again, and she felt Val's grip tighten around her fingers.

"Don't. Don't go," Val said. "Don't you dare leave me again."

She tried for another smile, but it slipped away before she could finish forming it. "Be back … tired."

"Promise me. Promise you'll come back," Val said.

This time she managed a smile. "I promise."

Peggy Coleman Photography

ABOUT THE AUTHOR

Maegan Beaumont is a native Phoenician, currently stuck in suburbia with her high school sweetheart and husband, Joe, along with their four children. She writes take-you-to-the-edge-of-your-seat-thrillers and loves action movies and spending time with her family. When she isn't busy fulfilling her duties as Domestic Goddess, she is locked in her office with her computer, her coffee pot, and her Rhodesian Ridgeback and one true love, Jade.

ACKNOWLEDGMENTS

I'd like to thank my husband, Joe, for his endless understanding and support while I spend hours and hours chained to my computer…and when he didn't understand it, he accepted my craziness and loved me anyway. To my beautiful children, Jaime, Julian, Sampson, and Mathew: no matter what, being your mother will always be my proudest achievement. For my family and friends, a heartful of love and gratitude for every word of encouragement and every second you believed in me. I hope I make you proud.

To my writing peeps: I may be the first, but I know I won't be the last. I never would have come this far if not for you guys. To my Annie: thank you for pushing me to spread my wings and fly. I'll never know what I did to deserve you, but whatever it was, I'm glad I did it. I'd also like to thank the wonderful team at Midnight Ink, who saw something worth sharing in the words that I write. And last but not least, I'd like to thank Les Edgerton for his boundless generosity with his time and talent. For giving me praise when I earned it and hard knocks when I needed them. You are my teacher, my mentor, and friend, Les—I hope you know just how much that means to me.